Rise

Awenmell Series : Book Two

Lisa King

Felen Press

Rise - Awenmell Series : Book Two

ISBN 978-0-6483026-4-3 (eBook)
ISBN 978-0-6483026-5-0 (Print)

A catalogue record for this book is available from the National Library of Australia

For you, dear Eariss . . .
We've been waiting.

M artha's hut is cold, but Thomas and I are warm under the blankets of her bed. Gray light gives shape to the hearth and signals dawn is not far away. I snuggle into his warm skin and his rhythmic breath passes across my cheek. My eyes droop in search of more delicious slumber, but now that my mind is awake, sleep seems improbable.

It must've been near dark when he left Sirban. I'm glad he chose to travel, even if it meant arriving in the dead of night. It was too late then to discuss Martha's pyre or how I retired straight to her hut and no one's disturbed me since. Not even that horrible tea drinking herder. I open my eyes a crack, the gray light lines the door and I silently dare him to try to force his way into the hut now. I smile. Thomas would rise from the bed and flatten him.

Wait, aren't I the Eariss? I expect legends destined to bring peace to the land aren't meant to wish others pummeled to the ground. Or are they? At this moment, I don't care.

I nestle into the crook of his arm and relax into heaviness. His skin warms my cheek and the rise and fall of his chest reminds me of all the simple things I've missed most, and hope to never miss again.

What *am* I meant to do now?

Move.

The Mystery drops the word into my heart. It's not urgent, just factual. I imagine the voice was just as firm when it told Martha she had to stay and wait for me. There's no way she could have explained it to someone else. The delivery of an impossible knowing, beating with the lightness of a thousand butterfly wings, yet coupled with the strength of iron. The light is brighter now, and I can make out the beams above us. Perhaps it's best not to explain what I know. To keep a secret. After all, my secrets are mine. Once they're shared, that's no longer true. They become everyone's, and I... well, I won't have any protection, any armor. Not even the safety of a flimsy shield to protect myself.

Thomas mumbles in his sleep. That face with the dreaming, fluttering eyelashes has *never* betrayed me. I wonder what it would be like to be bold for once? To be open and trust, instead of crouching and hiding, filled with suspicion. Thomas trusts *me*. I lean across and kiss his cheek. Today, I will return the favor.

He stirs under my kiss and arches his back in a stretch that spreads through his shoulders and arms.

I tap lightly on his shoulder. Not that he'd feel it. "There's something I've to tell you."

His stretch leads him to face me, his arm draped over my shoulder. "Mmm... good morning," he mumbles and plants a kiss on my forehead.

I move to trace my fingertips along the scar that runs the length of his jawline, but remember his aversion and touch his shoulder instead. My fingers slide down his arm until our hands meet, palms facing, our binding scars matching like imprints on our fingers.

Our fingers interlock and he brings my hand toward his face and kisses it.

Thomas studies my hands. "They're more scratched than usual."

"That's because I ripped all the chamomyle from their beds and scrunched them up."

He chuckles at me. "Why would you do that?"

"To throw them on Martha's pyre." He raises an eyebrow and I continue. "It was a statement, I suppose. The only one I was compelled to make at the time."

"And what kind of statement did you intend to make by throwing flowers around at a funeral?"

"I think Brenn got it, though. Actually, I'm quite sure she understood. She didn't seem happy with my discovery."

"And what discovery was that?"

I draw a deep breath. "That I'm the Eariss."

Thomas sits up so quickly I clutch at the blanket and pull it to my chest before more heat escapes. He leans over and takes my shoulders in his hands. The smile on his face is broad, but he blinks as if he's trying to wake up.

"You're the...?"

I smile and nod.

"Ha ha!" His laugh reverberates his joy and relief around the hut. "So, what do we do now? I imagine Brenn didn't take the news well."

"I haven't spoken to her."

"Are you safe?" He leaps from the bed and grabs at yesterday's clothes discarded on the floor. Holding a shirt in his hand and one leg in his pants, he tumbles toward the small window and leans heavily on the wall before peering out.

I sit up and tug the blankets to cover my exposed back. "I don't know. I think so."

"And what has the Mystery said?"

"*Wait*. And then, *Move*."

"Move?"

"We have to leave here."

He returns to the bed. "Thank the Stars for that! Where are we going?"

"I don't know."

He laughs and kisses my cheek. "Sounds perfect to me."

A few tiny coals still glow from last night's fire, and Thomas soon has some kindling alight. He shuffles the small logs around and coaxes the flames to take.

"So, tell me," He says, tossing my clothes from the floor onto the bed, "How did you know you're the Eariss. By the Stars, me telling you a million times did nothing."

"I just knew."

"Like when the Mystery speaks to you?"

His hands are busy with the fire, but his mind is already on his book. I slip my underdress on, taking a few moments to clarify my thoughts. "It was different than the Mystery's words. This knowing came from deep inside and took me by surprise." I tap my head. "It wasn't like Guthrie's head knowledge might tell me I was the Eariss, but the..." I stop and draw a breath, unsure of how to describe what I experienced. "It was so sharp it could slice you in two, but it's soft and tender... and more solid than anything I've ever known, but if you tried to touch it, it would be like mist."

Thomas's eyebrow is up again, and I realize my hands are grasping at the air. I drop them into my lap.

"It's not that I don't believe you," he says, "I just don't know how I'm meant to write that down so it's understood."

"I don't even know how to *say* it, so it's understood. It reminds me of the song in the forest. When you go to grasp it, it's just out of reach, solid but not there. But when you understand it, you just know the song. No one has to teach you."

"That doesn't help."

"Maybe we're not meant to understand it. Maybe we're meant to just let it be what it is."

Thomas stands and brushes the ash from his hands on his pants. "Well, we can't have you just *being*. We have to understand what happened." He looks out the window again. "You need to be safe. We need a plan."

I finish tying the sides of my smock. "We do?" I want to tell him he sounds like he's spent too much time with Guthrie, but he seems so serious and purposeful. I stand at attention. "So then, what are we doing?"

My question sends his face to the window again. "Wretched fog," he mutters. Thomas leans against the wall of the hut, rubbing his face. "You're still hidden, you know. But it won't be long until people find out. Were there lights?"

"Lights?"

"With your flower thing... rainbows... lights, anything like that?"

"Not that I noticed."

He rummages among bowls and baskets on Martha's table, discarding some old bread before settling on a basket of walnuts, speaking as he makes his selections. "Good, we might have more time then."

"For what?"

"To get you away from here." He cracks a walnut in his hand and lifts the meat from its shell in one piece. He's deep in thought, somewhere off with his plans, weighing up the treasures hidden inside the walnuts he holds. The next refuses to give way, and he squeezes and mutters under his breath. He swaps to the other hand and curses the unyielding seed, then clamps it between both palms. His focus is entirely on the single walnut in his hands, not any of the others left in the basket. Maybe some of Guthrie's eccentricities have rubbed off on him?

My brow knits at his reaction to this simplest of irritations. "I didn't feel any urgency or desperation with the Mystery's words, just that it needs to be done." Thomas grunts and I wonder if he's even heard what I said. "Are you feeling well, Thomas? You seem a bit agitat—"

"So, you don't know *anything* yet? Where's the army?"

I try a smile to ease the knot that grows in my stomach. "I thought me not knowing anything was the only thing we were actually sure of."

I flinch as he obliterates the recalcitrant walnut with his fist on the table. "Ha! Well, that got it out, didn't it?" He picks at the pieces of nut flesh among the shell and glances in my direction. No matter how hard I try, I still tremble. *Stay.* My body screeches at me to run. I inhale quivering air. *Stay.*

Thomas's shoulders drop and his eyes soften. "I'm sorry," he whispers, "Are you well?"

I nod, even though my body still screeches like a captured owl. I stayed, and I can stay again. Practice, that's all it takes.

Thomas holds me gently, telling me his list in calm, measured tones. "We'll need equipment. And supplies. I have some silver from my work in Sirban. There's a smith with a large forge camped just outside its gates, but he's moving on today. You wait here I'll be back as soon as I can. Can you hide in here?"

Hide? So much for being bold. Aren't I the Eariss? Perhaps I should start acting like it. "I don't want to hide."

"But it's not safe for you to come to Sirban."

"I don't want to go to Sirban. I want to speak to Brenn."

"Are you mad?"

"No. I'm the Eariss." I stand tall and step away from him. The screeching owl is silent. "Surely I'm meant to act like a leader. And I expect she's waiting to hear from me. I'll take her tea to her as usual, and perhaps we can find a way to work together."

"Work together? With Brenn? She hates you!"

"Maybe she's just scared about the prospect of the Eariss, like everyone else. I don't know what I'm doing, so if I meet with her, and I'm open and honest—"

"Open and honest?" he laughs "What would you know about that?"

His words might be true, but that doesn't soften their sting. "Look," he says, guiding me to the bed. "You can't be open and expect to change the world. They'll just trample you, and I'll be the one left to pick up the pieces. You're not to trust anyone, remember?"

"She said she'd never met an Eariss," I venture. "Maybe she'll be happy about it." I laugh at my own words. "There's always hope."

Thomas doesn't see the humor. "Fear and hope don't work together, Ashling. They battle until there's a winner."

Battle. How did the fire suddenly get so hot? Memories of that wretched scroll and all that slashing and burning flood my mind. My stomach churns. Where did those memories disappear to when I stood by her pyre and knew who I was? What made the fears disappear? If Thomas is right, it must've been hope. How do I find it again? How will I ever gain confidence if I don't take any chances... if I just hide?

Thomas interrupts my thoughts. "If I let you do this, then we can get to work on the army?"

Let me?

Do you know who I am?

The thoughts are new. And strange. I rise and look Thomas in the eye. "Go to Sirban and gather the items we need. I will speak with Brenn and meet you back here for our journey."

I know he wants to argue with me. His eyes narrow and he takes a few moments to reply. "Wait for the fog to lift," he says, "It helps if you can see where you're going."

"You're heading into the fog."

"Yes, but I know what awaits me." I hand him his satchel and he adjusts it as he speaks. "If she demands you leave, wait where I can see you. I'll be back well before the sun sets." He is almost at the door when he remembers to return and kiss me, then shakes his head and rests his forehead on mine. "I've been studying battle tactics with Guthrie; I don't have time to explain now. Just promise me you won't corner her?"

"You know me. I'll be the perfect guest."

The tea in Brenn's cup ripples as I place it on her desk. I'm glad to be rid of its responsibility. I shake the tremor from my hands and check her chamber door is still wide open. She's aware I've requested a meeting. This way, she can join me whenever she chooses. On the other side of the doorway, servers scurry around the main lodge, preparing for her arrival. They sneak glances at the incredulous young woman who dares to wait inside Brenn's chamber — and without a summons.

The wooden bench in front of Brenn's desk catches my shin as I pass, and I tumble sideways into the carved chair beside it. I scoot into a dignified sitting position. None of the servers noticed. I roll my eyes. Who knew the Eariss had such grace! I've only taken some skin off, and a quick rub settles the sting.

Was that Brenn's voice? No, just a server barking orders.

Nerves tumble in my belly. They're not the same as the ones that seized my body and brain at our previous meetings. They're softer, calmer. I'm quite content to wait here for her, especially if she thinks her delay will fluster me. I'm not flustered at all. Secure. Maybe it's confidence? I'm better at naming my feelings now. It feels strong. Strong and confident. Of course, that's what it is, that's what leaders are supposed to be.

I've only seen the Hall's version of leadership; as unforgiving and unmoving as the stones that create it. The stones that make up Brenn's chamber are earthier and brown, but they still suck warmth away. They're smaller than the ones at the Hall, but their sharp corners jut out and reach all the way to the roof. You could probably climb them if you had to, all the way to the top alcoves that hold dusty tomes and the seldom lit candles that stand half swallowed by the darkness. She should have installed more windows.

Books and parchments, flat and scrolled, line the walls, except for the alcoves set aside for candles. My lips pull into a lop-sided smile. Funny how I thought this chamber held all the answers when Thomas and I first arrived. And how desperate we were to find a way in here, to look at these dry scrolls. We expected them to feed us, but what we were searching for was growing in the garden all along.

A shiver runs up my back. I rub at my sleeves and tuck my smock closer to my thighs. Steam still rises in delicate wisps from Brenn's tea. The earthenware cup holds the heat well, but if she waits much longer, her tea will be cold. It looks out of place next to the polished pot that sits on a pile of manuscripts. I lean forward and catch my distorted reflection in its curves. My head-covering hides my hair and my hand reaches to where it sits now, just on my shoulders. Other than the fabled Crown of Fire, there's nothing that remarkable about me. I don't think I look terrifying. Why are people so scared of the Eariss? I turn my face this way and that, but the reflection doesn't get any clearer. Nothing gets clearer.

Brenn's footsteps stomp their way into the main lodge. Coldness spreads through my limbs and settles deep in my belly, then squeezes the truth into my mind.

I don't know how to be the Eariss! I sit among the evidence of her deep knowledge, seasons and seasons of study and contemplation, and these walls feel so much taller than before. Open and honest about my ignorance? They'll just trample you, that's what he said. What do I truly know? Nothing.

A deep breath fills my lungs.... I do know one thing. I know how to pretend.

I stand as Brenn enters her chamber. Engrossed in a parchment, her eyes flick sideways to me, and her steps falter. Was her huff at my presence or her misstep?

I do my best to sound cheerful. "I wish you a good morning, Brenn."

She bumps into her desk as she slides behind it and drops the parchment dramatically onto its surface. The parchment is safe, but tea sloshes onto her hand. "Just who do you think you—"

I raise my palm to her shocked face. "We both know who I am." Did she notice my widened eyes? Did I really say that out loud? Don't flinch. Don't flinch.

Brenn finds a cloth and mops the tea from her hand, only knocking the cup further, sending a cascade of tea onto her desk, which she mops in panic. "You!" she says "You, are a disruption to the running of this kinship!"

"I am."

"Yes, you are!"

"I wasn't questioning you, Brenn. It was a statement. I am."

"Well, I demand you leave."

I nod. "I've already made plans."

Silence. Her calm face belies the turbulence in her eyes. There's something at work here but I— She gives a tiny nod.

An agreement? What do I do now?

My shoulders tingle. Surely leaders with the same agenda shouldn't behave in such a manner. I sit, granting her the comfort of her familiar position behind the desk, and her stance softens slightly.

"Before I leave, I hoped we might discuss the workings of the Mystery... openly."

"And by Mystery you mean my Traditions of course?"

I don't want to lay claim to anything. "I've noticed changes among the kin I'd like to bring to your attention. You may have noticed too, which might allow a conversation, and if you haven't, perhaps we can give it some consideration."

"And why would I care what you notice?"

She catches my raised eyebrows in one of her furtive glances and directs her response to the table in front of her. "Hmm."

Our roles have reversed. It's interesting to watch fear from a place of hope. Every other time I'd seen the fear of the Eariss, I was drowning in fear myself; the bandits, the Tallefix. Her fear doesn't make me want to attack her. Sadness... no, maybe it's a kind of grief I'm feeling. That there's only half of her presence here. I'm not connecting with her, but only with her fear of me.

"Dear Brenn," I say, and gesture to her seat, which she refuses, "When Thomas and I first arrived, the kinship was a place of refuge, focused on the Traditions."

She stands tall, her chin lifting toward the parchments and alcoves surrounding us.

"But now it seems that the beliefs of the outer villages hold more sway here than your beloved Traditions."

"How dare you suggest—"

"You place your nurses in a row for silver, you court the knowledge of the Sirbahn over your own truth, and you use the kinship's silver to purchase mirrors."

Brenn's face reddens. "You misunderstand!"

"Brenn!" I stand and lean forward on her desk for good measure. "What I understand is that the kinship has discarded the Traditions and fortified the gates. At your insistence, entry is now only granted to the Sirbahn, and those with silver, or mirrors, in their hands. You send the wise away, mock their words and encourage ridicule." Her eyes widen and she fluffs herself up, positioning her fists on her hips. The words tumble from my mouth as if under fire, and I cringe along with them. "You have sold the Traditions for nothing more than your imagined status!"

Her voice shrieks and batters me like a thousand flapping wings. "Pathetic creature! Just look at you. Are you the one summoned to the tables of leaders among the unrest? And yet you somehow consider yourself worthy to tell me what you've noticed. How dare you offer advice and pass judgment on what you don't understand!"

I catch my reflection in the shiny pot again, caught up in the abstract shape of an object without a label. Heat flushes my cheeks and I want to shrink, away from her words, away from uncertainty. I have no words, no explanations. Nothing of value to offer as she continues, so loudly now the passing servers rattle and drop their trays as they scurry past the door. I'm in my seat again but don't remember ever deciding to be here.

"Never have I met such a pretentious and utter dolt! And to enter my chamber and accuse me, me, of not upholding the graciousness, and all-encompassing kindness of my Traditions. Your problem is you see circumstances that don't even exist." She taps a solid finger onto the desk to make her point and then points it at me. "You would do well to fear what you don't, or rather can't possibly understand."

I wait for her usual, Who do you think you are? and when I raise my eyes to meet hers, we both know why she failed to ask the question. I am so sure of myself I don't even bother to stand. "What I understand, Brenn, is that fear always comes from lack. A lack of information, a lack of perspective, perhaps even a lack of understanding." I lean forward to further my point. "Surely you understand I don't fear you."

Silence. My throat is dry, but she doesn't know that.

How has this happened again? Brenn... speechless.

Where are these words; this bravado coming from? Perhaps I am a leader, after all. One day I might take part in those meetings she speaks of, and others would take me seriously.

Don't corner her. Thomas's words remind me to leave her a way out. To save face, relieve the tension. Behind her desk, Brenn, as leader of the kinship, stands in white. But I see an old woman fighting to maintain her dignity. I offer her a gentle smile. We needn't be combative. To my surprise, the corners of her mouth lift, and she nods slowly.

"Very well." Brenn reaches for the shiny pot and considers it. Perhaps she's wondering about the truth of her reflection, too. She looks out the doorway to be sure it's clear before speaking softly. "There is validity in your observations." She breathes out a long, weary sigh. "It's been such a difficult path. And while this is painful for me to admit, I understand it's in the kinship's best interests to hear what you have to say." She's still carrying the pot when she calls out to the lodge through her open doorway. "The ceremonial tea please."

Ceremonial tea? That's for visiting dignitaries, nobility, and... *leaders.*

I've only just straightened my back and considered how one should sit for such a function when the tea arrives. They must have had it brewing already. A server places a small silver jug of tea on Brenn's desk and fumbles a little before placing the finer cups. I remember how intimidating Brenn appeared and how focused I was when I had to serve her. I try to catch the server's eye in gratitude, but she's too busy trying to impress Brenn, who started talking as soon as the tea entered the room.

"When we find our way to work together, everyone will be stronger. We must all play our part." The server dutifully bows her head and leaves, closing the door behind her.

Brenn studies the pot, adjusting its placement before speaking. "Martha told me the Eariss would come."

"She did?"

"I didn't expect it would be you."

"I didn't expect it would be me either."

She looks sad and tired, and I offer her another smile as she struggles with finding a satisfactory place to set the pot. I have no advice. What would I know of such things?

"Your presence brings many matters to a head," she says.

"I've been told that."

"It will come as a shock to many. I think if you announce this suddenly, you'll scare the more fragile. Some are just new to the Traditions, remember. Slowly, slowly, is my advice."

"I understand." It was awful trying to make sense of the Eariss; it still is. Brenn's right, they need no more confusion and the last thing I want is for anyone to suffer because of me.

"And what I understand of our meeting, is that if I wish to return the kinship to the Traditions, I must first return to them myself."

Is this how it should be? Two leaders smiling at each other in the presence of a silver jug.

Yes. Yes, it should.

Brenn lifts the jug, her hand wobbling as she prepares to pour the tea. She can't be that much younger than Martha. "Yes, let us work through this together." She stops before the tea reaches its lip and sets it back on the table with a thump. "You must learn this protocol. If you're ever to be summoned, of course."

Protocol? I nod.

"We serve ceremonial tea to honored guests and people of rank or influence. I would expect that at some time in the future, we will ask you to attend meetings where it is served. There are some regional differences, but the focal points of etiquette are that the visiting dignitary, or the most honored guest, always receives the first pour, the best of the tea as it were." Brenn moves the cups around and includes her earthenware cup for the demonstration. "Their cup is filled and set inside the circle of cups as the rest of the jug is emptied among the others. It's a lovely ceremony and speaks of our sustenance coming from a central purpose, a division of the whole into separate portions."

"How do they decide who is the most honored guest among many? The unrest must make these meetings unbearably tense."

"It's true. But if you stay watchful, you will learn many concepts simply by observing what positions people take in this ceremony. What demands they make, and those they could make, but choose not to. Often the ceremony, because it occurs before the meeting, foretells motives long before any discussion takes place."

Brenn pours the tea into the cup in the center of her makeshift circle of cups. "As you are the visiting dignitary in our case, I poured your drink first. Once the other cups are poured..."

The fine cup is warm in my hand. Brenn still holds hers aloft and smiles, and I'm not sure if there's another part to the ceremony. The jug, still half full, waits on the edge of the table.

"Oh," she apologizes, "The honored guest drinks first. Now here's an element to watch for too. The way a guest drinks exposes their willingness to take part in the discussion. Some like to toy with their adversaries in this part of the ceremony, but I would suggest you never sip. They will read it, particularly in your first appearances, as trepidation, uncertainty, perhaps even cowardice."

How a coward could ever make it to a meeting about the unrest is beyond me. I'm out of sorts learning about a tea ceremony. The tea smells a little bitter, but it has been steeping for longer than usual. I drink the full cup at once, practicing for the moment when I will be heard by other leaders who search for peace.

Brenn beams proudly. I must've impressed her. I smile and tip my head toward her, it's an uneasy truce but at least it's a truce. Drinking tea with Martha was always a sweet, kind, and warm memory. Yet here now, with this hot cup in my hand, the room feels cold. There's none of the openness or easiness I shared with Martha in the forest. I shiver, the bitterness of the tea dries my mouth. I bring the empty cup to my nose. The smell is familiar but I can't place it straight away, yes that's it! Soft earth. Soft earth and pine needles... and the little red caps hiding among them.

Martha's words sound as clearly as if she were standing beside me "... Thank you, but no, I don't drink tea... here."

And the room spins. My hands grasp at the hard edges of the chair arms, but I topple, collecting the jug of tea, its warmth spreading where it lands on my thumping chest. The shelves warp and drip like candle wax and Brenn's laugh cackles around inside my head, trapped inside a room it can't escape.

Why are the stones laughing? They mimic her voice and cackle and merge into one.

D arkness.

Voices.

What are they saying?

More sounds than language, like a conversation heard through walls.

Huh? Am I meant to understand? I don't.

I know the noises are words, but I don't know what they mean.

Why won't my eyes open?

So heavy. Like sludge that weighs me down. My hands won't move either. Do I even have hands? A body? Yes. Hard lumps press into my back, a breeze rustles at my ear, bringing with it the scent of straw... a field.

What's that smell?

Stars! I'm lying in my own filth like some untended animal.

The heaviness spreads over me and absorbs any concern, not that I can do anything, anyway.

Stop with the noise! Their sounds form words now, but even if I understood them, my mouth won't move to reply. I don't think it matters. They're talking about me, not to me.

Sunlight flashes on my eyelids with each of their movements as they hover above me.

Ow, my arm! Did someone just poke me with a stick?

Distant shouts draw closer and brightness and warmth splash my entire face.

A hand.

It brushes my forehead.

Breath on my face.

"Ashling?"

Thomas? This wretched heaviness won't let me open my eyes. I want to tell him I'm fine. Just so tired.

"Can you hear me?"

Arms scoop under my shoulders and legs, my neck strains as my head drops back.

I'm all right Thomas, really. I just need to wake up.

Each of his steps jolts my neck as he carries me across the field. He talks and shouts, but his words are fuzzy sounds that reverberate inside my head. So loud they overtake every other sensation.

Then softer words, I still don't understand them, but I can feel them.

I'm not afraid of the heaviness now.

"Thomas." The disconnect is so real I only think I say the words, but they must've escaped my mouth. His chest relaxes against my body and he responds with laughter and pulls me closer as he walks. I am not alone.

My breath catches in a gasp.

I twitch against the unexpected splashes and sounds of water. Cold water. Thomas still holds me, sloshing his way into the water until he releases me to float by his side. Sensations return slowly. I murmur, sometimes say words. His voice is soft and reassuring, soothing me as he wipes at my face with a damp cloth. My eyelids are still unresponsive, but some of the heaviness dissolves from my tongue.

"Where are we?" I slur.

"Martha's pond."

I can see it in my mind's eye. Thomas standing next to me as I float in the water and move my arms to help him remove my clothes. "It's wearing off."

"It'll take a little longer," he says and cups some water to my mouth and I drink. "I thought you'd feel more comfortable here."

There are many things I want to say. That I couldn't have made it here by myself. That he made a brilliant decision. How did he know? But all my body will allow is a mumbled "Thank you."

I squint and blink and adjust to the afternoon sunlight. It moves between flashes of brilliance and gentle shadow, streaming through the branches and leaves that overhang the pond.

Ideas and half held dreams and heaviness weave in and out of my body until the thickness of it lifts. My thoughts are more coherent. They seem in order and my senses return.

His hand brushes my cheek. "How are you feeling now?"

"Hurt."

"Where?" Thomas's hands scan my body and I brush them away.

"No. How could I be so foolish? I got everything wrong."

"You weren't to know."

"Martha said she didn't drink their tea. I thought Brenn was offering help. Advising me. Openness? I'm such a dolt!"

"Come now. There's nothing gained being so harsh with yourself." He plants a kiss on my forehead that makes my head bob in the water. "At least her 'advice' taught you to keep your wits about you in the future, didn't it?"

"Wits?" I scoff. "Don't think I have many of those left."

"True. They're probably scattered all over the field with the rest of your reputation." He's wearing one of his stupid grins. It drops when he sees I'm not impressed. "You've got to admit, she's done a good job. No one will listen to you now."

Thomas is right. She did do a good job. I know nothing about Guthrie's studies of great battles or the benefits of particular tactics, and so I have no idea whether I hate Brenn or admire her. There is only one certainty here; anything I say, any explanation I offer, will mean nothing.

The kin must think I'm a loon, albeit one who garners just enough respect to poke with a stick. She must have done the same to Martha. *Martha.* My tears run hot tracks from my eyes and I soothe them with cold water, but nothing eases the crush inside my chest. She lived each day as a spectacle, ridiculed and dismissed... waiting for me. And I've ruined everything about the legend in one day.

Thomas holds me as I sob. "You can't be open to the world. It's just not how wars are won, remember," he says. "Even so, it's a lesson, right? Mistakes aren't the end of the world... just don't tell Guthrie I said that. You even told me you didn't know how to be the Eariss, and I should've..." He's quiet, perhaps trying to find the right word, then takes my hands before I can ask what he should've done. "Can you stand?"

Silky mud slips between my toes, and my feet find some grip on the reeds that grow sparsely among it. "There." I say, standing waist deep in the water with only a slight wobble. I splash some water on my face. I'm done crying.

"We're ready then?" Thomas asks. "I'll get the things I brought from Sirban. I dumped them in Martha's hut when I heard... Will you wait here for me?"

"I can't very well walk back like this, can I?"

"Won't be long. We'll leave from here."

For a moment I agree, but a new determination forms even as I slip on the mud. "No."

Thomas catches me and I right myself. "No?"

"If you could just find me some clothes. It's late and we don't know where we're headed. Martha's hut will do for the night. In the morning, Brenn can watch me choose to walk under her threshold, not slink away from it."

"Are you sure?"

I stand tall and nod, even as a passing breeze causes an involuntary shiver.

"I won't be long." He sloshes his way to the bank as I drop my shoulders beneath the surface, grateful to be away from the breeze. Water cascades from his clothes, but by the time he's a few strides away from the pond, it's reduced to steady drips. "Wait here," he calls over his shoulder, as if I had plans of going anywhere else. He's almost out of sight, just a dark movement among the trees when he picks up a branch and smashes it into each trunk as he passes. He wields it like an axe, destroying some imaginary foe until he is completely out of sight.

I float again and try to relax my body. If we're traveling tomorrow, I'll need rest. Deep breaths fill my lungs and I imagine the air making its way to my limbs and clearing the last of Brenn's tea from my body. Another breath, then another, but my body won't settle. Tension centers in my heart as I fight the Mystery's insistence that we commune. I hold my shame up as a shield — the Mystery has made the wrong choice. Still, it insists. We dodge and weave until I exhaust my heart with my futile protection. I throw my shield down in disgust.

I ruined it all!

You did? I thought you learned something important.

Now you sound like Thomas. I'm meant to be the Eariss, aren't I? The powerful leader of some army. And where were you in all of this?

What did I ask you to do?

Move.

Did I ask you to visit Brenn?

I wanted to prove to her I could be a leader... but... ugh. So, this is my punishment for not listening?

There are never punishments. Just consequences.

The Mystery's words run like a loop inside my head. Punishment, consequences... punishment, consequences. Aren't they one and the same? Punishment was a way of life at the Hall, laced with anger and emotion... and control. What about consequences? You can't argue with them, I suppose. They just are. And I still keep my power to choose.

What you believe about yourself is what you will become.

They were Martha's words.

*And they are a choice. You must choose whether you failed in one task today or that you **are** a failure. Your choice. Your destiny.*

Blaming myself is easier, and familiar. It feels safer to me. Is that wrong?

See? A choice. The comfort of the old, or the possibility of the new.

I bet they both come with consequences.

Naturally. But now that you can see your choice, you're free to make the one you choose, not the one that you slide into as easily as you slipped in this mud. There are many lessons, and many choices.

But they're always mine?

As they should be. Are we ready to move forward now? There is much to learn.

Move forward. I know the Mystery is not talking about leaving the pond. There's a place within me that's as cold and dark as the deep river I discovered with Martha. That's where we are headed; if I choose. I tremble in the pond water although I'm not particularly cold; fearful and courageous all at once. I'm not afraid the dark river will sweep me away — the Mystery is here with me. Perhaps I'm afraid that once I wade into its waters I will never return, that its darkness and bottomless cold will trap me inside it forever. I see myself as one of the kin, prodding at it with a stick, unsure of what it all means and terrified of what might lie on the other side. What had refusing to acknowledge this hidden place inside me done for me until now? How did the Mystery describe it? The comfort of the old, or the possibility of the new. My choice.

A flash of sunlight through the treetops forces my eyes closed. "I bet there's no such event as a tea ritual."

The Mystery offers nothing and lets me stew in my own observations.

How could I be so gullible?

Can you feel the water?

Of course. Isn't that an odd question?

Describe it to me.

It's cold… and wet. When my body moves, I can feel it against my skin.

Good. Rest for a while. Feel the water. What needs your attention will soon be here.

The water slides between my fingers, and I recount the Mystery's words. Rest for a while, it said. My mind worries about the dark river and chatters constantly, but I'm more intrigued by a gripping sensation under my ribs. It grows stronger, twisting and gnawing until I can't dismiss it; until I'm convinced this is what the Mystery described.

Mystery, what is this?

It needs your attention. What is it telling you?

I feel into the gripping sensation, making no demands, just seeking to listen. It sits like a solid mass inside me, as if Feeney's talons themselves slice into it. I draw a deep breath, but it does nothing to ease the pain.

I can't do this. It hurts.

It's always your choice. Can you feel the water?

Yes.

Well, that means you're still here and not swept away, doesn't it?

The water ripples against my skin while the intensity of the sensation grows. I can sense both at the same time, a strange observance of both stillness and terror. I need to vomit, to purge the pain and be carried away, but the water keeps me here in this balanced state. There are no words, no explanations arising from the pain, just an awful feeling of trepidation in search of its own name, its own existence... *shame.* Once named, it spreads through my body like Brenn's tea, aching in every joint and weighing me down so I can't breathe. Panic rises from its sleep and urges me away for my safety, to turn away and not acknowledge its presence or the pain it brings. *Run away, now!* The panic demands as if I'm a bystander to some heinous crime, and like a frightened witness, I yield...

Can you feel the water?

The water caresses my shoulders while the fury of the panic rages within me, desperate that I don't expose the truth of my pain. But I see it. I name each claw and feel them as they rip into my gut. *Betrayed, Used, Exploited, Abused, Fool!* The panic fumes and spits, incensed that I won't turn away, then it threatens, and finally pleads; but I'm no longer afraid. I have felt my pain and we rest together as companions on the same journey who have witnessed the same atrocities and shared the same secrets. We see each other. We are part of the same story, once fractured into enemies but now allies. It eases into my body and has much to tell me, to teach me about myself. The Mystery was right, my heart needed attention, and I needed to discover the clarity on the other side of anguish. I go in search of the pain, to thank it for its lesson, but it's dissolved and untouchable, its grip a mere shadow. Even the deep breaths don't hurt and only bring about more lightness and relaxation.

Something else niggles within me, emerging as if it had left a gate open on my past. A diluted form of panic reminds me I have never-ending layers to work through. That this dark river I'm wading into might be bottomless and filled with pain I won't endure. I never want to return to the river, yet the dissolving of the pain was so sweet and liberating I'm eager to be free of every weight I feel inside.

Do you wish to return?

I should, shouldn't I? Isn't that what I'm supposed to do?

It's always your choice when to enter this river and how long to stay. Many paddle at its edges, but you're intent on discovering its depths without knowing what it contains.

It was awful in there... but worth it. That's what Martha was talking about, wasn't it? Embracing my whole story. Feeling into the parts I want to ignore or silence.... or wish away. It makes sense now, that when I appreciate them as part of me, they bring me together again.

My mind wanders back to the injustice of Brenn's behavior and it feels more like a factual event than anything I need to be ashamed of. My memories cause nothing but mild embarrassment about how naïve and stupid I was.

Hey, Mystery. Are you still sure you chose the right person to calm the unrest?

Owning your story gives you power. And is where you'll find the answer.

The answer to the unrest is in my stupidity?

Yes. You're learning to accept your pain and alchemize it away from revenge into a more powerful force.

But didn't I just ruin it all? You know, with the field and everything?

What if it isn't ruined at all? What if this moment taught you about not abandoning yourself when you're in pain? What if it allowed you to show some compassion for yourself?

I shiver in the water and consider the Mystery's words. The river runs silently alongside me but it's not a foe threatening to sweep me away, but rather a teacher, or an honest friend who cares more about truth than niceties.

How am I to be the Eariss, then?

Listen.

That's it?

Always listen.

And how am I to explain the unexplainable?

You don't Ashling; you live it.

I live it? I listen, and I live it. So, what do you need me to know?

I wait, but the Mystery doesn't answer. Instead, the familiar sensation of a waterfall flows over me, and bees buzz so loudly I open my eyes, expecting to see a swarm above my head, but there is nothing but clear air. The tree tops are clear with no signs of bees, or their hive. No bugs or noisy insects appear along the bank, not even among the reeds with the blue flowers. I frown. My ears are under the water.

Why are you filling my head with bees?

Watch them, they'll show you.

I close my eyes and let my mind follow the bees. They hover about the hive, as if they dance on air, a method in their comings and goings only they can understand. More bees arrive, one by one. Sometimes they nearly bump into each other, but they all seem to know where they're going and what they're doing. Their buzzing grows along with their numbers until an alert sounds, and the bees swarm, angry and defensive. A hornet is too close to the hive and they beat it down with their wings. By themselves, a bee's gentle wings move it from here and there, but among many, their effect is deadly. The hornet is dead, and the bees return to their gentle dance, in and out of the hive, almost bumping into each other as before. A fresh attack brings another response. The pattern of dance and defense coincides with my breathing, in and out, a mesmerizing pattern I don't understand but can somehow appreciate.

I don't understand what you're showing me.

Are you ready to trust me even if you don't understand?

But I'll find out one day, won't I?

Decide if you will be fine if you never find out, that's where you need to be.

That doesn't even make sense!

The Mystery doesn't respond. It takes a while for me to understand this argument could go on forever. The Mystery has said and requested all it needed to. Will I trust even if I never find out the outcome? What if I don't understand the outcome? What then?

"I'll trust you." I call out, and close my eyes, but no matter how much I try to summon the bees, they've left along with the waterfall.

⁕

"R eady?" Thomas calls. "I see you're still in the water. Had a good rest?" he approaches the edge of the pond carrying a small sack. His clothes are dry and even though I sit with my shoulders under the surface, I shiver in the cold water.

"I was dreaming of bees."

"So, it's bees now? I expect they spoke to you?"

"It would've helped if they did... but I know they were important... somehow." I splash water away from me in frustration. "None of it made sense. It must be the remnants of the tea that's making it hard to understand."

I imagine Martha shaking her head at me, but in a kind way. Yes, lessons hurt.

"See, you're braver than you think." She'd say it to me and I'd try so hard not to miss her.

Not to cry.

Not to wish she was right here beside me.

Grief rolls again, sweeping over me from head to toe, her loss so real I can taste its bitterness in my mouth. I wipe the tears away with wet hands and stand again, sliding my feet across the slippery mud, and wade toward the bank.

"Important... but mute bees," Thomas shakes his head and chuckles. "Sounds like the tea." He rummages around inside the sack. "I searched, but I could only find these for you. I hope they'll do." He holds Martha's simple brown tunic and white underdress bundled in his hand.

Grief can be the sweetest potion, too. "They're perfect."

The stone walls of Martha's hut are cold under my hand, but they're not filled with bitterness or harshness, just memories.

"You look like you're blessing the stones standing there like that." Thomas looks up from his packing. He's managed to fit all the goods he collected for our journey into two bales.

"Perhaps I am. Even without her, this place is sacred. Can you feel it?"

He lifts the smaller pack up for my perusal, then signals for me to turn around. "I've made these straps, see?" he says, tucking my arms through some leather loops so the bundle stays close to my back and leaves my arms free. "That looks adept. Is it comfortable?"

I bend and twist, and the pack doesn't move.

"Not too heavy?"

"No, it's fine." I say and reach my hands to the stones again.

Thomas jostles his heavier pack into position, clanging the small pot that hangs from its side against Martha's table, then quiets its ring with his hand. "Ready?"

Everything about the hut is still and quiet. Being shunned means there's no one to say goodbye to, no one to wish us well. Still, I chose to do this; to walk from here, not be carried out defeated. My heart expands with my breath. This is the first time I'll leave somewhere by choice, on my own terms. I adjust my pack and hitch the excess length of Martha's smock under a makeshift belt. It's just a tied strip of leather, but it lifts the hem well above the ground. "Ready."

The morning is crisp and the cooler air chills my face as we walk through the herb garden. Thomas places his hand over mine as I lift the loop to open the gate and holds it there while I survey the sheep track. He presses his hand gently onto mine and holds me in place while my chest constricts. I draw in a sharp breath.

"I wasn't expecting them to be lining the path." I whisper.

"Nervous?"

"A little."

"Isn't that what you told me all quests were like?"

I smile at him, remembering an early lesson outside Muscone that now seems a lifetime of road markers away.

He slides his hand from mine and stands behind me. "And it's my job to remind you of your courage," he whispers. He doesn't wait too long before offering his first reminder and a gentle nudge forward. "Lift that chin. Isn't that why we're doing this?"

The kin stand far enough from the edge of the sheep track that we can walk side by side, under their watchful eyes and slanderous mumbling. Once my beloved kith; the workers now avoid my eyes, turning away or looking to the ground. It's not because they're afraid of the Eariss, they believe the words of another.

"Fools," one says.

"Ours is the only way," boasts another.

Soon, a chorus accuses us of depravity. My body buzzes with a thousand of the Mystery's bees under my skin, and I wipe my hands harshly down the front of Martha's smock. What is wrong with me? I haven't done that in moons.

"Thomas?" I lean my head toward his, distracting him from his glares and visual challenges to the kin. "Do you think there's such a thing as a bad seed? Something that, even as it grows, can never be good?"

"You mean evil?" he says, jutting his chin in a challenge to a herder who instantly drops his gaze.

The kin murmur the word like a ripple, as if hearing it for the first time.

"Tell me, after I drank the tea, what did I do?"

Thomas shrugs.

"I know they told you. Look at them. They would have relished telling you every detail."

"There's no benefit in you knowing. You've no one to apologize to, and you've no amends to make."

"So even if I asked you once for every star in the sky—"

"Never."

The sheep track narrows as it joins the road that leads from the main lodge to the threshold. The kin are so close now I could reach out and touch them—if I wanted to, and knew they wouldn't recoil from me. Some turn their backs and Thomas tilts his head to remind me to lift my chin. I remember Abigayle's departure; grateful I'm clothed and not doused with icy water. Why didn't Brenn order a cleansing? That's right. She only orders them on the weak.

Won't one face in this crowd acknowledge me? Just a simple gaze? Eyes flick up once or twice, but never long enough for me to catch. Each step reminds me of my walks through the Hall's passageways, as though I was there, but I never really was, and making me wonder whether I exist at all.

"You don't need them, anyway."

"Huh?" Thomas's comment pulls my mind from the Hall and back onto the dusty road lined with angry faces. "A tiny jot of recognition might be nice."

"I'm surprised you relish it."

"I don't. Not really." Their eyes still focus on anything but me. "But I'm glad they've behaved this way, it's cured me of chasing it, thinking it's something I need. I don't need their respect. I just need mine." Thomas takes my hand and doesn't need to remind me about my chin as we focus on the threshold at the end of the road. A sudden rush of lightness and excitement sweeps my body, and a laugh escapes my mouth before I can contain its seeming disrespect. Brenn's shrill voice interrupts my frivolity.

"See?" she screeches. "If you weren't a witness to her behavior in the field, you have surely heard about it. And here now, before us again, she displays her irreverence for this exit path I demanded she walk! Don't trust a single word from her lips. Just as mad as the old crone, we're blessed to be rid of them both!"

The muscles in Thomas's jaw look like they're about to burst through his skin. He squeezes my hand so tightly it hurts. "You could fry her with the rainbow thing, you know. I wouldn't blame you."

"Martha said it was a sign, not a power. And anyway, what would it do other than create more fear. She'd love that."

The closer we get to the threshold, fewer kin line the road. Some have even made their way back into the fields. Thomas pulls me over to the grassy verge and wipes his boots on the grass. "If you step in something unpleasant, you acknowledge it, don't you?"

"We're about to leave."

"Exactly. Get over here and wipe the kinship from your feet, and move on."

The kinship looks sweet from the threshold. The main lodge sits proudly, with Brenn as a blob of white on the landing, watching us from her perch, while the tree reaches its arms down to the sleeping lodges. My sadness isn't about leaving, or anything that's happened here. I'm just disappointed it wasn't what I thought it was. "Oh well, it looked good on the outside."

Thomas walks on. "It's a good thing we won't have to strive anymore; I'm so done with striving."

"Me too." I smile and remember Martha's teaching about striving and resting, and her lessons about the dilution of power. For a moment, I try to imagine my bravery and power returning to me. Thresholds aren't only about stepping into something certain and organized. A step into the unknown is just as powerful. We're almost there when Thomas nudges me from my thoughts.

"You all right, rainbow girl?"

Herders, silent and uninterested, open the woven blackthorn gates of the kinship and take their position outside them, more worried about what might come in, than in what they are letting out.

"Well, at least this time I'm not alone and falling from a wall in the dead of night."

He steps back and sweeps his hand into our future. "And fully dressed this time too!"

His eyes are smiling. We have each other all to ourselves again.

All he wanted to do was write a book, and I have no idea what is about to fill his pages.

T he road to Sirban is just as I remember it; except for shorter grass between the cartwheel tracks, evidence of Brenn's profitable trading route. Tall trees festooned with vines line its grassy verge, and ferns and small bushes fill most available gaps in the understory. Thomas and I walk it as we'd done before, each in our own cartwheel track, alone with our thoughts. Our initial excitement about traveling waned along with our conversation several road markers ago, and we walk in an easy and comfortable silence.

Is it the trees I've missed? Perhaps it's Thomas, or traveling, or the notion of not knowing where we're headed that's filled me with such content. The forest surrounds me, hovers over me, and while this dirt path might take me through its middle, it doesn't lead to its heart. I need to hear the forest, not just watch the branches sway from a distant field, or enter only in search of nourishment or medicine. It requires an unfamiliar kind of listening, as rich as its loamy soil, scented with sweet decay and the fragrances of hidden blooms.

I fill my lungs with all the forest's possibilities; they pull at my heart and distract me from the road. Thomas might walk beside me, but I no longer need his escort and this particular road follows an intention set by others. It will only ever go in a selective direction, its entire purpose a method of getting from one place to another. A smile grows on my lips. More adventurous pursuits lay either side of its construction.

A tumble of joyous energy folds its way from my head to my feet. Under my skin, irresistible excitement compels me to step from the road. I'm certain the Mystery and this journey will ask more of me than any of the villages or even the kinship ever had.

Can I do this? Take every lead from the Mystery? A sense of calmness and unfathomable depth spreads over me. I don't want to visit with the Mystery, taking advice here and there. I want to live there. Is it possible? To constantly dwell together? To listen. I roll my eyes and sigh, as if I finally understood something simple for the very first time. That's all it ever required of me. *Listen.* Birds call in the treetops, insects hum as they move past me, leaves rustle overhead and our feet pad into the road, and behind it all, the forest's song. The Mystery's song waiting for interpretation. *Listen.* A bend approaches and the song pulls me from the road and into the forest's undergrowth. It's not difficult terrain, just some ferns and low bushes to brush through. Thomas stops at the edge of the road.

"Are you sure about this?" he asks.

"I followed you. Now it's your turn to follow me."

"Yeah, but I knew the way."

"I do too. I know it's this way... I just don't know where it leads."

"You don't know what *it* is either. I hope it's not one of those times you're not told, because if you were, you wouldn't go."

I run my hand along the fronds in front of me. I have no doubt that's exactly what's happening here. "It could be a bit like that." I side-step around a fern. "You can keep walking the road to Sirban if that's more comfortable for you."

"No... No," he says and ducks under a low vine, "We'll know it when we see it right?"

I don't even have the answer for that.

W e move through the rest of the day, following animal pathways, hopping rocks across streams and tumbling down dales. Our packs sometimes get caught between closely growing saplings, but other than that, we hardly notice they're there. Well, I don't. Thomas grumbles to himself occasionally, but his mood lightens after he retrieves some bread from the back of my bale. We don't stop; eating as we walk and marveling about how good bread tastes when it's not hard and straw flavored, but Thomas isn't himself. He seems distant and disturbed by something, as if he's only half here. The sun is lower in the sky when he brushes aside his distraction and clears his throat.

"It's getting cooler now. We should stop in the next clearing, and I'll get a fire going."

My feet are eager for rest. They seem to have heard his words and celebrate, pumping themselves with enough energy to make the extra distance. They don't have to wait too long before a clearing appears. It's only small, but perfect for a fire and a night's rest.

Thomas drops his pack and collects a few branches from the ground. "I'll start the fire. Tea?"

"I think I've had enough tea to last a lifetime, don't you?" I slide my aching arms from my pack and grin, hoping for a lighthearted response, but my smile is either missed or ignored.

"Yeah, I've been thinking about that tea," he says, snapping some smaller twigs into kindling. "Listen, I know you love Martha, but why didn't she warn you about Brenn's tea?"

"To be honest, I don't know." I drop my pack and move to help him gather, but he bids me to stay and rest by a tree. "We'll never know how that day might have been different if she'd told me to beware of poison. But the more I think about it, the more I understand it wasn't her job to warn me, it was mine to pay attention. I'm responsible for the position I'm in—not her. And that's something I had to learn for myself. She couldn't have taught it with a warning. There are a million lessons hidden in that day, and not just about not drinking tea with Brenn. Deeper lessons about trust and betrayal and intention... situations I had to experience myself, if I'm to learn from them." Martha's pond flashes into my mind, and with it a reminder of the sensation under my ribs. I had to experience it to learn from it. I had to embrace it, and once I'd received its lesson with no malice, it left.

"But your reputation. She could've saved that at least; they think you're out of your mind."

"My reputation's poorer, no doubt... but my experience is richer!" I laugh when I realize I've summed up my life thus far.

Thomas doesn't even smile and cracks a dried branch as thick as my arm. "We're already at a disadvantage. I just think she could've helped while she had the chance."

"It's fine, really, all going according to plan."

"And whose plan is that?" He sounds menacing, but I'm sure he's just tired from our day's walk.

"The Mystery's I expect. I've accepted I'm the Eariss—"

"That's right. So, you need to act like it!"

I snap back at him without thinking. "And right now, that means *listening*, and doing what is asked."

Thomas cracks another branch and an army of ants scurries from it in all directions. He flicks them from his arms and legs and slams the branch onto the ground. "No. We need to get you out of this forest and working with the elders to raise your army!"

What? "Thomas, you jest! Talk to the elders? Did you just hear what you said? Now you're the one who's out of their mind!"

He glares at me and brushes some leftover ants from his arms. I can't read him. Is he tired? Am I tired? Everything is cloudy between us and I sweep aside any hint that he seeks anything but the best for me.

"I'll gather some more, and then we'll be done." he says and wanders into the forest.

I shake my head. We must both be tired. *Elders?* What on earth was he thinking?

They should include full bellies after a day of traveling on a list of life's fineries. That, and how the blankets that once surrounded our packs, create a perfect haven for us to reconnect as if we are the only people on earth. It makes it easy to forget our earlier tension; and any pain dissolves amid tender words, gentleness and love, reinforcing promises of what we had known before. We lay together, rested and at peace, just like we had before. *Before.* I'd never had reason to look back with fondness. I think I can understand the obsession with nostalgia and remembrance of happy moments now. That my hope might bring something from those moments into the present one. A craving for comparison marking one moment better than another. Yet each moment *is* unique, and in this moment, Thomas's fire has cooked our meal, warmed our bodies and now dies down into coals. The sky changes color above us, moving through various shades of blues, purples, and grays.

"Stars are almost out," I say.

"That they are."

"It's so vast, isn't it? The night sky."

Thomas sighs and laughs a little. "It only reminds me of Guthrie's contraption."

I imagine him lugging the blasted thing from one place to another, with Guthrie following behind. For now, he watches the sky with me and points out the brighter stars as they emerge. His hand is warm in mine.

"Tell me he hasn't ruined it for you. Guthrie and his experiments can't completely dull the mystery and wonder of the stars."

He lifts my hand to his lips and kisses it. "What is the Mystery do you think?"

"I don't know exactly."

"But you say it's inside you."

"Yes, and outside too."

"So, it's not separate from you."

"It's not. But maybe it is. Sometimes I think it's been there all along, like a part of myself I'd never listened to, or a shard of glass like the windows in the Hall, splintered off but still part of the whole."

"But how can it be you?"

"What do you mean?"

"If it knows things you don't."

"I don't know how that works. It just does. It feels like home, like it's always been. Like I'm not complete without it."

Thomas's face goes blank and I'm desperate for him to understand. "What do *you* think the Mystery is? I'm sure you could hear it too."

"I have no need for your Mystery other than to have it tell me about the Eariss. Speaking of which..." Thomas flips the blanket open and reaches for more firewood. A thick branch lands in the coals, followed by another, and tiny flames spring joyfully to life along them. He wanders on the other side of the fire, searching among the objects tipped from our blankets, and holds his satchel up with a smile. Even in this low light, it seems more battered from his travels between the kinship and Sirban. It lands with a thud next to him as he sits beside me, his back slightly turned as he pokes among his writings.

"Ah, here it is," he says and produces a scroll. He beams as he unravels it, tilting it slightly so the firelight catches the soft cream of the vellum. Intricate colors and pictures line the borders and small icons rest among the lettering. It's almost too beautiful for words.

"I told you I'd make a copy."

"Your important work?"

"I was hoping to encourage you, for it to be a surprise, but it seems you were the one full of surprises today."

I run my fingers over the fine detailing and treasure the small pieces he's added to make it ours. There's even a cut apple among the letters. "It's so beautiful."

"But I left you alone. I won't do it again."

"None of us knows what tomorrow brings..."

"I thought about you with each stroke of the quill."

"And I get to think of you each time I admire this. Did you get any clues? Did Guthrie help?"

"He was too busy burning things with his oil of vitriol, clinking those wretched bottles, rearranging them. I was more worried he'd spill it on my work. But here, look..." Thomas points to the first line of lettering. "From darkness an escape to light—surely that means your escape from the Hall."

"Perhaps," but visions of the dark river that Martha led me to enter my mind. "There's lots of things that are dark and light. Can you read it to me again?"

"I could say the whole lot blindfolded if you wanted me to."

"From darkness an escape to light,
Hope armed across the land,
To run through all that stand before,
The change hid in our hand.

Slashed hearts and willing stretch of arms,
To fight a holy war,
Of stomping feet and chargers led,
Leave all unlike before.
"Anew!" hearts cry, for they are spent,
Sparks die for dusty ashen,
The alchemy of all to one,
Destruction for its passion.
The forest yearns to hold its own,
Saved blood, the crown of fire,
Yon bridge will rise despite itself,
With stars that lead to pyre.
A waiting oak at Awenmell,
Kind shelter through the mist,
Life of all lives scratched into stone,
The iris forms a fist.
The courage borne of sweetness charred,
Seized wheels that bear no turn.
The Acamar doth shine as guide,
On paths lit with concern.
Life from the ashes, burning flesh,
Stones weighed before their cast,
Of naked armies wailing deep,
The final storm has passed.
So far apart, yet just the same,
Hands hope into the past,
Betrayal and cinders fall like rain,
Till peace arrives at last."

I rest my head in his lap, looking at the words but unable to
read them, the light from the fire illuminating the back of the
parchment. This time the reading isn't so scary. Maybe it's the
warmth of the fire and being with Thomas, rather than a chilly

night under the stars with Guthrie. The sky is dark now and I wonder where the star Acamar is this evening, and how this moment fits into the scroll's meaning. Thomas holds it open while I run my fingertips against the ink. It feels real and my body rings with truth. Some might say it is only words on paper but there's life behind it, like the Mystery dwells within the ink, ready to reach out whenever welcomed. I trace the colorful flames he's inked onto the parchment, and quietly remind myself that my power is contained in all of my story, not just the parts that please me.

"Does it tell us what we should do next?"

Thomas shrugs. "No more than what you already know, but we're out here following some kind of lead, aren't we?"

"I suppose so."

"A stronger one than the Hall's I hope."

The fire flashes with heat and I close my eyes against its drying sting. "How does the Hall know what I'm supposed to do if I don't?"

"They've studied the legend too. Only they've concocted a story around its evilness so none would search for it. Or like in Brenn's case, primed it for ridicule."

"They've gone to a lot of effort for *just a story*, haven't they?"

"That's because they also know it's true, and how powerful it is."

The heat becomes unbearable. I turn my face from the fire and cool my eyelids with my fingers, remembering all the eyes that ever looked into them, searching and scanning. "If they were waiting for signs to kill me, why even let me live in the first place?"

"You're the only descendant of Brennyn Hall. You'd continue everything as normal, keep them in power. That makes you incredibly valuable to them—as long as you're not the Eariss."

"But I am the Eariss."

"So now,... you're more valuable to us."

I know I should be grateful. Happy even. Or relieved I'm considered valuable after believing for so long I had no worth at all. Instead, I'm a commodity; the bearer of a weapon no one knows how to wield. Do I belong anywhere? I don't even think I belong to myself. The forest tries to hold me but I move away, floating free of its groundedness and into a hidden part of myself, it's safe back here. I can watch and act, but I don't need to feel.

Thomas tucks the scroll away and stretches out with his hands behind his head. "Sometimes I wonder how it will all play out. Do you?"

I shrug and adjust my head on his thigh. The flames are smaller now, and flicker just beyond his feet.

"I do. I wonder where you'll find the weapon," he says, "... and more importantly, what you'll do with it once you've got it. What if the Mystery asks you to do something bad?"

"Don't think it will. We've talked about this before."

"But... what if it does?"

I sigh. "Why don't you tell me what you're worried about?"

"What if you get the weapon, understand who you are, and go mad with power? What if you turn out like Feeney?"

"Me? Power mad?" I chuckle at the thought. "I'm petrified of the whole idea. Can't imagine *me* being obsessed with power."

Thomas doesn't share my mirth. "But you couldn't imagine yourself being the Eariss either."

Silence.

"But what if it did?" he demands. "Would you trust it that much? You can do anything—remember the Tallefix? You asked for iron to release me, Ashling. *Iron.*"

I remember the moment, the silkiness and ease that existed simply because I connected to the Mystery and asked for help. And that because I had asked, iron obeyed my wishes.

"You have that power now, you should go and do it! Go and take the Hall!"

I shake my head and sit up. "I'm not meant to right now. I'm more than whatever power I have, and somehow more than what I do, and I don't understand it!"

"Neither do I!"

I've upset him again. I wish I had an answer for him; one that would remove his frustration, but I don't. We sit in silence until he rises to throw the last broken branch onto the fire. We're both tired, that's all.

How naïve of me to expect things to be how they were before, when everything is so different now. I'm the Eariss, and that's somehow made everything worse between us. What does Thomas want from me? Feeney's claws seize into my belly, sharpened with the message of other's expectations. *Behave. Do as you're told.*

The fire pops and I jump, shielding myself from the sparks and tiny embers that land around me. Pain sears through my body. I swipe feverishly at my ankle and free it from the tiny coal's piercing sting, but even after it's brushed away, the pain lingers. It reminds me of other attacks that arrive unannounced, fierce and unforgiving, with immeasurable consequences. This must be a physical taste of what comes to me in my dreams; the horror of the scroll that arrives with flames and swords, and the desperation of the people calling for an answer when I have none to give. Just a few moments ago, I was admiring the scroll's words and took comfort in its truth. Now I'm terrified beyond words.

"Tell me!" Thomas shouts.

"Tell you what?"

"I've been asking you, but you've been off into another world. Tell me you're powerful!"

His eyes hold every desperation I'd seen in my dreams, every hope he instilled in all he'd done for me. I smile at him, but it feels very much like the ones I wore at the Hall. "I'm powerful."

"Yes! That's right. Because you're the Eariss."

I'll make him proud. I wear a larger smile. "I'm the Eariss."

"That's my girl."

The fire pops again, and he laughs when I jump and prepares the blankets around us for the night ahead. I laugh too, but I don't brush away the tiny coal that lands on my leg. I soak into my pain and I let it burn.

The first birds call in the crisp air. I pull the blanket closer to my shoulders and listen to the sleepy stillness around me. Some stars linger but they disappear into the pinky gray that sweeps the sky. I dreamed of fire, and of bees, but this time I wasn't afraid. My dreams acted out before me like players in court and I was their audience; distant and uninvolved. I wiggle closer to Thomas, making the most of his warmth. He wants us to leave as soon as we wake. My ankle rubs on the blanket beneath us and pain shudders up my leg. The coal. Ugh, and all that tension. The familiar patterns I slipped into, as easily as I slipped in the mud. I rest my forehead into Thomas's back and listen past the birds, past the forest and into the Mystery.

I didn't listen.

You did not.

And I can't go back and change any of it now, can I?

That time has passed. But this moment is new. Take it.

I rest with the Mystery until Thomas stirs. He greets me with a smile. "Are you well? Are you safe?"

"I am."

We pack quickly and cover a reasonable amount of terrain by mid-morning; hiking through thick forest and woodland, following streams and climbing steep gullies. The sun is higher now and we follow a tiny track hidden beneath the leaves of waist high plants along a hillside.

"Look at that," I say, turning back to Thomas. I point ahead to the hillside covered with greenery except for occasional thin white-trunked trees. "You wouldn't even know this track was here unless you were walking it."

Thomas shades his face from the sun and looks into sparse tree-tops above him. "Goats probably."

I squint against the sun, too. The thick grove of trees in the valley below don't look that far away, but can't come quick enough for Thomas. He sighs so loudly it must be deliberate. "How do you *know* where you're going?"

"I'm listening to the Mystery. To my heart; to my body. It knows when something is right. I just have to trust and listen."

"So, it's knowledge that's in your body, not your head."

"But it's not like regular knowledge; knowing something with your head." I pat a white-trunked tree as I pass. "I know this is a tree—that's with your head."

"And no one will argue that. This *is* a tree..."

"But the knowing of your body can't be *proven*. It just *is*, and that's what makes it true and yours alone. It's believing something, trusting it without evidence—"

"I'm glad Guthrie's not here," he laughs.

"That's why we dismiss it, we're trained to ignore it." I turn to face him, making sure he understands my point. "Although I've noticed it does make your ideas and plans vulnerable to people undermining you, perhaps second guessing, maybe even making accusations..."

"I'm not doing anything like that," he says and rubs at his neck. "... you didn't have *plans,* anyway."

"But in the meantime, you're just teaching me things I didn't understand before."

⁂

This ravine looks familiar, and this tree; what if we've been here before? Pines line the gully, gifting it with a soft carpet of red and brown needles. Everywhere I look, every path I consider isn't right. Thomas watches me scan the area. His eyebrows are raised. At least I can be certain of one thing; if we've been traveling in circles, he'll be the first to let me know. My cheeks flush and I crane my neck and pretend to be interested in a distant tree.

Mystery? Why do I feel... nothing? No, that's not true. I'm pressured, like I need to perform. It sits on my chest like a rock. No wonder I can't find the way... my heartbeat thuds in my ears and I wipe my hands down my smock. I could just guess a direction, keep us moving, keep those eyebrows down and the flush from my cheeks. I check for a path between the trees again. Maybe it's this way...

Listen.

I close my eyes and find my way to the Mystery. It waits for me under my embarrassment, deep below my pride.

What if I ask you to stay here and admit you don't know the way?

I'd look foolish... and Thomas would think—

Would you trust?

I had no idea trusting the Mystery would also mean being willing to serve my pride up to someone on a platter. Someone with raised eyebrows. But I also agreed to trust, even when I didn't understand the purpose or the outcome. I unclench my jaw and let the tension slide from me. Yes.

I draw breath to say the word out loud, as if it contained some kind of eternal promise, and an insect catches in my throat. I cough wildly and gasp as Thomas pounds on my back hard enough to dislodge an army of bugs until I breathe easily and the compass inside me swings back to life.

"We're lost, aren't we?" he says.

I offer a final clearing cough and regain my composure. "This way."

We leave the pines behind, moving into a lower forest with lush growth and open loamy soil. Damp earth makes way to mud, then spongy earth that compresses under our shoes and leaves each footprint filled with icy water. Tree branches lose their uniformity, curving and twisting into thick dark patterns. The leaves, once lush and green, transform to moss and lichen with every slushy step we take deeper into the mire. At each turn, I look for something green, a patch of sunlight or warmth, something to lift the darkness that seeps over the ground and into the trees. Which direction did we come from? Everywhere is just as dark and damp as where we are now. How can we find our way out if we don't even know how we got here?

"It's this way," I say, and clamber over branches so intertwined they form an almost solid mass of black in front of us. The other side is much the same, but at least the trees aren't as tangled.

Thomas leans on the branch and peers forward. "What if it goes on forever? It won't do anyone any good if you go in there and never come back."

"We have to go through this way. Besides, isn't it customary to accept there's a dark night before a bright dawn?"

"A dark night? For the love of Stars, you *do* know there's daylight out there somewhere?" he looks around him, but sees the same as I do. Shadows and darkness. He shakes his head and his boots sink into the mud.

My teeth clench so hard I have to will them apart to speak. "You want proof?"

"Well," he begins, "Yes. Look around you! We're in a swamp. You can't raise an army in a swamp!" He stretches an arm and turns to make some dramatic gesture, but the bundle on his back catches on an errant branch, knocking him off balance. "You can't even *move* in a swamp! But you!" he says, pointing at me and climbing through the branches to the other side, "You can ask material to move and it moves! See over there, that mass of twisted, ugh, whatever that is... You could just blast a hole right through there." He wiggles his pack from his shoulders. It lands with a slop into the mire and he moves toward the target. "Yes.... right there," he points and steps over a thick root and disappears from sight.

Thomas!

His curses reach my ears before I can form a sound. Not that he'd hear me. On the other side of the root and chest deep in a pond of bog mud, Thomas thrashes, grunts, and bellows about his predicament. I clamp my hand over my mouth, hoping my eyes convey concern and not the merriment that bounces through my body. I wait for a gap in his tantrum and try to speak, but laugh instead, and set off more of his frustration.

The bog is large, well it seems that way. Gnarled black trees, fallen branches, and rocks line its boundary, but with both the surface of the ground and the bog looking so similar, it's impossible to tell. Thomas grasps at branches around him and grunts against the sludgy pressure of the mud, but can't advance. Every movement makes it worse. The fallen branch beside me isn't long enough to reach him, but there must be more around.

"Now Thomas, just because the path isn't smooth and beautiful, doesn't mean it's the wrong path."

"Yeah. Hilarious," he says. "Try over there... Wait! Shh.."

A soft wind groans through the limbs that creak above us. Sodden branches drip their excess into the slosh and Thomas pants, scanning the swamp in every direction.

"I can't hear anythi"—a low grumble, a growl. More than one. "Wolves," I whisper.

Thomas launches himself at a floating branch and swings it toward the approaching wolves. "Yah! Yaaah!" The branch doesn't reach the edge of the pond, but still he swings it about and shouts at the three wolves as they move closer, menacing, growling. "Stay back! Yah! Yah! Ashling Move!"

I stand still, watching it all unfold like one of my dreams.

"Move!" Thomas screams at me, "What are you doing? Ashling! Ashling, get up a tree!" He lunges and shouts at the wolves, swinging wildly and almost reaches the one by the edge. His free hand scrapes the surface around him and bombards them with lumps of mud, all the while yelling at me to arm myself.

Finally, some silence.

"Come along," I say. "Stop teasing him."

The wolves vocalize their disappointment and join me, prancing and playing at my feet. Thomas pants, his face splashed with black mud, still gripping the branch above his head. His eyes narrow, and he blinks several times. The stick splashes onto the surface of the bog.

"We're on the right path," I say.

Thomas wades toward the center of the bog where there is more water and it's easier for him to move. "And how do you know that?"

I stroke the coat of the wolf next to me. "Wolves don't lie."

"Is that so?"

The wolves nudge me. They walk a short distance around the pond and I hoist Thomas's discarded pack onto my shoulder. "So, Thomas," I call, "Who should listen to who?"

"Whom."

"What?"

"Guthrie says it's *whom*."

"And Guthrie knows everything?"

I follow the wolves' every step around the bog. Sometimes the way seems obvious; relatively solid ground, logs, and rocks. Other times, they detour around an area that I would have charged right through.

"Don't step there!" Thomas calls, now waist deep and halfway across his muddy hole.

I don't move. I wait until he looks into my eyes, and I step directly where the wolf suggests. There's barely a splash of mud on me when we reach the other side of the bog and the wolves go on their way. "I'd trust a wolf before I'd trust Guthrie."

"It's getting firmer here," Thomas wades closer to the edge. "No, wait. This is like the mud on the other side, it draws you and holds you." He frowns and watches the surface water.

I can't imagine what answers he'll find doing that. There are some long branches nearby and I search among them for one that might reach him.

"I've got it," he calls to me. "I'll stretch out across the mud. That will even my weight across the surface. When I'm ready, grab my leg and pull me across."

Stretching out across the mud sounds simple, but it takes Thomas several attempts before he floats upon its density rather than sinking into it each time he moves. I'm tired of his explanations about why it's not working and just wish that it would. He's almost within reach now and the cold black mud sloshes to my thighs as I wade into the bog.

"Careful you don't get stuck."

My arms strain as far as they can, but I can't reach his leg. I pinch at the cuff of his trousers. Got it. "Can you move your other leg over here? Slowly." I pinch the other cuff between my thumb and fingers. "Got it."

"Pull."

Dragging someone across mud is harder than I thought it would be, my fingers strain to hold on... then snap! I fall back, mud splashes onto my face and I sit chest deep in mud.

Thomas clutches at his loose pants. "Ashling!"

I snatch at them but miss. "Thomas!" He's pulled them out of my reach and I'll have to wade further in. My fingers pinch around the cuffs again. "Hang on to your pants this time. Never in my wildest dreams would I have imagined this!"

"There was a lot less mud in mine."

We laugh so hard it saps our energy, and I drop back into the mud before trying again. I'm still giggling when he makes his way to my arms. The black smelly mud coats our exhausted bodies.

I flick some mud from my chin. "I thought being the Eariss was some kind of noble adventure. Not this."

"Tearing my clothes off isn't a noble adventure?"

Lumps of sticky mud form inside my shoes. They squelch with each step, but it's a relief to finally be walking on solid ground. For a while I thought Thomas might be right, that the swamp and darkness might last forever. But the light came, softly at first, breaking through the dark canopy. The further we walked into it, more objects came to life around us; leaves appeared, branches straightened, and the earth returned to its form. I pressed my hands into it, pushing into the soil, grateful for every moment of resistance.

A soft breeze drifts through the birch grove, meandering its way around the trees and brushing at the dry grasses that cover the rise. It jostles my hair, but my skin is almost numbed to its passing by all this dried mud. Thomas points to the ridge and I nod a confirmation. He hasn't complained once.

"Want me to take your pack?" he offers.

"There's rest waiting for us over the rise," I say. "Maybe after that."

The trees at the ridge thicken, yet they're spread evenly across the level ground. Birches mingle with tall ashes and some wide-reaching hazels form a canopy above us. It's cooler here, and so quiet it seems the trees listen for our steps in their fallen leaves. The brighter light of open space points through the edge of the woodland and ahead of me, Thomas halts; just a few strides from its boundary. I stand beside him, silent.

A huge open meadow, larger than the lands of the kinship, slopes gently away from us. A breeze sweeps up the field, pushing against its grasses like a giant hand enjoying the texture of a pile. Elation floods my body, tingling all the way to my fingertips as the wheel turns inside me, just as it did beside Martha's pyre. I draw a shuddered breath and try to speak, but my mouth is too dry. Thomas fumbles for my mud encrusted hand and takes it in his. He stares at the field, perhaps worried it might disappear and turn into a bog if he removes his eyes from it. For there, in its center, stands the object of our attention. A large tree, unbothered by the winds, solid and unfailing.

"It's a waiting oak…" I whisper.

Thomas squeezes my hand. "… at Awenmell."

Awenmell. I draw a deeper breath while my mind tries to make sense of dream, reality, and legend.

Awenmell.

There are no beams of sunlight or frolicking lambs. There doesn't need to be.

Thomas stands solidly beside me. "So, this is it, then? Are you sure?"

"This isn't too strange for you?"

"I think I gave up the notion of *strange* when you knew where to find those berries outside of Smoutlea." He leads me into the sunshine and erupts into laughter, so uproarious, so joyful, it's contagious. "I can't believe it! I mean, I always believed it—but… Stars! This is Awenmell!"

A fresh breeze winds playfully up the slope and my feet hum with the forest's song. It's not that the land is heavy and drags me, it's more like one of Guthrie's magnets, that snaps my feet solidly into its earth, as if I'd lived here my entire life, as if my heart has made it home. "So it is."

Thomas grunts with every elongated stride as he measures a space near the oak tree, then stops and squints up at the sun. He tracks its transit across the sky with his face.

"We can set our lodge here," he says.

"Our lodge?"

"For your army." He thumps his way through the grass, stepping out imaginary lodges and outbuildings and calls out his discoveries and ideas as he goes. "The doors should face South," he says, pointing down the meadow. "... snowdrifts." he explains.

I push our packs away, recline against the oak and watch him lunge his way through the waist high grasses. He reminds me of one of the spinning tops I'd seen village children with; wound up as tight as possible before all his energy is let loose in a flurry of ideas and calculations.

Underneath some fallen leaves, the soil calls me to press my hands into its coolness. The same captivating sensation my feet experienced when I stepped into Awenmell runs through my hands and into my arms. A warmth, thick with knowing, covers me like silk. The song envelops me and I see the tree through many seasons, patience at its heart. I know this oak has waited for me—just like Martha. This *is* the waiting oak. This *is* Awenmell.

"Trees. Over there." Thomas points to the forest on the other side of the pasture and beckons to me as he hurries toward it. His enthusiasm pulls me to my feet and soon after I join him in its shade.

We wander among the trees and Thomas explains to me the benefits of each type of timber. I copy him, leaning my body into the tree and staring straight up to its height. I try to understand and find the clues he looks for, but only end up making myself dizzy.

"There's more than enough good lumber here," a satisfied smile spreads across his face.

I want to tell him he sounds just like a carpenter, but decide on a firm "Good," instead.

As we walk, he slaps his hand onto the smooth bark of a good-sized rowan and turns to face me, "You know, I was just thin—" Thomas freezes. He flicks his hand up in a signal to halt, listening intently. "Can you hear that?" he whispers.

Noises flutter through my head. Forest sounds, breathing, my heartbeat. He looks at me expectantly, but I don't know what I'm listening for.

"Water." his eyes widen and he follows the fall of the land toward the sound. I track his steps through the light undergrowth and find him standing, hands on hips, beside a small stream. It's lightly pebbled and small branches make graduated steps along its course. The water babbles its way past us, trickling at each variation and step.

"Can you hear it now?"

My hands are already in the crisp water, washing the last of the dried mud from my hands. I scoop the clear water to my mouth and wipe the excess with the back of my hand. "We won't need a well at least."

A well. I hadn't considered a well... or the hard work of digging one. A yellow leaf bobs past on its way. How many other things haven't we considered? Just moments before, Thomas stepped out measurements for a lodge and noted what timber to use, but we didn't stop to think about food and water. His eyes are on the stream too. I wonder if he's thinking about what lies before us as well, and how this is meant to unfold. We have no idea what we are doing. Unease grows in my chest and I close my eyes, observing it as it tightens into a knot. *Listen.* All is well.

Thomas whispers. So softly I can barely hear him amid the noises of the stream. "Thank you," And I can pretend I didn't hear it at all; it wasn't directed to me.

The stream runs the length of the meadow. We chase its meanderings, leaping from one side of its bank to the other when larger trees overhang its edge and we can't pass. One trunk with deeply grooved bark leans almost to the other side of the stream, so I balance against it and spring from one large stone to another until I reach the other side. Behind me, Thomas's boots pad onto the same stones. I squint in the sunlight. A clearing? No. The ground falls away ahead of us, but it's not a valley; I can see the trunks of the trees but not their roots. Thomas brushes past me on his way toward the dale and I follow him through the trees and down a short embankment to the edge of a pond. It's not much larger than Martha's. A fallen tree reaches from one side to the other, its head hidden somewhere in the forest beyond. Grasses and occasional boulders line its banks.

My breath catches in my throat and warmth shoots from my chest all over my body. "Thomas!" I squeal, "A waterfall!"

"I've seen bigger."

I don't care that I just squealed, or that I've pushed past the irises that line the bank and now wade thigh deep in the pond. I need to get to that waterfall. "They don't need to be big and spectacular," I yell. "They just have to follow the form of the earth!" I giggle, then laugh with complete abandon, but sound more like a madman as I lunge through the water, tripping on my waterlogged clothes.

"Fine, then." Thomas says, sloshing through reeds and knee-deep water, "But you seem to know a lot about waterfalls for having never seen one before."

At the base of the waterfall, the water comes up to my chin and I have to turn my face from the constant splashes as the stream meets the surface of the pond. It doesn't leap directly from the top, but cascades over rocks and old branches before landing here. A large gray rock sits near the bottom of the fall and collects most of the stream before passing it into the pond. *I must get there.*

I bounce in tiny increments toward the rocks at the edge of the fall, frustrated by the weight of my clothes. My feet fumble under the surface like a blind man searching for treasure. A foothold. The next one raises my shoulders from the pond. My hands latch onto the rough surface of a protruding rock and my knees find a ledge to rise from. Now waist deep, water drains from my shoulders and the sensation threatens to pull me back into the pond. This will not do.

"What are you doing now?" Thomas calls from the pond.

"Catch."

My sodden clothes land with a splash beside him.

Splashes from the waterfall flick at my feet and knees as I stand an arm's length away and the gray rock holds my soles firmly in place. If the only concern that existed in my life was this moment, I know I would be grateful forever.

A stream has no choice but to follow the form of the earth. Words from my childhood. A tale about not fighting against who you are, and the things you are here to do.

The waterfall rushes past me, compelled by laws it doesn't understand but obeys. My hand reaches gently toward it, dotted by spray and random droplets until it's caught in its force, fingers pushed back before my hand resists and attempts to control the weight of the flow. The water lands in my palm with such force that it can't be contained and anything I seek to hold on to leaves me with emptiness. Once I understand this, I can enter fully. The water pounds along my arm and into my shoulders and almost knocks me off balance. It travels along my neck, forcing water over my face until I'm ready to draw a deep breath and raise my head as it floods my entire body.

This waterfall isn't as smooth as the ones that come to me at irregular times, or in my sleep; the ones that feel like warm oil. This one is forceful, eager, determined; but still welcome. Perhaps the time of gentle waterfalls is over. Perhaps something new is on its way.

Our clothes, scrubbed clean of bog mud, lay scattered over branches, bushes, and rocks beside the pond. I stretch out on a warm boulder, dried by the sun, and kept snug by the stillness of the air. No wonder lizards are always sunning themselves on rocks; not a care in the world, no kinship, no Sirban. I flop a lazy arm over Thomas's chest and the rumble of a growling stomach echoes against the rock face.

"Was that you or me?" he says without opening his eyes.

"I think it was me."

The fallen tree leads away from us and disappears into a collection of trees on the other side of the pond. I focus on some branches, partly obscured, but shaped like they might bear fruit.

"Is it too early for apples?" I say, and Thomas shrugs.

Clear water and flecks of broken bark roll across the top of my foot as I press it into the spongy base of the fallen tree. Away from the water, the log looks firm with just a few patches of drying moss. I take a few steps, slip, and regain my balance. Over on the rock, Thomas rises on his elbows. More likely positioning himself for the best view of a hilarious tumble than checking on my safety. The water slides under the log, like one massive sheet on its way to be shredded into smaller trickles downstream.

My bent arms bounce up and down at my sides like Guthrie's brass scales. "Whoa no... I'm fair. I think I'm balanced now."

"Balanced? Are you sure that's the word you're looking for?"

"Yes. Why?"

"You would have said it differently before."

"Before what?" I take a few steps along a drier patch of wood.

"Before everything, before the kinship, before Sirban. You wouldn't have said *balance*, you would have said something like..." he looks to the sky for inspiration, "something like... you've achieved satisfactory equilibrium," and laughs so loud several birds take flight.

I laugh too and nearly topple into the water. Everything in my life is relaxed now, even my tongue, and why wouldn't it be. "I don't have to be so careful now. My life doesn't depend on getting it right."

"What does it depend on, then?"

I think he'd like me to say him, or maybe Awenmell, but the answer is simpler than that. "Listening." The word is embedded in my heart as if a hot iron branded it there. Its charge is not negotiable, even if I don't understand what it means. *Listen.*

"Are you well?" Thomas calls.

I didn't grunt that loud. It must've been the snapped branch that woke him from his sunny slumber on the rock. Getting from the log to the trees was easy. They were right beside me, but reaching for the fruit is another matter. The stem of the first apple broke easily. This one has decided I should stretch precariously over thin branches and involve myself in a game of tug of war before I'm rewarded. *Snap!* Finally.

Halfway across the log, I show Thomas the apples in my hands and he beckons for me to throw one to him. "Oh wait," he says. "Are you going to talk about apple seeds again?"

The crisp apple slaps into the palm of his hand. He laughs and takes a bite.

He's happy and relaxed. I may as well tell him now. "People are coming. Here, to Awenmell."

"Now?"

"No, not now, we're not ready."

"When will we be ready?"

I shrug, seat myself on the log, and let the water drag past my toes. What are we meant to do for these people? They're coming for something, but why? Whoever they are.

"How are we meant to train them?" he says.

His question jars me. It feels out of place.

"How are we meant to *feed* them?"

I pinch the apple between my thumb and forefinger and spin it with my other hand. I don't know the answers to his questions. I can only try to explain the sensations and understandings that roll through my body. Even when they make little sense. In fact, they always seem to make more sense once I've uttered them, like they're a stopper on a bottle.

"They're coming to cross this log."

I don't need to look at his face. He'll be trying to figure out what crossing logs has to do with the army, the unrest, and the legend. He'll think about asking me what I mean and then remember that most of the time I don't know, anyway. I hope he'll also remember to be patient with me. He crunches his way through the apple and tosses the core behind him.

"Tell me about this log," he says as he reclaims his clothes and dresses himself. "How much do you know?"

I run my hand along the log's bumpy edges. There's not really anything to know about this particular log; it's just like any other, slimy patches, hard wood, moss scraped clean where I slipped and nearly fell... "It's about the *crossing*, not the log."

"Right then, tell me about the crossing."

I take a bite of my apple, thoughts arriving as I chew. "Well, no one crosses a log unless they want what's on the other side, right?" I present my apple as evidence.

"Go on."

"There's a decision there.... but the first step is always terrifying. Well, it always is for me. I worry about slipping, falling, doing it wrong. You know what else?" My thoughts tumble over each other, morphing and connecting in unusual ways. "Once you step out, there's only you. Open and exposed and vulnerable. What if people were to throw rocks at you? How would you dodge them and stay balanced? If someone had pelted me when I crossed that first log at the lake, I'd be at the bottom of the ravine. If not by falling, then by jumping in complete horror."

"Sounds like it's about bravery. That's honorable."

"What if you watched other people fall? Screaming to their deaths. How much harder would it be to cross then?"

Thomas looks pale. "That would take..."

"Courage."

"It's important not to look back," he announces.

"Or too far forwards. There's enough slippery stuff under our feet."

Thomas nods. "I think I'm understanding this."

"Have you noticed when people get scared, they grab on to things? Anything. When you're on a log, there's nothing to hold on to." I throw my apple core into the forest and stand. "You know what's left? Trust. Being in the center of the log, with nothing to hold on to, perhaps having rocks thrown at you, and believing the decision that brought you here will help you stand." Thomas watches as I walk the rest of the fallen tree and take his outstretched hand. "Then there's the people who love fiercely, the ones who remind you to stand when you can't see a way through the horror and slime ahead of you." I stop at the very end of the log, take his face in my hands, and kiss him. "They're the ones worth keeping."

"They're the ones worth being."

I dress quickly and we choose a direction back through the trees, traveling upstream toward the oak.

"Looks like we're really doing this then?"

"Yes, Thomas of Feldston, we are."

"**I** had a dream last night."

Thomas stirs at my announcement, and I turn my head. "Mmhmm," he nods with his eyes still closed.

Broken leaves rest in his hair, an inevitable result of sleeping in the forest. I gently clear them out, one by one, and speak again "I had a—"

Snoooore!

Fine, then. But I'm only indignant for a heartbeat. Appreciation takes its place and I try not to move, hoping that every breath of sleep brings him rest.

It's hard to believe two moons have passed since we discovered the waterfall. All the trees we've felled in that time, dragging them from the forest to the site of the lodge. The decisions we've made about what to plant, where to store seeds and how much food we'll need. My hands are scratched and calloused, but they're strong. It surprised Thomas how much he remembered from Guthrie's lessons about agriculture, and he laughed when he remembered being oddly interested in marketplace conversations about weather and crop rotation. From all of this, we've developed a plan to get us through the short and mild winter.

I prop myself on my elbows and look out from our forest shelter to the meadow in the distance. Other eyes might see a half-built lodge, logs lying in mud, partly dug fields and a holding pen for non-existent animals. I see a completed warm and welcoming refuge for those who will come. The vision sustains me. No matter how many times I try to push it out of my mind and see all the mud and mess, the vision overlays it and becomes more real than the mud squelching under my feet, or the ache in my back. I've given up fighting it and it's become a part of me.

We usually gather our morning meal together but occasionally, like now, I hold my breath and sneak away from our shelter and wander the forest alone. Everything we need to collect is here; even this wonky woven basket I carry came from the branches of that willow just over there. I'm sure she laughs at me and my lop-sided hamper each time I pass. I'll get better at weaving, I promise. For now, there are more important things to do.

The berries drop straight into the basket, and the walnuts are plentiful. The apples, though, are not quite ready. I check behind me and around each side of the tree. "May I help them along?" I whisper to the tree and once I have permission, ripen them under my hand. The forest still holds my heart even though I spend most of my time in the meadow, and I revel in listening to its chatter and hearing its tales. The song is always clearer in the morning and leaving feels like pulling away from a lover's arms.

Thomas stands outside the shelter. He's started a small fire for tea and rubs his hands together when I return with the basket. "What did you find?"

"Nuts and apples—"

He reaches into the basket. "How come I never find fruit like this?"

"And some roots and herbs for the perpetual pot."

With our bellies almost full, Thomas cracks the last of the nuts open on a large stone, and I sip tea close to the fire. But not too close. The dreams still come most nights. Bright oranges and reds color the darkness and heat sears through my body.

"Move closer to the fire, it's a cool morning," Thomas suggests.

"I'm fine. Tell me, what are the plans for today?"

"We're almost ready to—"

Crunch! Snap! A yell.

What was that? We're on our feet in an instant. We stand perfectly still, straining to hear the slightest movement. The hairs on my arms stand on end. Friend or foe? We've seen no one in moons. My tea hisses into the soil. The voice seemed far enough away, yet we talk softly and creep among the trees. We listen hard and shrug at each other. Nothing sounds unusual.

Arghhyahh!

My eyes bulge. Someone is out there. On the other side of the meadow. They scream, grunt, and yell, and move closer. We step toward the boundary of forest and meadow. Thomas picks up a branch at his feet and hands it to me. He finds another for himself. A fist closes around my heart and squeezes all blood from it. Did a Trothsman find his way into the valley? Is it one voice or more? The voice is getting closer, angrier. Perhaps they won't cross the meadow. They won't want to reveal themselves. Yes, they'll travel around the meadow. Good! We'll have time to hide in the forest. But they'll see the lodge! An icy coldness drips from my head to my feet, and I feel as bare as the lodge that stands exposed in the middle of the meadow.

Thomas urges me back from the meadow's edge. He douses the fire and secures the satchel high in a nearby tree, and drops to the ground. His eyes are concerned but strong. "Ready?"

I can just make out the rough edge of the satchel cradled above us. It didn't matter how many nights Thomas pulled that scroll out to encourage me, I only took comfort in the detail of his work and tried to block out the violence it contains. Now this, how does this fit into the legend? How does being found before we're ready help anything?

"Do you want to do this?" he asks.

What do I want? I want to know why we've been led to this field in the middle of a valley. Why we're compelled to build a lodge for people that don't exist. Why I can't sleep at night because of the fires that come for me.

I squeeze the branch harder.

Awenmell has answers, and I'll die before it's taken.

"Ready."

A donkey's bray screeches across the meadow. That *was* a donkey, right? Thomas looks as puzzled as me.

A shout chases the bray down to our hiding place. "Confounded beast!"

On the other side of the meadow, a figure covered in bog mud tumbles out of the forest, cursing in ways and methods I've not heard before.

I straighten my back. "Is that... Guthrie?"

"No, it can't be."

The man, almost entirely covered in black mud, rises to his feet and catches the errant donkey's reins. "You are the most insolent beast in Sirban. No, no wait! In all of this world, just look at me, you imbecilic creature!"

I snort, and tension slides from my shoulders. "Sounds like Guthrie."

"But he's talking to a donkey."

True... and I clench a thick branch ready for violence and Thomas's fine hands are calloused and dirty. "Things change."

My grip on the branch is strong; thanks to Thomas. He was determined I should learn to fight, or at least defend myself. At first, I resisted, then agreed just to amuse him.

"I can't do that," was my excuse.

"Why not?"

"I don't have that kind of confidence, or the strength."

"What makes you think you lack it?"

Why did I think I lacked those skills? "I haven't ever lived that way."

He threw a branch to me. "Well, it's time to actually live it, and prove to yourself you can."

I'm more comfortable holding a weapon now, confident perhaps. I release my hand's pressure on the branch and clutch it again. It still amazes me how something as simple as moving my body in a new way can override what my thoughts had convinced me of for summers.

Is it really Guthrie? The man draws closer to the lodge; the donkey happy to wander behind him into the open field. He seems interested in one of Thomas's logs. He stares, tips his head to the side. His mud-covered hands lift the end of a log and repositions it slightly, then adjusts the angle of a post with a hammer. It only needs two slight taps.

We exhale at the same time, and Thomas shakes his head. It's Guthrie all right.

Thomas calls from within the trees. "What wonders have I performed to deserve a visit from the wisest man in Sirban?"

Guthrie strains his neck and scans the trees as we emerge. He greets us with a smile that lights through his muddied face. "My friends!"

Friends? He must've banged his head on an old gnarled root in the bog.

Guthrie scoops us into an embrace. The wafts of mud force a wretch from my gut and my shoulders squeeze into my neck. Everything in my body feels squeezed shut. Trapped.

Thomas flicks Guthrie's arm from my shoulder. "Tell me, what brings you here?"

Guthrie scratches at his cheek. "Well, I had to find you, you see."

"You've gone to a lot of effort. *We* don't even know where we are."

"Yes, you left these." Guthrie rummages amongst the bags on the donkey's back, mumbling incoherently, his eyes darting between us and the pack. "These," he says, holding brushes and quills in his trembling hands.

Thomas looks confused.

"And these." Guthrie pulls parchment and reeds and brushes from the packs. "Perhaps these then," He holds them out to us, his teary eyes pleading for recognition. Anything. Panicked. *Guthrie?*

Thomas gently places his hand over his. "I thank you sir, but these are not mine."

"Oh," Guthrie nods slowly.

Oh?

Guthrie twitches at the sight of the implements in his hand as if he'd never seen them before, smiles at us and returns them to the donkey's pack. "Not yours? Oh, well."

Every sensation inside me is tied into a million knots, and no matter how I scramble, I can't find the end to unravel them. Thomas's careful eyes watch me stroke the donkey's neck, remove his pack and guide him to the pens. I'm leading myself away too; away from Guthrie and the tangle that hovers about him.

Deep breaths open my lungs like gates swung wide at the end of a siege. The donkey wanders between his stall and the open field, but the heaviness that Guthrie brought with him still hangs in the air. Thomas waves and I draw another breath. Resignation, I suppose. Some host I am; preferring to run away than attend to our guest.

Guthrie barely looks up when I return. He's made himself at home, eating, and drinking; but doesn't seem content wherever he sits. He settles on a thick log next to Thomas and uses his knife to slice at the lump of bread in his hand.

Thomas catches my eye and directs his attention to Guthrie. "Guthrie?"

"Hmm."

"How goes Sirban?"

Guthrie's eyes widen at Thomas, as if perhaps he didn't understand the question. He considers the bread in his hand and raises his face to Thomas again. This time his mask of gray mud darkens at the corners of his eyes; he clenches his knife and growls. "Burned to the ground!" His dagger blade hacks into the log beside him and all the knots inside me explode into a million flailing ends. He half-grunts, half-screams as he wrests it free and waves its glistening point at me. "*Your* Trothsmen!"

I buckle under the pain of his words. A blow straight to my gut. I absorb the blame as if I had commanded the Trothsmen myself. His beloved Sirban. *Fire.*

Thomas snatches the knife away and leans over his frame. "They're hardly *her* Trothsmen!"

Guthrie drops to the ground. His quivering arms raised over his head, his body curled and protected. I think he's whimpering. Stars! Guthrie? Thomas stands down and offers me a cursory nod. I nod back. I'm fine, I'm fine. But what about Guthrie?

Thomas places a hand on the old man's shoulder. "Come then Guthrie. Your bread is all but finished." He takes Guthrie's trembling elbow and helps him to his feet. "Let's get you to the pond and out of all this mud."

I collect extra clothes from the shelter and follow a distance behind. What's wrong with him? What's wrong with *me*? I'm bound with invisible ropes and can't draw breath past my throat. I stop and make a concerted effort to breathe. It hurts to inhale, as if it's something I shouldn't be doing; like I should only breathe in secret. I shake my head. I should think of Guthrie, not myself.

I hurry to catch them before they enter the water and lay the clothes on a wide rock, hoping the sun warms them enough to bring Guthrie some comfort.

I've tended the donkey so often he's sick of me. I've tended the pot... and the fire. There's no point trying to move the heavy logs by myself. They must be finished by now. Guthrie had no more mud on him than we did. I'd wager they're sunning themselves on the bank and chatting about old times!

They stand waist deep in the pond. Guthrie mutters incomprehensibly. I'm too far away to hear Thomas's words but his tone is gentle. He scoops water over the old man's bare skin, letting it fall gently... what is that? My breath catches in my throat and I drop behind a boulder near the edge of the pond. The burns are unnatural, like nothing I've seen before. Oddly placed and various sizes; yet deep and open. How? They need tending. How can I offer to tend them without him knowing I'd seen them?

"That should do it." Thomas says.

Water sloshes amid Guthrie's grumbles and Thomas's directions to be careful. If I move now, I'll see more of Guthrie than I ever intended. I'll wait until he's covered himself. But then they'll know I was here while he was bathing. Ugh!

"Do you need help to dress?" Thomas asks.

"I didn't believe her, you know."

"About what?"

"About everything." Quiet grunts and chupses fill the air, and I wince in sympathy.

"Remember how she was always trying to tell me about things that can't be measured, can't be seen? Well, I saw it."

"Saw what? Where?"

"Something that can't be measured. In that man, Feeney."

"Feeney was at Sirban?"

Feeney at Sirban? A cold force crushes my chest and a cry lodges in my throat. *Run!* I grip onto the grass to make myself stay.

"He came with the Trothsmen, when they couldn't find you. They did... this."

"Guthrie, I..."

"No need." Guthrie sighs. "They would've burned it all, anyway. Feeney's book is all that matters to them."

"He had the book with him?"

"You know about it?"

"Yes, I've had the displeasure of meeting him."

"Then you've seen it in him? The meanness that seeps from the pores of his skin."

Thomas doesn't reply. Perhaps he's caught up in his own rendition of the meanness that pours from Feeney's skin, enveloped by his own visions like I am.

Guthrie's voice breaks through my memory. "He knows she's the Eariss—she is, isn't she?"

My heart pounds in my throat. Thomas?

Guthrie's voice is loud now, passionate. "He'll kill her, you know that, don't you? They're looking for her. They'll find her, you know it."

"Not while I'm here."

"That's why I had to find you; to warn you."

"You weren't followed?"

"The kinship welcomed me, then shunted me out when I asked after you. Rest assured, no one could have followed me where I wandered. I've had a merry journey, thinking I had gone mad and following the most peculiar of impulses. At one point I imagined I had a compass point inside me." He offers a small chortle. "I thought I'd lost all my sense, completely, but I got to match wits with some wolves near that awful bog. They'd meant to round me up and devour me, but I outsmarted them by traveling through the bog. You see, they didn't follow me then."

Thomas snorts, "Aren't those wolves something?"

Tears prick my eyes. Yes, they are. Those wolves *are* something. Reminders. The crushing cold lifts from my chest and horror evaporates with it. I've no idea what the Mystery's scheme is, and I don't need to know; I need to listen. Comfort waits while I chase away the last of my fears. What matters most in this moment?

Thomas and Guthrie tarry their way toward the fields of Awenmell. How to tend those burns? There's wormwood growing near that short cliff. I rub my chin. Yes. And there's benne in the same area. I won't need a basket.

⁂

The herbs were perfect. I've enough to make the salve and some tea... but how can I let him know about the burns? Thomas and Guthrie are discussing roof pitches when I return. Warmth spreads through my chest to see them together again, acting like the brains and brawn of a balanced team. Thomas steps forward to meet me but repels me with waves of anger that crash into me, one after the other.

"If you've got plans, you better get them going. Where's your army? We need weapons. We need—"

"We need to listen."

"No, we need to protect you! We need an army to go out there and wipe Feeney and the Trothsmen off the face of the earth." Thomas points over the mountains surrounding us.

I try to imagine a battle, but my vision stays firmly on this field. I can't see beyond the mountains. Nothing calls to me. The longer I try to search for something outside the field, the more anything beyond it disappears.

"Are you listening?" Guthrie shouts at me, his panic stinging me like a thousand needles. "They want you dead and they'll do anything to achieve it! If you don't go out there—" he swings his jabbing finger from the mountains and aims all his terror directly at me. "They will come here for you."

They'll come for you! Guthrie's needles blast into me and congregate in my stinging fingertips. I rub them on my smock, but nothing eases the savage memory. How they sting..., scratching so desperately at the floorboards in my chamber until they bleed. How did they find me? I was so far under the bed. I claw for anything to grasp. Anything to hold me still. But nothing meets my desperation. Fingernails maul the boards, trying to carve something out of them. The truth. Anything.

Thomas grabs at my hands. They sting.

Searing heat throbs at my fingertips.

His eyes are strong, solid.

Something to hold on to.

Air fills my lungs and I pinch my mouth into a half smile. I ignore the flush that rises inside and collect the dropped herbs from the ground in front of me. "I have a salve to make."

I know he'd never hurt me, but I'm not going anywhere near Guthrie while he's stabbing that dagger into the wood. The salve has mixed nicely and I intend to soothe those burns, whether he thinks I saw him naked or not. But *not* while he has that knife in his hand. What a funny distinction; to be wary of an object, not a person's action.

Thomas and Guthrie sit near the lodge and discuss the seasonal variations of recent times. Not boring, but not interesting either. A debate over the melting rate of fresh snow distracts Guthrie enough for him to forget about the dagger.

I approach him with the salve. "May I?"

"May you what?"

I swallow hard. "Your burns." There. I said it.

He frowns and shifts his eyes from side to side. He rolls his sleeves high enough for me to access the burns on his arms. Thomas continues their conversation as if they were resting at the table inside Guthrie's cliff-side home, not among the rubble of a half-built lodge. Guthrie seems softer now. Softer? No, probably just more like himself.

"So what is this place?" he asks me.

"It's Awenmell."

"Awenmell?" he chuckles, "From that frivolous scroll?"

"It's a place of inspiration." I flick Thomas a hopeful look, but his face is stern.

Guthrie scans the field, the mess, the mud. "Hmm, quite fitting."

Thomas leans forward and rests his arms on his knees. "This is where we'll be training the army."

Guthrie scoffs at him. "You imagine yourself a leader and you can't even lay a pole straight on the ground?"

I thought Thomas was doing a brilliant job. Yet a strange relief floods my body at the idea that Guthrie has returned to his normal self. Yes, this is safer. Please stay a while longer, old Guthrie. I need the breathing space.

Thomas laughs at Guthrie's correction. "Of course sir, and after you've straightened the poles, you can put your hand to felling the trees and carving and building the lodge. I'd appreciate the help."

"I—I—"

"My aching muscles thank you."

"No. No. No. All I meant was you're yet to measure and test your ideas. Everything must be measured and tested. How will you know anything otherwise?"

"I will know... dear Guthrie... because you will undoubtedly tell me everything I need to know about it. And then even more on top of that!"

I press my lips together hard and try not to snicker as I dab ointment on the last of his wounds... it's no use.

Thomas laughs too, and I clear my throat and prepare myself for Guthrie's tirade.

Guthrie flusters, slaps his leg and laughs at himself. "That I will!"

Their conversation returns to agricultural practices, and I try to imagine the odd mix of Awenmell and Guthrie.

Guthrie of all people.

Here, at Awenmell.

We're building it for *him*? I shake my head gently and remix the salve, ready to store it away. There's a small jar in the shelter, I'll use that. Guthrie's face seems smoother now, calmer perhaps. He returns my smile and though I still hold mine, an unease spreads through my body. It creeps quietly along my limbs, it's not a frightful dread or fear, it just is.

I hold my hand up and shield my eyes from the early sun. This lower corner of the field still has high golden grasses that bend and sway, and reach almost to my knees. From here, Awenmell looks just as it stands. Nothing's finished, there's mud and chaos everywhere and somewhere in the distance, the donkey is lodging another complaint. A smile draws across my lips, but its beginnings come from a warmth deep inside me, not unlike roots that support a flower. Maybe that's what true smiles really are, blooms from deep within.

I stretch tall to the sun and close my eyes against its brightness. Martha would be proud of my morning routine and what I've learned so far. *What do you notice?* I hear her say. In my mind I tell her about the scent of the grasses; musty yet light and sweet. The breeze that plays with a loose strand of my hair and sweeps by me with such a perfect temperature it almost ceases to exist. I bend my body to the side and my muscles lengthen in delight, pulling playfully against my reach. My hands draw slow arcs high above me in the air. I'm not even sure what they're doing, but it feels... good. A body can feel good? Not only pain? Interesting.

On the other side, I listen hard for the rustle among the grasses, for when they whisper secrets to each other. Ah, there it is. Their secret whispering that Martha said I still needed to learn. Just like the whispering within my body that I can hear now, too. Pain and terror shout so loud it's hard to hear the whispers, but they're always there. Waiting. Just like the grasses.

It's quiet moments like these I'll enter the dark river and become acquainted with the deeper pain inside me. Sometimes we converse in a way where I'm free to cry and be angry, sometimes we sit in silence together, sometimes it shows me things I'd never seen before. The deeper I go, the more open I feel. It's an interesting paradox. Paradox. Yes. I think that's the word for it. I take all the time I need, moving from the depth of the river and then back to the grasses, or the warmth of the sun, or the stretch in my muscles. It's like floating in the water; I can be in both places at once. Yet at the same time, it's as if I've stepped through the veils that surrounded the Tallefix, it's another world. A safe and powerful one where I always feel welcomed and loved, no matter my mood.

Bending over now, my muscles pull from my legs and down my back and into my shoulders while my fingertips touch the soft earth. Grass crunches beside me, and Thomas's boots appear at the edge of my vision.

"What are you doing?" he says.

I smile to myself, even though I'm doubled over. "I don't know. It feels good."

"But there're reasons for everything you do—should I get some parchment?"

"What makes you think there's a reason? It feels like something I need to do, so I'm doing it."

"But you don't know why."

"Do I need to know why?"

He reclines in the grass and watches me stretch; his eyebrows raised in a quaint form of anticipation. "Everything's a talking apple seed to you. I'll just wait here."

I shake my head and reach higher, drawing arcs with my arms from one side of my body to the other. If I focus on my muscles,

I might forget he's watching. Back inside my body, I'm larger, expanded. As though I'm here, and that I truly exist; not that I'd ever try to explain that to him.

"So, tell me, Ashling of Awenmell, what are you doing?"

I return his smile. "Me? I'm taking up space. And I'm taking up as much space as I like."

"And it feels good?"

A familiar sensation clamps around my heart. How curious that I immediately want to deny what I feel. To hide it away for fear of it being taken away or used against me. I force myself to be truthful. "It does."

"And what have you learned?"

"That my body doesn't only send warnings and pain. It has a quiet voice if I care to listen."

"And what has it been saying?"

I wait a few moments, sorting my thoughts into an order he might understand. "It's been teaching me about pleasure."

"Pleasure?" He props himself on one elbow. "Go on."

"When it's denied to you, you don't know what it is, or even how to react to it. Now I get to define what pleasure is to me, not anyone else's idea of what I should like or dislike. What *do* I like? It's like experiencing life for the very first time."

"Wouldn't everyone just know what they like or dislike?"

"When every choice is taken away, every piece of you is taken away, too. It was easier to like something because you were told to, or it was expected, not because you actually did."

"So how do you find out what you like and what you don't?"

"By experiencing it without any pressure, like this. Feeling my body and listening to it. I know it enjoys stretching."

He watches me for a while. "So, everything is new then?"

"I'm experiencing it differently, in my own way, for the first time. And for the most part, you've been pretty patient with me." I push away memories of his anger and he returns my smile with a gentle nod.

I bend forward, and my fingertips draw lines in the soil. "If you find the tools you seek, will you be brave enough to use them?" I didn't mean to say it out loud.

"What?"

"It's what the Mystery said to me on a few occasions. I was just thinking of it now."

"What does it mean?"

"I don't know." Thomas inhales and before he can sigh, I add, "... yet."

"This'd be easier if you just trusted yourself."

I continue to move and think about the notion of trust, while Thomas lies on his back in the grass, eyes closed to the sun. It's good to see him rest. He looks so peaceful; I'll save my questions about his plans for later. I chase my thoughts about trust as they weave their way through my mind.

"You can't just think it better." I say.

"Think what better?"

"Trust,"

"And?"

"You can't just decide with your head that you're going to trust, or be strong, or whatever. Your body has to live it for you to believe it."

"Go on."

"Like with the branch, when you taught me to defend myself. I got to live it, so my body knows it's true. If you don't get to live it, how do you learn to trust yourself and your decisions? If your survival depends on giving in to another's demands, what practice do you ever get in making your own decisions? To know whether your thoughts are trustworthy? Particularly when you're being told the opposite. It takes practice." I stand straight. That's enough for today. "I think trust is formed by living it, not just deciding it."

Thomas lays still in the sun. Perhaps I've put him to sleep.

Feeney chuckles inside me and demands to know why I bother to speak my thoughts when no one wants to hear them.

His words crush my body back into the safety of a small and quiet existence.

I try to coax it to happiness, but it has already shrunk too far away from me.

I n the forest below the field, a breeze pushes its way through the trees. Their tops sway and move in playful bursts. When this day's work is done, I'll join the breeze, the forest and its song. So many things have changed since we first stepped onto this meadow. There's now a threshold at the gate, and fencing surrounds most of the meadow. The donkey didn't object too much to the plowing implement Guthrie created, and now most of the field set aside for grain is turned over. The doubts in my heart about anything here dissolve with each passing day.

I tie the last of the reeds together. Hopefully, this will be the last of the yelms Thomas needs to finish thatching the roof of the smaller lodge. No more sleeping in that big drafty lodge. I'm sure it will be fine, filled with lots of bodies, but the cooler weather is already here and I can't wait to feel the security of a smaller den for us all. It only took two moons of Guthrie's continual questions to finish the main lodge. I don't know if it was his questions or all the yelms we made that made it seem like time had stopped still. Like the Mystery was playing some kind of jest and there'd never be an end to either. The lodge sits in almost the center of the meadow, under the protection of the oak. The leanings of the Mystery led me from the path to Sirban, and continue to lead us now as we build and hope and dream. At first, my requests seemed odd as I'd walk through what we'd devised and make adjustments.

"There need to be more doors and windows," I'd say.

"It'll be too hard to heat."

"Doesn't matter. We need more doors and windows. There must always be a way out."

"Why?"

"I'm not sure. But it's important. Do it."

It felt weird giving orders; telling them what to do, as though I was someone who knew what they were doing.

As if the words I say should be taken seriously. It was almost like another strange person stood tall inside my skin, with an odd fire in their belly that knew what was true. Thomas and Guthrie would sometimes look at each other and roll their eyes, and I was terrified they might defy me.

I know I'd back down if they did that.

I think they knew that too.

From here in the field, it's easy to see all the work that is incomplete. Items and ideas waiting for attention and time. An awful wave of ingratitude washes over me. It comes from focusing on the end and not on what is right here in front of me. I've been wishing it was something it's not. Finished. I know I'd be quick to correct Thomas if he complained; I need to listen to my own words.

So, as I change my thoughts, and concentrate on the truth of what is here right now, seeing it as it perfectly is, appreciation and love take its place. I'm still amazed that a simple change in thought can alter my life so much. My emotions, my upsets and my pain, all changed by my thoughts.

What you think of yourself is what you'll become. Was Guthrie the wisest man in Sirban simply because he told people he was, and they believed him? Was I always the Eariss? Or only the Eariss because I believed I was? *Ugh*. I've spent too much time in this field. I bundle the last of the grass reeds tightly together and carry the yelms toward the smaller lodge where Thomas and Guthrie can distract me.

Thomas is high on the pitch of the roof and Guthrie calls up to him, frustration in his voice. "Why didn't you build a smaller lodge for yourselves first?"

"And have the army move in with us? Not likely." Thomas laughs and twists the hazel branches together on the final run along the roof of the lodge. It doesn't look like a lodge, it's more like a cottage. I like the sound of cottage. It sounds as warm as we'll feel inside. There's just enough room for some pallet beds and a small fire, but that's all we'll need. Stiff wind crosses the field and blusters into my face. Our first night inside cannot come quick enough.

"Whoa," Thomas calls, and the side rake thuds onto the ground beside me; its nails pointing to the sky.

"Here," he calls to me, "Pass it back up."

"You can't say that!" Guthrie says. "You can't order her around. You forget who she is."

Thomas laughs as I hold the rake up for inspection. "Hey you, Eariss—pass the rake back up."

I toss the side rake to Thomas and plant a kiss on the old man's head. It's good to see him smile again. He still argues when he's unsure of himself, puffing himself up like a peacock that's easy to ignore. He naps more too, at least he's sleeping, and not wandering the lodge as a shadow at night muttering to himself. Sometimes it's his thrashing that wakes me, other times I pretend I haven't heard his screams and Thomas settles him. He still refuses to discuss what comes to him at night, and I worry that his heart or mind might break before his silence does. I know the self-destructive terror of forcing your body to stay awake. When sleep terrorizes more than it rejuvenates, the body tumbles into a self-betrayal where safety doesn't exist in any form. One day he might catch the lines we are throwing to him.

Guthrie pours some water from the jug, sips from his cup and scans the mountains that surround us. "Are you really sure this army's coming? And how are they going to get here? This could all be a waste of time."

"We don't know exactly," Thomas calls from the roof. I shoot him a look; he knows uncertainty sends Guthrie into a spiral of panic that grasps at anything on its way to rage. "But we're confident they'll come," he adds.

"But it's dangerous out there, they'll die on their way. The strength required to get here…"

"It's all right, old man. They'll be fine. Now tell me, how is that water, have you left me some? Should I come down before it's gone?"

Guthrie frowns at his cup, as though rounding up his thoughts and focusing them. One thing takes all the energy he can muster. "Yes," he answers, "Best come down before I finish the jug."

The whole idea of *not knowing* is freeing for me. It means anything can happen. Yet the same idea terrifies Guthrie. I expect it doesn't fit his predetermined idea of how things should be. I hold a cup out to Thomas and he pours, there's enough water for me too and I sit and rest with them. Guthrie shuffles along the ground to make room for me and his hand squelches into a patch of mud. He shrugs and wipes it on his trousers. This is not Sirban and I forget how far he has traveled. How far we have both traveled.

"Guthrie, do you think it's possible to grow without uncertainty? I mean, isn't *not knowing* something the basis of your scientific endeavors?"

"I expect it is."

"So what's uncertainty then…, how would you describe it?"

"A problem that needs to be fixed."

"Intolerable then?"

"Like a lump in my gut."

"What if you just let it be there and tried not to fix it? What would happen then?"

"I've never tried it."

Thomas joins in. "You know what I do? I get busy. Logs and reeds, fields and fences. Then I don't have to think about what I don't know. I don't have to have an answer. I just need to keep myself busy." He takes a drink and his eyes widen when he realizes what he said. "Oh, I get it. It's still there, the uncertainty. Guthrie attacks it, I cover it up, but it's still there."

We watch Guthrie, ready to backtrack if needed. He looks at Thomas, then meets my eyes. "So how do we get rid of it?"

"We don't. It's not a fiend to ignore or banish, it's an ally."

"But allies are meant to help."

"Allies teach trust. When you're stricken with uncertainty, use it as a reminder that when things are certain, there's no room for the miraculous. Uncertainty is proof that anything is possible."

Guthrie tips his head from side to side. "I could try that... as an experiment you understand."

"Do I need to be writing this down?" Thomas asks.

I nod at Thomas and wait until he's ready. "Uncertainty is like being at a crossroads. Old is gone, new is yet to come. It's always so dusty and quiet, there are never any signs. We need to celebrate the uncertainty even though it's uncomfortable. Listen to it, it's an ally. This is where growth is, and anything becomes possible. We only need to know what to do in this moment, even if this moment wants us to be with the uncertainty and trust it. Then our own uncertainty becomes an adventure, not a chore, not something to be fearful about, chased away or covered up."

Thomas looks up from his parchment. "That's it?"

"I think so." I can still see the crossroads and feel the dusty path under my feet. A knowing rises from deep in my bones. I need to understand this more than Guthrie does. The knowing seeps from my marrow and floods my body. *Listen.* My life depends on it.

G uthrie paces in the old lodge. A chilly wind whips from one end to the other and sends invisible tendrils out to toy with dry leaves on the floor. Tonight will be cold and I want to be safely inside the cottage before the sun sets. Thomas gathers the remaining items destined for the cottage. He balances some of Guthrie's instruments on top of his satchel, while I hold the blankets and resist the urge to wipe them at my nose that runs in the cold air.

Measured thuds beat through the whistle of the wind as Guthrie's knife stabs small notches into the logs along the wall. He's wandered into his own world before, but the promise of warmth should pull him back.

"Coming Guthrie?"

No answer.

His agitation means he's lost to us now. Many nights we've paced with him and watched over him until he feels safe enough to rest.

Thomas loads his armfuls on top of my blankets. "My turn," he whispers, "You get to the cottage."

Guthrie storms past us, slams his knife into the doorpost and heads into the fields. Thomas shrugs and follows him. I hope they're back before dark. I toddle carefully toward the doorway, weighing and balancing the charges that wobble and slide atop the blankets. The knife vibrates with the leftover energy of being thrust into the wood. As I pass, I catch the reflection of my eye in its blade. I have no free hand. I leave it there, standing watchful, like a soldier on guard.

❧❧❧

Cold air rushes into the cottage and if I stay completely still, Guthrie will think I'm asleep. I'll be one less concern for him as he tries to settle. Thomas speaks in calming tones and directs Guthrie to his cot and then crawls under the blanket to me. His skin is cold and I press myself against his shivering form. We strain to listen for Guthrie's sleep. His telltale rhythmic breathing that soothes our nerves and helps us to relax, too. The brightness of the full moon distracts Thomas and I hold my breath as he hangs a shirt over the small window, willing him to not make a sound. Maybe this smaller and warmer space will bring Guthrie some comfort, and for us, some sleep. Some warmth escapes from the blanket as Thomas climbs back into my arms. A gentle snore rattles in Guthrie's corner and I breathe the easiest of breaths. At last, the cottage is complete. It's not grand, but I have a place that's mine. If the future never arrived, I could be happy right here.

Thomas's warm breath puffs onto my lips. He whispers and for a moment, I'm simply me, not a legend, not information on a scroll.

"Are you safe? Are you well?"

"Of course. You?"

He nods. "We must speak in the morning about Guthrie."

Guthrie's gentle rumble continues. He's safe from himself for now. "Has anything changed?"

"No, but we need to make some decisions."

"Decisions? You're better at them than me."

"Shh. You've made some good ones."

"Like you, I suppose."

"You decided to be the Eariss."

I'd like to think I didn't decide to be the Eariss, that it was all thrust upon me. But Thomas is right. I made that decision. I decided who I would be. "Do you know how we decide who we are? And when?"

He shakes his head.

"It's when we look into the eyes of those we love. The earliest reflections sear into our hearts and make us who we are. If we only see hatred and disapproval... well, what can I say? The decision is made for us and also by us."

"And what do you see in my eyes?"

I'm braver with what I will admit now; to him, as well as myself. The moonlight dulls his eyes, but they still hold every promise he ever made to me. "That you love me, and trust me, and you believe I can do this. Whatever this is."

"Of course, you can, you're the Eariss. Besides, it doesn't really matter what I think, it matters what the scroll says."

But the scroll can't look into my eyes.

The scroll doesn't see me.

"Of course." I whisper.

My eyes snap open. Moonlight glints off the blade next to my head. I didn't dream that thud! Guthrie curses and tugs, but the wood won't release it.

"Guthrie!' I croak. Torrents of rage pour from his mouth. Blankets tangle me as I try to escape, pushing Thomas off balance in my leap to the door. I'm out. Cold wind slaps my face and I run. Grasses sting, whipping at my shins. *Run!* Where? *Run!* Guthrie curses behind me. So close. Lungs sting, I tumble. No! Get up, get up! I scramble with shouts behind me, more than one. My feet slide on the grass. *Run!* I turn from the field to the closest part of the forest. Guthrie charges toward me with Thomas following. Just over this log. I slip and crash sideways into the earth. Run! No, maybe he'll leap right over me. I pant into the dirt and listen for his footfall. Shouts.

The moon bathes the field in blue. Thomas catches Guthrie's shoulder and lands a blow to his face that sends him and his dagger to the ground. Thomas shouts at him, but I can only hear my desperate gasps for air and the blood that rushes in my ears. I don't understand. Maybe this is a dream, like one of Guthrie's nightmares. I wipe the tickle at my ear. My blood looks oddly vibrant and red against the grayness of everything around me.

I catch my breath, but my mind won't move beyond this moment. I force myself to think of Thomas or the cottage or the field, but nothing catches, and it slides right back to here.

I wipe at my ear again, distracted by humming. Bees buzz so loudly I think it must be the blood in my ears. Bees? At night? There's nothing in the trees. The sound heightens and crashes like a wave, flooding me like a waterfall.

Mystery?

Bees? Why are you showing me bees? I slump with my back to the log. Help me understand.

"Ashling?" Thomas calls to the forest.

"I'm fine."

Thomas steps aside for me to draw closer to Guthrie. He wouldn't move unless it was safe, unless he knew this old man who sobs quietly with his head in his hands was no longer a threat. I reach down and rest my hand on his shoulder and kiss the top of his head. He cries louder now, his head bobbing with each sob. It's more comfortable here on the ground in front of him. I lean my head against his and feel into his lostness. There's no 'Guthrie' here. Just bewilderment.

"Do *you* cry?" he asks between sniffs.

"Almost every day Guthrie." We weep together for this moment. Mourning that we are here; grieving for the events that led us here. "I had a wise friend called Martha. She told me tears were healing. That those who refuse to cry believe their tears might overwhelm them and wash them away, when really the strongest among us allow ourselves to feel, and honor, our grief. She said that when we show honesty and kindness, especially to our hearts, we build bedrock to stand on. And just like Thomas's scar, we are stronger for being touched by the Mystery."

Guthrie wails, and sobs some more. The cold wind chills the tracks of my tears, and swirls at my shoulders, but I don't shiver.

"I was going to hurt you. What is *wrong* with me?"

"Guthrie, let us walk." I help him to his feet and slip my arm in his. We become companions in this moment, in conversation as we stroll through the field in the moonlight. Ahead of us is a mist we can't see through, yet head towards. Thomas follows a step behind with the catalyst for our conversation safely in his hands.

I pat at Guthrie's cold hand. "Will you be open to a conversation that may appear illogical to you?"

He nods without a defiant bone in his body.

"You've studied bees?"

"I have."

"Have you ever noticed how bees will attack a hornet that gets too close to the hive?"

He nods. "Yes, they're very efficient. They swarm on it and kill it."

"Because the hornet is a threat?"

"Yes, if the hive's in danger... as I said, they're remarkably efficient."

"Guthrie, I'd like you to consider yourself as a beehive." He halts, considering it just for a moment, and walks alongside me again. "Think of whatever upset you as a hornet that has come too close. The bees charge into every part of your body, buzzing you into action as if there were a deadly threat to the hive. You panic, ready to fight off this attack, sure that your death is imminent. Only you're not doing any thinking, with that beautiful brain of yours; you're *reacting* to the presence of the hornet and the bees that create all the commotion inside you. Please know that your reaction was out of your control. The bees took over your brain to keep you safe."

Guthrie moans and missteps, but I catch him before he trips. My throat constricts and a fierce ache shudders from my heart through my body. The moonlight reflects in his welling eyes. "My brain?" he breathes, "My brain is broken?"

"It's not broken; just confused."

His eyes plead with mine, and another explanation comes to me. "You know when ants are trailing on the ground, and you move a stick or a leaf and they scatter because they've lost their path?"

He nods.

"They always find their path again, don't they? They work at it; they figure it out."

"There is a path back?"

"I'm sure of it."

We walk on in silence, our steps lulling us into calmness.

At the cottage, Guthrie squeezes my hand and opens the door for me. "I'll stay with the donkey tonight."

Thomas puts a hand on his shoulder. "Let me be sure you're comfortable enough. I won't leave until you're asleep."

Guthrie nods, and tiredness seems to pour over all of us in one breath. "You'll tell me more in the morning?" he asks.

"Of course."

This time, I shiver when Thomas's cold body arrives under the blanket.

"Did he speak much?" I ask.

"Not a great deal. I checked his face. Nothing seems broken, but we can check again tomorrow. He's so tired, he dropped straight off." Thomas flings the blanket away and positions Guthrie's cot so it blocks the door. He seems satisfied. "How did you know to do that?" he asks as he climbs back into bed. "All that stuff with the bees?"

I shrug. "Remember when the Mystery showed me those bees at Martha's Pond? They're starting to make some sense. Tonight, it was like I stepped inside his mind and watched the bees scatter. Bees scatter through my body too, although I never really knew how to explain it."

"Do you know what made his brain go like that?"

"When he's rested, and ready, he may tell us—if he knows. I react to the strangest things and sometimes I don't know why." I sigh and roll into Thomas. Tomorrow will be a big day. In fact, it's probably tomorrow already.

"I wonder why the scroll doesn't say anything about rounding up bees?"

"It doesn't say a lot of things."

"Which is kind of like you. Why don't you say the things you know?"

"Maybe the things I know are of no consequence."

"You knew things at the Hall."

"Yes, but that only concerned me, not other people."

"So what's the difference between knowing for yourself, and knowing for other people?"

I'm too tired to think of an answer. There must be a difference, though. I remember my throat constricting when I caught Guthrie in his pain, the shuddering ache through my heart. I could never tell him I felt what he felt. It feels like an imposition, a privacy invaded. Just like the knowing and understanding of motivations. "But what if people hate me for knowing?"

"Do you really think Guthrie hates you for helping him to understand what he just went through?"

"So I should tell him what I see?"

"If you don't, who will? You might be the one to say just one word that helps him do something great." Thomas props himself up on one elbow and points to me. "You don't have to do the great thing to be the great one."

We both consider his words. He raises his eyebrows and I smile and nod.

"Really Thomas? I'm impressed."

"I should write that down."

"I think you should."

⁂

The waterfall bounces down the rocks and into the pond. Each time I'm here, whether to collect water or bathe, or simply to sit in my morning routine, it still amazes me how the water leaps from its ridge, not even knowing where it's headed. There must be a great deal of freedom in such abandon. This morning Guthrie is beside me. We spoke little on our way. I sense he's a little apprehensive about how I might explain this "bee thing" as he calls it, and gives me a quick smile that doesn't quite reach his eyes. My own bees terrify me at times, and I hope I can explain it well, and gently. He watches the water cascade, and my heart swells with love for this odd little man. The wisest man in all Sirban is proving to be its bravest too.

"Have you ever stood under a waterfall, Guthrie?"

"As a child."

"They're new to me. Well, these kinds anyway. Their power surprised me. Shocked me really."

His eyes follow the water from its first leap to the pond. "It's the gravitational forces you see, it gathers momentum—Yes, they are surprisingly strong." He smiles. "I remember being a little scared of them too, as a child."

"What made you venture in?"

"Curiosity I suppose."

"Even though you were afraid?"

"Curiosity is often stronger than fear. It's what propels us forward, advances us if you like."

I know he's talking about his beloved experiments, but all that comes to mind is that moment when I left the road to Sirban and headed into the undergrowth. "Can you apply that same curiosity to the kinds of places we're going to? Even if you find you lose your footing now and then?"

The tumbling water is a convenient distraction while we wait for his answer. He rubs at his cheek and inhales deeply. "I am willing," he says.

He finds a seat on a boulder, rests his hands on his knees, and watches me like an expectant student. "Tell me what I must do."

"You're keen." I claim a seat on the log next to him.

"Let's get on with this. Fix my brain."

"It might not be as simple as one of your experiments, Guthrie. Some things aren't clear cut. You need to be prepared for unexpected moments."

"Regardless, let's get on with it. No time to waste."

"Guthrie, are you well?"

"Yes." His legs jiggle and his fingers drum on his knees.

"Guthrie?"

He pushes his palms into his thighs, exhales deeply, and lifts a hand in front of him. "Look how it trembles."

I reach forward and hold his trembling hand between mine until it stills. "Why don't we talk about what you love most? Your magnificent brain."

"I'm not sure it's so wonderful... after last night."

"We'll give it what it needs; an explanation." His body softens at the thought, and he rests back on the boulder.

"Remember how I said to think of your body as a beehive?" I catch his eye. "And I want you to know it's a healthy beehive, doing all the things it should be doing. Fear, or the buzzing that agitates the hive, is perfectly normal. It's here to protect us and keep us safe. But sometimes the bees get out of control, and if your brain understands why they do that, it can help to calm the bees down."

"I see. And the hornets?"

"From my experience, they can be anything. A smell, a look, a spoken word, a situation that *reminds* us of another. That's important to remember Guthrie. The bees buzz through your body to protect you from the original situation, not the one you're actually experiencing."

"The bees can't tell the difference?"

"The bees don't think, they just react. When a hornet arrives, the only thing they're interested in is keeping you safe."

"So, the hornets are reminders?"

I nod, suddenly aware of how many hornets still affect my every day. They wait for me where I least expect them and set the bees inside me into a flurry of stinging panic at a moment's notice. As much as I'm explaining the hornets to Guthrie, I'm taking comfort in how the process works for me. "They're many things, but mostly they remind us of what we *couldn't* do. Situations that are unresolved for us, or moments we associate with danger. They might be things we don't want to face, or refuse to face. It doesn't matter how or what made you feel powerless, or whether you might consider the incident small or huge, it's the sense of powerlessness and fear that seems to sit inside us and keep the bees on guard."

Guthrie perks up, rubs his chin, eager to solve a problem. "It seems the bee's function is to keep us away from the true source of the agitation?"

"To keep us safe, because to return to that sense of powerlessness is painful and fearful. They're only doing their job, remember."

"So, what do I do when the bees feel like they're stinging me all over? Making me rant and rage—"

"Or run like a deer, or freezing me so I can't move—"

"Or making my head spin and I can't catch my breath—"

"My stomach churn and my heart race. Until I'm so exhausted, I don't know what to do."

Our tightened smiles match.

They're not particularly happy ones, nor are they sad. Yet they pass between us as an indestructible bridge to another's heart.

"Yes." Guthrie nods, "So, what do I do?"

"You listen to your bees, Guthrie. They lead to honey."

"Here's the secret to your bees Guthrie." he leans forward, his brow furrowed in concentration. "They're teachers. Here to teach us something; not terrify us out of our brains. We've been looking at them the wrong way."

Guthrie pulls away from me, sits up on his rock, and glances around the pond. I expect it's the way I said he was doing something the *wrong way*. I should have chosen other words, but I can't change that now. I need to be more careful, gentler. Every step we take is his, not mine. He exhales and looks directly into my eyes. "Go on," he says.

"When the bees cause a reaction to guide us away from danger, they also show us a path to our healing. We're just too busy panicking along with the bees, to notice it. When you learn to stop and look for the path, it's like a huge road marker or sign, and you wonder why you hadn't seen it there before. It's always been there; we just haven't been paying attention."

"Looking at it the wrong way," he admits.

"Well, not exactly *wrong*, just not noticing anything else but the sensation of the bees under our skin."

"Which is perfectly normal."

"Perfectly normal," I assure him.

Guthrie shakes his head. "In my panic and rage I've not seen anything, least of all a road sign."

"But before that? Before the bees overwhelm you?"

"Nope. No road signs... not that I've looked."

"Here's where your beautiful brain gets to shine. Rather than being taken over by the bees, we need it to step back and watch them. Watch how they feel in your body, where they buzz, and let them buzz. You'll be amazed at what they show you. Remember the ants and the broken pathway? Every time we watch the bees and listen to them, it's like replacing a missing leaf or stick for the ants. They'll find their way again."

"So, this is the honey you were speaking about?"

"Almost. The bees have always shown me sweetness, even if I have to endure stings to get there."

Stings. The word seems to hang in the air between us. If Guthrie is going to lose his footing, it will be now. The bees hurry us away from danger and to turn against them, without knowing the sweetness of their message is terrifying. I try to swallow, but my mouth is dry. Guthrie fidgets and swings his tongue wildly around in his mouth. The tickle in my throat distracts me until Guthrie clears his throat to speak.

"So, how does this work exactly?"

"We are going to go looking for the bees and let them show us the way."

"Looking for them? Deliberately?" his face pales and he stands and paces.

"I know it sounds terrifying, but we'll just search for one or two; not the swarm. We'll ask them what their message is."

He lifts his trembling hands toward me, but he appears more interested in them than afraid.

"We can listen to your bees another time if you prefer. There's no rush," I smile at him, "They're not going anywhere."

Guthrie chuckles lightly and flips his hands from front to back, watching them as his bees buzz ever so gently in his body. How do I know that? I can feel them too, just like his dry mouth and the tickle in his throat. My eyes widen at my discovery. What does this mean? What am I supposed to—

"I think I'll stroll around the pond. Let my brain absorb what you have told me."

"Of course."

Guthrie wanders the edge of the pond, stopping here and there to investigate his discoveries on tree branches and at the water's edge. He inspects reeds, pulls some from their beds and tests their strength. He measures the wind and checks the position of the sun. All the things that bring him strength and comfort. He looks up at me and smiles, and I feel as hopeful as he looks.

Mystery? I ask through my smile to Guthrie.

I'm here.

And all at once, I understand Martha's description of me as a bridge. Of me being neither here nor there, but in both places at once.

Guthrie steps around the small rounded boulders near his seat and wipes his hands on his shirt. "So, what do we do when we find them?"

"Have you ever noticed when bees are around a hive they follow each other, almost in lines. They know where they're going and what they're doing? They're like the patterns in your brain, the way we think and breathe and react. The hornet makes them scatter and nothing makes sense."

"True."

"So, we need to get the bees back in line first, then we can listen to them. When you're good at this, the hornet can walk among the bees in your mind, and they'll be aware of the hornet, but not react to it, and you'll be able to hear what they're telling you."

Guthrie is wide eyed. "The bees will really talk to me?"

"Not in a way you're used to communicating. It could be frightening, perhaps uncomfortable." Their stingers and bramble fences come to mind, but I don't mention them.

"So, we find them..."

"Ask them why they're upset, what danger they want to keep us from."

"And they just tell us?"

"More like show us, in our bodies. It might be painful, but you have to stay and listen if you want to reach the honey. Even for the things you don't want to hear."

He considers my words. Weighing them as carefully as he would his ingredients. "Then what do we do?"

"We thank them."

"Thank them?"

"For protecting us, for showing us something we couldn't see before, for being there with answers if we care to listen."

"Ah, I see," he says. "Gratitude for their message. The one we first perceived as bad, but is, in fact, good. That whole wrong way thing."

"Only because we were reacting, not listening."

Guthrie nods. "Yes, yes, accurate enough. Come along, let's get to work." He stands and considers his boulder, walks around it twice, and pats the surface. "Here? Should I sit here?" He plonks beside me on the log. "Maybe here would be more expeditious? What about over there?" And he is off the log before I answer.

I call to him before he has gone too far. "Don't fuss about where. You just need to be comfortable. Where will you feel most relaxed?"

He makes his way back to me. "Here I expect," he says as he wipes his hand across the boulder and settles himself, reclining across its surface.

"It's important you're not agitated Guthrie."

He takes a deep breath and sighs it away. "I'm not agitated."

"Remember, we aren't looking for a swarm of bees, just one or two to train us to listen. Can you think of something that bothered you recently? Not enough to send the bees in flight, but enough that you noticed their buzz."

He pulls his lips to the side of his mouth, deep in thought.

"What happened with Thomas this morning? You grunted at him, something passed between you."

Guthrie sits up and pokes a finger at me. "I told him the lever he was using wasn't strong enough, and do you know what he said? 'Off with you, old man.' That's what he said, like I was some kind of imbecile!"

"Well, this seems like a reasonable place to start."

"Upstart young man! Making me angry like that. I was having a good morning!"

"Guthrie, can you feel the bees related to that moment?"

He rubs at his arms. "They're all under my skin."

"I need you to get the bees in order. Can you do that? Relax again on the boulder, take a deep breath. Would you like to close your eyes?"

"I don't need to close my eyes! I'm not an imbecile."

"Very well then. Breathe gently until you have those bees in order. If your mind wanders to Thomas, bring it back to getting the bees in line. Let me know when you're comfortable with them."

I sit quietly and feel Guthrie's bees settle within myself. I don't understand how or why I should feel his bees. My mind takes me back to when he first arrived and how disjointed and out of sorts I felt. I'd wondered what was wrong with me, when it wasn't me at all. It was Guthrie's disordered presence that had me reeling and wanting to avoid his company.

"They're in line now," he says.

"Can you think about this morning, but imagine yourself standing in the field and watching it from afar?"

"I can do that," he grumbles.

"As you watch, take note of any bees that buzz inside you. Can you feel them, just find one or two? Concentrate on what they're doing."

"Just buzzing lightly."

"What does it feel like inside? How would you describe it?"

"So this is like a report, an experiment?"

"If you like."

Guthrie closes his eyes and rubs a hand on his stomach. "They're in my belly, buzzing a bit harder now."

"Just watch them Guthrie. You don't need to be carried away by them, just watch them."

He pulls a few faces and I reach out and pat his arm. He speaks through clenched teeth. "This isn't very pleasant, is it?"

"It's one of the reasons why we don't want to listen. Don't try to change the buzzing or wish it away, or demand it be something else. Just stay with it and listen."

"They're not talking to me."

"They will."

Guthrie draws a deep breath. "I feel like I've just taken a blow to the stomach."

"Are you still with the bees?"

He nods, his face grimacing in pain. "It's changing. Why is it changing?"

"Because you're listening Guthrie."

"Now it's tight, pulling, twisting." He hugs his body and groans.

"What are they telling you, Guthrie?"

"They're reminding me of how angry I was at Thomas."

"Angry?"

"Now it's more akin to frustration. It's changing again."

Guthrie sighs a long, staggered breath. "Oh Stars," he whispers, "I wasn't frustrated. I was embarrassed." His face flushes, and he closes his eyes. "Why was I embarrassed?" There's no need to speak when he turns to me for an answer. "Right, ask the bees," he reminds himself and returns to his inner experiment.

It's always fear. It seems like a bold statement for my mind to make as I watch this sweet old man sort through his emotions, but it's true. Underneath the layers of everything we ever tell ourselves. Every lie that has ever caused us pain. There it is. Fear. It wears many robes, dresses itself in finery and calls itself by many names, but its bones stay the same.

Guthrie's face contorts and grimaces as the bees reveal the truth of his reaction to him. I'm glad he chose a gentle incident to explore first. I've come to appreciate every one of the buzzes. Even the swarmings that leave me gasping for breath, I don't welcome them, but I don't fear them either. I've accepted they're only here to help.

"Ashling?"

"Yes."

He turns his head and faces me, his eyes wide with the wonder of discovery, and whispers his conclusion. "I wasn't angry, or frustrated, or even embarrassed. I was scared."

I nod at him and touch his arm. He used to be so confident about his world and how everything operated inside it. Now even his own emotions have appeared as charlatans, dressed up in anything more appropriate to admit than fear. I'm surprised he's taking it so well, but I'd never thought about what I'd expected from him, anyway.

"I was scared I wouldn't be useful anymore, an old useless man, that's what made me angry at him. It had nothing to do with Thomas himself." Another discovery brightens his face. "It's more than that. I was scared that without my brain, without others relying on it... I'd be... nothing."

Each time I've come face-to-face with the lies I've believed about myself, I cry. I can't help myself. It's almost like they wash away the remnants of denial, that something once seen, especially when it's about yourself, can't be unseen. Guthrie seems to delight in finding the answer and setting things right. Perhaps that's his way of being sure things can't be unseen again.

"What do I do now?" he asks with the face of an excited child holding a new toy.

"Investigate those fears and see if they stand up to your scrutiny. Are they true? Here's one. Would you truly cease to exist without your label of intelligence? Or is it possible you're a valuable and wonderful man with or without the label?" I'm glad he thinks this is a game. What an introduction to listening to his heart. He found his answer quickly and without too much pain. I smile as he frowns through his internal questions and understandings. More pain will come soon enough. At least he knows the way out, and more importantly, the way through.

"I don't believe my only value lays in my intellect," he announces.

"You believed something that wasn't true. It was just a story you told yourself."

He flushes. I didn't mean to have caught him in an error, but he is safe here. It would normally mean a barrage of insults, as he protected himself from his fear. Today it is different. His eyes are sad. "Yes. Yes, I did."

"Can you forgive yourself for believing that lie?" he shakes his head and I catch at his arm, "Knowing that you didn't know any better. Your story protected you."

"I should've known better."

"But you didn't, you sweet old man. That's entirely the point. Be kind to yourself, Guthrie."

His face pinches at the thought of compassion and unmerited favor. He weighs up his punishments and failures and benefits. He's still an intelligent man, laying on a rock beside a pond with his heart wide open. I lift his hands and place them on his heart. Tears tumble from his closed eyes.

"You and your blasted bees," he mumbles.

Guthrie and I take pause at the edge of the bottom field. Awenmell looks somehow grand in the afternoon light. A couple of wooden buildings, fences, and a large oak. The grandest home I've ever seen. Thomas works in the distance, a tiny figure among his levers and pulleys.

Guthrie nods toward him. "He'll have that done in no time."

As we walk, I slip my arm into Guthrie's. He pats my hand. "The bees will be back, won't they?"

"It takes practice Guthrie. Each time you learn something new." Thomas curses somewhere behind the lodge in the space ahead of us. "Tell me how you feel about your incident with Thomas this morning. What does remembering it bring up now?"

"I don't feel any tension, if that's what you mean. I can see it for what it was, a reaction to my thoughts. It had nothing to do with Thomas, yet I blamed him for it all." He chuckles to himself. "It's an amazing tool. Do you think it changes the past?"

"The way we think about it at least."

Thomas stands at the edge of the lodge yard, hands resting on his hips, and looks down at us as we arrive. "Stars! It's about time you got back. Could've done with some help." He flings his arms in the general direction of the mess about him. "The lever broke, we're out of water, and your brainless donkey Guthrie!... he's set me back at least a day knocking things over every time he moves. How are we supposed to get that fence finished by tomorrow at this rate? You need to do something with that beast, old man!" Thomas storms off and kicks the empty water bucket in our direction and Guthrie collects it as we enter the lodge yard. He's taking Thomas's outburst very well.

"Are you well Guthrie?" I ask.

He raises his eyebrows and the empty bucket. "Seems our young upstart needs to listen to his bees."

T homas's side of the blanket lands on top of me with a thud. I crack my eyelids a little. Ugh, morning already? He shuffles in the half light and snorts at every slight distraction to his dressing, and stomps from one side of the cottage to the other. Moving Guthrie's cot to the donkey's stall was supposed to give us a sense of space, not provide room for his surly pacing.

"This can't go on," he says, louder than my mind is prepared for before sunrise. "I know you think you've got it all sorted with this bees nonsense, but it's not working, is it?"

"The bees were just an introduction. Guthrie has more problems than a few harsh words with you about a lever."

"What? And he's blaming me for that too?"

"No one is blaming anyone."

"Is he up yet?"

"It was a long night. I think we should let him slee—"

"Get him up! If he can scream and not give us peace to rest, then he can start the day with us."

"But Thomas—"

The door slams against the wall as Thomas strides through on his way to Guthrie. "Get up old man!" His words fill every quiet space within the meadow and any quiet space within my heart. I swing my legs out of the bed, and my feet land on the floor with a weary thud of their own.

By mid-meal, the work we've completed has appeased the worst of Thomas's impatience. He jokes with Guthrie around our small fire and speaks hopefully about his future plans. Our future plans.

Guthrie sets aside his bowl and waits until he has our attention. "I apologize for the annoyance my particular situation brings."

"Guthrie it's—" I begin, but he cuts me off.

"I can't keep them away. When those damn bees come at night, they swarm, they sting. They're just there. There's no warm up, no trail to follow." His voice cracks, and he sobs into his hands. "I'm so tired."

Thomas stares at the ground, his lips pressed tightly together. I hope he keeps them that way.

"You must rest."

"But how?"

"Dwale." I say without thinking. "Let us make dwale." They both look at me now, wide eyed I would suggest such a dangerous brew without a need for surgery or imminent death. "Small amounts. Small increments until we know what is best."

"But the ingredients?"

My memories scan the forest, the dales, the cliff edges, the pond, but I don't recall seeing anything there. Thomas frowns, and Guthrie scans the horizon. His pointed finger follows the mountain range. "We may find some mandra along that ridge."

"There's some at Sirban." Thomas says.

Guthrie shakes his head. "Sirban, no. It's gone."

"Outside of Sirban. That small junction with the blacksmith and the tavern."

"I know of it."

"They grow helpful plants there. If they don't have mandra, they'd know where to find some."

I snap some small sticks and drop them into the fire. It doesn't need more fuel, but I need some kind of distraction. What began as an unchecked thought has too quickly become a plan; and a perilous one at that. I think of red-capped mushrooms and Martha's rebuke, Brenn's tea and lost days. Mandra is gentler, and mixed with other herbs, loses its ferocity. Not that I ever thought I'd need to recall Martha's lesson. Yet here it is in my mind, clear as the sunshine that brightens the field. Yet clarity never dispels danger.

The flames have distracted Thomas and Guthrie too, and my words rouse us again. "Do you wish to try the dwale Guthrie?"

"Wish?" he replies with a heavy sigh. "I wish I didn't fear sleep. I wish I could remember what it felt like to relax, to not fear my mind." He rubs his forehead. "I wish for the impossible; that things were as before."

As before. Guthrie and I couldn't have more contrasting '*as befores*' if we'd tried. We can change none of that. But we have this moment, and the irrefutable forward motion of our lives, and a choice.

"The dwale may help with some of your wishes, but others might never be granted." The recognition in his eyes pierces my heart. "You understand, don't you? Some *are* impossible."

He wipes his face with the back of his hand. "That's something, isn't it? Coming from you."

"Wishing is beautiful, and hopeful, and dreamlike. But when the time for wishing is done, acceptance rouses us with its gentle tapping. It taps so quietly at our heart we might not even hear it at first. It's polite; never barges in and always asks if we're ready to receive visitors. The trouble is, acceptance always brings another guest. Acceptance and grief always travel together. And while we may only want to welcome the first visitor, it's not until we've wholly embraced and even delighted in the things grief shows us, that we can move forward."

"Acceptance, you say."

"When wishing is done."

"Then grief."

"When you're ready to welcome acceptance."

Guthrie watches the fire, nodding gently. How did a discussion about dwale end up being about grief? And a plan to ease his pain thrust him further into it? How did the beauty of wishing become stark reality? Perhaps he isn't ready for any of this. Thomas offers me a half smile. He doesn't know where any of this is going, either. Was the idea of dwale wrong? Did I just offer him hope and then smack it to the ground? Everything feels raw and open, then shut tightly and bound. Sharp and true. Then shrouded; but never soft. My breath only reaches my throat as if a deep breath would scare whatever this is away. Whatever this is.

"They held me down, you know."

His words punch a hole so deep into my body, I might tumble into it and never return.

I want to hear. I want to stay, but his pain sets my own bees into a flurry of panic that threatens to whisk me away to a safer place. I blindly reach for Thomas's hand and find his searching for mine.

Guthrie's eyes wait for me to flinch, to turn away and prove his story unworthy of telling; to prove the damage doesn't matter, to confirm he's safer in silence. I hold his hopeful gaze. I can't swallow, but it's not my voice he needs.

He runs his finger along his forearm and stops at a scar. "This one was first. You never forget that sort of thing, do you?" He pulls one side of his mouth into a half-smile. "Oil of vitriol."

That's the oil I spilled on his desk! It burned through the wood. Tears prick my eyes and I can't breathe. *Oh, Guthrie.*

"You're right," he says, his own tears brimming, "I can't wish for the impossible."

There were so many burns on his body. So many drips of that wretched oil. They used his own works against him. They used his own love against him. "Guthrie, I—"

He holds a hand up to shush me. "You told me yesterday about how we get caught in the things we couldn't do. The actions we couldn't take. They held me. It was impossible for me to fight back, and I understand that." He taps at his temple. "But there was a dagger there, just outside my reach. If they meant it to bedevil me; it did." His fists open and close in quick succession and we sit in silence until he takes a deep breath and continues. "The bees," he says, "The night bees are done with the torment. They want the dagger, they want the action!" He pounds his fist into his thigh several times and sniffs his quiet tears away. "My brain was useless. I was useless. I couldn't work out any formulation that could help me. They wanted battle tomes, they wanted strategy. They wanted answers, and I couldn't give it to them. Me! Guthrie, the smartest man in the village." He stares at me now, and all the stubbornness I had ever seen dwell in the old man comes to the surface and embodies every part of him. "They wanted something I couldn't give them. But even if I could have; I *wouldn't* give it to them."

Stubborn old man. Hateful, even. I wince, just remembering when I first saw his burns. Tending to them, watching them heal. That one on his forearm took the longest. I used to only see the brightness of the scar, not what put it there, but now all I see in them is Guthrie's torture. Didn't anyone in Sirban come to help? Surely someone would have heard. I imagine the sound of his screams and they consume me, clawing at my insides.

"I would never give them what they wanted," he whispers, "Because they wanted *you.*"

⁕⁘⁂⁘⁕

I don't know how I got to the forest, or how I ended up here, curled into a ball among the ferns by the stream. I rest my arm over its bank and let the ripples drag at my fingertips. It doesn't seem to matter how I got here. Just that I am here. Memories of this morning fade in and out of my mind, like someone telling me a story, and I remain distant and unaffected. The water brushes by my fingers, sometimes swirling around them like tiny eddies before heading into the distance, where it will eventually become part of the waterfall and the pond. A small leaf floats past; off on a journey it might not even want to be on. *Marigolds?* I smell marigolds. But if there are some in this forest, I've never seen them. I don't see any orange flashes of color anywhere, yet their scent lingers slightly in the air, fading now. Replaced by a whisper of Martha's voice.

Whose hand controls this cup? She asks, as quietly as the breeze.

"Yours," I dutifully reply.

And whose hand controlled the oil that caused Guthrie's pain?

I breathe my words in a sigh, knowing her presence will soon be gone. "Not mine."

Old patterns are comfortable, not always truthful.

I nod, concentrating on the memory of her voice, and how heartened I felt standing beside her. *Snap!* A stick breaks behind me and I'm on my feet.

A short distance away, Guthrie smacks Thomas's shoulder and shakes his head at him.

Thomas shrugs at me. "We followed you when you ran off from the fire."

"You've been here the whole time?"

"Hope that's all right," he says.

Guthrie chimes in, "We just wanted to be sure... you know... that you were well."

"I'm well now, thank you."

We leave the stream, the ferns, and the forest, but I carry the faintest hint of marigolds within me. Thomas wraps his arm around my shoulder as we approach the field. "Are we still intent on addling the old man?"

"Not addling, Thomas... Calming. Guthrie?" I ask.

Guthrie shows me his trembling hands. "I feel hollow. Perhaps you're right. I'll leave for the blacksmith outside Sirban in the morning."

"Don't leave," I say. "You're already weak from lack of sleep."

"Well, *you* can't go," Thomas says to me, "I'll do it."

"They won't sell the mandra to you, and besides, you don't know what you're looking for."

Guthrie flicks Thomas's shoulder. "Then you come with me. We'll take the ridge."

I laugh at them. "What? You don't want to go back through the bog?" but they ignore my jest and continue their plans.

Thomas rubs at his chin. "If we don't find those plants—"

"Mandra, oh, and some henbane. The ones with the creamy flowers and dark eyes."

"I know the ones. If we don't find them on the ridge, we'll continue along it until we reach the blacksmiths."

A plan. A new focus. Something to dwell on other than mud and bees and Guthrie's night cries.

We spend the rest of the day shouting our thoughts to each other as we work.

Are there any supplies we need?

How much silver do we have?

No doubt we'll hear about the unrest.

No, we're not taking that awful donkey Guthrie. He'll slow us down. Lock him at the back of the lodge in that pen.

But I've just put all the pots there.

It's not like he's going to eat them... is he?

It's quite possible knowing that animal.

The dwale....

Yes, the dwale...

I hope it works...

A beetle buzzes past me. It probably wants to leave the heat of the field too. My hands slide on the handle of the hoe, and I stop to wipe their perspiration on my skirts. There's only this small section to finish and I can plant those seedlings. I stretch my back and survey my work. I've done quite a bit since they left.

I was glad to see them go. Glad for them to be off on their adventure, and to leave me with mine.

"I worry that I'm leaving you here." Thomas said.

"At Awenmell? No need for worry. I am safe... and I am well. Because of you."

That seemed to cheer him, and I walked with them down to the threshold, encouraged them to support each other and once I turned from them, I turned to what I might accomplish while they were gone.

They carted water from the pond for me before they left. That was one practicality out of the way. The donkey grazed free for a short while, but he soon discovered the seedlings nestled inside the lodge and I lured him back into his pen with some fresh vegetables.

The day is my own. No Thomas or Guthrie to interrupt or add to my concerns. So while I till the soil, I commune with the Mystery. Together we consider Guthrie's bees, and the flurries and stings of mine. *What you do for yourself, you can do for others.* It reminds me.

I ask questions about the lodge, the wolves, and the bog. The answers fill my body with understanding, not always words, and not always in a way that I can explain. I'm grateful for the solitude, particularly when I answer a question out loud and then laugh at myself. There's no need to rush, I'm reminded. Whether about the lodge, Guthrie's dwale, or this patch of hoed earth for the seedlings. I hold a seedling to the light, just as I did in Martha's garden. We protected them along the garden edge there, and here, we protect them within the confines of the large lodge. Now it was time to introduce them to the wider world. Time to see if that early protection had kept its promise and provided the strength they need to withstand whatever comes their way.

The first one drops gently into the soil and holds its form, standing straight and strong. It's quite brave, this tiny thing in an enormous field. It looks so vulnerable, and just a misplaced footstep away from destruction. Yet it needs this vastness around it to grow to its best. Without the light, warmth, and rainstorms, it can't produce what it's destined to produce.

A wave of uneasiness rolls over me. It still looks too tender to be this far from the lodge. No protection, no armor, nothing to shield it from any adversaries. Don't be a dolt. It's a balance. How can it grow if it's hidden behind shields, how can it produce if it doesn't stand in the sun's heat and be stormed upon as the seasons pass?

The lodge looks so much bigger from this angle. The Mystery nudges at my heart, but I don't understand it. Something ties the seedling to the lodge, but I'm missing it. I shrug. Some things are clear as stream water, other things only come into view as I get closer or dwell on their connection. For now, all I have is a feeling they are somehow one and the same, that they come from the same place. I scoop some water in my hand and settle the seedling into place.

"It's a good thing I put the donkey away," I tell it. "He's most likely your greatest adversary."

Movement darts in the corner of my eye. Intruders! Every nerve in my body jolts into action, and bees surge through my veins. Two strangers stand at the threshold. I'm on my feet, shallow breaths in my throat.

Mystery?

I am here.

I beg you, tell me they are only in search of food…. Mystery?

Trust what you know.

Bees charge unabated, stinging and scraping through to my extremities as what I *know* comes to light. The thin man takes an odd stance. His raggy clothes emphasize his only arm, and he uses it to awkwardly pull his companion's shoulder away from Awenmell. The larger man shrugs him off and saunters under the threshold and up the rise toward me. One Arm follows behind, head down.

The lodge beckons but is too far away. A race for my life that I won't win.

The first man is solid and wears a vest of fur over his garments. He thinks it makes him look bigger and more brutal. My body shivers. It works. He's not tapping at his body. Thomas says tapping's a sure sign of a weapon. My heart is about to beat through my chest.

Mystery?

I am here. What do you know? Think!

Thomas said there were five to remember. Five. My fingers drum gently against my skirt. One, two, three, four, five. Knowing how many doesn't bring them to the surface. The five are hidden; drowned by bees.

The men close in. Think!

Be kind. I'll offer them food and they might...

I reach down and scoop a handful of soil to examine. If I'm unconcerned about our meeting, they might be too. The dirt trembles in my hand.

"Nice lodgings," the fur vest says as he approaches. "Lots of space for just you." One Arm halts behind him, hidden in his shadow.

"There's not just me." My words sound far more confident than I feel.

Fur Vest looks around the field. "Seems to me you're all alone."

"Things aren't always as they seem."

Fur Vest raises his eyebrows and his sly grin exposes rotting teeth. The seedling pops under my feet; a sacrifice for my firmer footing, and I squeeze the tremble from my other hand into the wood of the hoe. It reverberates back into my body, but Fur Vest seems unaware. They only see their prey. They don't see 'me'. The bees drown in something calmer than a tremble. Something calmer, but more terrifying. Something new.

"A meal gentlemen?" I suggest, but this is a formality; a kind warning, and their last chance to back down.

The fools don't take it.

The dirt leaves my hand and fans over Fur Vest's face. He reels backwards, eyes closed. No time to lose.

I swing the handle like a sword into the side of his head. The deep thud shudders into my hands. He screams an obscenity, half-blind, and grabs at his head.

Where's One Arm? Retreating. Good.

Fur Vest lunges at me. I duck sideways, and stab the blunt end of the hoe into his gut. Hard. He staggers back, enraged. Eyes white against the mud on his face.

He latches onto the hoe and shoves it back at me. He's too strong. My arms collapse. The flat metal hoe punches into my stomach, forcing air from me in a yell.

I step back from his motion, my hands gripped around the weapon. If I let it go, I'm dead. He releases his grip and I reel. My neck snaps back.

My hair! I swing the hoe blindly behind me. He shouts in pain. My hair is free. Got him!

He wrenches the staff from my grip and flicks it away, scraping the metal blade on my shoulder as it passes. I scramble after it. I need my weapon. One stride lands me on my face. Aghh! Skirts. I dive for the hoe. Get off the ground! *Off the ground!*

I roll on the lumpy earth. Fur Vest lands beside me with a roar. I smack the metal end into his back over and over. I can't get up. The hoe just bounces on the fur. Aghh! He snatches the pole and snaps it in front of me. No!

I scramble to my feet, hunched over with no plan. Clods of dirt hang in the strands of my hair. I pant and watch him rise. The victor's grin spreads across his face. My energy drains into the soil. Blood drips from a gash on his forehead.

I back away, but these wretched skirts trip me and land me on my back. Fur Vest looms above me. I grab handfuls of dirt. Futile.

What's this? My hand latches onto the broken handle. I aim as he dives.

Stomach?

No.

Eye.

The heat from his scream cascades down my neck, and I push him away from me and wretch.

I scurry backwards from them both. One Arm helps his wailing friend to his feet. Fur Vest curses with a mix of spittle and blood on his lips. The blood drips from beneath the hand on his eye and makes bright stripes on the fur.

I wave the bloodied stick at One Arm like a madwoman.

The curses continue all the way to the threshold. Mostly from One Arm now that Fur Vest is ailing. I can't hear what he's saying and I don't care. They couldn't see me; I bet they can see me now.

My eyes sting a little. It's probably dirt. Lights? The lights were just a sign, not a weapon. That's what Martha said. They should take it as a sign to never come back.

I can't see them anymore, nor hear their complaining. I gasp as my body makes itself known again. I tense against the pain in my belly, blood trickles from the wound on my shoulder. I collect the broken hoe and take refuge inside the lodge.

The cottage pulls at me. I want warmth and tenderness and...

But I can see better from here.

The rag I use to clean my shoulder turns the water in the bucket red. I should have thought to keep some separate for drinking. Too late now. Too late for many things.

I laugh, I cry, I tremble even though the wind isn't cold. What on earth is going on? I curse Thomas. I curse him for forgetting to tell me about what happens afterward. I wretch again. I'll do it alone.

I say the word out loud, even though it comes as a croak. "Deception." It means the truth isn't told. Some surprises are pleasant, but a handful of dirt in your face is not. The five come back to me now; did I complete them?

I welcome the distraction and count them out on my fingers with a dreamlike quality, as though their meaning is there, but I am not responsible for them. Do something unexpected, and follow with a blow. I hold my thumb and forefinger out. I did that. The third was don't stop. I shuffle my legs about and confirm their freedom as the panic of the tangled skirts shoots through them. Four. Act on a tell. I shrug, I don't know if I did that or not; I don't think I care anymore. And the last one; number five... number five has gone; it disappeared into vapor before I even got close.

There's still no one in the fields. I rest in the doorway and let the aches move across my body like waves. I heave again, it's not from blood or pain, but an awful sense of betrayal. It bites into every part of my being, far worse than the bees ever could. My arms squeeze as best they can around my body, and I groan like an animal. I'm glad I'm alone. I toss the broken hoe out into the yard. I give up my weapon. If there were dwale here, I'd drink it by the cupful. How can a victory feel like a bitter betrayal? Aren't I supposed to feel invincible or something?

Tell me the last one...

The Mystery cuts through my agony with a voice like warm oil. There's nothing sharp, nothing harsh or blameful about it. Just inquiring. I search my mind, but I can't find the last one. Number five. It's wandered off into a fog, and I've no wish to go after it. "I don't want to." I whisper. The Mystery waits; in infinite patience for me to search. If I stayed in this doorway for a thousand moons, all would be perfectly well, but I already know where I must look. There's no point fighting what you know.

"Number five..." my throat constricts and I force the words out, "... was, don't let the battle linger. If you get a chance to end it..." I heave again and a shiver triggers aches through my body; a punishment for acts I chose to perform. Deep breaths agitate the bruised portion of my stomach but eventually return me to a calmer state where I'm less defensive and ready to hear again. Ready to listen, ready to be honest.

Who did you betray?

"Myself."

How?

"I always thought I would never harm another. So much harm was done to me. Look what I did! I thought I was a peaceful person."

You weren't peaceful. You were harmless.

The reality of the Mystery's words seeps into my body in tender and stinging correction.

It's only when you know what you're capable of that you can choose to be peaceful. It's not a choice otherwise. Your power lives in the choices you make, not in your circumstances.

I think about everyday choices I make. How I speak and act. It's true. I have the power to choose peace, only because I have the option to choose otherwise.

Tell me what you did this day in the field.

I think about how I charged, raised the hoe, and waved it at One Arm as they left. They were the things I did, but the Mystery is asking me something else. I smile at the dragonfly that hovers near the open door as a courage I didn't know I had makes its home in my bones. "I defended myself."

And what you can do for yourself, you can do for others.

<hr>

Two days of rest is enough. That's if you call carting water and tending seedlings rest. There's still a few hours of daylight left; I can get something else done. Slowly, but I can get it done. I gather the pieces of broken hoe from the yard using the hand of my 'good' arm. This morning's paste of crushed yarrow cracks and tumbles in pieces from the wound on my shoulder. My hand rushes to it, warms it; it's still tender but on its way to health. I bite my bottom lip. Any task that hinders my recovery is my new enemy. I won't tolerate the thought of making this worse. The hoe was my weapon, but my choices have become my shield.

The sticks roll slightly on my palm. I don't know what I'll do with these pieces. They're both stained with blood, two sides of a story that will be told in a million different ways, but no story has the power to erase stains. Stories explain, but they never dilute.

They don't belong in the lodge. I drop them beside the door just as a breeze whisks the sun's excess heat from my back.

It's too hot to work in the field. The breeze brushes the tops of the grasses and I gladly accept its invitation and leave the lodge behind and wander through them. A section of the boundary fence has a rail missing. It lies just to the side and all it needs is some propping up. I lift it with my good arm and a surge of pain shoots through the muscles of my stomach. The rail lands with a thud onto the grass. It can stay there until Thomas and Guthrie return. I follow the fence line, noting any tasks they'd want to know about. I wonder how they're doing?

I must ask Thomas to read the scroll again when he returns. Did the scroll talk about the army, or was it just Thomas's idea? I run my hand along the rails as I amble the rise along the back of the lodge where we first landed our feet on Awenmell. If Fur Vest and One Arm found us, who else will? Thomas might be right after all. It's time to focus on the army. My mouth pulls to one side. I can't believe I just thought that.

The view from here is remarkable. The oak stands like the kind shelter the scroll promised it would be, but there's also the completed main lodge, and the beginnings of another. Our cottage sits off to the side and we're working on dividing the fields, or at least creating a larger pen for the donkey. Are we ready for an army? Something tells me we're not, that there's something we're forgetting; a piece missing. There aren't gaps in fences, and Thomas's plans are in order. Yet something is unfinished, untended; but I'm not exactly sure what it is.

I gasp and drop to my knees beside the fence. A rider atop a dark horse walks under the threshold. *Not again.* The thought of another fight saps all my energy. The branches above may hide me if I can get high enough. My gentle dive between the rails jars my shoulder and searing pains rips across my stomach. I won't be climbing any trees today.

The Trothsman's black cape covers his body and the flank of his horse and makes them look and move as one. Like black silk sliding across the meadow. I swallow hard. I could spot those horses anywhere. Especially if all my fears have come true and they are here for me. Did the bandits tell him I was here? I scan the lodge in my mind. The fire's cold. He might think I left. Fire. What if he burns the lodge? The scroll's in there. Bees scurry through my veins, searching for non-existent answers.

Mystery? Nothing. The bees are too loud. I scrounge around me for a solid branch and come up with a pathetic, uneven one. I've seen Trothsmen up close; they break sturdy branches as easily as looking at them. What if I run?

Wait.

A man follows behind. A familiar gait.

Guthrie. *Guthrie?*

Betrayal surges into my heart. My jaw clenches against the tears that form in my eyes. *You lead them here?*

Guthrie, why? An invisible blow hits my tender stomach, and I land seated on the grass.

They've got Guthrie... but where's Thomas?

The setting sun dazzles my eyes. Stripes of orange and flashes of light through the distant treetops make it hard to follow their path to the lodge. The Trothsman dismounts and they enter the largest building. What's in there? I run my list again. Seedlings, water, yarrow, Guthrie's cot, tools. Anything to give me away? What will Guthrie say to him?

They're out again. On this side of the lodge, scanning the fields.

"Ashling!" Guthrie calls. Surely he knows I won't answer.

Take him to the pond, Guthrie! Oh, he must think I'm there. No, no! Don't walk the boundaries.

But wait; I focus...

Heat flushes through my body and I jump to my feet. I shout the pain of my movement away.

Guthrie jumps, and Thomas flicks the last of the Trothsman's cape from his shoulders. They both run toward me as I rage.

"Did you not for one moment consider how I might have viewed this arrangement?"

They could've reached me by now, but stop short.

"We, err," Thomas says, "… wanted to surprise you."

Guthrie nods behind him.

"*Surprise* me?" The word drums up pictures of Fur Vest swatting at the dirt on his face. "Well, that's one word for it. You dolts!" I clench my teeth against passing through the fence again. My heart beats hard against my chest. It's not just pain, I should bang their heads together. Where to start with my abuse?

The bees sting and flutter, then dissolve at their cringing faces. How I've missed those lovely faces. They're home and safe. For now. "We have work to do," I say and kiss Guthrie's head as I pass. His eyes are brighter. How I've missed Thomas! I take his hand with my good arm; I don't need to worry him with my injuries right now. Our feet trample the grass path back to the lodge. Thomas smells of horsehair, a scent that works its way into my bones. "We need to prepare for the army," I say.

"See? I told you, didn't I?" I don't know if Thomas talks to me, or Guthrie, but it doesn't matter, anyway. "Did you see the horse?" he asks me, "Isn't he a beauty?"

"I saw him."

"You've always admired Trothsmen's horses."

"I have." Sleek memories of that dark silk, majestic movement, hooves on cobblestones… I shake my head before the blood trickles between them.

"Can't you see?" Thomas bounces with energy. "It's all coming together. The plan. Slowly, but it's coming together."

I scrub my hands down my skirts. My palms don't burn, but the action pains my shoulder enough to provide some relief and the cobblestones disappear. "Tell me about your journey," I say. The question distracts Thomas from my behavior.

"Wait until I tell you about the horse."

"The ingredients. Can we make dwale?"

"Yes, yes, we can make dwale. Now, come and see this horse I brought you."

The hearth in the main lodge holds the fire well. Its light warms our faces as we sit in an arc around it, devouring our first meal together in days. My heart swells with how much I had missed these two, and how glad I am that we're side-by-side once more and that we're all safe together in the twilight.

"So the horse is really ours?" I ask again. It still feels like a dream; as if a priceless gift was accidentally tossed my way. My stomach twists and cramps. I should eat slower.

"The law says it is," Guthrie says and licks the back of his spoon.

"His rider took an arrow under the arm." Thomas diagrams the angle of the arrow. "Pierced his chest and finished him quickly. He left an unattended horse with no other Trothsmen about, so we claimed him."

"Did anyone offer to hear his confession?" I don't know why I'm intrigued to hear what a Trothsman's final thoughts would be. Would they be proud of their service or filled with doubts like the rest of us? They're always so sure of every punishment they dole out; every decision they make.

"He said he wished for a freedom he never found." Thomas shrugs.

"How odd that a Trothsmen would think of freedom."

Guthrie leans toward the pot and helps himself to another scoop. "They're certainly not applying those thoughts to anyone else."

"But death brings honesty, doesn't it? He died in his safe lie."

"Safe lie?"

"His life was a lie. But he was safe. Look at what I endured at the Hall."

"That wasn't safety," Thomas says.

"I thought it was, and that's the point. This Trothsman thought he was safe somehow. Only he wasn't."

Guthrie shakes his head. "No one is safe out there right now."

"Were you two in any danger?"

They look at each other, and Thomas nods to give Guthrie the floor. "The travel along the ridge was tiresome but uneventful. But once we were close to the trading point..." Guthrie shakes his head. "The air was so heavy. A strange phenomenon. Our main objective was the plants, of course, and the plan was to appear unobtrusive and move in and out of the trading area without detection. The stall by the blacksmith's, the one with the helpful plants, was just where Thomas said it would be. So we put our heads down, purchased the mandra and some ale for celebration when a misunderstanding between some men about seeds erupted like one of my steam experiments." Guthrie shoots his hands in the air and whooshes like escaped steam. "Peculiar behavior, and might I add, with disproportionate results."

Thomas takes over. "I grabbed Guthrie's arm, and we ducked under two waves of men as they met each other with daggers and hatchets."

"Hatchets? Over seeds?"

Thomas nods, wide-eyed. "We met many running in as we were running out. All with that same vengeful look in their eyes. All wielding something."

"They acted like my magnets," Guthrie adds. "All converging to the same source, but without reason."

I rest my hand on Guthrie's arm. "You were well through this?"

"Once we were well away," he says. "... and the ale came in handy for calming my nerves."

"And mine," Thomas says. "It's said bandits have a lair in the Trecian caves on the next ridge over. You can bet they watched us on our way there. I tried to keep close to the forested parts of the ridge on the way back."

The next ridge. I've seen it when I gather near the cliff edge beyond the pond, but I'd never paid it much attention. My eyes were always drawn to the village that lay in the valley far in the distance. Sometimes I could see wisps of smoke, or what I thought were flickers of light at dusk. Thomas said it was the village of

Lewtshire and I needn't bother about it. Anyone would have to scale that great cliff to get to us. I hope bandits aren't good at climbing.

"Won't they move on now?" I ask, "If it's common knowledge they're in the cave, surely they'll be ambushed by the Hall."

Guthrie taps his spoon in the air at me. "It's a labyrinth in there. Some say the tunnels link and come out on the other side of the mountain. Others try to map their way through and aren't seen again. Either way, it's madness. They launch attacks on the Hall from the caves, and the Trothsmen chase them down like rabbits."

Thomas pours ale into our cups. "Occasionally the rabbits strike true, and this time we were in the right place to benefit."

Guthrie pulls a quick uncomfortable smile. Being so close to a Trothsman would have frightened him more than angry men wielding hatchets, yet he showed compassion for the dying man. "Arrow helped carry our purchases along the ridge, and he'll be of great assistance around here."

"The horse's name is Arrow?"

"It is now. A fortuitous meeting if you ask me," Guthrie says, and they bang their cups of ale together. "To fortuitous meetings!"

I wait for their chuckles to subside before I speak. "I had a meeting while you were away, too. Only I'm afraid it was a little light on compassion."

I stand and tell my tale, complete with animated swings and descriptions as my injuries will allow. Their expressions contort between frowns, shock, and horror and I smile at the faces they pull and the pure relief of having them home with me.

Thomas leaps to check my injuries, "Thank the Stars you're well," he says, and kisses my forehead, but his jaw clenches and he doesn't seem proud of me at all. I've disappointed him. Maybe it's because I couldn't remember the five.

I smile again at Guthrie's wide eyes and the way he jests and distances himself from me; about a hoe's length away. "So hoes aren't those tools you were seeking?" I shake my head, and he laughs and brings me my cup. "I never expected to hear such a story from you."

"And I didn't expect both of you to be so compassionate toward a Trothsman."

"The strangest story of the day," Thomas says, "Is the one where you stormed towards us and announced we need to prepare for the army."

I swallow my ale quickly. I don't think I stormed, but that doesn't matter now. "Where's the scroll? Remind me what it says about armies."

Thomas moves to the other side of the lodge and finds the scroll tucked among his parchments. Guthrie leans in to me, the effects of the ale softening the edges of his usual clipped speech. "It's not all about battle plans with him, y'know. He believes in your army. He thinks I didn't see, but he traded his beloved vellum for extra bowls and blankets. He thinks I didn't see, but I saw."

"Here," Thomas says, "It says you'll run through all that stand before you. Sounds like you're already practicing for that part. You'll fight a holy war, whatever that is, with chargers. Arrow might be the first of many. And naked armies... what's that supposed to mean? Guthrie?"

"Naked armies?" he shakes his head and doesn't even try to make himself pompous. It's comforting to know he's as lost as we are. Thomas frowns at the scroll and shakes his head.

"Wasn't there more?" I ask Thomas, "Other things you've told me, not in the scroll. Hints about what we do now?"

"Not really. The tales only speak of the actual army, and its remarkable power, not how it begins unfortunately."

The fire is suddenly too warm for me, and I seek cool air by the open door. "So we've got all these pieces of information, but nothing that's solid." I say and rest on the door-frame. The combination of ale and cool air makes me less interested in involving myself any further in their conversation.

"Some from the scroll, some from Martha, some from my travels... and from Eshnae." Thomas says.

Guthrie sits up straight. "Eshnae?"

"Ashling's maid. She told her to search for what was hidden. Turns out it was her." Thomas calls out to me. "You know that's what she meant when she said 'it's you', not that *you* were to blame."

I nod. Hidden in plain sight. Like everything else until we have the eyes to see it.

"What other things did she tell you?" Thomas asks.

Patches of memory, distant words, flashes of color swirl in my head and I clamp my hand against my stomach's retching. Pieces float around inside me, waiting to form something usable, but nothing connects, and I give up without trying. "Let's concentrate on the things we already know. They must add up to something."

"You're still confident they're coming here, though. We don't have to go and find them?"

The sensation I felt when I crossed the log returns. At least something is strong and true. "No, they're coming here."

"When?"

I shrug. Thomas's face is hopeful, but I have nothing to offer him. "There's something missing but I don't know what it is."

"Missing? From here?"

"There was a large window in the Great Hall. Made up of lots of smaller pieces of glass. It always amazed me how it held together and how the light would fragment as it entered the room. The light still came in, but in diverse strengths and on distinct angles. All the various pieces made up the whole, but you couldn't see that if you just focused on one piece of glass. You had to see the whole pane to understand how it all fit together. Like our stories tonight, and pieces from the scroll, and our memories. I think we just need to trust that all the pieces are somehow bringing something together. I don't know how. But it feels close."

Thomas and Guthrie shrug at each other. They've both heard stranger things from me. Their conversation blurs into the background and I lean my shoulder back into the door-frame and try to make sense that the impressive black beast that wanders our moonlit field is real. A Trothsman's horse - mine. He's so majestic, yet a stab of panic hits my heart and floods into my extremities; it's not right that he's here! A chill pours over me and pools at my feet.

It's not a good thing to be mine. He must go.

Thomas interrupts my thoughts, tidying a curl behind my ear, and stands close behind me. My hair's long enough to tie up now, but loose strands are often free. His lips brush my temple and I recline into his embrace, letting the safety of his presence and the effects of the ale lull me into rest. He still smells of horses, and I scrunch my nose against the scent.

"He's grand, isn't he? Just look how the moonlight reflects off his coat."

My lips pull into a tight smile. Not that Thomas can see it. I fight against the horror that rises again, over and over, until the agitation ends as my stomach heaves. "I don't want the horse. You should release him."

Thomas's body tenses behind me. "What are you saying? You've always wanted one."

"It will only bring pain."

"I thought it would make you happy."

His movement floats a trace of hay and horsehair over me, and bile rises and churns in my gut. My body tightens, but the ale has loosened my lips. "Get rid of it." There's no point grasping for something that will only be ripped away.

"What's going on here?" Thomas turns me and frowns, waiting for an answer, but the bees that storm through my veins have silenced my voice. He makes sure our eyes meet. "Do you trust me?" I know the words came from Thomas's mouth, but the Mystery is here too. "Do you trust I wouldn't have brought this horse to you if I did not mean it for your good?"

Especially if it causes dread to power through your body? Thomas didn't know to say that part, but the Mystery makes sure I can't deny its words. Unacknowledged memories slide against me and the ale makes it easier to surrender to whatever the Mystery wants from me. I nod my head to both of them.

"You're afraid of Arrow because happiness terrifies you?"

"People will die." I know the words don't make sense, but I let them tumble out.

"Look around you. No one will die because you dare to be happy."

He's right. Guthrie sits by the fire watching our conversation, and Thomas is safe right before me. Yet as he moves, earthy scents waft by and send more bees scurrying through my veins. I don't want to follow them; I fear what they might show me. My breath slides in and out of my body and keeps their stings at bay, for now. I must decide where to go from here; listen to my bees and let them lead me, or deny the Mystery's gentle tapping at my heart and find a way to cope with their incessant stings.

Thomas brings his face closer and speaks softly, "Is the Mystery saying anything to you about this?"

My eyes narrow. How did he know to ask that? The bees buzz slightly, a tiny reprieve and warning before their reaction to my choice. They scatter as heaviness crashes like a wave above me and pulls me into the iciness of the deep river. There are no shallows to wade in this time, only its darkest depths that lure me so powerfully I fear I might not rise again. Will I release the weight that drags me into its depths? Will I surrender? Trust? You want to know what the Mystery says, Thomas? My hands rub my skirts feverishly, and I force the words through my clamping throat.

"It's telling me about the power of stories."

"Stories?"

"How they bond us together. Cleanse us. That horrors are diluted by hearing ears."

Guthrie nods gently at me. Does he feel the thickness that surrounds me, and the pressure that crushes my breath? The tension of fruit about to burst its skin. I force air into my strained lungs and release it as a statement. "I must tell you." In my mind's eye, blood seeps around the cobblestones, and I refuse to shake the vision from my head. I see them clearly now.

The stench of blood calls the bees to return, and I gag violently. Thomas waits while I compose myself; for my throat to cease constricting, and for the bees to leave the last of their stings as an ache in my bones.

I need air.

Thomas's hand is warm as I lead him through the doorway. "Guthrie, will you join us?"

We walk the short distance to the field where Arrow stands. The moon is round and lights the way, a safe place for confessions and full deep breaths. My heart thumps with shock and so much jagged energy I can barely feel the wound on my shoulder.

Guthrie refills Arrow's bucket and joins us at the edge of the field. There's no sound other than some crickets and the wind rustling the leaves of the oak.

Thomas breaks the silence with a whisper. "Are you safe? Are you well?"

I trust these men with my life. Why is it so hard to trust them with my heart? Their faces are gray blue in the half light. Will they mock me? The Mystery nudges me into my bravery.

"I have a tale I must tell; will you hear me?"

Thomas and Guthrie sit on the ground and wait for me to speak. But where to start? How to start? I reach for Arrow and he doesn't shy when I rest my forehead on his slender neck. His coarse mane ruffles under my hand as it slides towards his shoulders. My fingers instinctively scramble in search of bumps and a tender smile stretches my lips.

"Did you ever believe you could fly?" I say to them. "I mean as a child. Really believe you could fly away and never be found?"

They shrug and mumble softly to each other.

"I did. I believed it so much, I thought the truth of it would burst through my skin and I'd soar and then..." I pull a momentary smile. "I expect when you're six summers old you don't think about what you'd actually do if you flew, the most important thing was that you did."

I purse my lips together and join the men, facing them on the grass. The ground is cool and solid and holds me like cupped hands. I can't fall any further from here.

"I had a pony once." I say.

"You did?"

Their eyes watch me, so much closer than I anticipated, and more intense than I'd imagined. It's easier to tell my story to the patch of ground between us.

"A shaggy, fat black pony," I say. "He was black, but when you slid your fingers through his coat, his hair stood up like little rows of soldiers between them, and it had a red tinge to it. You know, like he was two things in one. I thought he was magical. Made of every magic substance the world contained. Sometimes, when the Hall was near empty, Eshnae would sneak him into the courtyard. 'His name is Dhu,' she said at our first meeting. His muzzle was so soft and warm on my face, the softest thing I'd ever felt in my life. I loved him at once and insisted he was *my* Dhu."

"Sounds delightful." Thomas smiles.

I nod, careful not to catch his eye. "I don't even know where he came from, but I knew he was mine, and I was his."

"He was a gift from Eshnae?"

I'd never thought of him as a gift before. "I expect he was. Eshnae wasn't always so shut off from me. Her laugh was like a melody. But I can't remember how it goes now. And she was generous. Well, as generous as her life at the Hall allowed her to be. There were other gifts, too. She'd sneak flowers into my room and show me how tight the buds were and how they would explode into color when their time arrived. She said I was a flower, and if I opened, I could fly. And you know what? I was six summers old. I believed every word she said. Mardu had the deepest, darkest eyes, as if the night sky lived on the other side of them and he just went on forever. And I lived on the other side of them too, you see, because he was so full of magic there was room enough for both of us." I chuckle a little at myself. "I also thought my shaggy, fat, black pony would grow up to be a Trothsman's horse. He was just a smaller version of one, right?"

Thomas and Guthrie both wear a gentle smile for my childish understanding. I share their humor for a moment and focus again on the patch of grass between us.

"You see, Mardu was so full of magic he could fly. But not yet; he just needed to be a bit older, perhaps. We couldn't tell anyone, of course. His wings were growing in secret, and I'd feel along his shoulders for the bumps I was sure were about to appear under his skin, like the tight buds ready to unfurl. We'd practice flying though, Mardu and I, while we waited for that marvelous day to arrive. The day of his wings. The day we'd fly high enough to leap the walls and be gone forever."

I'm still relaxed from the ale, so I don't hesitate to tip my face to the stars and lift my arms at my sides. "Did you know that when you hold your arms out like this on a horse, it feels like you're flying and nothing can touch you? No one can touch you." My eyes close, and the wind rustles across the field toward us. "This breeze is just like the breezes that crossed my face in the courtyard with Mardu, bringing scents from outside the walls. Windy days were the best. The noise was so loud in my ears I couldn't hear his hooves on the cobblestones at all. We were so light I was sure we were flying, only I was too scared to open my eyes.

I always had to flee to my chamber before we were discovered, but each time I made sure to check for the buds one last time. It became a silly ritual; me burying my face in his mane; my fingers desperately feeling for the slightest bump. If I couldn't find them that day, hope was not lost. They might be there next time. I would never stop searching for them.

I once asked Eshnae if it was possible to fly over the walls. I didn't mention Mardu's wings, of course; I was already good at keeping secrets. She held a finger up to her lips. "Shh," she said, "It's always best to fly quietly." I had no idea what she meant."

"I was too happy. I laughed too loud.

Maybe that's what Eshnae meant by flying quietly.

I missed her signal. The one where she'd press her hands down on her skirts and swipe them out. It always looked so very graceful to anyone else, but it meant *Beware! Solemnity now!*

I missed it. Maybe she didn't even do it. I don't know now."

I still can't look at Thomas or Guthrie. My heart hurts with each beat and I draw a deep breath and dilute it, or maybe it just moves the ache around. The grass feels damp now and I squeeze it between my fingers. I can be *here* and tell a story of *there*; the Mystery has shown me that it's safe to move between the two.

"It's odd that I remember it being dark, yet it couldn't have been," I tell them. "It was morning; but there's no brightness in my memories.

The sun was warm on my face. Mardu and I were flying. So, so high. I laughed. I must've been too happy.

Mardu stopped, and the momentum flung me forward. I latched onto his mane to keep from falling.

Feeney was there. Right by Mardu's head. Scowling at me.

All the lightness fell from me, dropped through my belly and down to my feet - and it kept going. We were falling. Why? Feeney was so loud, squawking and shouting, but I couldn't understand him. We hit the cobblestones hard. The fall trapped my leg under Mardu. Why won't he move? I wiggled and pulled at my leg until it was free and scrambled to him. There was so much blood. I can still see my little hands trying to hold it together; little fingers trying to seal the gaping wound across his neck. I tried so hard, but the blood ran through my fingers and along the cracks of the cobblestones. In little straight lines. There were tiny bubbles in the blood from his nose, and tiny bubbles in the lines of the cobblestones. I scraped at the blood and the grit and tried to push everything back.

Feeney kept shouting. So much noise. He handed me a loose cobblestone. I nearly dropped it; my hands were too slippery, too small. The grit dug into my skin as my hands clamped around it.

"Most wretched child - put him out of his misery!"

Strange. I can't tell you the shape of Feeney's blade or what clothes he wore, but I remember how the edge of the cobblestone split Mardu's eyelid and how no blood seeped from it.

That's how I discovered that cuts don't bleed when your heart is dead.

His shouts reverberated around and around my head until they made sense. "Hand it to me, child!" he squawked again. The stone almost slipped from my hands as I stretched to obey his command. Normally, I would have cowered waiting for a blow, but he demanded something different this time. "Say thank you."

I frowned and hesitated, but as ordered, the words fell from my mouth. They came from me, but they didn't belong to me. Nothing did anymore.

I couldn't see a thing. I wiped my tears and pushed the grit from my face. All I wanted was Mardu's eyes. I hovered over him, moving closer and closer until our eyes almost touched. But all I found in his eyes was myself, and that the night sky that went on forever was gone."

"I don't remember how I ended up in my chamber. But I sat there forever. In the middle of the room. Blood and grit to my elbows, its stink crusting in the creases of my skin."

Thomas moves to comfort me, but I hold my hand up to keep him at a distance. My hands rub on my skirts just as they did when I pleaded for help. "I called for Eshnae, but she didn't come. I begged for water. Surely someone, anyone, would hear me. But no water came. I rubbed at the stains, harder and harder, but their stink and horror overwhelmed me. I watched myself from afar, as if I'd floated to the ceiling. I thrashed and raged like some broken animal in a trap. And then it all seemed to stop. The broken animal stopped screaming, stopped whimpering and slept in its own blood.

I didn't speak to Eshnae the next day. I didn't want to talk about the horrible things I'd done. Without a word to each other, we found a new way. She pretended her bruises weren't a result of my behavior, and I pretended to be alive."

My hands are hot now, burning against my skirt. I bunch some fabric in one hand and feel a stab of pain through my shoulder. The other hand cools on the grass. I am still here.

"That's when she stopped telling stories about life outside the Hall. She still sang that little song with me though, Open flowers, crown of fire, taught by stars and fueled by pyre."

I smile to myself. I can't remember the last time I heard it. "She made me promise to only ever whisper it and to never ever sing it where I might be overheard." Thomas and Guthrie look blurry through my tears. "I never thanked her."

Moments pass before Guthrie speaks. "Mardu was already dead before you hit him, you understand that?"

"I understand that, now." My heart warms at his offering of what comforts him most; facts. "Yet a shell formed around me that day, like a walnut, and I clung to it as the only thing that was mine. It turned out this shell drove Feeney to rage. He fed on my reactions and responses, so I refused to give him any. It became our contest. I didn't see all that at first. As a child, I just knew the shell was my only protection. It kept me from him, it kept me alive. His last words may have been, 'You will weep!', but I will never shed a tear in front of that man. If he wins our contest, he wins me. I will never let him win, ever."

And with that, my story is done. The moon is higher in the sky now, the breeze a little cooler. I inhale deeply, hoping the air dislodges the last of the ache around my heart. Thomas and Guthrie watch me intently. The moonlight glistens in their eyes, and I can't imagine a safer place to be. I relax and push a smile from my lips, and relief floods my body. The tears flow freely now as images and emotions flash through my body. The bees lead a charge and sting with lightness, perhaps a farewell to their torturous dragging to this moment I had fought until now. My wounds are just like Guthrie's. They needed exposure to the air and washed by tears.

Martha was right, it's silence that keeps hearts in chains. I wipe the last of the bees from my hands on my skirt, feeling strangely heavy and dense, but lighter than ever before.

Thomas takes my hands and caresses them so gently I barely feel his touch. I want to pull them away; hide them. I force my eyes closed and concentrate on dismissing the urge to wipe them, to let this excruciating urge to recoil ebb and flow in time with my breath. He kisses one hand, and I break into sobs before he kisses the other. The urge to run away from his kindness and compassion almost overtakes me. I force myself to stay, to be calm, and to receive.

Water drips on my hands. Tears? No, it's cold. Guthrie dips his hands into the pail he's moved beside us. One after the other, they dip their hands into the water and cover my arms and hands. They wash the length of my arms, my elbows, my wrists, palms and between my fingers until every trace of blame is gone. Each stroke, each cool drip diluting every lie I'd ever carried with me.

A sensation moves like a breeze inside my body. It feels alchemical. I'm turning into something extraordinary, altered from one creature to another, an act of transmutation as blatant as one of Guthrie's experiments. Who am I becoming? I don't need to know. I stay quiet and feel the sharpness, the pain, and the purity work through me.

The dwale recipe comes easier to me than I thought. I mix the ingredients with Martha's instructions coming to my ear as easily as if she was seated beside me. Once boiled, I drain the liquid into a glass bottle from Guthrie's collection.

"Here's the stopper," he says.

The cork molds to the narrow neck and we step back from the table and consider the fluid before us.

"How much again?" he whispers.

"Half a spoon to a full jug of ale." I reflect on his slighter frame. "But let's start with quart a spoon tonight."

"That's fair," he nods.

"Did you sleep?"

"Well enough," he answers, "the ale helped. And you?"

I don't have to pretend with Guthrie. He knows the exhaustion that follows the wars that battle inside us; the ones that no amount of sleep will ever refresh. "I'm drained. Weary beyond comprehension."

"Then you shall rest."

"But there's—"

"The dwale is done. You said yourself it was this day's priority." He leans through the doorway and calls to Thomas in the field. "I'll be along to help soon!" The old man turns back to me. "And you," he says, "Where will you find your help? Where is your rest?"

It's like bathing, but I'm not at the pond. It's a specific kind of cleansing, not one that washes the skin or any visible thing, but an invisible restoration of everything that holds me together. When I close my eyes, I can feel it knitting me back together, pulling gently to close rips and tears, applying balm to irritations.

The musky scent of the windflower brushes past me. I imagine them nearby bobbing their little white heads and announcing spring is on its way. I won't go to find them. I'll stay here and let them come to me. It's been an age since I've slept in the embrace of strong roots. It's a deeper sleep than usual, mixed with dreams, instructions and wanderings that fill me with wonder and understanding. I move in and out of my sleep, sometimes aware of my adventures, other times blissfully surrendering to wherever I may go. My bedding is spongy, soft fungi and chips of soft decomposing wood. Even from underneath me, they tell their stories as they change from one form to another. Just as I have. The Mystery wanders alongside me in my dreams, guiding me, speaking and teaching without words. I know I am changed. I am new. I am strong.

I wake and find food and drink beside me. I didn't even hear Thomas and Guthrie stow it here; proof of the depth of sleep and my safety. The food is just what I need; now there's nothing to distract me from my rest, or my wanderings. Each time I close my eyes, I step into another realm, one where all possibilities await. I know they can exist in this world too, as real as the tree I lay beneath. Must I choose? How do I bring one side to the other? The Mystery shows me a walnut tree and we stroll around it together. I admire its branches and hold my palm up, and fruit drops into it effortlessly. Just as anything that is for us should be. But how can the walnut bring this realm into my world? I'm shown the far-reaching expanse of its limbs and the meat hidden within each of its shells bursting with energy. My heart dances with the joy of recognition, but my mind strives to understand and tries to grasp at the walnuts on the tree, but they disappear like mist. Crunching sounds turn my head this way and that, but no one walks this way. The sounds arrive again. They're not from this world; the footfall comes from the place where I sleep at the base of a tree. I smell the windflowers again and feel the lump of the trunk at my shoulder. Thomas and Guthrie's voices grow louder as they approach. I sway between the two worlds, pulled this way and then that, until the potency of the Mystery fades. I have returned whether I want to or not.

Thomas's voice is distant but gruff. "All I'm saying is once the army's here, we'll grind Feeney into the ground. It'll be his blood on those cobblestones."

Their voices quieten as they move closer, and I win over my resistance and open my eyes.

"Shh!" Guthrie tells Thomas as they slow their walk.

The shadows are long and stretch across the small clearing they pass over. "How long have I rested?"

"Most of the day it seems," Thomas says, "Are you well?"

"And I am safe."

Guthrie lands beside me with a tired sigh and rests his head on the trunk, "And I am done."

"Did you raise the roof frame easily enough?"

Thomas nods, "The second lodge will be done before we know it." He checks over the food I've eaten. "So do you know what we're meant to be doing now?"

"She's meant to be resting." Guthrie says.

I pat his arm. "I am. I have. Today was perfect. I can't remember the last time I just lay around and listened. It's the most powerful tonic."

"Listened?" Thomas says. "What did the Mystery say?"

"Lots of things."

"And...",

"I'm trying to sort it out in my mind."

"You need to just trust yourself more."

Just trust myself? He has no idea. "Has a friend ever betrayed you?"

Thomas frowns at me. "Of course."

"And after the betrayal you got to choose whether to walk away or continue that friendship, and if you did, no doubt you were a little wary, untrusting, perhaps on the lookout for the next betrayal?"

Thomas shrugs, waits a moment, and concedes my point with a nod.

"So then, consider my predicament. To survive, I've betrayed myself too many times to count."

Thomas shuffles his feet in the undergrowth, "I didn't mean to—"

"It's all right, really. I need you to understand this. I destroyed my trust in myself in the same way your friend's betrayal did. Only mine was over and over, and it's a relationship I can't walk away from. It takes practice and painful tiny steps to develop that trust again, and I'm making progress; however painfully slow it might appear to you. Please understand that each time you flippantly tell me to trust myself, you're actually reminding me that I can't."

"I had no idea," he says, "So how can we help? How do you make progress?"

"By keeping small promises to myself; abiding by my decisions."

Guthrie nudges me with his shoulder. "You decided to come here. That was an excellent one."

I let his words soak into me. "Yes, it was. I followed the Mystery."

"But you still made the decision."

"I did. But I think even my confidence to follow came from the Mystery as well."

"Perhaps it just lent you some of its confidence until you find your own."

What a remarkable thought. Empowered by the Mystery in the places I surrender. The thought still floats around in my mind when Thomas speaks.

"Look at what that one decision brought you. It was well informed."

I love Awenmell and my decision to come here. It's mine. Regardless of scrolls and legends, the moment of decision was between myself and the Mystery. It was about trust.

Thomas sits on the other side of me. "I for one trust your decisions." He leans forward, "You Guthrie?" he asks and Guthrie nods. "So, tell me, what did the Mystery say about the army?"

"Walnuts."

Silence. I knew this wouldn't work.

The men look at each other from the corners of their eyes. I don't give them the chance to speak. "And something about armor. But it's a picture that hasn't settled yet. Like the waterfall is blocked and only trickles make their way through, or it gushes in fits and starts. Just speaking it aloud adds to its strength, but it still doesn't make sense."

"Walnuts! We're going to throw walnuts at our enemies?" Thomas says.

"Idiot!" Guthrie shouts back, "Just listen!"

"No!" Thomas paces in front of us. "We need fortification and weaponry, not tales about walnuts as if we're a scurry of marauding squirrels." He points his finger at me. "Your Mystery jests!"

"The Mystery *is* speaking of fortification, armory and shields."

"And?"

I try to form my thoughts into words. "It's about how we arm ourselves with shields. We create a fortress around our memories. We hold shields up to stop people from seeing our wounds…"

Guthrie sits up and nudges me, "Like the walnut shell."

"That's the connection! When you provided a safe place for me to give air to my wounds, I was able to put my shield down and rest my arms. I could recover and discard the walnut shell. The secret is in the shield—and the walnut."

Thomas shakes his head. "Now we're making shields from walnut? I mean, it's a sturdy wood, but shields?"

"No, you misheard." The waterfall floods into my system. "The shields have to *come down*. And regardless of what you think, it *is* a strategic move. Without that action, what we build here at Awenmell will be just the same as the Hall." Thomas scowls at the suggestion. "The Hall makes everyone protect themselves, close themselves off in order to survive its harshness. We raise shields to deflect attention from our weaknesses, our wounds, thinking it's the strength of the shield that fortifies us, but all the shields do is isolate us. We hide behind them, terrified we'll be seen, that our most raw and tender parts will be used against us. But what if we dropped our shields? What if we not only let our truth out, but allowed healing in? With our shields up, we rot inside our own walnut shell, and no one even notices." I feel like I've just made some strange, impassioned plea and I'm not sure any of it made sense. "The army will come, not because we're fortified and have our shields up, but because they're down."

Thomas still shakes his head at us. "Anyone would think she's been testing that dwale. You sure she didn't?"

Guthrie catches my eye. Can he sense the bees flying through Thomas's veins? He faces me. "How do we do it?"

"We start with a pledge to honor each other's truths; however uncomfortable they make us."

Guthrie nods firmly.

Thomas crouches next to Guthrie. "But this is the *opposite* of what we should do! Tell her Guthrie!"

"I know firsthand the immeasurable importance of dropping one's defenses."

"See?" Thomas pleads. "Guthrie knows this is a monstrous plan too."

"No, you misunderstand, young man. The monstrous plan is to stay closed."

"You're mad. Both of you." Thomas storms away from us, grumbling as he goes.

For a moment I think of following him, but what would I say? Best to leave him with his own thoughts for now. I sigh, and Guthrie pats my hand.

"Are you ready to honor my truth, even if it makes you uncomfortable?" he says.

I sigh again. I didn't for one moment think this would be easy. "I am."

He points to Thomas in the distance. "This may be the very end of you."

"I know."

⁂

The sun has almost set as Guthrie and I make our way back to the lodge. Thomas didn't return to us, but it was just as well. It gave us a chance to explore what it meant to live a life free of shields. I shared my memories of stretching my arms wide with Mardu, and with only a twinge from my shoulder, stood in the forest in the same way. "See how open I was? See how my heart was capable of anything? I wasn't shielded in that moment. I was free."

"So to drop the shields is to be open? But what of your defenses?"

"What if you didn't need any?" My arms drop to my sides and I walked back to the tree. "What if we lived with hearts so open that the battle with our own bees helped others with theirs? You know what was interesting? You commented on Thomas's bees only after you had seen your own. What if the people with shields are the ones who haven't listened to their bees?"

"Projecting and deflecting their pain onto others. Anything to avoid those blasted bees."

"We know why they do it. We've done it ourselves."

"What you're asking is terrifying, you know that?"

I know it. I pull a slight smile at the man. He knows the answer too and doesn't need me to say anything. Yes, it's terrifying. A powerful word to use when talking about something that's just a thought; a plan. But a lesser word won't do. I think of the shields that lay at the bottom of the walnut tree, and how the fruit dropped into my hand. An open heart is terrifying, but there was something courageous rising from those shields. Something released only once they hit the ground.

The lodge doorway glows with warmth in the twilight. The fire must be settled by now. Lovely hot coals waiting for us to admire them and their changing colors. I ignore the times my feet slip on the damp grass, but now that the old man slips too, I take his hand and help steady both of us up the rise to the lodge. His hand is icy. "Almost at the fire." I say.

"What will you tell him?"

"That depends on his questions, Guthrie. I can only answer what he asks."

The warmth calls to us as soon as we enter the building and we hover around the fire enjoying her comforts, rubbing our hands together and pressing them to our cold faces. Thomas has added more to the pot and the scents of chestnuts and freshly cut watercress trail in wisps of steam. Thomas brings our bowls to the fire, and I kiss his cheek as I take them from him. My nose is cold against the warmth of his cheek. I scoop and hand out the filled bowls.

Thomas prods his potage with his spoon and leans forward in his chair. "So, you're both still as mad as when I left you in the forest?"

Guthrie's overly interested in a lump of parsnip and won't even meet my eye. Looks like I'm answering this one. "I expect so."

"Hmm," he says.

I don't know what *'Hmm'* means, so I become overly interested in my parsnips too. We eat in silence, mouthful by mouthful, with only the crackling of the fire for company and conversation.

"Hmm," Thomas says again. "It appears I'm outnumbered."

I scrape at my bowl. "It's not a case of being outnumbered, it's about your decision on how you move forward. I'm choosing to drop my shields."

"And I'm not."

Guthrie coughs and shuffles in his seat. "It appears there's no middle ground. Whatever behavior each of us chooses will show our intention. Let's keep it simple. Walnuts or shields down? Closing off and living inside the protection of the shell, or the bravery of exposing our wounds so others feel less alone in their battle with their bees. Every day I intend to choose, and no doubt every day I will get it wrong, but my intention is to drop my shields and allow myself and my heart more freedom."

Thomas shakes his head at me. "It's not safe for you to be exposed."

"Would you prefer me to remain safe in a nutshell?"

"No, of course not... Yes!... no..."

Dwale. I'll prepare Guthrie's dwale. I step around Thomas and away from the fire, anything to get away from the ache in my chest. But I carry it with me to the bottles of ale, it's already begun to settle. I can raise a shield and deflect the pain, or wrap it inside me with a hard shell so I don't have to feel it again. Ugh. *Shields down* is so much easier to say than do. I draw a deep breath. There are no bees directing me. It sits like a lump in my chest. Stubbornness and anger. I invite the bees to join me while I measure Guthrie's ale, and I listen to their fears as I collect the spoon to measure his quarter dose. As the dwale drips into the spoon, I take a moment to thank them for their offer of protection, and then I let them go. The lump in my chest lightens and dissolves. I breathe without agitation.

"Guthrie?"

He takes the jug of ale and wiggles himself into a comfortable position in his seat. "The whole jug?"

"It's only half full."

"This'll keep me occupied. Perhaps I shouldn't have eaten so much," he says and pats his belly.

"So how then?" Thomas says, "How am I meant to do this marvelous thing you two speak of?"

Guthrie quickly sips on his jug. It's up to me again. I don't feel any resentment now for Thomas choosing his own way. It must have been tangled amongst what I worked through as I prepared the dwale. "For me," I say and sit next to him, "It starts with realizing I'm holding a shield up. It's difficult to let go of something you're not holding, don't you think?. Then I consider why I'm holding it. What part of my heart feels the hurt and why? And then I get to choose. Before that, without knowing I'm holding a shield up, I don't even have that choice. But now I do. I choose to drop the shield and feel the pain move through me. I let it sting me if it needs to; I hear what it wants to tell me. And just when I think there's no end to it, I see the other side. The real magic is the story that trapped the pain stays, but the pain no longer controls my actions. Of course, I could choose to raise my shield and curl inside my walnut shell at any time, or I can enjoy my escape and vow to never willingly return."

Guthrie raises his jug. "It's a hard practice young man, but made much easier with support."

Thomas rubs his chin and watches Guthrie take another swig. He leans toward me. "And you say the army knows this?"

"I don't understand how they know. All I know is our shields repel them somehow. We must drop them if we expect Awenmell to prosper."

"I'll do anything to get that army here."

Now it's my turn. "Hmm," I say.

Arrow thunders through the forest and I thunder with him, convinced we move as one force. His hooves sound on the earth, but my soul flies above us, untouched by anything that might draw me from this moment. I weave and duck a low branch without thought, as deep in the flow of his actions as I am with the Mystery. Peace and pure delight overwhelm my heart as we wheel around an old oak, charge past the pond and set our heading toward the far cliff edge.

He feels it too. This maddening energy that causes us to blast free of the lodge each morning, exhausting ourselves of it before the sun has risen. We greet the sun each day as if its first rays bestow some kind of blessing that keeps us whole. The lodge is somewhere behind us, almost complete and waiting for an army that is yet to appear, no matter how long Thomas stares at the threshold. Leaves whip at my face and I crouch low to Arrow's mane as we bolt through a grove of low hazel trees. His scent acts like a balm on my heart as the sun's rays flicker between their trunks. My shoulder is strong now.

Arrow is strong too. He may have learned to plow, but that doesn't mean it's his only purpose here. He winds through the trees and shakes off the last of what holds us down. At the grassy verge, he slows to walk the last distance to the edge. Our breath puffs into the familiar mist of the cool light of morning.

Another routine takes place deep inside my heart.

Good morning Mystery, I call.

Do you trust me?

To the ends of this earth.

❧❦❧

Thomas blocks the sun's rays as he trips through the lodge door and lands his open sack of produce on the table.

The vegetables bounce and tumble toward the table's edge and I lunge, just catching them in time. "How did we end up with so much parsnip?"

"I only planted a *little* more, thought I'd see how well they grew here."

Guthrie snorts, unimpressed. "*Prolific* is the word you're looking for."

"We could always eat them." Thomas suggests.

Dirty vegetables of differing sizes cover the table. What a joyful thought; a lifetime of parsnip meals. My stomach contracts and my tongue pokes out of my mouth in disgust.

"I saw that!"

"We can't eat them all. Not right now, anyway. And there's not enough salt left to do any good." I nudge Guthrie's attention from his book. "What about pickling? And Thomas, could we leave some in the ground?"

"Pickling?" Guthrie rises from the table in a cloud of excited mutters and toddles to his bed on the other side of the lodge. He rummages among his goods, clattering items and making selections based on, well, I don't know what they're based on. His level of '*ahas*' perhaps?

"Here," he says, holding a scale aloft and a pile of books under his arm. "Time for an experiment."

Thomas folds his arms. "Another one?"

"Better than your frivolous planting of those pond flowers by the doorway."

The blue flowers in the planter were a sweet idea; just not a very practical use of our time. He confounds me with his rush to arm us all, and then the next, he's kind and thoughtful. Thomas squeezes his arms shut tighter.

"Well, "I say, "It's still nice to be reminded of beauty now and then."

"True, true," Guthrie scans the parsnips. "We'll discover what method of preservation is optimum for duration... and taste of course."

I'll wager he's thinking about a lifetime of parsnip meals, too. He pushes the loose produce across the table and sets his goods down as Thomas and I catch the wayward parsnips before they hit the floor. His biggest book, the one he records everything in, lies open across the sea of produce. First, it was only the seeds that captured his attention. They now accumulate at an alarming rate and hang protected inside the black Trothsman's cape that sags from the roof. 'That's the new harvest in there,' he keeps telling me as it bulges with the smooth roundness of a babe in a sling. Sometimes I run my hand under the bulge and wonder what it's like to carry your own flesh and blood on the outside of your body. It must be an odd sensation; and while everything else around us seems to multiply and enlarge, Thomas and I can only wait and wonder when it will be our turn.

Guthrie sorts through the parsnips, inspecting and selecting the best for his experiment. He flicks the smaller ones to me at the end of the table. "They can go into the pot; they'll be ready in time for mid-meal."

"Ah, blessed equilibrium," he says and holds his scales up in perfect balance. "Stability is the center. And within that, is the beauty of benefit to both sides."

Thomas rolls his eyes and I wash and toss Guthrie's discarded vegetables into the pot on the hearth. This experiment of his will take some time. Didn't he say 'optimum for duration', or something like that? Yep, this will be a long one.

"Hey you two. Look at this." Thomas beckons us to the open doorway but stands back from it, his eyes narrowed in focus and concentration.

A handful of people stand at the threshold. They shuffle and rearrange themselves in their rags and traveling clothes. Two wear robes; a tall man and a child, but the rest appear a mixture of sizes. Is that a dog with them? A shadow flits around and behind them.

Guthrie taps my arm. "Are they lost?"

"No. They're not lost." I know that much, but little else. We speak without taking our eyes from them.

"The man on the left," Thomas says, "Isn't that the leather sash of the North?"

Guthrie nods. "The fighting's bad there. There's not one among them who would not have seen atrocities."

A lump forms in my throat. "Most are children. Can you imagine what they have seen?"

"I don't want to think of what they've seen."

Thomas continues. "At the back in white. Or what used to be white. That's a Fercie, I'm sure of it." He gives a quick chuckle. "And I thought we were a bunch of misfits."

Guthrie moves closer to me and whispers. "Why are they just standing there?"

"They want to come in."

"They outnumber us, they could just charge in."

"Perhaps they're polite."

Thomas shakes his head. "Polite starving waifs and scoundrels in the middle of the unrest?" He grabs a weapon and hands one to Guthrie. "We shall see."

We cross the lodge yard together. Guthrie and Thomas flank me in a slow and cautious walk while the visitors hold their ground. Bees flutter in my veins but don't cause me any alarm. Perhaps it's because I have the men by my side. The closer we get to the threshold, the more the bees move... but gently, almost courteously, in nature. They tickle! Who would've ever thought they'd tickle? Guthrie's face is stern; he won't want to hear about the bees.

"Wait!" The youth in the robe calls to us and we stop short. We're halfway between the lodge and the threshold, the perfect place for both groups to decide on an attack or retreat. Guthrie and Thomas tense. The youth steps in front of his band and defiantly throws his hood back. He squints in the brightness as the sunlight flashes on his white hair. Guthrie gasps and Thomas curses under his breath. A child of the invaders. A walking death sentence.

"How is he still alive?" Thomas whispers.

"What in Stars is this about?" Guthrie speaks and turns his head to me, but his eyes don't leave the threshold.

The gentle bees make way for the blast of a waterfall that covers me from head to toe and disappears before I can acknowledge it. "Do you see their robes?" I whisper to the men.

Thomas tips his head in my direction. "Only two of them are wearing robes, Ash, the tall man at the back and the invader waif. The rest are in rags." He grips his weapon tighter. "Why? What's under them?"

Guthrie's response is gentler. "Tell us what you see."

"A swarm of bees so thick I can barely see through them. They wear heavy robes, like the fear robes I told you about, but these are much heavier, like armor."

"Do they mean us harm?"

"No, if anything they fear us."

"Us?"

"What are we to do with them?"

Thomas readies himself. "Send them away?"

"They're *fear* robes Thomas, and they're the ones wearing them, not us."

Is everyone in the group holding their breath, or is it just me? Every gaze is lowered, every stance readied for escape, like the moment you come across an animal in the forest. Who will move first? And what will the outcome be?

Thomas watches them closely and switches his attention between me and the gathering at the threshold. "You used to be like that."

"Like what?"

"All hunched over like you were protecting something."

My heart. I was protecting my heart. "I didn't know I did that though, and they won't either. They'd be just as bewildered by their behavior as anyone outside of them." Pain radiates from my heart. My body aches being so close to them, like when Guthrie's confusion managed to confuse me too. "We must invite them in."

Guthrie relaxes. "If you're sure."

"What do they want?" Thomas asks.

"They want to rest."

"So just for the night? I suppose we can help them with that."

"We're going to do for them, what you did for me."

His eyes widen. "We're what?"

"We're going to tell them we're glad they're here; we're glad they survived. And we're going to keep telling them until they believe it. Right now though, we're going to give them what they need more than anything."

"A wash?"

I roll my eyes. "Safety." He's lucky I know a flick across the top of his head will send our visitors scattering.

Our guests sit around the table inside the main lodge, heads lowered, with their eyes never settling on a single item. If they felt safe enough to speak, I'd wager they could tell me every way to escape this room, and how to use every implement they see as a weapon. I guide Thomas a few steps from the doorway. "Be on guard if you must, but don't block the doorway. You'll be trampled if they take flight." I know they've seen me clear this route even if they don't acknowledge it. Not acknowledging every detail they notice has kept them safe; it's not rude - it's survival.

Guthrie answers their furtive glances at the hearth. "We'll just add a few items and your bellies will be full in no time." He scrapes the last of the smaller cut vegetables into the pot and nudges Thomas as he passes by. "Seems you were right about how many bodies would fit around your large tables."

Thomas stands taller and nods at himself. "Now for those extra bowls."

The table used to feel so huge with just the three of us. It looks tiny now that it's surrounded by people of all shapes and sizes. And those bowls. My cheeks flush. 'What are we meant to do with all these bowls?' I asked Thomas on his return from the dwale mission. What would we be doing now without them? Serving pottage into our guest's hands? It's as if all the ideas and plans he worked on constantly, the same ones we wished he would shut up about, have leaped from his head and become solid right in front of us. He returns with bowls stacked in his hands and his face free of its usual scowl.

Our guests sit tight, like one of Guthrie's springs waiting for release. If I touched them, I'd wager they'd be hard as rock and bounce straight out the door in fright. A motion near the door catches my eye; must be that dog again, the one that plays in the shadows, but no one moves to chase it. The silence isn't awkward, it just is, and anything else seems intrusive right now. The tall man in the robe rises and moves toward Guthrie. He speaks in hushed tones and bows his head several times and Guthrie replies gently, "No, no. You are our guests. We will serve you." The robed man returns to his seat for a short while and then repeats the process.

Guthrie rubs at the back of his neck and I join him in the guise of checking on the meal. "Are you well?" I ask him.

He nods and stirs the pot and then tilts his head toward our guests. "And our guests? Are they well?" he whispers.

I'd briefly checked each of our visitors as they entered and asked if anything ailed them. "Nothing urgent. But the children with the slash scar across their cheeks; their wounds look the same. A little familiar. Almost uniformed."

Guthrie sighs gently and returns his gaze to the pot. "It's a mark of ownership. Still used in the northern holdings."

That's where I'd seen the mark before, the lackey who accompanied the Northerners to council. I'd only seen it once and thought it a war wound. I was a fool. "Slaves?"

"For whatever purpose their owner requires."

My heart aches. I have no outward scar that tells everyone my station, but I've been owned too. I manage to catch the eye of one of the scarred children and slip them a slight smile, and their gaze drops directly to the table. Their facial scars have healed well and don't require tending. The inside ones are a different story. Another shadow darts across the doorway, but this time I'm sure I glimpsed slender arms or legs. A child.

"Almost done," Guthrie calls to the room. "Thomas has your bowls."

They line up without word or complaint and once pottage fills their bowls to the rim, rush toward the table, eager to begin. The line dwindles as the table fills.

"I'm glad you're here," Thomas says to a young girl as she passes with her hands cupped around her bowl. She flinches from his words as if he'd struck her, and Thomas recoils from her reaction, eyes wide.

I take his hand and draw him away from the table, closer to the doorway. "You first said those words to me in the darkness, when I could pretend I hadn't heard you. I had to get used to your kindness. They don't understand what you're saying to them.

Look at them. They're not glad they're here, and alive. No one's told them that before, they've probably never considered it. They may even think you're mad and deluded. I know I did." He smiles and I kiss his hand. "It will make sense to them, eventually."

"When?"

"When we've gently shown it to them. Not just told them."

A shadow brushes past the open doorway. "Look at this one darting around outside."

"You've seen it too?"

"I'm glad you're here!" he calls to the ragged waif skittering around the fields. The waif drops in fright at his words and hides among the tall grasses. "Won't it be hard to show him if he won't stay still?"

"Him? You sure?" I'll never hear the end of it if I say I thought our busy urchin was a dog. "It's hard to tell anything with all that flitting around. Kind of like a sweet field bird."

"Like one of those little wrens. Should we try to catch it?"

I blink hard. "Catch it?"

"Isn't it better to have it in here with the others?"

"If that little wren felt safer in here with us, don't you think that's where they'd be?"

"But we've got food. Look how hungry everyone is. The wren must be starving too."

Wren pops up above the grasses and runs a scant distance and disappears again. "When your survival is tied to another's bidding, every tiny choice is taken from you. Let Wren come for food on their own terms. Give them back this one choice, no matter how outlandish it seems to us."

Thomas fills a bowl and places it outside the lodge. "There's a bowl here for you!" he calls over the field. Grasses brush against each other in the breeze, but there's no sight or sound of our little wren.

Guthrie greets us as we enter the lodge. Most of the bodies around the table are finishing the last of their meal, and he has arranged a ladle and bucket of water for their thirst. He corrals us from the doorway. "They need more than one night's rest, agreed?"

"Agreed," I say. "Isn't that what we decided Awenmell was meant to be? Honorable and kind shelter?"

"No," Thomas says, "It was meant to be about the army."

I lower my voice. "The scroll says Awenmell is kind shelter, remember? Besides, this situation is beyond the army."

"There's something beyond the army? I thought that was our main objective."

Guthrie ignores Thomas's staunch designs on the future and takes his elbow. "Look at these souls around your crafted table. How much food will your army need? Where will they sleep? Our current guests can help you answer those questions."

"Like an experiment," he says. "I can practice on them."

"That doesn't sound very honorable."

"Maybe not," he says and lifts Guthrie's scales. They wobble until they restore their balance. "But I need to prepare, and they need support. Equilibrium, right old man?"

Guthrie gives him a half-hearted shrug and turns his attention to me. His brow furrows in soft lines over his eyes. "You look concerned."

The energy in the room has changed. I used to believe it was my madness that made me sway according to the company I was in. Working with Guthrie's bees and my own has given me a keener insight into which bees belong to me and which I have no control over, or responsibility for. This lodge is full of painful stings, ready to show themselves. "It's just their bees," I tell him, "I hope we're strong enough."

"**M**ore?" Guthrie sits in front of the hearth and holds a scoop of hot vegetables above the pot.

Expectant eyes light up at his suggestion but defer almost immediately to Cal, the white-haired youth who defied us to let them under our threshold. Thomas and Guthrie dart their eyes to mine. Cal's slight nod frees the group from the table to refill their bowls, and the younger children squabble and fuss to get to Guthrie first. I didn't see who replaced Cal's bowl with a steaming refill, but he leans over it and takes a mouthful and fixes his eyes on mine.

Yes, I know who you are to them. What I don't know, is why you have that position.

Maybe he's proved himself braver, more trustworthy than the rest. The tall man spends his time hunched over and apologizing and even eats his meal completely covered. He must have his own reasons, yet I can't see this troop following him anywhere. Cal shares some jest with the companion next to him. Imagine the tales they could tell; the good and the horrendous. You'd need a certain bravado to withstand his life, one rigid enough to survive being hunted; a shield so impenetrable it becomes an act of defiance to wave your otherness around on. Like he did at the threshold. Daring us to reject him, and if we had, gaining comfort from the stability that he was right all along. At least that's something he could count on. At least meanness is dependable. I decide against offering him a smile. Kindness can be suspicious and unnerving.

"Another? I'll bring it to you." Thomas collects a full bowl from Guthrie and places it in front of a wide-eyed child. I smile at him from across the table. He looks pleased. This isn't so bad after all.

Cal's eyes narrow and move between the pot and the smiling child. He charges to Guthrie and leans over the pot, their foreheads almost touching. His clenched teeth don't hide his words from anyone on this side of the table. "I decide who gets more; not you."

"A person's hunger can never be adequately determined by an-other," Guthrie says, his knuckles whitening on the ladle. "That would be a rather incorrect assumption young man."

Cal frowns, and they lock eyes. "A what?"

"An incorrect assumption. You decide nothing here."

Bodies scatter from my side of the table like a flock of birds and almost knock me off balance on their flutter to the door. Cal seizes Guthrie from behind. A tight choke hold and grip that immo-bilizes the old man. Guthrie's eyes bulge and he kicks in panic. Sparks fly around the people rushing to the door. The loaded springs are free. The pot spills to the floor. *Guthrie!* I lunge at Cal, taking aim at his neck. Thomas shouts and trips over the robed man, cleaning up the spilled pot. More bodies scramble past as Cal dumps Guthrie to the ground and latches his hand onto my throat. Thomas bellows something unintelligible. I smack down hard on Cal's elbow and twist his arm up behind his back and almost throw him through the door into the lodge yard. In a few steps, I am beside Guthrie on the floor. "Are you well?" I pant, and relief floods me as he nods.

"Just get out, get out!" Thomas yells and shoos the robed man, who bows in apology even as he walks out the door. He turns to us on the ground. Food drips from his shirt, but his rage is palpable. "What in Stars was that all about?"

"Bees," Guthrie mumbles. "My bees... and his bees... and a few hornets too I expect."

Thomas storms to the door and stands firm. No one is coming back in. No one would dare. His shoulders raise in time with his puffing breath and he shakes his head at our callers. Did he hear Guthrie's explanation? "So this is how you repay a kindness, is it?" he shouts at them. I guess not.

Cal nearly tripped over his own feet as I threw him out the door. I didn't see where he landed; I needed to get to Guthrie. He'd just grabbed my throat and threatened me, and I sent him on his way without a second thought. How did I become this person? One capable of protecting myself and others? I could never have done that before. Why now? The answer stands admirably at the doorway, a barrier between me and danger. He taught me how. He showed me how. From sticks in the forest to lessons in the field, it was when he trained me and explained why, that I could do it physically. I was strong. My body believed it was true because it had lived it.

Guthrie squeezes my hand. "You were right about the bees."

I nod, bringing my mind back from the field and into the lodge. "They're always our first line of defense. We're all hunched over protecting our wounds and we'll do anything to keep people away from them. Cal's attack on us was the same as yours."

"I wonder what his wound is?"

"Whatever it is, his rage keeps everyone away from it."

"It's doing an outstanding job, that's for certain." Guthrie clambers into his seat and adjusts his clothing back into place. "It's interesting to consider that boy and I are the same. That our attacks are defense. I imagine as all attacks are."

Thomas strides from the doorway and stands above us with his arms folded. "So what about people who attack you for no reason other than they want something from you?"

"Secure people have no need to attack. The insecure live with a hollowness inside them, and it's crammed full of bees; stinging at them constantly so they never stop reacting. They never get to listen to their bees. Look at Cal, 'if I rage, no one can get close enough to touch my wound', or the wren 'if I keep moving, no one can catch me and touch my wound'. I was frozen, afraid to do anything, hoping no one would see the weakness of my wound."

Thomas flicks a stray vegetable from the sleeve of his shirt. "And the robed dolt that's always in the way and apologizing?"

"If I keep everyone happy, I'll be safe. No one will ask about my wound."

Martha said I'd prod people's wounds, and they'd hate me for it. Is this what she meant? Our visitors mill about in the lodge yard as if waiting for something. To be sent away, I expect. They move together as a swarm, the little ones striving for the comfort and protection of the center. It seems none have left us of their own accord. White hair flashes among them; not even Cal. Chaos, pain, bees and wounds fill the space between the lodge walls and the fields. We understand the bees... but they don't. How could they? No one had taught them, no one had shown them. It's impossible to make a choice when you don't know there's another option.

"So what do we do now?" Guthrie asks.

Thomas's arms remain folded. "Send them on their way to bother someone else." He looks down at me and waits for my response.

"We could always offer to help them understand—"

"That they're rude and ungrateful and don't know how to behave?"

"My normal was never the same as others. Don't punish them because theirs isn't the same as yours."

Guthrie taps on the table with his reacquired ladle. "Think beyond this moment, Thomas. Life will be easier for them and everyone they meet, not just us, if they understand their bees."

"So my experiment gives way to yours?"

"I don't consider this an experiment."

"What is it then?"

Guthrie's eyes mirror my own trepidation. "I don't know," we say in unison.

The swarm of bodies congregates in one section of the lodge yard. Some sit huddled on the ground, others pace nearby. "They'll expect us to mistreat them. To somehow punish all of them for Cal's behavior."

"Why aren't they gone then?" Thomas says, "I'd be far away by now."

"Because they expect it. Have you noticed life feels safer when we know what's coming? When there's some kind of order to our turmoil."

Guthrie frowns, deep in thought, and places the ladle silently and carefully onto the table. "It will terrify them," he says, "I know it will. But if we continue in the pattern they're used to, it will only perpetuate the problem. We have to interrupt the pattern they expect, only then can they acknowledge their bees."

"And once they acknowledge them," Thomas says, "they can listen to them, and move on?"

Guthrie smiles. "Correct."

Thomas's shoulders soften and he sits on the table edge, his arms loosely crossed. "So how do you plan to interrupt this pattern of theirs?"

"Unfortunately for them, we're going to give them what they don't expect. And they're not going to like it."

Our visitors flinch as we casually enter the yard and seat ourselves on the logs beside the ashes of last night's fire.

Guthrie shields his face from the sun. "My word, it's warm out here today. Still, it's always nice to see some sunshine and brightness." Our first foray into living the idea of having our shields down. No deflection, no protection. A test for us as much as for them.

We settle into a cautious silence and Thomas looks over my shoulder into the field. I know there are plenty of other things he'd prefer to be doing than sitting here at Guthrie's request. I'd expected an argument from him, like the one about the shields, but he's remarkably gracious and slips a half smile to me when his focus returns. There are many things we all could be doing, but this seems the most important work of this moment. It's unpleasant, this sitting here doing nothing; no fixing things, or making announcements. No demanding and no explaining. Just waiting while they work through the strangeness of this moment, with the least amount of pressure as possible. Guthrie warned us it could be too much for them. They might panic under the pressure of uncertainty and we need to be prepared for anything, but I hope their exhaustion might sway them into staying.

They watch us with narrowed eyes, waiting for the trap to spring on them, but not quite understanding where the trap is. Cal paces and fidgets and seems confused. At least if he was goading us, he'd have some measure of control but he isn't even resorting to that. He throws some insults indirectly that we take no offense at. He mumbles insults under his breath as a test of sorts. A rising sense of panic and confusion and curiosity wash over him in waves. Now we wait to see what he decides.

"Caltrop, what's going on?" someone whispers.

I strain to hear his response. They're waiting for him to decide what they should do when he's not sure himself. We offer no threat, nothing to defend against, we make no demands. He mumbles and there is a sigh. They separate themselves from him, the huddle forms ever widening spaces.

Cal watches Guthrie, but not with menace, as if he wants to approach but is unsure. Guthrie leans across to me. "What should I say to him?"

"What do you like most to hear after an encounter with your bees?"

He nods. "That it's a normal response; and there's a way out. Yet there are always consequences aren't there?"

I pat Guthrie's hand and make a dramatic gesture of wiping my brow. "Do you know we have a pond here?" Several faces light up. "I think I'll head there now. You're welcome to join me."

Thomas and I stroll hand in hand toward the pond, followed by the band, who didn't even wait for Cal's permission. He releases my hand at the fence-line, satisfied there's no threat among those who follow me, and eyes the yard. "You go ahead. From here, I can be at his side almost immediately."

The pond is almost still. The cascades of water at one end seem to be absorbed by its stillness as soon as it breaks the surface and slides almost silently out the other end, weaving its way through reeds to continue its journey. The water is cool on my feet, a welcome and short-lived surprise from the heat of the day. My charges stay well back from me, as they have the entire way here, and I move slowly and deliberately through the water and find a shady place to rest out of their way. They enter quietly and timidly, gently goading each other until they forget I am there and splash and laugh as they play. Wren even makes an appearance, dipping in and out of the water as quickly as her namesake. I leave them to their play and wander close enough to see the fields of Awenmell. Cal and Guthrie wander the fields, followed by the robed man. He's probably more interested in Guthrie's lecture about soil properties than Cal would ever be. I release the tension from my shoulders and draw slow, deep breaths. In my mind's eye, fewer bees hover over the whole of Awenmell.

The warm air stays until evening. No cooler breezes this time to brush away the day and mark the transition from day to night. Even the stars twinkle in the twilight, not sure of their place.

Thomas nudges me. "Looks like someone's got a new lackey."

Cal carries lopped branches and helps Guthrie prepare the fire for an outside meal. We'd normally eat and discuss our day and plans for the next around this fire, but we're all too exhausted for words. Blankets and places for sleep are organized, all that is left for this day is to eat and retire. Guthrie concedes help from the robed man who serves our meals with a bow of gratitude and continues his low conversation with Cal. They seem like firm friends. A shared experience and deep understanding can do that.

"Will you tell the others about the bees?" Cal asks Guthrie.

Guthrie looks at the stunned faces around the fire, all caught in various stages of eating but awaiting his answer. "Well, if they'd like to listen," he says. "I'll gladly ... err." Seeing Guthrie lost for words always makes me smile. "Tomorrow in the lower field then," he announces, "Whoever would join in can meet me there."

⁕

The lodge looks strange; filled with bodies after seeing it empty for so long. Beds line the walls, and blankets and skins cover the bodies resting for the night.

Guthrie spreads the cooling coals in the hearth. "All is well," he assures us and nods toward the door. I can't wait to retire to the cottage away from this day.

Thomas holds me close on our brief walk and kisses my temple. "Guthrie will keep them safe."

"I know."

"I find this bee thing odd, though. Some of them don't have any scars or burns at all. How can they have a problem with bees?"

"The bees care little for the outside tale. Whatever happened to them, they were powerless to stop it. The terror lies in the stripping away of any power or choice they had. That's the battle line, it's not so much about the tale."

"Don't we have to know their stories?"

"They will tell us if they choose to. Others will never tell, and that's their right."

"How can we help if they don't tell?"

"A well doesn't ask a thirsty traveler how they got so thirsty, it just provides the water."

The cottage is a welcome sight. A refuge from our regular days and now from our most irregular one. Each day when the door closes, I relax, knowing it's just the two of us again. No fields, no lumber, no chores, and now no visitors.

Thomas lights the candle and rifles through the parchments and collections he's borrowed from Guthrie. He pulls out the book he's been studying most nights. Something about grand battles and strategies. He coped well today, under trying circumstances that seem almost foreign to him.

"Oh, I forgot to tell you," I say and climb under the covers, "When I pushed Cal out the door today, I noticed something in the yard."

"What was that?"

"Your little wren's bowl was empty. Seems like you're the one who's a step closer to their battle-line."

He purses his lips and waves the book at me. "You attend to your bees and I'll attend to my preparations. Although what you're dealing with is not exactly a war, is it?"

"When there's a forced defeat—you can be sure you're in a war."

"Facts are wonderful things," Guthrie says. We're seated around him in the field just where he'd promised he'd meet us. Some sit up and lean forward, others lay back and watch the sky and I recline into Thomas's chest. I find his hand and squeeze it. He didn't want to be here, but relented before Guthrie could lecture him on the importance of solidarity. I just wish he'd understand how his narrowed eyes unnerve us all.

He bends and whispers close to my ear. "Over there." Wren pops in and out of view, moving closer with each sweep past. "Probably going to hear every tenth word at the rate she's tearing around."

"It must be all that extra food you ladled into their bowl at mid meal." I gently elbow his ribs.

He clears his throat. "Maybe."

Guthrie is in his element. His face practically glows with the joy of sharing all that knowledge jammed inside his head. "Now, facts are information you understand. We don't have to decide anything about them, they just are. The sky is blue, the sun is out today, we are presently in a field. There's nothing to challenge us or frighten us in those facts, are there?" Some shrug and murmur, but all are attentive, so he continues. "Today I will present you with facts. There won't be anything to fear, nor will I ask or demand anything of you. We will use our brains today and," he pauses for a moment, "This part is important; you may decide for yourself to leave at any time. Understood?" Heads nod around him. "Now, get up and follow me."

The group straggles and trails behind him, but comes together again when he stops at the edge of the forest. He waits for us at the back of the group to arrive before he speaks again. "It was on my morning walk that I discovered something I felt would be pertinent to our lesson."

A child's voice raises at the front of the group. "A what to our what?"

Guthrie considers his students. He scratches behind his ear and a smile lights his face. "Ah! There's something I thought you'd like to see. I want to show you something."

A murmur of approval sweeps over the group, and they follow him into the forest; the younger ones jostling for position alongside him.

We're only a short walk in when he stops and faces the group and holds his finger to his lips. Somewhere behind the rustling of leaves, there's a faint buzzing sound. So quiet at first, but soon we're all searching among the trees for the source as if it were a prize at a village fair.

"There it is." A child points high up a birch tree.

"Where?"

"Where? Oh, I see it,"

"There."

It seems every finger points to the tree until all eyes have laid eyes on the prize.

"Right under a beehive," Guthrie chuckles. "It seemed like the perfect place to conduct our lesson." He gestures for everyone to sit and many take their places against trees or on the smaller mossy rocks around us. Thomas leans against a tree and I lean into him. Guthrie has all their attention. Time for quiet. I rest my head on Thomas's shoulder and focus on the sounds of the forest, the chatter, and the song behind the scenes. The bees hum alongside the bird calls, and the leaves rustle according to the strength of the breeze that passes by them. Everyone settles and listens to Guthrie's wise voice.

"Beehives are filled with honey, such wonderful sweetness, but they're also filled with bees going about their bee business and part of bee business is protecting the hive. If they feel there's a threat; perhaps a bird is hovering around, bouncing on the branches, or a hornet comes too close, the bees will do anything to protect the hive. Can you imagine their hue and cry? 'Protect the hive! Keep the hive safe!'" The younger ones laugh at his panicked bee impersonation. "Sometimes they're so worried about the hornets; perhaps because they've seen so many, they get confused over shadows and things that hint at the shape of a hornet, and they'll still attack and swarm, even when there's no hornet there. The message still goes out loud and strong 'Protect the hive! Keep the honey safe!' but for no proper reason at all. Can you imagine how exhausted those bees get?"

Guthrie reaches toward the child that rises and removes the stone from his hand just as he takes aim at the beehive. "Ah no, we don't need a demonstration. I'm sure we all know what swarming bees look like." He pats the child's shoulder and directs him back to his seat. "Besides, you can run a lot faster than me."

Guthrie surveys the group before him. "Granted, I know it sounds strange, but just for a moment, I'd like you to think of yourselves not as a child, or an adult, not as a Northerner or a Fercie, but as a beehive. And seated beside you are other beehives filled with wonderful sweetness, and you're all just going about your bee business.

Now, consider the times when you've behaved in ways you didn't understand, moments that left you shaking your head, times that frustrated you. Think about the times you fight among yourselves, when you're terrified of certain things and not others, when you don't do the things you set out to do, or when you rage at things considered petty by others."

I'm not the only one who sneaks a glance at Cal. He knows eyes are on him, yet he watches Guthrie steadfastly and nods gently at his mentor.

"You might ask yourself, 'Why did I do that?' or get frustrated and blame everyone else, because we surmise if they hadn't acted that way, then you wouldn't have acted the way you did. Maybe you think awful things about yourself and others." Wren chooses the perfect time to flit past. "Or perhaps you keep yourself so busy, always moving with so many things to accomplish, you don't have to stop to consider your beehive."

"If you think of yourself as a beehive, you can see these reactions as stinging bees, swarming at shadows. When something unexpected happens, or challenges you, the bees kick up inside you and cause you to behave in ways you'd prefer not to, or just wouldn't do if the bees weren't charging through your system. But they're not bad, they're coming out to protect you. Sweeping you and your conscious thought away with your emotions of fear and anger and frustration and helplessness, or away from you by attacking someone else in an effort to keep you safe. You see, the bees are just doing what they're supposed to do. They think they're keeping you safe. It's all the same bees, whether you're attacking someone else or curling into a ball and hoping it will all go away." Guthrie taps at his chest. "My bees make my heart race, like it's about to pop right out of my chest."

"You have bees too?" a small voice asks.

"We all do." Cal says and directs attention back to Guthrie, "It's what we do with them that matters, right?"

"You know what happens when my heart races and the bees are charging through my system? My brain stops thinking. It's like I can't get to it at all. It's of no help to me. What the bees want is the only thing that matters. They might want me to run as fast as I can, or to hurt someone before they get a chance to hurt me. Other times, they freeze me standing still and I can't talk or move. It's like a million of them have swarmed into my body and taken over, and I'm so terrified of their stings I'll do anything they tell me to do. Anything to stop this awful sensation. I say and do things I wouldn't do if my brain was there to help me. But it's not. All that matters are the bees, and doing what they tell me will keep me safe. Once they've overtaken me, there's nothing I can do, but fix up the mess I've made of things afterward."

Guthrie did a splendid job of explaining the bees. He wasn't condescending, and it's clear that his audience is deep in thought.

Cal speaks to the surrounding group. "You'd think the answer would be to fight against them, stop them from coming. But it's not." He waits until he has everyone's attention and adds, "We have to listen to them; pay attention to what they're trying to tell us."

Someone shivers. "How are we meant to do that?"

Guthrie stands tall, as if a weight has lifted from his shoulders. "Oh, I'm only here to explain them to you. Ash is the one who'll show you how to listen."

I jerk back into Thomas. Huh? I will? Faces turn and catch me off guard. Oh, of course I will. Somehow. But not now. I nod at them and then remember to smile, too. "Not yet, but soon," I tell them. "Guthrie's given us a lot to think about. Thinking differently about the bees was my hardest challenge. So Guthrie, what's your next instruction, while we wait to be shown how to listen?"

Guthrie rubs at his whiskered chin. "Those bees are tricksters. Just notice them. Being around people usually brings them out, but sometimes the way we speak to ourselves does too. Watch for them, and observe them, as a scientist like myself would. Where do you feel them in your body? What was it that made them buzz or swarm? Don't go searching for them, just notice them, and talk to each other about them, too. Understanding each other's bees will help you understand yours."

Thomas pushes me away and stands and claps his hands together. "So, we're all done here?"

Guthrie nods.

"Good, I've got a list of things that need doing, and I've delegated who can help me with what."

They jump to their feet and surround Thomas, intent on finding out their assigned task. He'd better not complain about a lack of eager hands ever again.

❧❦❧

I sneak behind Thomas in the early morning light and follow him into the main lodge. I grab his arm just as he wakes a sleeping guest. "Let them sleep." I whisper.

"But the sun's almost up."

They stir and I cover them. "Shh," I tell the blanketed form, "Sleep until you don't need to anymore. Ask your body what it wants to do. You may only rise when it asks you to, and not a moment before." I wipe my hand across my eyes.

"But you need your sleep too," Thomas speaks softly but sternly, "Don't think I haven't noticed."

"It's not just me. Guthrie's been tending to their night terrors as well." I rub my eyes again. I wish there was a way to end this fog in my head. This kind of tiredness was once normal for me, but the peaceful life here has softened me. "If they feel safe enough to sleep heavily, it's a good sign."

We move toward the door and Thomas spies a child asleep on the floor. He hugs a blanket. Someone next to him has also left their bed to sleep on the floor beside him, and shared their blanket with him. "What's with the blanket?"

I smile and a tired warmth spreads through my body; I take Thomas's arm and lead him outside. "He wouldn't take a blanket from me last night. 'You're shivering,' I said and tried to drape it over his shoulders, but he kept pushing it away. I folded the blanket and placed it on his legs.

'There,' I told him, 'It's yours. I won't take it back. Ever.'

'Not even when I'm warm?'

'Especially if you're warm.'"

"So he's going to drag a blanket around with him all day?"

"If he chooses. But he'll let go of it once he knows it's truly his. He knows the blanket is his, but he doesn't believe it. There's a difference."

Guthrie stokes the morning fire in the lodge yard. He's perfected a way of rising without alarming any sleeping bodies. There's a soft mist in the field below. This day will start like any other we've recently experienced, with us tired and trying to keep up, and ending with us tired and trying to sleep. We speak quietly, but Thomas is still distracted by what he found inside the lodge.

"They're on the floor. I made them beds and they sleep on the floor."

"It's where they're most comfortable."

"For now." Guthrie chimes in and completes my thoughts.

"I know you'd think they'd revel in comfort, and they will, but comfort is foreign, it's been denied them or comes with strings attached. It's easier to not get used to something that can be taken away or used against you."

"What do you mean?"

"If someone knows that these little ones want something, or need something, even something as basic as comfort, it can deliberately be used against them to cause them pain. It becomes shameful to seek comfort. A weakness. It's safer to not want anything at all, to not care at all. When they trust us, and know we won't cause them harm, things may change."

"And you understand this?"

"As if it were my own story."

"And you, Guthrie, do you understand this too?"

"A little. But I trust what she sees. As you do as well, I assume?"

I catch Guthrie's raised eyebrows as he turns away from us. It's not lost on us that Thomas doesn't answer his question. I know he trusts me, the stories of the Eariss, and that the army will arrive, but his eyes dull when I try to explain the sometimes inexplicable behaviors of our guests. I wager he thinks I'm mad, making up wild stories to... why would anyone make this up? Perhaps that's the exact question he's trying to sort out himself. Once he finds his answer, I imagine him clinging to it. What we understand is so much easier to welcome. Less of a battle. Less wearisome.

Guthrie stands alongside us as we look into the first rays of this day and lets out a weary sigh. He's making a declaration for all of us. "You know what happened to me, with the Trothsmen?" he directs his words to the fields, but the conversation is with us. "I'm a grown man."

We nod and assure him we're listening.

"I thought I was going to die. It was over. And that was one time... those urchins..." his voice breaks and we keep our eyes on the field, "They faced that terror every day. Under whips and in any split second. How do they do it? How do they keep going?"

"In whatever way got them through." I whisper.

"Fantastic little creatures." Guthrie shakes his head, "Inspiring."

"And whatever way got them through is perfect. Now we just need to help them understand the truth of what they see and feel. When you're constantly told the sky isn't blue, it's green as the darkest moss, and no matter how many times you scrub at your eyes you can't make them see green, you question and doubt your eyes, not the lie teller." The sun breaks through the clouds in slivers of light. Beams of the morning not fully itself yet, like all of us.

"Constant denial of truth wears the strongest of us down. And each agreement with a lie, often under horrible duress, forces them to reject and hate the part of themselves that hungers for the truth. And when that part speaks to them now, they disregard it. They not only don't trust us. They don't trust themselves. They numb their bodies in protection, but even now, they can't feel a thing. And they're terrified to feel."

"Don't they understand how strong they are?"

"They believe they're weak and that the strongest are the ones who battle, not those who survive."

"And what if they were given no chance to battle?"

"Martha told me to never blame my heart for what it did to keep me alive. It was my greatest ally, and yet I treated it like the enemy. We have to introduce them back to their hearts." *Introduce them back to their hearts.* The words fall out of my mouth and cycle back inside me with the same magnetic motion I felt as my feet stepped onto Awenmell. Finally, something solid among all this madness.

Guthrie exhales. "They always tell us facts, don't they, with their stories? I would normally have adored all that information, but now I see how safe details are. It's easy to hide in facts. Trust me."

"They can't tell us how they feel about anything because they don't know. They won't allow themselves to feel it, and if they did, they probably wouldn't have the words to describe it."

Thomas seems agitated. "And you know this because....?"

"My tale is similar, and while the facts may differ, the effect often is not. Waterfalls still arrive and pour over me and show me occurrences as if I was watching. Other times it's as if I am right there with them."

Sights, sounds, conversations, and smells from the stories they tell latch onto my body as if looking for another home. My chest constricts and I force air into my lungs and focus on the field in front of me. Beyond the misted field, the dark spires of the forest wait. As they always do, for me to wrench myself away from the lodges and the aches and the busyness of each of my days. My body aches for the peace its canopy brings and it calls me like the hearth of a warm home, yet I can't reach it yet. Not yet. Maybe later today, maybe tomorrow.

Thomas dumps some stale bread in my hand. "You haven't been eating either."

It doesn't look at all appetizing. Dark bread with dried edges that might serve better for scraping bowls, or mud off boots, for that matter. Still, food in my mouth means I won't have to talk to anyone, and I can go in search of the stillness that was once inside me but now is buried under a list of too many things I must accomplish before this sun in front of us goes down.

"Did you hear about the massacre at Talcasty? Those five who arrived yesterday filled me in on how it came about."

He's probably thinking about strategy and troop numbers, but the pictures come flooding in again, the cries, the smell, the terror. I squeeze my shoulders together to contain the tremble that creeps through my body and clasp desperately to the pendulum that swings inside me. The wanting to know, but not wanting to know. The way I bandage their wounds and daydream about taking the bandages and wrapping them so tightly around myself that I feel solid again. The way the smoke of burning villages burns in my nostrils and makes me gag for air.

I pick at the bread. "I did."

Thomas shakes his head. "The madness of it all. No man trusts another, not even his kin. Betrayal, that's what it's about. The elders want the land, the farmers want the land, the lord pays his guards for service, the guards desert to the farmers, the farmers become guards. How do you make sense of that?"

I can't make sense of it. Thomas chose the right word. Madness. There aren't enough bandages in the world to hold me together.

"They're waiting for you," he tells me.

His eyes are expectant, as if I'm about to stand up and declare war and lead him off to some enchanted victory, but his words land in the pit of my stomach and punch their way into my shoulders.

I'll add that to my list, shall I? Guests emerge from the lodge and distract me from saying something I'll assuredly regret later.

The pond is always at its prettiest in the afternoon. That's what I think, anyway. The shadows fall across the water in graceful patterns and the sun captures the water movements that move across its surface as we fill our buckets to prepare for supper. Claudia and her tiny thin arms have joined me for this task. Two less buckets I have to carry.

"We should just jump in," Claudia says.

I splash water from the pond to my face. It almost stings against the heat on my skin. "We need to get the water back to Guthrie," I say to her disappointed face. "Maybe tomorrow." A deep and distant rumble resonates through the air. An afternoon storm. It can't get here quick enough.

The buckets are too heavy for a young girl's frame and we take our time crossing the field back to the lodge. The beauty of the afternoon sun disappears under its relentless baking in the open field.

"Let's set the buckets down and rest for a short while," I say.

Claudia drops the buckets to the ground with an appreciative grunt. Even though they're half filled, only a little splashes out with the momentum. She tilts her head to one side. "I don't think you're anything like they say." Claudia says.

"Me?"

"Aren't you the Eariss?"

Her eyes hold an expectant look. I'd been so caught up with bees and settling everyone that the name of the Eariss seems almost foreign among all this disarray. Thomas had already stopped writing about it. He said our guests were just a byline anyway, a distraction until the proper story picked up again. "Well, yes," I reply, "That's what they say."

"The scroll in the lodge, the one that's nailed onto the wall, Guthrie read it to us the other night."

"I see."

"But I still say you're nowhere near as bad as the stories."

"There's bad stories?" The pendulum swings again. I want to know, but I don't want to know. But I've asked her the question without giving it thought. Perhaps this is perfect. A child's gentle version of a terrible story.

Claudia shields her eyes from the sun and squints as she looks to my face. "It's all your fault, you see. All the unrest. All the people dying. That's what they say."

Brilliant. Childlike. No nonsense. Brutal. "All of it?"

"Well, that's what everyone says, even the kinship told us."

"You've been to the kinship?"

"They threw things at us."

Of course they did. "I see."

"But they still made sure we knew the song."

"The open flowers song?"

"No, this one sounds the same, but it's different. Everyone everywhere knows it. Have you heard it?"

I pull my lips as tight as I can and shake my head.

"It goes like this …

Eariss tales and Crown of Fire
'but poisoned words from a liar,"

I nod, but the lump in my throat won't allow me to speak. Everyone knows this song, that's what she said. How will an army come now? Claudia continues to gossip, unaware of the knots twisting in my stomach. The weight of the buckets pulls my arms straight and creates a sense of solidity in my body as we dawdle our way closer to the lodge.

"Lady Ashling's in hiding and when the lord dies, she's gonna return and kill everyone who disobeys the Hall."

It sounds strange to hear that name again. Almost as though I'd forgotten I'd ever had it, or that life. Does Claudia realize who I am? I clear my throat with a slight cough. "Do you think she'll really do that?"

She shakes her head, and her shoulders give a halfhearted shrug under the weight of her buckets. "Doesn't matter. People are either scared of her or want to kill her. Whichever way, she's dead, isn't she?" Claudia toddles straight ahead. There is no fear in her body, no worry in her bones. Just the matter-of-factness of living with death daily.

Bees swirl inside my belly. They don't sting, but I know they wait. On edge. Ready. I swallow, but my mouth is dry even in the heat. The weight of the water buckets pulls at my shoulders and perspiration slides down my inner arm. A misstep and the bucket scuffs again into my calf. We're almost at the lodge yard. "And what do the people say about the Eariss?" I ask. Memories of Bez and villagers and secret pacts come to mind. Surely they still sing songs of hope and change; that they see blaming the Eariss for the unrest is a distraction.

Claudia places her buckets in the yard with care and watches them until the water settles. For someone so talkative, it's almost as if she's not sure how to answer my question. Again, the swing of my inner pendulum asks whether I want to know or not.

Claudia shrugs again. Her movement seems exaggerated now she's free of the buckets.

"Claudia," I ask, "If I inquired in a village about the Eariss, what would they say?"

"They would laugh," she says and offers me a sad smile. "Who chooses to be poisoned?"

Who indeed? Feeney's rage spreads out from the Hall like its own poison, stopping in at the well of every village and offering cups of gossip and slander to thirsty minds. They'd take comfort at that well, drinking something solid to believe in, an explanation for their peril. I watch the faces of the guests mill about me, preparing for Guthrie's talk around the fire this evening. How many of them has Feeney poisoned? How many sing Claudia's song? A slap in the face, harder than any Feeney had delivered, reverberates into my soul. The air stifles my breath, its thickness suffocating me. I watch them through narrowed eyes, gleaning my memory of their stories for betrayal or a misspoken word, but revisiting their tales only brings their pain to me again. Like the waves at Ferce Point, I feel every crash, every accusation, every violation, every cut, every burn and every rejection. My body burns like fire, yet a breeze touches my skin. Cool and gentle. From where? The forest. I step away from the throng.

"Ash, there you are. We'll need some firewood, not too much." Guthrie says, "And get the rest of it under cover before the storm comes." And then he is gone. Off on some other errand.

I close my eyes and gently shake the pressure inside my head away. "Of course."

At least the wood is cut. It could be worse. These small lumps of wood could be heavier or need chopping. A small amount for a small fire, just cooking tonight. The storm will shorten Guthrie's talk. A tremor runs through my arms under the weight of the wood. It's not that heavy, but everything in my body feels tremulous right now. Nothing's solid, as if I bounce on a tightrope and I could tumble at any time. Maybe Thomas was right. I need to eat. I hope it's not parsnips.

Riotous children run past me as I deliver the first armful of wood to the open fire. "Slow down!" I call, the last thing I need is to be tending to burns. A trip and an accusation develops into a tussle on the ground and Thomas arrives by my side to help separate them.

Damp hair sticks to the side of his reddened face so close to mine I have to stop. "Is this really what we're meant to be doing here?"

Smoke stings my eyes and takes my breath as Guthrie appears and points at the dropped wood. "We'll need more wood than that!"

I turn on my heels and stride to the loose wood. Thomas pants alongside me and motions to the threshold. "There's more of them," he says. "Where are they coming from? How come they're clean? Why didn't they have to go through that bog like we did?"

"How am I supposed to know that?" I cough the smoke from my lungs.

I scoop the wood up while Thomas watches. "Here!" I say and dump the wood into his chest.

"What if they're all still here when the army arrives? Where will we put everyone?"

Pain slices into my finger. Splinter. I shake the pain away and answer with gritted teeth. "I don't know."

With armfuls of wood, we charge toward Guthrie's meeting and nearly crash into the robed man. He bows and scrapes as we maneuver around him and continue on our way. "And what's with that man's robe? Isn't he hot under that?" Thomas demands. "You never see him with the others. He spends all his time in that forge Guthrie made. Do you know anything about him? Are we just letting anyone in?"

"I don't know much at all." I've never seen the robed man's eyes. He reminds me of something, a recognition, but it seems as deeply hidden as the heaviness of that robe that hides him.

We dump the wood with a clatter. I can still make it to the forest. Water first. Thomas follows me to the barrel outside the lodge and I try to keep my thoughts on the forest and not on his incessant chatter. People gather for Guthrie's fireside talk. What was it this time? Honesty, I think.

"The unrest," Thomas continues under his breath, "We've got to do something other than play with unruly children!"

I gasp in impure air. How can the smoke have followed me here? Sharp tingles scratch their way across my shoulders. I'd prefer the smoke to Thomas.

"People are dying and we're sitting here doing nothing."

"I don't know what you expect me to do," I say and dig fervently into the splinter under my skin. Pain shoots into my hand.

"Call your army."

I don't know how to call the army. He knows that. Perspiration stings at the corner of my eye, and I'm so invested in the splinter I don't wipe it away. I shake my head. Not at Thomas, at everything. At children brawling near open fires, and night terrors and more and more people arriving and no sleep and this ache in my eye and my tired eyes and fuzzy brain and weakness and this wretched smoke that follows me and this abysmal heat. And that the forest is only a short distance away and I can't seem to get there no matter how I try.

"Are you scared?" he leans on the lodge siding with an air of smugness that makes me want to hit him. "I think you're scared."

I'm not scared. I know scared. I knew it in the Hall; I knew it in the field with the man in the fur vest and his one-armed companion. I'm tired. Too tired to respond to him. Martha told me only I get to decide whether I'm too scared to move or too scared to stay still. I'm honest with myself enough to know that if I had the means, and I knew it was what I was meant to do, I would call the army in a heartbeat. It's not what I'm meant to do right now. "I'm not afraid."

"I think you are. Otherwise, you'd do something. You're the Eariss, remember."

I turn from the barrel, not sure whether I can flee to the forest without being seen by Guthrie's group seated around the fire.

Thomas grabs at my arm. "Well, make sure you let us know when you're ready. How many more will die? Tell me that?"

His words have a life of their own, as if they've grown hands and strangle my chest and throat. His eyes show he was sorry the moment the words left his mouth, but I couldn't even spit out a reply if I wanted to. They embed themselves into me like hot coals.

I need a distraction. I force my eyes to absorb my tears and take a seat at Guthrie's circle. He looks concerned when I wipe my hands on my skirts. It's just the dirt from the wood. That's all. Focus. Honesty, wasn't it? Who's speaking next? Oh, the robed man. He rises, and his hands tremble along with his profuse apologies. Bees stir in my belly and I battle to keep them under control. Concentrate. The tremor in his hands increases as he reaches to undo his cloak pin. Time to focus on something else for a change. The robe drops from his shoulders and I'm aware that his countenance changes, but I don't notice his face.

He has one arm.

Where is it?

The words hiss through my teeth. Bottles rattle and clang into each other under my scrambling hands. Guthrie couldn't have had it all himself.

"Calm down, child. What's wrong with you?" I jump at Guthrie's voice and a bottle chatters onto the floor, telling a tale of its own. Of course, he followed me from the fire. He knows what I'm looking for. My hands clench the edge of the table. If he can escape whenever he wants, so can I. I made the damned liquid. "You tremble."

"I don't tremble, Guthrie. I'm traveling in ten directions at once!" Energy crackles through my veins in a frightening paradox. It bids me to scream for years without end, while it urges me to tuck it all away and shrink into the tiniest jot on one of his parchments; unneeded and unnoticed.

His eyes show deep concern, but no clues for my prize. "You concentrate so much on making us safe, you've failed to make it a safe place for you."

I rummage through his bottles again. Maybe I missed something. I can't stand around wasting time while he speaks. He pats my forearm and I flick away his concern.

"Don't you usually find your answers in the forest?"

Of course. The forest. Little red heads poke through pine needles. "Namatia!"

"That's not what I meant—"

Distant lightning brightens the lodge, and I wipe my tears with the back of my hand. "I need to gather." I push past him with more force than necessary. Guilt thuds briefly into my chest, but rising panic claws it away and claims me. I can't take the chance that anyone would hold me down and keep me away from a place where nothing matters. Nothing at all.

I take the path away from the fire, past the darkness of the forge. If no one can see me, no one can stop me.

L ight rain precedes the coming storm with as much vigor as trumpeters marching before a battle. They announce greatness but never really embody it themselves. Branches sway in occasional gusts and dump light showers of collected water, sometimes catching me, sometimes not. I don't care. I frantically search the ground for my treasure, slipping on pine needles and imagining my prize around every trunk, or hiding behind every rock. I toss the basket aside and crawl through the wet undergrowth; only stopping to peel wet leaves from my cheeks. It's all these scents, strong pine and dirt, that's why I can't breathe. Where is it? My fingers dig through layers of wet needles. The storm moves closer. I can feel the rumbles through the earth and into my body. Light flashes brighter in the sky. The rain grows heavier.

It was here. Somewhere. Anywhere. Panic surges, as no relief appears. I scramble now, more like an animal. Desperate and driven by an insatiable hunger. My mind whirs, never settling on anything, with odd flashes and visions and emotions that flood me to my fingertips. I am no longer myself, but a congealed mass of pine and mud and terror longing for release from the horror that stalks me. It's only the namatia that can save me from the wave about to crash over me. I'm on the verge of hysteria. It's not here.

I stagger to my feet, soaked through now from the heavier rain, and the approaching storm cracks over my head. "Where is it?" I shout into the thunder and there is no response. I try to reign in my panic, but the bee's stings surge through my veins and strip them raw. Guthrie's disappointment and Thomas's anger, the people that just keep coming with their pain and stories. A waterfall knocks me to my knees and I fight against falling to the earth where I know I'd be totally consumed by the visions and emotions that smash into me with as much force as the storm that I'm not sure what is within and without me. I need to escape from this crushing, from myself. What begins as longing soon turns into panicked desperation from an enclosed room. A window, a door, a hole — anything. It's a familiar panic I've brought from the Hall. Yet a child has no means of escape. I do now. And I *will* find it.

Wind blows wet leaves that slap into my face like a correction. I peel it off and demand to know.

"Why do you hide my escape?" I shout at the sky.

Silence.

I search in all the common places, and strain my mind to produce it. If I imagine it hard enough, it will be there. But it's not. Time after time, slip after slip, tree after tree. Not one dot of red among the needles on the floor. Hot blood pulses in my veins and pushes the panic aside in favor of rising anger.

"It was here yesterday; you know I saw them. Where are they?"

Thunder rolls, but behind its commotion, there is only silence.

"Fine!" I stomp through building rain, sloshing water up with each step. "I'll find it myself!"

Desperation consumes me again, like a fever that's taken my senses. Namatia is my answer, my cure. I curse at the Mystery for hiding my relief, and when I run out of curses, I make up some of my own. The harshness of the weather matches my tone and thunderclaps hide my rage at the Mystery. Lightning flashes and mud splashes up. I pull wet strands of hair from my face and arms. My trail leads me to the edge of the pond. I snatch a handful of iris blooms and crush them into my hand. Pathetic. The iris is weak.

My hand creeps open to splashes of raindrops and the crushed petals roll like a soggy lump into the pond. My feet dent into the mud. Realization breaks my ego's heart in two and a heaviness drags me to my knees. There will not be any namatia. I could search forever. There will not be any escape.

I roar into the night sky, a raging inferno that terrifies me with its force. The storm above me swallows the sound, mixes it with the reverberation of thunder and flashes its energy back through the night sky in sheets of energy bright enough to make it feel like day. The redness engulfs everything around me, forcing its energy through my throat and burning everything to ash inside me. A grief for all the times I should have been safe but wasn't. For every moment of being so terribly horribly alone in a world that was so much bigger than me. The shame that embedded itself in my powerlessness. The pressure and punishment of having no answers. Will I never be free of the Hall's torment?

How long have I screamed at the surrounding storm? My throat is hoarse. I pant, water runs down my forehead and face as though I rain tears myself. My rant has exhausted a little pressure, but anger still simmers in my veins. My jaw pains with clenched teeth.

You need to feel.

"You need to provide me with namatia!"

Silence.

I pant, sullen. A flicker of embarrassment at the curses I shouted crosses me but is soon swept away by irrepressible and irrational bravado. There will be no namatia. Of that I'm sure, yet I still pout like a spoiled child who doesn't get their way.

I wiggle my knees and feet in the mud. They're not going anywhere.

"I think..." I whisper, drips dropping from my lips into the pond, "I think I'm scared."

Of what?

My hands slide into the pond water in some kind of cleansing ceremony and wipe my tears from my storm-soaked face. "Weakness. Being swallowed whole by Awenmell, the decisions, the pressures, the uncertainties. One arm! I can't see the way out. I just stood on my feet and now here I am in the mud. I'm failing them and I don't even know how. How can I tell them what's coming when I don't know anything?"

Do you really want to know?

A cheek muscle coaxes one side of my unruly mouth into a slight smile. "No." I say. It's barely audible, but I know I'm heard.

My shins squelch further into the mud, and I have no inclination to remove them. I wipe a trickle of water from the side of my face, but only smear more water on my skin. The storm is quieter now; the wind arrives in slight blusters here and there, but the rain taps onto my head. Uniformed and patterned, cold and unrelenting. It drips down my back. I should shiver, but I really can't be bothered.

Finished?

"No." I want to hold on to some last remnant of... I don't even know what it is, but it keeps me suctioned here, sodden in the rain. Not moving forward or backward, like the old ewe in Martha's garden. What a stubborn creature she was.

"Where were you?" I finally mumble. "I wanted help to find the namatia, and you didn't answer."

Would you have listened?

"No." I smile at myself. My ill placed bravado has made way for gentle honesty.

When was the last time you listened?

"In the field. My mornings." I draw a deep breath through my teeth. "I've been busy. With Awenmell..." I think of our guests, Cal, Thomas, Guthrie, Wren, the constant busyness, food and teaching and building and cleaning and explaining. "... there's been no time for mornings."

No time for mornings?

Rain tickles down my nose, and I itch at it. What a dolt. I say there's no time to connect and refresh myself with the Mystery, yet I've found the time to throw a tantrum in the middle of a night storm. The Mystery doesn't have to explain it. I brought myself here.

"Where to now?"

The stream.

I lift my head and water trickles down the sides of my face. The waterfall continues its flow throughout the storm as if it hadn't even noticed its presence. It might surge with more water volume from run off, but continues as it always has, pouring water from the stream into the pond. "You want me to climb up to the stream?"

It's the source of the waterfall, isn't it?

I suction my feet from the mud and step gingerly away from the edge of the pond, correcting my balance for slips and holding my arms out into the relentless rain and find my way back into the forest and the stream above the waterfall. Within the shadows and darkness of the forest, I make out a section of the stream, a small straight that runs between two trees. It appears lit up in confirmation by occasional and distant lightning. It doesn't seem too deep; I step into the water almost to my knees; smooth pebbles are under my feet. At least it's not mud. I hold my skirts above the waterline — a rather pointless exercise. I shake my head at myself and release them.

"Fine. Now what?"

Sit.

I'm not even surprised. Sit in the middle of a stream, in the middle of a storm, in the middle of the night. Why not? I plop into the water; my skirts rise like a pillow of air and I smack them into place to submerge them. I strain to see if anyone watches me from the dark. Why would anyone be here? Only mad people sit in streams in the middle of a stormy night. I resist the urge to fold my arms and pout.

The water current tugs lightly at my clothes, bringing them to order. Comfortable pebbles form my seat. There's warmth in the water, more than what's above it in the rain and the nearly exhausted wind. I relax into the strangeness of this moment. Just like any storm, there's a point where you stop running for cover and just let yourself get soaked. I know I passed that moment long ago somewhere in the depths of the forest tonight, but it's comforting to acknowledge it now. The tender moment when you stop fighting the wetness of the storm and just let it be part of your experience, and let it soak into your entire body.

Tell me about the stream.

"It's wet." I bite the inside of my cheek. Stubbornness rides in my veins like a mule, ready to kick when I least expect it. Just when I think I'm a good student, I ruin it for myself.

The stream?

I close my eyes and try to push the left-over angst away. The stream. "It's moving," I say. "Gently, but moving. I don't expect it ever stays still." I wipe my hands over its surface. Rain breaks any smoothness that might be here on a normal day or night. Larger droplets from the trees fall regularly and push deeper into the stream than the rain. "There's more going on at the surface than underneath." My skirts drag in the gentle tug of the current, but other than the silky sensation of water passing them, there's no turbulence, a notion of movement, but warmth and so much less discord than above. A gust of wind dumps heavy dollops from the trees that fall over me in a burst of activity, creating a sense of great agitation on the surface, but underneath, you wouldn't even know there had been a gust of wind. "It's almost as if there are two distinct streams running the same course."

Which feels more secure?

"Definitely the gentle current under the surface. The surface is always agitated and changing depending on what's going on up here." Raindrops land and wind blows, and I focus on comparing the two streams again. The agitated surface, and where I sit in the stillness underneath. It reminds me of something familiar. "This is the place I hear you clearly, like my mornings in the field."

Storms will always agitate the surface, big drops from trees, and windblown, pelting rain. Other times, the tiniest of sprinkles hits the surface and leaves tiny circles so soft they barely radiate out from themselves. Underneath the surface, under all the commotion, that's where you find me. I never left. You just changed your focus to the surface. You focused on the storm instead of the stillness.

"But storms rage, and when they do, they sweep all common sense away."

Only if you're watching them from the surface. From the depth of the stream, there is no agitation. You can watch the storm pass by without longing for it to be any other way. Observe the storm, but don't be distracted by what's going on at the surface. It will try to pull you in like an eddy. But this place, this is where your decisions are unbiased and unravaged by what's happening around you.

I'd left it behind. All of it. The stillness of the field, and the forest, in my rush to prepare Awenmell. Every time I deferred the silence, I floated closer to the surface, closer to agitation and being unsure of everything; including the Mystery. I can't believe I missed it. It was right there in front of me. I drop my hands into the stream. "Idiot."

Without this storm around you, and the one within you, would you have found yourself sitting here in this stream?

Distant lightning crackles enough light to highlight my predicament. I must be a sight. "It's hard to imagine any other reason for it."

Each tale, even of woe, brings you to the next. Each experience is another stepping stone. Without them you stay still and make no changes, you don't get to see the other side; you don't learn to trust. You won't learn, can't learn if you don't experience. Discomfort is never punishment, it's a reward; it's a hint of coming greatness, giving you experience and preparing you for what's coming next.

It's hard to imagine I'm prepared for anything. Embarrassment pushes aside the remnants of my anger. Martha said I shouldn't ever blame myself for not knowing something. 'Once you know, you can do better, but it's impossible if you don't know, and pure insanity to blame yourself for the impossible.' I can't promise it'll be better, but at least it'll be different. I hope it'll be different. Ugh! How many more storms will I have to sit through?

As many as you like.

"I wasn't really asking. I was just saying…"

Storms are not punishment, remember. Look around you. The stream, the trees, the forest; there is not one moment of shame or guilt, blame or fault in their existence. They aim for growth, but don't strive to be more than they are at this moment. Have you noticed they don't grasp for some measured outcome? They're not attached to an idea of being anything other than they are. So tell me now, what are you attached to?

I draw a deep breath and spray rain droplets from my lips as I exhale. "Doing everything the proper way. Not being enough of whatever it is I'm supposed to be; not calming Thomas, or being helpful to our guests. If the unrest is my fault, aren't I supposed to be the one to fix it?"

And all this worry and fear. Does it come from this moment in the stream or one in the past? Do you find it at the surface, or in the depths?

"The surface."

Try looking at it from the depths.

I submerge my fear into the depths and sit with it in the stillness. It dissipates, diluted into the mass of water that gently washes it away until there's nothing to grasp anymore. Even when I try to conjure blame for myself, it doesn't exist, just compassion for my intention that got distracted and overwhelmed. The same feeling of grace and understanding I offer to our guests rises in my heart and acts like a balm as silky as the water flowing beside my skirts. I am worthy of compassion too.

"But the waterfalls," I mumble with my head low, rainwater drips from my nose and chin, "Not the ones filled with information, but the ones that sweep me away...." Visions of massacres and our guest's tales of mistreatment find their way to me in the stillness. Their barbs don't tear at my flesh here, but hover over me menacingly. "What good is this torture if it does nothing but overwhelm me?"

Would you choose to never deeply know another soul?

There are many, many times I longed to be free. I try to weigh up my yeses and nos like Guthrie's balancing scales, but that means denying my experience. I shake my head gently; the Mystery was right. Experience is a stepping stone. "I fear it's who I am, whether I choose it or not."

Acceptance. The lightest heart is the one that's stopped fighting its destiny and starts working with it.

"Work with it? I wanted to get rid of it."

Do you remove the bees from your guests, or do you encourage them to become quiet, and listen for themselves? What good would it do if you heard the bees and not them? It wouldn't do anything for you, or for them.

"I understand."

Put their stories down. You needn't immerse yourself in order to know their pain. Some acts of mercy require you to carry another's pain, but not as often as you might think.

"But I can't just not listen to them, or not know things when I touch them."

Listen and feel from the safety and depths of the stream, not from the surface where the eddies wait to draw you in. Hear them from that gently flowing space of compassion and they'll feel seen. You being in the depths of the stream invites them in, you're making a place for them in the stream, not holding their pain for them and damaging yourself. You're not doing anything, not fixing, not healing, not judging. You're simply there, in the stream. The most powerful place to be in the face of great pain and anguish. That connection, you couldn't wish it away, it's what lights you up and draws them to you. When you're in the stream, to them, you're as safe as the stream.

My hands raise and lower, alternating between the depths of the stream and the agitation of the surface. Everything makes sense here. The rain has slowed to drizzle, and the clouds - once heavy and dark - are thinning out and letting strains of moonlight through. Lulls in the wind silence the trees and let voices and noise from Awenmell reach me in the stream. I'd like to return to Awenmell, but I'd also like to stay here. Sodden, but complete.

My lesson is done. I'm not the same person who entered the forest as the storm arrived. I close my eyes and concentrate on the wisps of movement along my legs in the stream, the stillness and the depth under the agitated surface.

I will never keep you from your own decisions. Wisdom decrees the best ones emerge from the stillness and not from the restlessness at the surface. Here...

Moonlight shines in slivers along the edge of the stream. Just among the ferns, a slight movement brushes the tiniest of delicate fronds aside. I lean forward and watch a perfectly formed namatia grow before my eyes, its red cap promising short lived oblivion.

Your choice is your greatest power. How will you wield it?

Out of the water, the hem of my skirts feel like they're laden with rocks. Water pours from them at first and then settles into steady drips as I hurry my way to Awenmell, hugging myself against the wind. I pull at my soggy sleeves and relieve their cling for a moment. My feet slide inside my misshapen shoes and throw me off balance. They kick off easily and I scoop them from the ground. I don't need an injury.

The constant pull of the water as it drains down my clothing feels very different to the pull of the current in the stream. How am I meant to carry the depth of the stream in my heart? That stream back there somewhere; a magical strait between two trees where the namatia grows untouched by its side. I stop moving and concentrate. Can I conjure that same silkiness out of the water? My hand finds its way to my heart and I hold it there until the imagined depths settle inside me. "Here." I announce it to the forest around me as if sealing it into my body. "Here. Dwell here." Is it enough? A solemn vow with my full attention. It's all I have. I shiver in a blast of wind and hop from tussock to tussock on the edges of the field. The warm heart of Awenmell glows yellow through the cracks on the door frames. Splinters of promise from the hearth that both warms and chills me at the same time. What am I meant to say to them? Thomas will ask me about the army. So many questions and no answers.

Clarity is coming.

"Let me guess," I puff, and leap from one grassy mound to another, "I'll find it in a cloudy stream on a foggy morning." I snort at my jest, but the Mystery seems unimpressed.

Like a crisp breeze.

I shiver again, and my steps become more urgent. "I won't mistake it for something else?"

Not if you're in the depths.

The lodge yard looms closer with each step. Am I just returning to the chaos that sent me on my way into the forest? Pressure. Pain. Things that weren't mine to begin with. I draw a breath that pulls the bees from my veins and back into the depths.

One Arm. I'm not overwhelmed now. Just curious about why he's here. Why he'd stay here. There's no point telling Thomas. He can't even cope with an unruly child, or how people travel in perplexing ways. And why don't they come through the bog? I forgot to ask. It would be good to give at least one solid answer to Thomas. I stop and speak to the clouds, although I'm sure that's not where the Mystery resides. "Can you at least tell me why they don't come through the bog?"

Clarity is coming.

"So you say."

The lodge door swings open and illuminates part of the yard. Guthrie's form rummages under the covers that protect the firewood pile on the side of the lodge. He mumbles to himself and emerges, cradling the split wood like a child, and stops short at the sight of me. I halt at the edge of the yard, unsure of how to make amends. What to say? I lift my soggy shoes by way of random explanation as the water continues its steady drip onto my bare feet. His eyes alter from concern to compassion. A smile crosses his lips when he realizes I am unaffected by anything unworldly.

A shadow blocks the light from the doorway, and Thomas's chuckle fills the air. "Well, would you look at this," he says and steps toward me. "Seems weathering the storm in an incomplete forge wasn't such a great idea after all, was it? You should have joined us in the lodge."

"I did advise her not to take refuge there," Guthrie offers a sly wink, "But she had other plans for this evening."

Thomas puts his arms around my shoulders and leads me inside, where the warmth away from the wind soothes me like a blanket. I collapse into the chair like the sack of sopping clothes that I am, while Thomas gets me a bowl and I smile and nod at our guest's concerns and the youngster's giggles at the sight of me drenched to the bone.

Guthrie places his hand on my shoulder and speaks low into my ear. "You visited with your Mystery?"

I nod and pull some limp leaves from my hair. Each time I come back, I'm refined, purified, a tiny bit more. Like I bring a little more of the Mystery into this world, into this lodge and this moment.

Thomas places the bowl in my wrinkled hands. "Are you safe? Are you well?" I nod and thank him before he registers what Guthrie asked. "The Mystery? Any news of the army?"

The room falls silent, as if the entire building holds its own breath. Even Wren stops her flitting and waits for my answer. "No, not yet," I say. Thomas is disappointed, but the building breathes again, safe in the knowledge they can stay a while longer. Hot food radiates heat from the inside out and as the others mill about me, moving in and out of the lodge, enjoying animated conversations and preparing themselves for the night, I draw on the stillness of the stream again. Thomas is back to his watchful self, checking, nodding and watching me while he helps the others. I itch. First, it's my arms, then my legs. The heat from the fire and the dampness of my clothes prods me to move. I return the bowl. "Time for me to remove these wet clothes. Goodnight, all."

Voices chorus a warm and restful night and Thomas hastens his work to join me.

Guthrie catches me at the door, concern for unanswered questions about my search for dwale and namatia in his eyes. "I've heard it said wanting to disappear really means wanting to be found. So your Mystery has found you. And Thomas found you, and I found you, and now the others have found you."

I pat his hand and smile. "You needn't worry. I am found."

Thomas closes the cottage door behind us and helps me out of my clothes. "I meant it, you know."

"Meant what?"

"Are you safe? Are you well?"

My outer skirts peel off and land with a thud on the floor.

"I'll admit it. I've been distracted. What with the preparations for the army and my reading," he gestures to the books on the floor and I almost expect him to pick one up and start lecturing me on the importance of radical defense. "But tonight, as the storm raged, Guthrie asked me questions."

"Questions?"

"About you."

"I see." My arms pull free of the sleeve's clinginess into the open air of the cottage.

"And I'm ashamed to admit I had no answers. I couldn't answer them. Simple questions."

His hands are warm against the goosebumps on my shoulders and arms, his embrace protective and tender. My ally and comfort in this strange world. The future doesn't matter, neither do droplets and streams, currents and thunder. There's a depth between us too, one that goes beyond surface agitations and annoyances. A bond that moves as deep and as gentle as the deepest current. I've been focusing on our guests; he's been focusing on the army. Now we must focus on each other again.

"Truly, are you well?"

"I am now."

⁂

I wake to Thomas, kissing me.

"You were smiling in your sleep," he says, "Must've been thinking of me."

I stretch, "No, sorry," he looks disappointed. "A circle of logs, actually."

He falls onto his back. "They weren't talking to you, were they? We've only just got settled here... no, wait. You don't know where they are or what they're for."

"That's where you're wrong, Thomas of Feldston. I know exactly where they are, and what they're for."

I try to get out of bed, but he pulls me down into his arms. "That's *Thomas of Awenmell,* thank you very much."

⁂

Thomas wipes his brow in the midmorning sun. The tall firs I led his troop to in the forest were now felled, dragged, and lying in the lodge yard. "This reminds me of moons ago. Watching you in the field every morning, me dragging lumber through the forest."

I remember those days, though I'm not sure if it was yesterday or a lifetime ago. "It seemed simpler then, didn't it?"

People work in the fields; taking advantage of the storm softened soil. Another group trails in a loose line, bringing water from the pond, behind us some older children chatter and giggle while preparing vegetables for the mid-meal. A shout in the lower field puts Thomas on alert. There's a scuffle between two men, but it's soon quelled by... "Is that Cal?"

"Sure is," Thomas says.

The men shout, with Cal between them. A brave and wise negotiator, a tamer of bees if ever I'd seen one. Soon they're shaking hands and working side by side. Cal looks up toward the forge where Guthrie nods his approval. Cal always was a leader; he just didn't have the right mentor.

Wren zips past us, fleeing the tension of the field, and hops from log to log on her way across the yard.

"Well, Wren appreciates the logs." Thomas says.

"I do too. Can we cut them, though? They seem a bit long,"

"See the men over there repairing that fence?" he lifts an arm to them and they return the acknowledgment. "They'll be up here soon with their axes to do exactly that."

"You've thought of everything, haven't you?"

"Except why it's so important to lay these heavy logs around the fire."

"For open discussion."

"I know, you told me. Like a town square, only this is your version... so unsurprisingly, it's round."

I can see it in my mind's eye even as the logs lie haphazardly across the yard. "It's more about conversation, and community, and oddly enough... defense." His eyes light up, just as I expected they would. "Just not the kind you're anticipating."

He leans his elbow on the yard fence and scratches his head. "You're going to tell me something about defense?"

"Remember when you taught me how to wield a stick in the forest?" I pretend to swing a large stick and suppress a smile when I remember how that lesson ended, "... and then again, here in the field." I flick my head and free it of visions of One Arm and Fur Vest. "You said I needed to protect myself against unwanted things in my life, and that the best way to keep safe is to not find yourself in that predicament in the first place. But, if you find yourself there, you must be prepared to defend yourself, or there will be unpleasant consequences."

"Sounds like something I'd say."

"Well, look at them." I turn back to the lower field and as if on cue, Wren barrels past us back into the field but slides to a stop and tracks sideways when tensions in Cal's work party erupt again. Among the vegetables, a young woman throws a basket at another and storms away. "They don't want to be in this predicament, but that's what life has brought them. Hornets, and bees, and constant tension that's just as dangerous and life altering as meeting a bandit in the forest. They need to know how to defend themselves, not against another, but against their overwhelming reactions." All is calm in the field again, but a rumble is never far away. "They're like individual storms, but they don't have anywhere to shelter from themselves."

"And the logs?"

"Remember when I couldn't feel anything, couldn't trust anything? I had bound myself up so tightly, I wasn't prepared to let anything in, because everything hurt. Everything. The bees were my constant companions, directing me here and there, causing more pain than they'd convinced me I was avoiding. They were hovering over a wound, embedded like a deep splinter that irritated me, but was so tender I couldn't bear to let anyone see it, let alone touch it. The bees make it easy to believe that destroying myself or everything around me is preferable to facing what was causing the deeper pain."

"And that's what they're doing. But how will the logs help?"

"You and Guthrie created a safe place for me. That's what this is. A place for them to acknowledge the bees that rage through their veins. A place to understand the person who sits beside them understands the bees and won't blame them for surviving the best way they knew how. We can make knowledge of the bees our normal and take the lessons of what they teach us to help others thrashing in their stings. We keep our shields down; the ones that would hide our bees from each other, or stop us from the pain of seeing the bees at work in others. When we belong to each other, and we have each other's backs. We become safe."

Thomas nods slowly. Can he see it? Or is he just humoring me? "And how do you know all of this?"

A question like that would have filled me with sadness a while ago. The Mystery's prompting now fills me with hope. "I feel their pain; because they are me, as much as I am them."

"Then we shall cut these logs," he says as he steps forward to embrace me, "and make a circle of your town square."

A loud stomach grumbles between us.

"Now that was me." He says.

I pull away from his chest and laugh. "Remember that awful straw bread at Smoutlea?" My eyes widen and my mouth waters. His eyes widen too. There's bread on the table in the lodge. He remembers it as well. We both start at the same time and trip over each other, but I reach the doorway first. Thomas pushes past me and claims the bread. "Aha!" he cries.

Wren's tiny feet disappear out a small window halfway along the lodge.

"Sorry little one," he calls and holds up bread she can't see. He tears at it and passes the rest to me.

"Did you see how quick she did that? Like leaping through windows is normal."

"If it's her normal, she wouldn't know any other way."

Thomas chews his bread thoughtfully for a while. "Have you seen her run and weave in and out of Arrow's legs? He doesn't mind at all."

"Arrow's a patient teacher."

"We kind of messed it up, didn't we, charging in here like that?"

"One day she might stay..."

"But not today."

I shrug and place some torn bread in my mouth. It tastes heavenly. Nothing like straw at all.

"You know what else isn't normal?"

The lump of half-chewed bread in my mouth won't let me answer. What could I answer, anyway? Nothing here is normal. Surely Thomas hasn't just figured that out.

"That weird robe guy."

The bread gets stuck in my throat. Weird robe guy. One Arm. A flurry of bees explodes from my heart and nestle in my shoulders. They flutter but don't sting, waiting, hovering gently.

"He doesn't fight with anyone, or do anything other than get in the way with all his apologizing."

I swallow hard and pass the bread back to Thomas. "I expect he feels safer blending in."

"But he stands out, doesn't he? Having one arm and all? I wouldn't even know if he has eyes; he never looks at anyone. If you're reckoning on normal behavior, there's something hidden there for sure."

I nod, remembering how One Arm moves away whenever he sees me. I expect there's been many times he's disappeared without me even knowing he was there at all. He's been so scarce that if not for our history, I might not even know he exists, yet Thomas has noticed his behavior too. "I don't see that much of him, to be honest," I say.

"You know what's fascinating? He spends all his time in the forge now. Guthrie's set him to making all manner of things. Apparently, he's quite good. Have you been to see his work?"

I shake my head.

Thomas stops to think for a while. "I wonder how he does it? You know, one arm and all?" Thomas snatches my hand and pulls me toward the door. "Let's see what he's up to!"

I choke on non-existent bread, and Thomas's momentum draws my staggering feet toward the doorway. Toward the forge, toward One Arm, toward I don't even know what. My brain scrambles for any excuse as the bees raze my blood and shut off any connection to my mouth.

Cal crashes into Thomas in the doorway, and we bounce back amid his flustered panting. "Need help!" he gasps and directs our gaze with his thumb pointing over his shoulder. His field melee has turned into a brawl. Thomas calls over his shoulder as he charges after Cal and we tumble through the doorway. "Another time!"

Air rushes into my compressed lungs. I can breathe. Another time. Gladly! I lift my hand in acknowledgment, but words escape me. That was close.

"Ashling!" Guthrie barks at me from beside the lodge. His strides place him next to me before I can return his greeting or avoid the agitated shaking of the wooden frame he clutches. "How am I expected to exact my knowledge without a precise time of delivery of the hinge required for optimum observations!"

I blink hard. What has come over this place? "Guthrie, I—"

"I can't leave now!" He checks behind him for some unknown pressure, and stomps towards it. "You find out! How can I make the required adjustments without a completion parameter from the forge?" It wasn't a request; it was an order.

There's no one else. Anywhere. Everyone is either involved in the melee or disappeared from the face of the earth, and it roots my feet to the ground.

"Well?" he turns back and demands.

"You need a hinge...?" I repeat.

"No! I need to know when it will be ready."

"You want me to go to the forge?"

He looks at me red-faced, a tiny twitch in his cheek muscles, and speaks through clenched teeth. "Now would be good."

"Yes, Guthrie," I say, my heart thumping in beats of pain. I wish there was somewhere else I could be right now; like Wren's feet disappearing through the window. "Of course, — now." I turn on my heels and console myself with a raspy whisper that covers each step that takes me closer to the forge. "Yes. Now would be good." I repeat.

But I don't believe a word I say.

The forge lies to the south of the main lodge, a hodge podge three-sided building whose dirt floor was leveled by cutting into the surrounding slope. The open side faces the field and gives it a pavilion kind of air, like if it were grander, you'd sit surrounded by food and be entertained by activity in the field, and not just stare at crops growing and people working. Guthrie ordered its hasty construction in an uncharacteristic fit of impatience, leaving the walk space around the three walls ripe for water overflow. Even I knew it needed channels. It wasn't worth arguing with him then. He waved his 'wise and unapproachable' shield around, just as he did a few moments ago. The forge is so new, there's not even a track to follow there yet. Just a padding down on darker grass that shows someone has passed by.

"Now would be good," I whisper again. I might have been whispering it all along. Just unaware. As if it was some unconscious and peculiar mantra that would suddenly make it so. I scrunch my fingers into my palms, rhythmically kneading them as each of my steps takes me closer to the forge. "Now would be good." Guthrie needs to know about his hinge.

Who would've guessed a one-armed man was a blacksmith?

And a journeyman at that?

Who would've guessed I'd be standing a few steps from the side of the forge and unable to enter?

Kneading my hands provides a comforting distraction. What do I say?... Hello? No. What are you doing here? Why were you with Fur Vest? Isn't it a lovely day?... Stupid brain. My hands knead themselves hot and my brain refuses to focus. It's not fear... intrigue perhaps, apathy? There're no bees. Nothing. Just my shallow breath and my clenching and unclenching hands.

Wren flits past my side and I return the quick smile she offers; she does a lap of the forge, then back to me before darting ever so lightly in and out of the forge proper.

"Now would be good." I whisper. I would never have forced myself to this moment. Never have made the effort to confront him. Yet here I am. Hiding is just another shield. Protection? Definitely, but I need to realize I'm holding a shield in order to put it down. So, why don't I want to be here? I don't want to feel uncomfortable emotions. At least now I know why I hold it up. And now I'm free to choose whether I put it down.

Wren pops out of the forge, circles me and flits back inside.

"Hello there little Wren," One Arm's voice is deep and worn dry. I twist and press my back into the forge wall. "That's what they call you, isn't it?"

Her feet shuffle on the ground, a soft padding that never stays still behind the walls. The acrid smell of fire and molten metal seeps through the thin cracks of the boards behind me.

"Do you have a name?" he asks between taps and heavy bangs onto the metal. "You must have one all of your own. It's probably as light as the breeze, too. Just like you."

She bounces out of the forge and checks on my position before returning to the sounds of hissing and clanking behind the wall.

She must be watching him, but I can't imagine her standing still. Perhaps she's swaying. She does that from time to time.

"See how the metal changes? That's how we can make new things. It's got to get hot first." He bangs hard and I jump and slide my back carefully down the boards.

I can't imagine how loud it is for Wren, or whether she covers her ears, but she appears to the side of me and flits in and out as though it doesn't bother her in the slightest.

"For anything to change, it has to go through discomfort. That's what I've been thinking, anyway. Look how hot this metal is; it's like soup, isn't it? The heat's completely changed its form. Don't get too close now... you see those wiggly lines, that black stuff? That's called dross. It's the stuff we don't want in the metal. It weakens it. It rises to the top so we can see it and remove it. But here's the secret... without the heat, the dross won't rise. We can't see it, or fix it without all that horrible heat."

I could go in now. I could stand up, brush down my skirts, step into the forge and say... what would I say? I bite my lip. Nothing.

One Arm chuckles a little. "Did you hear Guthrie talking about those bees? Sometimes I think I'm made of them."

The sound of Wren's feet pads away from me and then she appears on the far side of the forge, scampers around the forge's makeshift path, leaps over my legs and darts back inside.

"Ha! You got me!", he greets her in surprise as she enters, "I'd say you buzz just as much as them."

Among the clanking and shuffling, her feet pad gently on the dirt floor.

One Arm sighs and speaks softly. "Oh little Wren, look at them all out there in the field. Keeping busy and living as though they don't have stingers charging through their veins every second of every day. We survived, right? But our broken pieces make cracks for the bees to follow, and the bees get confused and stampede along the wrong lines. They tell me I'm safe when I'm not, and tell me I'm in danger when I'm safe. I don't know where you get your energy. I'm tired, Wren, so tired. I'll do anything anyone tells me, even you. That's not much of a man, is it? I don't even own my life. I may as well be bound in these chains here, dragged around at anyone's bidding."

The chains rattle and clang as he moves them around inside the forge. I turn my head this way and that, expecting to see Wren out and about, but she doesn't appear.

"It's weird, this place, isn't it?" he continues, "I'm no one important, but I feel I'm needed here. Like any one of these links in this chain. There's no shame in being a link, little one. You're one yourself, you know, even if all you ever did was flit in and out of here and run among the fields for the rest of your life. Everyone has a purpose, even if it's listening to another's thoughts... that's what they say."

Wren bursts from the forge and sprints to the main lodge. Birds resting in the nearby grasses take off in flight, and I am at once on my feet.

"Well?" Guthrie's voice booms inside the forge. He must've come up from the field. "The hinge."

I cower and clench my teeth. I creep to the back of the forge and peek through the cracks in the boards.

"I'm onto it right now, sir," One Arm's voice is nothing like it was before. Timid, scraping as low as his bow, "I'll deliver it to you myself. Promptly."

Guthrie rambles the kind of nonsense that rolls out of his mouth when he's under pressure and storms to the main lodge. Wren has seen him coming. A trail of frightened birds and general disarray betrays her escape path. She zig zags through the field before I lose sight of her, then delicately circles the forge in large arcs, moving closer with each pass, like a bee attempting to land on a flower head. When it is safe, she lands.

I can see how he works now. His back blocks most of my view of the forge itself, but he works over the fire with a heavy wooden contraption that reeks of Guthrie's brilliance. One Arm's feet control it; standing on it causes it to act as a large vice to hold his work steady for all manner of beating and pouring. He pushes his boots onto foot operated bellows and encourages the fire to take hold of the new wood and rests on a rickety chair while he waits for the coals to form. He sighs so deeply it almost forms a groan. Guthrie could never have known the moment he'd interrupted. We never do unless we're paying close attention.

Wren makes a star shape with her body and rocks from foot to foot.

"You know what, little bird? I've been thinking that broken chains are stronger." He holds a short chain loosely in his hand. A few black links writhe on the dirt floor as he examines the middle links that lay flat across his palm. "You see, when they're broken, they have paid more attention to their weakness, they're aware of it. It's one of those great mysteries. Learned men like Guthrie call them paradoxes." He shows Wren the links that lay across his palm and she hovers around it, looking at it from all angles. "See how I fixed this broken chain? I spent time with it. I found where it was weak and strengthened it, and now it's doing the work of ten chains. It was hot and hard work. Should it break again, there's no need for devastation. I know the repairing process. Breakages happen, and repairs happen. Some links were rushed; weren't given the care they needed for strength, but that doesn't mean they can't be strong now, does it? Still, I've seen some of the strongest chains break under the right weight. Maybe we're all broken, every one of us with cracks and lines and ways of behaving that keep us away from the heat that wants to change us. A bit like how those bees dig deep inside us and bring things to the surface, just like dross. What do you think, little one?"

Wren's eyes widen and she scoots back to a bench that holds his tools, running her hands across them and using two hands to pick up a heavier one before she discards it and moves to the next.

"Do you think some things might be too heavy for the bees to lift? I mean, look at you. You're light as a feather and I'm as heavy as these chains. Sometimes I think my bones are made of dross, as if the times I lived through rotted them to their core. There are moments in time I would give anything to put into hot coals and beat and reshape as though they had never existed. But I can't, that's the worst part Wren. The time has passed, I can't fix it, and the bees come for me and sting unmercifully. I was weak, and others suffered for it."

A scent of marigolds twists my stomach into tight knots and I clutch at it and lean back into the forge walls. Martha's words soothe me and the bees dissipate.

"Cursed Stars!" I jump at One Arm's curse. Or perhaps it was the crash and loud thud onto the ground that accompanied it.

Wren runs past me in her arc of the forge.

"Sorry Wren," One Arm calls as he gathers the dropped items; one handful at a time. "If your purpose is in your hands, what does that make me?"

Her little feet scoot through the grass outside the forge and then come closer, trotting around the makeshift path, mostly avoiding the puddles that formed from last night's storm. She is almost ready to land again.

"Look at your hands Wren," he calls to her as she passes his open side of the forge, "No one else on earth has those hands, and can do what you can do with them." She slows her trot as she passes me, watching her hands flip from front to back as One Arm continues. "You can create beauty wherever you go. You needn't be a tailor or a craftsman either, more beauty is created by hands of kindness, than at the end of a brush or chisel. Your hands show your purpose...."

She flutters and lands back in the forge. "... and they are strong. Just like you."

I turn my hands over in front of me, just like Wren did as she passed me. If your purpose is in your hands, what do I set mine to? What have I set them to? I wipe my skirts frantically, trying to rid myself of the sensation that etches into my skin. A deep calmness patiently waits for me to understand that the water and grainy mud that covers them is not blood and grit, just splashes from Wren's passing. I hold my head in my hands and try so hard to remember the stillness in the stream, the depth and the water, gently pulling everything straight. I am there within a few breaths, then swept back to the sensation of Thomas and Guthrie washing my arms and giving me permission to forgive myself, not only for the things I'd done, and blamed myself for, but for surviving.

My hands don't look any different than they did a few moments ago. Yet I'm another person who looks out at them. I'm not the same person the Hall created. I am who I am now, at this moment. I'm different to who the Hall told me I was, but I could never have discovered that if I was still there, surrounded by people who followed the Hall's agenda. Berating myself didn't help at all to make me better or provide any relief. It didn't lead anywhere but to an endless circle of pain and regret. For the things I did, and even those I didn't, the bilious sensation and churning self-hatred remain the same.

I focus beyond my hands. Wren's sweet face watches me. How long has she been there? I smile and she raises her eyebrows. Great. Challenged by a child again. Ugh, I know. Now would be good. I adjust my skirts and pretend I haven't been eavesdropping the whole time.

Wren beats me to the forge and waits just inside, watching me as I approach.

One Arm's work noises stop as he notices her. His tools drop with a thud. "Is someone there, Wren?" he asks.

I catch the smallest glimpse of his face before he groans and drops his head so low I fear he may tumble forward. There's no heavy robe for him to hide in, no dark corners, no stretch of distance between us. One Arm's empty sleeve is tucked inside his shirt, his other hand rests on his crouched knee for support, his back rises and falls with tensioned breath. We stand silent for a while, sharing a strange moment of shared history, of shame, of both wishing a moment had never occurred, but no way of erasing it. The coals glow and the wood, not yet transformed, crackles as a breeze comes up from the field and sweeps some of its heat away.

Should I pretend I haven't heard his words, or that I don't understand the reasons for his anguish? Perhaps I should take one of these iron rods and beat him with it. That is the Hall's way, the proper way, and what is expected. Yet I understand now, every blow that lands on his back, lands just as harshly on mine.

I pick at the dirt under my fingernails and force the confession from my mouth. "I've also done awful things to survive."

One Arm doesn't move from his position. The wind creates a small whirlwind, picking up traces of dust and grass that capture Wren's attention and leads her outside and back into the field among the workers who greet her with a wave.

"There wouldn't be one among those in the field that can't tell a similar tale. That's what the bees excel at. They convince us we're alone, separate from each other, and compel us to attack each other for the very wrongs we're guilty of ourselves. It's easier somehow, more righteous, to wield an iron rod in our hand than hold compassion in our hearts."

His head remains bowed. He seems tense and unsure.

"I believed many lies, behaved in unbecoming ways because I didn't know any better," I say. "How could I? How could you? How could any of us? We did what we needed to, and when we learn a new way, we know better and we do better. Would you blame Wren for her survival behavior? Or me?"

His body jolts with horror at the thought, yet he doesn't lift his head. "Never!"

"Then why do you not deserve the same compassion for the same behavior?"

"But I...", his voice is barely audible as he haltingly searches for words. "Forgive me, for being so bold in this circumstance, but you have no idea..."

We all have no idea. About anything. This is why the logs are so important. "You might be surprised".

"None deserve more punishment than I."

"So, you would choose to stand still in your life? Stagnant. Offering nothing to the world, including recompense, because you'd sooner pummel yourself at every opportunity? Let me ask you this. Has your self-hatred made you a better person? Has it done anything for you other than keep you trapped in a prison of anger and remorse?" The words tumble from my mouth, fold back on themselves, and return to my ears. It's quite convenient really, how most of what we say is what we need to hear ourselves. "Anger can be a shield too, a way of protecting ourselves from the stings of self-betrayal. It doesn't matter whether that anger focuses inward or out, if you're using it to deflect pain, you'll stay trapped until you choose to put your shield down."

He glances to the field and tips his head slightly, "Are you sure about the others; that they feel this way too?"

"We all have these old foundations, the way we used to see and react to the world. You didn't create yours, just as I didn't create mine. If you look, you'll see it in all of us; our habits that protected us, now seem to destroy us. And a new way is just out of reach, just waiting... hating ourselves drives us back to those old foundations and patterns, and there's comfort in the familiar, even when it tortures us." He nods gently and I add, "But you have a choice now."

"A choice to do what?"

"To take the amount of compassion you hold in your heart for Wren and extend that to yourself."

He shakes his head at the impossible thought. I know it well; how insurmountable and foreign it seems. How I could never look into another's eyes lest they see the offensive stain that lingered on my soul. For what I did. For what I didn't do.

He scoffs respectfully. "You expect being kind to myself will make me a better person?"

"I know how unbelievable that sounds when punishment is all you've known. But self-forgiveness actually makes us more responsible, not less. When you accept your own pain and short-comings, you're able to accept them more readily in others. You won't seek to cause them any further pain because you'll see how similar we all are. Think of all the interior battles we face all day, every day. We need more compassion, not more iron rods, wouldn't you agree?"

"For others, yes."

"And for you." He doesn't see it yet. How wisely he'll be able to respond to his own bees. How he'll enjoy following their trail out of the prison he's built around him, and how he'll teach others to do the same. "I once had a friend who told me to imagine our lives as rivers; always moving forward. Regrets act like boulders that dam up its flow. They make us cling to them, to keep all our focus upstream, so we never know the joy and freedom of moving downstream."

"But it's impossible to go back and move the boulder. Nothing can change it."

"That's true. But you can let it go."

He shakes his head.

"Don't shy away from the painful things, the hard things. Whether you like it or not, you're aware now. You get to make a choice." The wind carries laughter from the field into the forge. I can't tell if it's a jest or Wren's funny ways that has brought everyone together as they work. "You know what's most important to reclaim? What was taken from us. Our ability to choose. Whoever chooses has the power, and right now, that's you. What you choose is what you become."

Wren bustles back into the forge as a welcome distraction and One Arm is on his feet but will not meet my eyes.

Thomas appears by my side, "Ah, you made it here yourself," he says, "Couldn't wait?"

One Arm attends to his coals, "I must get to Guthrie's hinge."

Thomas holds my arm and draws in closer, speaking just loud enough to be heard over One Arm's clatter. "Everyone scatters when they see the old man coming. Do you have what you need for more dwale?"

"I'll start right away," I nod, and Thomas approaches the fire.

"Well met," he calls to One Arm and extends his hand.

One Arm stops his work and takes his hand in a weak shake. "Well met, Thomas."

"We haven't been introduced."

"Silas," he says, staring at the ground.

Perhaps one day Silas will know himself well enough to own his story and meet my eyes. He reminds me I need to own every part of mine, too. I'd never seen him as a person. *One Arm*. I'd assigned him a label, not a name.

Thomas seems a bit perplexed at our lack of conversation. "We'll let you get about your work then, shall we? We've things to attend to before this day is done."

Silas bows, his eyes firmly on the dirt floor as we leave the forge.

The weather has been kind to us. There's only been one moon since the harvest, and our sheaves are ready for threshing. Guthrie made us lay them out for inspection before we bundled them for drying. I expect everything is cautionary the first time you do something. Like how we forgot a barn would be best for this purpose and we've lived amongst drying sheaves in the lodges and unused cottages. We've done well, what we didn't know, we learned. The logs came in handy for that. We'd gather around the fire each night and plan what was next. A rousing cheer always greeted the person who said they could teach us a task. Other times someone had at least witnessed it and we worked it out from there with Guthrie's oversight. Between the mixing and matching, creating tools and learning from each other, we had just brought in and protected our first harvest. We had no idea what we were doing, other than relying on each other. It now lay in the lodge yard, dried and ready for threshing.

"Is that all of it?" Guthrie checks the spinning tubes and dials attached to a fence post at the edge of the yard. I don't understand the whirring and notifications of his weather machine, but he's adamant we have two clear days ahead of us. He scans the congregation that gathers around the fallen sheaves, waiting for their signal to beat the heads loose. His brow furrows when he spies me. "Did you retrieve the sheaves from that far cottage?"

My blank look gives Thomas a chance to interject, "We'll get them now." He takes my hand and we hurry up the slope.

The far cottage lies at the highest point of Awenmell, one little room that overlooks the whole parcel of land.

"I still think we should've taken this far cottage," he says, "It's more private."

"But—,"

"Yeah, I know, you prefer to be close and among the others." He turns to walk backwards up the slope, "Just look at all of that. We've accomplished quite a lot, you know."

The view is impressive from here. Two lodges, the forge; one day, there'll be a barn too. Stubbled fields being cropped low by a grateful Arrow and donkey, gardens, a scattering of cottages and our little home under the oak. And this top cottage. Below us, two children run hand in hand from a cottage and join the gathering in the lodge yard.

"It was a good idea to build the extra cottages," he says, "Glad I thought of it."

I ignore his bait. "I just remember how awful it was when the kinship separated us. Who knows what they've been through to get here. Why pull them apart? They only stay in the cottages until they relax, and then they join the others, anyway."

"Ugh! Brenn and all her star-forsaken rules." He thrusts his fists into his hips and performs his impression of Brenn surveying her workers and I laugh at him as we continue our climb, walking backwards and enjoying the view.

Awenmell is beautiful from here. There's no mud and sore hands and backs, no nightmares; only morning sunshine and whatever this day will bring. The harvest has grown with the people. First, it was all those extra vegetables when Cal and his group arrived. Today, it's sorting the sheaves and preparing them for threshing. Thomas opens the cottage door and pulls the sheaves clear while I admire Arrow's shining coat in the lower croft. I've got this notion that if I keep him groomed, he won't forget who he is. Working next to the yoked donkey seems undignified for a horse of his beauty and stamina, but he copes well. Even a horse isn't allowed an ego here. Something moves in and out of his legs. Wren. He's never once minded her flighty presence, or the way she almost smothers him as she strokes his mane.

"Here, hold your arms out." Thomas says. We stack the sheaves on our arms, Thomas uses his belt to loop some on his back "No need for a return trip."

Guthrie's organized everyone in the lodge yard. Sheaves are laid out ready for the threshing, and he demonstrates the action he's decided will be most efficient. It seems easy enough, beat the wheat stalks until the heads come off. Then another collects the heads and begins the winnowing process, tossing the heads high in the air on rough sieves to loosen the chaff and leave the grain behind. Our focus is the threshing. We can do the winnowing in batches if we must. The novelty soon wears off, it's dusty and warm and Guthrie wanders among us, correcting our form and posture, generally being his annoying but ever productive self. Thomas works beside me. We've managed to fall into a rhythm with the other partners around us, concentrating on the whacking and thumping and not hitting ourselves or our partners' heads or anything else we shouldn't. I wipe my brow without losing momentum. Thank the Stars, this is only two day's work.

"Pity there're no apples about," Thomas says.

"Wrong season," I say, my mouth dry from the dust.

"No, then you'd have something to talk to."

I smile at him. Maybe he's trying to annoy me.

"So, do these seeds talk too?"

"Not so much, but they tell the same tale. Everything you need is already on the inside waiting to become something wonderful."

"Fair enough. Only this time it seems you've gotta be beaten around a bit to release the good stuff."

Guthrie passes by and chuckles. "Don't we all?"

Wren sweeps through the threshers to calls of "Wren!" and "Watch out!" and manages the run without getting hit once. She scoops the loose heads as she passes by and delivers them to Guthrie before her descent back into the field to Arrow. On her next swoop, she pauses to gather some large heads in front of Thomas. "Arrow likes you," he says, "You look like good friends."

Wren's broad smile catches him by surprise. He waits until she's skipped away.

"Did you see that?" he nudges me, "She smiled at me. Ha!"

We thresh and weave and swear and sweat and laugh for most of the morning. Silas bothers everyone asking if they need water, Guthrie now jots notes in his big book. Wren flits in and out, and Cal tries his hardest not to boss people around. Adults move from chores in the fields to the threshing yard. All ages work to get the chore completed, swapping jobs one for the other so no one gets worn out. The youngest swap more often than the adults.

"Those kids," Thomas says, "The new ones, they're watching everything I do. I mean everything."

"And?"

"It's unnerving." His eyes dart from me to them and back again. "Why are they doing it?" his eyes grow wide. "They're looking for a weakness, aren't they? An opportunity to attack."

"No. They're just waiting for you to mess up."

"They're what?"

"Remember the first night Cal arrived? And after the tussle, they didn't know what to do because we weren't behaving how they expected we would?"

Thomas nods and side-eyes them.

"This is the same thing. Their world is safer if they can predict what will happen. Even if it's bad, at least it doesn't take them by surprise. Predictable means no surprises, and no surprises means safety. They're watching for you to prove to them that their version of the world is correct. That you, like everyone else they've encountered, can't be counted on, can't be trusted. They'll do things to aggravate you, in an attempt to feel secure. Being here is turning their world upside down. A secure place can be a misery infested dungeon, if that's all that you know."

"So physical danger and stress can make them feel safe?"

"When it's all you've known and you can predict it. Yes."

"But we told them they're safe. We haven't hurt them."

"They still need proof they're not being lied to, trust me, just because someone says something it doesn't mean a thing."

"So you didn't believe a thing I told you when we first met?"

"Probably not."

He stops and thinks for a while. "But you believe me now, don't you?"

I wonder what his face would look like if I said 'probably not'? I smile at him. "Of course."

He watches them and tries to put the pieces together.

"Here's a thought Thomas, what if everyone around you had a wolf—,"

"A wolf? Oh, like a companion animal?"

"Yes. And everyone's wolves played with them, and they laughed, and were a constant companion who offered warmth and protection. But your wolf bit you every time you got close. What if it held your throat in its mouth occasionally, to let you know how powerful it was and could be at any time? What if you couldn't leave your wolf, it was attached to you by bond... rather than affection?

You'd look at all the other people with their wolves and wonder why it is just so hard with yours. There must be something wrong with you, surely? No matter how much time you spend trying to find out how to stop the wolf biting, each time you try, you fail. Soon enough, you receive a slower bite, a gentler one that hurts so much less than the others that it feels like kindness. The wolf could have bitten harder if it truly wanted to, but it didn't. Somewhere underneath all the terror, maybe everything will be alright after all. But you've learned your lesson. You never reach out to pet your wolf, you simply survive alongside it. Now Thomas, do you think you'd be happy if you came across a wolf anywhere on your travels?"

"No, I'd be terrified."

"What if I simply told you wolves were cuddly and kind and protective, are you going to believe me?"

"Not on your life!"

"What if I told you a hundred times?"

"Nope."

"Well, they're not going to believe what we tell them, are they? We have to show them. They have to live around kind wolves so many times that the biting wolf becomes a fading memory and becomes their new normal. Then our way won't terrify them. But for now, nothing about this place makes sense to them. This is hard work, for them and for us. And Thomas..." I wait until he looks at me, "No matter how much they 'unnerve you', please don't bite."

We continue working, take some water from Silas, Guthrie's now enthralled in taking his measurements and recording weights. Thomas huffs but it's not from exertion or the irritation from Silas, or Guthrie's mutterings. I try to brush off his agitation but it settles in my shoulders, deeper than their ache from threshing.

"Something bothering you?"

He stops his work and considers whether to speak. "Well, yes. How can you know so much about them, and all this craziness, and not know when to make way for the army?"

I don't know why each mention of the army always lands deep in the pit of my stomach like a cold rock. I shrug. Not that it's very comforting for Thomas. "I wish I could tell you something substantial, something to help with your plans. But you're learning what you wanted, aren't you? Measures of food, carriage of water, blankets, medicine, tools. It can't all be for nothing, can it? Perhaps it's like your book. You had the instrument before you had the knowledge, only this time it appears you have the knowledge before you have the instrument. Things have odd ways of coming together."

He grumbles. "You're going to tell me to trust, aren't you?"

"I'm not about to tell you to do anything."

A shout from the lower field grabs our attention, and the bees that had been on alert in my shoulders shudder through my veins. The deadening smack of a fist meeting another's flesh carries to us, and the men charge into the field to help. I cringe at the violence that sweeps on the wind as two men raise their fists and incoherent shouting begins. The bees settle and sting softly now; I find my way to the depth of the stream easily and acknowledge I am safe, but the bees are ever present and on alert. I don't bother looking for Wren. She would've darted away at the first hint of a tremor in the air. I'm not in danger, and my reaction is normal. My bees stir again at another shout, but I don't need to let them carry me away, instead I follow them to my fear. A deep breath calms their way and I follow their channels to my secrets.

The panic weaves its way in and out of my skin, but I watch it move, observing its stings and flurries. I grimace and clench my teeth, and soon the stings have made way for heavy flutters. There's nothing gentle about what they wish to show me, it's hidden deep inside and if the bees are leading the way, it's something I've been avoiding. I stay with them, following the pain as it spirals down into the dark places I don't dare to look. There it is. The powerlessness that overwhelms me in the face of violent anger, the way I fold in the company of rage. None of these reactions are of my doing, yet here they are, a part of me. A reaction embedded like the deepest splinter that the bees now hover gently around.

Feeney threatened and raged and my tongue became bewitched, silent and unworkable, as if it wasn't connected to my mind; as if I wasn't connected to anything in this world. Powerless, betrayed by my own reactions, and abandoned by my own self. And here it appears again, visiting me because of someone's anger in the field. This time I stay with the sensation, and I don't shun what my body needs to feel. The bees have shown me the way into this memory my body holds, and I can visit here again when I need to learn more. They flutter away with each deep breath I take. I've done nothing but stand here for a few moments in the lodge yard, yet I'm exhausted; and I'm proud of myself. I stayed, and I lived through one more time that my very own wolf memory didn't bite.

My hands clench the fence rail, and as I release them, color returns to my knuckles. In the field, the worst of the melee is over. Some men stand and talk, others seated on the ground support each other. There is wailing and shouts of grief and frustration, not anger.

Some bees sting harder than others. And the process of opening up those channels isn't always pretty, but welcomed. The men are patient, knowing it could be any of them in need of support the next day, maybe even the next hour. Maybe it will be any of them. Maybe it will be me.

Thomas looks for me and I nod. I hear his words in my head. Are you safe? Are you well? Gratitude floods my veins and washes any trace of the bees away. For all his misunderstandings, he seems to instinctively understand the medicine found in compassion, and the healing that takes place when anger and outrage are given their due. Everything is welcome at Awenmell, especially the parts of us we hide from ourselves. Martha was right about the dilution of the herbs. The whole plant needs to be present, or it loses its potency.

Every night, we sit around the fire. What an odd collection we are; young, old, tall, short, thin and plump, yet we gather our bowls and eat in the twilight together. Summer days seem like they'll unfold forever. The light from the flames, barely visible on our faces at first, grows bolder as the sky darkens.

The logs have been good for everyone. Even me. Confessions and stories still cascade over me like waterfalls, so vivid they etch themselves inside me like they were my own. But I observe them from a distance now; or at least I try. Some secrets tumble and share themselves easily, others the words remain stilted and incomplete, as if some moments in time are beyond explanation. Guthrie's tears give them permission to gently expose their wounds to the air, to be witnessed, and treated with tender care. We celebrate our victories, however small. Our weariness will always need someone at the ready to praise us, to cheer loudly, and make the next morning bearable. I don't know how our habit came about to end our nights on a cheery note. Perhaps it was one of those things that grew of its own accord, a confidence we all needed, a moment we pretend the nightmares won't visit tonight.

Every night we sit around the fire, and every night I wonder if I heard right; or if I'm mad. If this strange family we've grown here is just some delusion, some happenstance that benefits us all. We're supposed to be preparing for an army; perhaps my imagination has run away with me. Imaginings can do that. They can make us believe in things that aren't there, and believe the things that really are there, away. I wager if I tried hard enough, I could find a way to explain everything about this place as a figment of my imagination. This is nothing at all like we expected when it was just Thomas and I sleeping in the forest and building the first lodge. He looks up from his ale and winks at me, and I think about seeds, and harvests, and streams. My imagination can do many things. It can trick me into believing many things, but there's one thing it can't do, no matter how hard it tries. It can't make a mushroom grow before my eyes.

Every night after the fire, Thomas pores over the scroll in the cottage, hoping his army will soon arrive. It's his army now. It was never mine anyway. Perhaps it'll change once they're here and he begins to teach me how to lead an army. I imagine I'm supposed to thrust a sword in the air and shout courageous things, and have people die for me. I wretch so suddenly it catches me by surprise, but I cover for my actions by collecting one of his books from the floor. Thomas paces and mumbles about his figures, thankfully unaware.

Every night before I go to sleep, I open the door and check over the field, thank the moon for lighting the way, and smell the air. And every night, I notice something. Is it always there, or does it only appear for my noticing? The freshest breeze blows across the field. It tumbles over every part of Awenmell, sweeping and cleaning just like the winnowing of the wheat heads blows away the chaff to leave only the newness of the grain in its place.

The morning breeze is so crisp it makes my eyes water as it sweeps up the croft and into the lodge yard. Guthrie appears beside me.

"That's not normal." He points to the threshold where a small child sits just outside, next to one of the poles. "How long's he been there now?"

Thomas pushes between us for a closer look. "It'll be three days at the end of this day." He shakes his head, "I'll tell you what's not normal, the wind at this time of year."

Guthrie stands to face me, probably to prove he's earnest, but I'm more grateful he's blocking the wind. "Someone should go and get him."

"We've been taking him food and water, he'll come when he's ready. Besides, he's not in danger. He has his own guard."

"Hmmff," Guthrie snorts. It's been a while since he was so close to a wolf.

"They're fine," I assure him.

"But the boy hasn't spoken."

"They're fine."

"How can you tell if you haven't heard it from his mouth?"

"They're fine, Guthrie."

Thomas interrupts. "The boy may not have spoken, but my guess is that gray wolf has." He notices my smirk, "And if you continue to press her, Ash will remind you that wolves never lie—and you can't argue with that. Believe me, I've tried. It won't end well."

"Wolf or no wolf, there's something fragmented about this."

"Fragmented? Really, that's the word you choose, Guthrie?"

"Unsystematic... Out of order, then."

"You're always in such a rush to fix things. Waiting and watching often reveals more." I pat his arm as I pass. "He'll come when he's ready."

Guthrie's eyes widen and he sucks air through his puckered lips so fast he almost whistles. "Maybe he's waiting for us to be ready."

Thomas laughs uproariously and slaps the old man's back. "Well, that's very Eariss of you, Old Man!" Guthrie's wide-eyed wonder breaks under Thomas's laughter and they chuckle together. Thomas pulls a few faces behind his back without him seeing. I'm not so sure about this level of mirth. The old man is right about the child's behavior being unique. Not that I'd call it fragmented or unsystematic or whatever word he used.

The waif can't be more than eight summers in this world. No one saw him arrive, and no one has heard him speak. For two full days we've taken food and water to him and his wolf, and the servers all return to the lodge shaking their heads. He won't come in. Guthrie may well have it right. Maybe we're not ready for him. And a wolf? Well, that's an interesting development. But who are we to say who our travel companions should be? After all, Katteryn brought chickens with her and no one complained about that.

Still, I'm glad he's here, leaning on the threshold upright, his patient and vigilant wolf by his side, and the open grass strip between the lower fields that leads straight to the lodge should he choose to take it. For all the lad's bravery in staying outside, he will probably need care. I feel like one of Katteryn's fussy chickens wanting to shield him under her wings. Guthrie and Thomas chuckle behind me. I'd love to interrupt their animated conversation and tell them I think someone traveling with chickens is far more odd than traveling with a wolf, but I'm really not in the mood for one of Guthrie's debates. I stretch my neck for a better view of the child. He must be lying down now. I can't see him, but the wolf remains on guard. It seems odd to think he'd be bringing something to us. But Guthrie's right. It's not normal, but that doesn't mean it needs correction, or that we do. We just need to be patient. I grab a woven basket and land it on my hip, and sigh. Curiosity won't get any of our work done. "Well, come along then," I tell the others. "Let's get on with it."

I've only carried the basket of plump beans the short distance from the garden up to the lodge yard, but it feels like my arms are about to fall off in protest. It's not so much the weight, but how awkward this wide basket is to carry. I gladly drop it on the sorting table outside the lodge. "Thank the Stars that's ov—"

"Ash... Ashling." Guthrie calls in a panicked whisper. "Look."

The boy and the wolf walk along the strip that leads to the main lodge. They move slowly, scanning all the faces that have stopped their work to watch. Even Wren stops her fluttering and watches from a fence rail along the side of the grassy verge. The air is silent apart from the wind that gently batters our ears. He seems skittish. Perhaps that's what everyone is responding to; holding firm lest their movement be the one that sends him back to the threshold. He places his feet carefully on the path; one after the other, and it feels like everyone is holding their breath. The faces in the fields and along the fences begin to turn, one by one, to follow the line of his gaze to where it has ceased its wandering. To where it has settled. Me.

Thomas gently nudges me. 'Go' he mouths.

I almost fall as my feet touch the path; no one else notices my grip on the rail, or my legs that wobble under this warm dizziness that settles over me like a thick cloud. They're all still watching the child. The giddiness floats me toward the waif as if I'm disconnected from my feet. Yet they know exactly where they're going. How could I possibly explain this disconnection to Thomas? I don't care. Whatever this is, there is something so true about this meeting it seeps into my bones like warm oil. I step smoothly, carefully matching the boy's pace, terrified if I act abruptly, I might scare this moment away.

He's closer now. The wolf walks beside him, with alert ears almost as high as the slender boy's shoulders. Above his shoulders, dark hair that's been slashed into points falls around his face. His arms are scarred and need tending, burns probably. Underneath his tattered clothes will no doubt be a damaged body, but something more hovers about him, something bigger than the size of his body, something deeper than the darkness of his eyes. Breathe. That's better. I part my lips to exhale quietly and sense the middle of our distance, the place where I stop and lower myself to my knees. His eyes remain on mine, as steadfast as his wolf.

Mystery?

I am here.

Level now, his eyes seek mine for some kind of awareness, as though he might suddenly recognize me but is still unsure. His eyes share the same darkness as Mardu's; deep and so impossibly filled with the whole of the universe. Waterfalls trickle within me, but more like the spray when it breaks upon the rocks and hangs in the air. Light and gentle. He seeks trust, something solid. Will he find it here? More importantly, will he find it now, in me? This is what he's searching for. His heart fills with questions that words will never answer, ones that only presence can understand. How brave to still reach for a connection on a thread of spider's silk. So easily broken. So fragile.... I didn't miss it. How could I? Like a crisp breeze. That's what the Mystery said.

In my mind's eye, I not only drop my shield, I fling it into the farthest field.

Are you in the depths?

What if I say the wrong thing?

Stay in the depths.

He walks tentatively, still searching my eyes. Waterfalls stream through my senses: horror, strength, and bravery. Glimpses of scenes that make me more determined to never look away. He marches closer, each step bringing more pain to my body but strangely dissipating it in us at the same time. An ebb and flow I know nothing about. The wolf is satisfied and stops, leaving the boy to continue a few steps beyond it before he halts.

Still out of arm's reach. Wise child.

Tears prick my eyes for his need to be so clever.

I blink my tears away. He sniffs and wipes at the side of his eyes. Fear and courage have an amazing ability to blend and create the bravest of tears. They're altogether remarkable, and more powerful than any other tear we cry. They cause us to stand; and to stay. I fight the urge to reach out and take control of our meeting. This moment is his, and I honor his terms.

He stops there and considers me, tracing my features, searching for some connection, some confirmation. He lifts a dirty hand and holds it flat against his chest.

"Here?" he asks.

A burst of delicious pain shoots into my heart. A surge of connection, of instantaneous understanding. He is aware of me as much as I am of him. I didn't expect clarity to be so painful, or so truthful.

I hold my hand to my chest. "Here."

Slowly, one tiny pace at a time, he moves closer and places his hand over mine, watching it as if it might produce some sign or understanding. He draws a deep breath and releases it, and curls into my arms. I press his head to my shoulder and kiss it. Unashamed tears roll down my cheeks and relief floods my body. I know nothing other than this moment is perfect.

No one moves as I raise myself to my feet. The wolf walks beside me as I carry the child toward the lodge. I smile through my tears at their murmuring conversations as I approach.

"That's a wolf he has with him."

"And what do wolves bring with them?"

"More wolves." Someone answers.

"No," Guthrie corrects them, "They bring messages."

"What was that all about?" Thomas whispers as I walk past him and into the lodge.

"I'm not sure."

"What do you know about him?"

"Not much."

The child is already asleep in my arms. As tired as any other traveler we've seen. There's a burden within him, but it's not the child's weight. I feel like I'm holding the entire world in my arms. Thomas offers to take him, but I'm not ready to give him up.

"What are we to do with him?" he asks.

"Keep him safe—whatever the cost."

Thomas eyes me for some kind of explanation, but I don't have one. I shake my head just as Silas bustles up to us. "I've made up a cot for him already, — the cottage next to yours." He jolts at the sight of the wolf and is gone.

The bed looks well prepared and comfortable, but I don't want to put him down. I'm stronger somehow, that in taking him in my arms I have set root. Will he be safe here if I let him go?

The wolf lies beside his bed.

Perfectly safe.

I stretch in the field. My morning exercise that I've kept up since the Mystery's insistence that connection is far more important than weeding and working. I frown and try again to think of something other than the child that lays in the cottage. I leave my mind to wonder its own things and settle into the stillness of my heart, the depths of the stream. I take my place in the bottom of the far field, a hefty enough walk to keep anyone strolling by from disturbing me. If they make the effort to get here, their message must be worth my attention. Yet still, I hear crunching steps and boots appear in my vision. I roll my eyes at the grass. Good thing I'd almost finished.

The crunch of an apple bite crackles to my ears and Thomas speaks with the piece lolling about in his mouth. "So, what's happening with that foundling and his wolf?"

"He's sleeping."

"The wolf's not there. You know, outside his cottage. I thought he must be up and about somewhere. Intriguing child, don't you think?"

"I took him some food, he seems well."

"He's just tired then, like the others?"

Like the others. Interesting turn of phrase to describe someone who is so unlike the others, yet so alike in many ways. I stand and smile. "Yes, just like the others. He'll be out when he's ready."

"But there's no wolf."

"Try approaching that cottage and see if there's no wolf."

He nods thoughtfully as he chews. "Hmm."

Surely he's not weighing up that challenge.

Earlier this morning, the wolf greeted me outside the cottage door. Only a few people milled about in the early dawn and the wolf moved aside for me to enter, carrying a small bowl of food. The child jumped in his cot at the opening door and I stood perfectly still while the wolf made its way to his side. Calmer now, he stroked the fur of the wolf and surveyed his surroundings, and me. There were no words again, just as when we first met. Perhaps

I couldn't find them, still worried they might push him away. So I stood there mute. Yet there was something else. The same connection, the *'here'* he had asked about, felt as tangible as the stillness in the depth of the stream, as if it had taken over the whole cottage and that he dwelt in that space too. Words? It was as if we didn't need them. No perfunctory 'good mornings' or 'how do you dos' they were already taken care of by our own proximity. He was safe, he instinctively knew that, and I was safe, too. We stared at each other for a while, an extraordinary kind of looking glass where the things you see aren't made of things from this world. It was odd and soothing all at once. Words formed as I placed the food next to his bed.

"I'm glad you found your way to us."

"I followed a path where there was no path."

"How so?"

"I didn't know where I was going, but my feet knew the way."

"I'm pretty sure that's how we found this place too."

We shared a smile, and I produced a small jar of ointment from my apron. "For your wounds?"

He nodded and pulled his shirt over his head. Some wounds were crusted and wept, others bore the grayness of charred flesh and healed scars. He didn't flinch as I applied the ointment as the others had done. Instead, I was the one who flinched at the resounding waterfalls of smoke and flames that poured over me at every touch.

"Tell me about the pyre." I was horrified I'd spoken so brazenly and bit my lip so hard I tasted blood.

He didn't react at all to my query, or seem to wonder why I asked. "There was lots of angry shouting and noise, so many sticks. Branches so heavy I could hardly breathe." He drew a deep breath and relaxed into its exhale.

An additional level of dread reached my system. "They were going to—"

"But they didn't." He sipped nonchalantly at his ale and, after a bit of organizing, found a place to rest the bowl among his bedclothes.

Horror filled me, and no words arrived. The thought of being burned alive choked me as much as the heat from a fire might sear my voice from me forever. Yet there were no bees within the child. Maybe his close call with the pyre burned them away. He ate with serenity, a surety that I can't even begin to comprehend or explain. I returned the ointment to my apron, "Let the ointment dry before replacing your shirt, and then sleep as much as you need."

He nodded with a mouthful of pottage.

"Do you have a name? What are you called?"

"Oren."

"Oren." I let the name sit on my tongue.

I turned and walked to the door, a whisper on my lips. Soft enough that we could deny it at any moment, quieted so as not to scare him away. "I'm so glad you're here."

❧

A wolf is simply a wolf. It's only people's experiences of them that show in their reactions to it. The wolf roams among the people as they gather for mid meal in the lodge yard. Some don't care, some show affection, some are wary, and the wolf respectfully keeps a distance from the terrified ones that huddle with their meals at the far end of the logs.

Guthrie arrives from his workshop behind the lodge and takes a large detour around the mass of people to avoid walking in front of the wolf. He scoops his meal from the pot. "Some protector that thing is, shouldn't it be with the child?"

"Ah, here's a new game for you, old man," Thomas says, and waves a strip of bread at him.

"I don't play games."

"An experiment then."

"Go on."

"It's called find the wolf at any time of day."

"And how do you suppose I know how to do that?"

"It's easy. Just start striding toward that cottage over there."

Knowing heads nod and a few chuckles and exclamations fill the air. It's been a trying morning for those whose path would normally take them directly past Oren's cottage.

Silas appears outside the forge, again. He checks on the lodge yard but disappears back inside. The next time he appears, I hold a bowl up to him. He nods and begins his walk to us, but turns and retreats again. Eventually he makes it to the far end of the lodge and peers around the corner, only lifting his head high enough to eye the position of the wolf. He beckons me to him and I fill a bowl to take with me.

"Look, there!" he whispers loudly as I get closer. "See, that's what I was talking about."

Sure enough, it was just as Silas had explained it. Wren stops her flitting and gazes into the sky, not for too long, but she stares long and hard, even when there are no clouds to watch pass by.

"Are you ready now? You have time?" he asks with his eyes on the ground.

I nod, forgetting he can't see me and hope he doesn't sense the truth. I'd forgotten he needed my help today. "Let me finish here and I'll meet you in the forge."

He takes the bowl gratefully. "Just don't let that wolf follow you."

I can't believe I forgot. No other chore was pressing, and Silas had been patiently waiting for me to be available.

When I first found him raiding the contents of the apothecary, I was suspicious. Was he searching for dwale? It's easy to be suspicious of items or guilty secrets you've thought of yourself. Our minds always go toward our own weaknesses. How we love to see them in others, just so we don't feel so bad. Why would they come to mind otherwise? But it wasn't dwale or anything other than woad that he sought.

"Woad leaves? Are you injured?" I grabbed at his arm and turned him, looking for signs of blood loss. My eyes then scanned the outside yard, panicked at what I might find. "Is it someone else?"

"No." His reply was coy, "It's just Guthrie explained to me how to make a dye vat."

"You want to dye something?"

Last Spring's woad had dried nicely. There was enough to see us through until its season passed by and I could gather again. As long as there were not multiple injuries. Did I need it all? What was this wasteful business of dyeing? Why didn't he ask for the woad instead of behaving like a thief, an opportunist? My mind tipped and toppled like one of Guthrie's balance scales as Silas held a bunch of the leaves in his fist. He wasn't about to let them go. I gestured to the table. "Sit. Tell me what this is about."

"If you need me for anything, I'll be in the forge," I call to Thomas and Guthrie. I'd never thought of Silas as a mother hen, but he'd fussed so much over the vat. Keeping it warm, moving it close to the fire and dragging it away, covering and testing it for warmth. I wasn't surprised when Thomas mentioned Silas had slept some nights in the forge.

Silas hovers over the vat as I enter. "You've done a superb job." The fire is low and a large pan of clear water sits next to his beloved vat. His dark, repugnant smelling vat. I didn't expect a collection of urine and other elements to smell like wild flowers, but I wasn't expecting this. I hold the back of my hand to my nose. "You checked with Guthrie? You steeped it for the required time?" Silas nods, and I hope he understands I don't mean to order him around. I know how desperately he wants this to work and we can't spare any more woad.

Silas churns the vat with a wide paddle. "I've lost count of how many times I've stirred this. Is it mixed well enough?"

The dark green dye hides how well the ingredients have integrated into each other. What an odd combination, fresh and dried, old and new, sweet and pungent, all blending, hoping to create something anew. Guthrie said we couldn't do without the urine, we needed it to set the dye, and without it, any new color would wash away. Seems we need to accept the awful stuff for the good to stay. "Looks fine," I say, although I immediately regret the use of the word fine.

Silas tilts his head toward the pan of water. "I've soaked the wool. It's ready to go," he says.

I raise the small woolen cloak out of the pan and let the excess water drain from its cream texture.

"Katteryn gave it to me," he says, "You know, the lady with the chickens."

"She's very generous," I tell him as I lower the garment into the repulsive waters of the dye and wonder why Katteryn isn't plunging this herself.

"Careful! Guthrie said air pockets might ruin the color."

The wool sits there, doing nothing but absorbing and changing. Moving from cream to a strange form of gray.

Silas stirs the vat, and a splash of dye hits my skirts.

"Sorry Ash, I didn't mean—"

"It's fine. We're almost done."

He stirs gently now, paying close attention to the placement of every trickle of water inside the vat. Once he's satisfied with the cloak's position, he draws a deep breath and raises his head. I'm surprised by his unexpected bravery. His chin is quite proud, his eyes as gray as the wool in the vat. "Will you—can you ever forgive me?"

It would be easy to go along with his charade and pretend we're talking about the splashed water. But we're not. We spend much of our lives talking about the things that are not, instead of the things that are.

"For the splashed water?" I dare him to take one step closer to honesty.

He almost dips his face again, but corrects himself. "I'm so sorry for what happened. I can only move forward from now and be who I couldn't be before."

"That's all I ask. Did you know taking responsibility for your actions is a sign of leadership; if not of others, then at least of your own life?"

Silas breathes an audible sigh of relief and shakes his head.

"It'll be hard work, Silas, changing your ways. But all of us are doing it with you. Are you ready?"

He squares his shoulders. "As ready as this wool looks."

We lift the gray wool together, freeing it from the vat into the air. The dye draws down through the cloak and changes before our eyes, shifting from its dullness of gray to a startling gray green, into shades of blue.

"Do you think Wren will like it?" he asks, worry in his moistened eyes. "She spends so much time watching the sky. I just want her to be wrapped in it when she needs to sleep and the sky is dark."

I cross the fields in front of the forge on my way to the pond. The forest beckons me as clearly as Silas did earlier, but I carry the dripping sodden cloak, desperate to wash the stink from it and me. Wren flits about in the farther field. When we don't have the luxury of woods to hide in, we hide inside. She stops to focus on some clouds and I hold my hand up to block the sun. Is it the clouds or the color of the sky that fascinates her? One day, she might tell us what she sees up there. There's something sweet about it, dreamy even. I hope she teaches me to see it too. Then she's off again, brushing the tops of the grasses as she runs.

Some days it's harder to be still than others. Sometimes the need to move, to busy myself, keeps me away from the stillness, as if when I stop, all the things I don't want to feel will overwhelm me. The momentum of the day pulls me out of the depths and I get caught in the surface drops, the splashes and agitation of the people around me. I imagine it's the same for Wren; we run so fast to stay away from what plagues us, chases us.

I flick my shoes off and enter the pond. The coolness acts like an irresistible balm that spreads into my body and once the wool is rinsed; I plunge myself headfirst into the water. Everything stops here. I'm weightless, and no sound reaches me.

Silas has a journey ahead of him. Listening to the bees that rise in his body and not running from them, but sitting with his pain as he listens to their tales and reminders. Feeling his way through moments he'd rather forget; facing the shameful parts of himself and greeting them with kindness instead of reproach. Every part of the journey requires patience and practice. The way he operates that forge contraption proves he has both. He just needs the courage not to turn away from himself. That's the harder part. He's so close. So close to discovering how a slow exhale relaxes the body as if by magic, and that he'll soon welcome the bees, knowing they lead to the sweetest honey; his own freedom. Like a wide, expansive field. A lush one, just as Martha said, waiting on the other side of that wretched bramble fence.

The mind can understand the lush field before the body does. The bees still charge sometimes as if they didn't get the message, rampaging through the veins with no concern for anything else going on around them, running a completely separate agenda. It's the uncertainty that's unnerving, like two specific pieces trying to become one; like Silas's vat.

I've lost count of how many times I've stirred this. That's what he said. It was the integration that took the longest. That all our half-connected thoughts, our pieces of ourselves that haven't died, not yet fully formed, are in some kind of stinky mix like Silas's dye. It takes all that mixing and stirring to become whole again, the good and the bad blending together without the labels that others piled upon us. And like Silas's dye, it takes time for things to disappear into each other, for things to settle. To come out changed for being dunked in the waste and stink of the dye. It's a process you can't get out of order. Wanting to be well without facing the pain is trying to dye something blue without the stink. We can fight it all we want, but there's only one way there. And it's through that Star-forsaken fence.

Silas is busy at the forge but meets me with a huge grin as I hang the almost dry woolen cape on a hook in the forge wall. It's a beautiful blue, albeit more like the heads of the cyanus field weeds than the sky, but at least it won't be mistaken for anything other than blue, even if it dulls over time. I'm so pleased the process worked, and so is he.

I arrive at the lodge yard and take a seat next to Guthrie as he heats some experiment by the open fire. I don't bother asking him about them now.

He looks toward the threshold. There are only a few newcomers this time. We've got enough food and places, but Thomas always gets upset when more people arrive. I'm torn between understanding him and reminding him he wanted practice in logistics. But perhaps it's just me and I'm seeing things that aren't there.

An older child squeals and tears across the croft in front of us, followed moments later by Thomas, and sends Guthrie into a series of snorts that roll into a chuckle.

"What's so funny?"

"Young Thomas has been whittling stakes. Just like the one we saw go past in that child's hands. What he means to create is a collection of training weapons, but the children use them to stake their plants."

I purse my lips and stifle a smile. "He's trying."

"I'm well aware of that," he laughs. "He lived with me in Sirban, remember?"

"What do you think it is—this agitation of his?"

"He's always wanting to do, to learn things, be busy with things... conquer things. The closest I've come to seeing him rest is with you."

"There's plenty to do here. More than enough. But it seems it's never enough for him."

"He's so focused on the end result he doesn't see the information in front of him. He'd make a terrible scientist. That's no way to learn; not wanting to do experiments to discover the truth, just wanting the results. And deciding what they should be ahead of time."

"Has he spoken to you about his own bees?"

He shakes his head. "You?"

"He always changes the conversation or else becomes defensive."

"I know that pressure well."

"He doesn't rage, he simmers and keeps himself busy."

"It's a distraction that works for him now."

Thomas stomps back across the field with only one stake in his hand. At least he didn't pull the stakes up with the plants attached.

"It's odd, Guthrie," I say as Thomas disappears behind the other lodge, "At times it seems Thomas is split in two. I wonder which one I speak to each time I open my mouth. If I raise my shields against his agitation, I'll miss the moments when he's open, contactable... lovable. Do you see it too, or is it just me?"

"It's not your fault if things don't go the way he expected; the way he decided ahead of time they should be. His bees certainly ravage him, we can both see that."

I feel less alone now, knowing my mind isn't imagining things. I can't force him to listen to his bees. I can only show him the benefits I receive when I listen to mine.

Guthrie taps on my knee. "Don't you stray off course to cater to him."

I smile and shake my head gently. *Don't stray off course*. I don't even know what course I'm on.

Uncertainty means possibility, but it doesn't feel like it right now. It feels like I'm standing on the slippery mud at the bog and there're no branches to hold on to. Or I'm all mixed together in a vat, not knowing what the result will be. The Mystery is my only constant. Things change. Thomas will get over whatever is bothering him today. Guthrie will make new discoveries, and people will arrive, and people will heal. And everyone is on their own course, including me. Wherever it might lead.

The wolf appears beside me and pushes her nose under my hand. I knead the fur around her ear and wonder what clarity I should expect from a child who has only spoken a handful of words and what his arrival means for all of us.

❧

Thomas grunts as he splits the wood next to the lodge and I stop collecting the dropped pieces for a moment and admire the reality of Awenmell. It's in my pores, as much a part of me as the air I breathe and the blue sky above me. The fenced fields, lodges and cottages, and the people that wander among them all. Purple mountains in the distance that act as a border to our reality and for the first time I'm curious about what's beyond them. Not curious enough to act on it, though.

The wolf passes by and stops to roll in the grass along the fence line. Silas is yet to make her acquaintance, but for the most part, she's adapted and become part of our weird clan, sleeping on her back, paws in the air in the sunshine. Her presence soothes me and reminds me of this moment now, where life is happening. Not tomorrow or the next moon, but here.

"Come along then," Thomas gestures to the wood that lies haphazardly around the chopping log.

I scramble to collect the pieces as Guthrie passes us by. He snorts and lifts the bucket he carries toward the sleeping wolf. "How about that for shields down? Maybe we need to make our insignia a sleeping wolf."

I laugh along with Guthrie as Thomas rolls his eyes and slams the axe into the next piece of wood. Oren scuttles past us on his way to the field. His wounds have healed, and he moves freely with an exuberance for life I wish was contagious. I'm glad he moved into the main lodge with the others, and my heart swells as I watch him make his way to join them.

Thomas reminds me of the wood again. "What's with that waif?"

"I think he's delightful."

"He's weird... that's what he is."

A little different, true, but not what I'd consider weird. "You know what he reminds me of? A surprise. Like when you taste an odd fruit and what you thought about the outside doesn't match the experience of the inside."

"That's just what I said. Odd. Weird. And small. You should ask your Mystery why it keeps sending us weaklings." He grunts again, and the wood splits into three pieces with the force of his blow. "And that boy says even more convoluted things than you do. Is it because he's so damaged, he makes little sense anymore?"

"I enjoy listening to Oren. I think his voice is soothing, his words and ideas make me think they're not actually his own, like—"

"Yeah, like there's a creepy old man stretched under his skin."

"Something like that."

"See? Like I said, creepy."

'Creepy' is not a word I'd use to describe Oren, either. Serene, calm, perhaps complicated... maybe even wise. I pull on Thomas's arm and direct his attention to the field. "Look at this."

Wren and Oren play together with Arrow. They run around the ever-patient beast and weave in and out of his extended legs, then he trots a short distance away and waits for the game to begin again. Wren runs with both of them, in play, not fear. Her short blue cape flaps from her shoulders as she darts and changes directions. I smile when a memory of her little feet disappearing out the small lodge window rises in my mind.

Thomas pulls his arm away from my hand. "Maybe he should just let her play, like we do."

"She doesn't seem to mind."

"But he's taking over her game."

"It looks as though she's enjoying the company."

"He's changing what she does."

Wren's laugh carries on the wind and heads raise from their work at the new sound. Smiles spread across faces and share her joy. Thomas smiles too. That kind of joy is irresistible, no matter how hard your heart.

I pat his arm. "We both know what she'd do if she felt uncomfortable."

He takes up the axe again.

"Look at all the space around her. Nothing is stopping her. No one is stopping her."

He balances a piece of wood and readies himself to split it. "You should put him to work, not have him gallivanting around in the field with Wren."

"I believe he's doing more good there than he would be carting water."

Thomas chops the wood into shards, and I collect them and stack them beside the lodge. I can't help checking on Oren and Wren's game each time I can see them. I've almost completed the stack.

Thomas puffs and rests on the axe handle. "All I want to know is if he knows anything about the fires in the East, and he keeps talking to me about putting out my own fires. Whatever that's supposed to mean."

"The fires in the East? Honestly Thomas, haven't we heard enough already?"

"It's just someone mentioned small renegade groups, small armies if you like, and some larger ones too, moving about. They might turn up here. An army, already trained at the ready. Just waiting for your orders. And all I get from the kid is talk of fire."

"He knows a thing or two about fire."

"I'm talking about armies here. You do remember the scroll, don't you? The one that says nothing about some weird child taking over and doing whatever he wants and you hanging off his every word."

I dump the wood on the ground in protest. "The scroll doesn't say a lot of things."

I step away and lean on the yard rail, resting my chin on my forearms. Wren and Oren play along the edge of the strip of grass that serves as the road to the lodge. Their game seems to wash away the frustration I felt with Thomas, or perhaps it just doesn't matter in the face of their joy. The Mystery said clarity was coming. Surely, that means Oren has something to teach us. Can the Mystery speak through a child? I pull my cheek into a half smile. Silly question. I talk to apple seeds, don't I?

There is something different about Oren, whether Thomas likes the idea of his presence or not. The way we speak together, like we are both foreigners in a strange land, or that we grew up in the same village and drank from the same well. I never have to consider the words I choose when I'm with him; as if they are of no consequence.

A small cart ambles under the threshold, it's laden with thin logs for a new cottage roof frame and the half smile returns to my cheek. I still think it amazing that they got the donkey to comply. The cart rocks under the weight as it traverses, not helped at all by the large man aboard who's just spied Oren and Wren at play. He pulls the pipe from his mouth and stands to wave. In his exuberance, he trips and tumbles from the cart just as it rocks from a bump in the road and tips. Donkey screeches in protest as the cart hangs there, mid balance, as if it was taking forever to decide whether to fall and unleash its weight. I'm already running as it tips and sends its goods crashing down towards Wren.

Bodies appear from every direction and shout instructions that blur into noise. On the ground, a wide-eyed Wren tugs feverishly at her trapped foot and frees it from a fallen log just as the crowd arrives. She's off before I can check on her, but there seems to be no change in her gait, and for the first time I'm relieved to have her run at full pelt from our presence.

Oren hadn't been knocked over. He'd stayed beside her with his arm extended toward the cart and only now drops his arm to his side and lets the rest of the cargo fall where Wren had just lay moments before. People step back from the commotion as the contents of the cart crashes, bounces and settles from the momentum of its fall.

Smoke. I can smell smoke. Flames take hold from where the driver's pipe had landed in the stubbled field. The wind encourages the small blaze up the slope toward the main lodge, fanning it out in size as it goes. Oren runs toward the flames before I can latch onto him. He passes the flames and faces them and their run up the slope. Again, he raises a hand and the flames stop their run, as if he might command an attack dog to stand down. The flames settle, reduce to small licks of fire and disappear into nothing. Thomas and I arrive by his side just as the last of the red sparks are defeated into the black of ash.

Thomas attempts to speak, but his mouth hangs open and no sound comes out.

Oren considers the patch of black straw and directs his attention to Thomas. "Fire only burns when it's fed. Stop feeding your fires."

Thomas nudges me and puffs. "See? Weirder than you."

I drop to my knees and search him for non-existent injuries. What am I meant to do now? How can there be no injuries? "How did you do that?"

Oren frowns for the tiniest of moments. "I do as you do. I simply ask."

There's nothing for me to do but nod. I remember the silky veil at the Tallefix's camp and freely stepping into that same place to ripen fruit or speak with the Mystery. Is this what I might look like to others? A deep knowing spreads a smile across my lips. That pyre wouldn't have stood a chance against him.

Thomas kicks at the blackened stubble and Silas stands a distance away with the others, wide-eyed at the whole circumstance.

Wren whooshes past with her arms out at her sides and Oren joins her in a new race across the field, oblivious to all the 'what ifs' still circulating through the minds of the adults.

Thomas joins me to watch their antics and catch our breath. He shakes his head and rests a hand on his hip. "Did we really just see what we saw?"

"Seems that way, doesn't it?" In times past, he would have written all this down, filled with the passion of discovery, but instead he has a troubling demeanor. "What are you thinking?"

"We could keep him."

I raise my eyebrows. "*Keep* him?"

"You know, train him. He'd be—"

"Ugh!" I turn on my heels and stride back to the lodge. Thomas's footfall sounds in the dirt behind me. Bees swirl through my body, but I'm not sure if I'm angry or devastated or bewildered by his response.

"It's just it'd be a shame to waste—"

I spin and step toward Thomas. Our momentums cause us to meet abruptly face to face in the middle of the field. Thomas steps back from my anger. My teeth clench so hard I fear they may crack. "He is a child." The bees rage through my body, not stinging and attacking, but energizing. I pay attention as they swirl and dive and strengthen and make me feel ten times bigger than I am. "We are charged to protect him!"

"Well, I—"

"Not *use* him!"

"You're right, I—"

"You will protect him? At all costs?"

"He has the wolf. He won't need me."

"He needs you. He needs all of us."

Thomas frowns at me, seeking more answers I can't give.

"Will you protect him?"

"Yes. Yes, of course," he says and rubs at the back of his neck.

I turn again, and he doesn't follow. I don't want to talk to him, anyway. I stomp my way to the lodge. Something just changed between us, but I don't know what it was.

The growth of a plant, from its first incarnation as a seed, through its cracking open and reaching its first shoots through the soil to the sky, moves from potential to existence. Some seeds we sow directly into the soil. They're sown that way at Guthrie's insistence, of course, according to his weather machine and knowledge of the seasons. Others, like the seedlings I hold in my hand, need extra care and protection to reach their full potential. It's vital they reach maturity, he explains, so we can collect an abundance of seeds for next season. Even at this first instance, some appear more robust than others. They remind me of the little pots in Martha's garden, nurtured until the time comes for them to face the open sky and turmoil of the weather. But there is no turmoil today. Just the welcoming soil, still damp from the morning dew, that sticks to my fingers in tiny clumps.

Thomas works a row away from me. He moves faster than I, being far too practical to stop and bestow a blessing and a wish of abundance on each seedling that leaves his hands. Everything planted is sown in hope. Little green shoots that don't reward our hope overnight. We must wait. Who plants apple seeds and doesn't dream of the day when they'll eat from its branches? We imagine that first bite, feel the crunch. It's impossible to plant without thinking of what might be. Isn't that the whole point of planting? The intention to make something from nothing, to make something better. Just by intending it.

I stand and brush the dirt on my skirts and tip my head sideways to consider my last planting. "I might find a small stick to stake this one."

"Don't waste your time."

It looks forlorn, head bowed and balanced on a precipice of whether or not to give up. "It doesn't waste my time when I follow my heart."

"Suit yourself. It probably won't produce any yield."

"Ha! It'll probably produce the highest yield just to spite you."

"There's a lot that can be said about you darling Ash, and much of it under the breath, but you'll always be a dreamer." Thomas chuckles to himself, looks up from his planting and groans. "I just wish you'd stop dreaming these people."

My shoulders drop. More people are at the threshold. Only two this time, but I sigh, and tiredness sweeps over me even though it's early morning.

Thomas brushes loose dirt from his pants and offers me his hand. "So, feed the hungriest? Isn't that the plan?"

Thomas took quickly to Guthrie's adage about finding out each visitor's pressing need, and meeting that, regardless of how ridiculous it seems to us. What do they hunger for? It's such a simple notion that's often overlooked when someone's eagerness to help means they disregard the wishes of our guests. For some, it may be warmth, a listening ear, or to be busy with a chore. It doesn't matter what it is, as long as we listen. Once their overwhelm is calmed, we are able to move forward. Oren is especially good at listening and will quietly drop a blanket next to a new guest, or introduce a particular person to them.

Our new guests have no injuries, or urgent requests, and we lead them to the main lodge.

"You're in luck," Thomas tells them. "It's Katteryn's turn to create our mid-meal today. She devises the most delicious fare."

Katteryn bustles between the warming pot in the lodge yard and the doorway of the main lodge, cradling chopped vegetables in her apron. "Oh my dear heart," she says and plops her hand on her generous bosom, "Look at you two." Everything is generous about Katteryn; her compassion, her waistline, her eyebrows that raise up and down at the slightest hint of news or provocation, and her serving sizes. No wonder her chickens follow her everywhere. There is no one more tender or unassuming to leave to the care of our new guests.

"They've just arrived this moment," I tell her. "Can you organize a meal, any other needs, and cots for them?"

Katteryn fusses straight away. "You sit right here," she says and guides them to the logs around the fire. "My hearty bread and pottage is only a moment away."

"They've traveled far," Thomas tells her, "Be sure they rest when they need to."

I'm impressed. It's probably one of the nicest ways Thomas has ever told anyone that their love of talking can be detrimental to others.

Katteryn nods and trots back into the lodge. "I've been chosen, and charged, to prepare meals and anything else for the new guests," she tells whoever is in the lodge and within earshot. "They've traveled far. So you must leave them be for now. Don't tire them out with your nonsense. None of you. Now where are the bowls. They chose me to collect the bowls. Ah, here they are."

Guthrie ducks out of the main lodge and looks over his shoulder as he walks to us. "She clucks as much as those chickens. So, seedlings done?"

"Almost."

Katteryn arrives with her bowls and ladles the older pottage into each and hands bread to the guests.

Thomas hovers over the pot. "That's a fine meal you're preparing, Katteryn."

She raises a bushy eyebrow and smiles. "It'll be ready for you at mid meal." She turns and heads back to the lodge with a finger held above her head. "I forgot the guest's ale." Her voice echoes through the main lodge. "Oh, I forgot the ale, but they all think I make the finest meals. They said they can't wait for mid meal today. They said I make the best pottage."

"Did I say that?" Thomas asks.

"No, but you know it's all true."

He laughs. "Katteryn is chattering. That's what they say. She repeats everything she hears."

Katteryn's voice still bounces its way around inside the lodge, little inflections of excitement raise it here and there. Guthrie chuckles to himself. "And to think I spent time trying to invent a method to best communicate a message among the people here. Katteryn does it for us with no invention required."

"And no effort, it seems to happen of its own accord." Thomas says.

"Unlike those seedlings."

Thomas concedes with a nod to Guthrie and we return to the lower field and our planting.

It's well after mid meal and I'm back in the lower field waiting on Katteryn.

"Don't forget me next time you're gathering. You won't know what you did without me!"

There are only a handful of us and some pace, eager to embark on the extra distance we'll need to cover to where the last of the yarrow flowers bloom. The colder weather is almost upon us, and it won't be long before their petals start to brown and their goodness decay. Our supply is almost depleted and this chance to forage deeper in the forest gives me the opportunity to explain to those interested in nursing the ill, not only what to look for among the yarrow, but of the various stages of growth in other plants we'll pass along the way. It's the same way Martha taught me. Asking and answering questions and watching and observing the growth patterns of flowers, seeds and roots that we use every day.

"Finally," someone mutters, and we all raise our heads as Katteryn approaches.

Wren arcs around us in little scoops, but doesn't come close. Some in the group are new to her, so I don't expect her to get any closer.

"Katteryn," I greet her with a smile.

"They needed me to—"

"Come along!" a voice calls and we wind our way into the forest.

Our trail takes us past the stand of pines with their noble covers and deep into the birch grove. There's no time to dawdle today, but we keep busy discussing plants of interest and the best methods surrounding their use; steeping, drying, balms, and concoctions. With so many voices chattering and making observations, it's easy to accept Katteryn's usual comparisons and puffed repetitions about the length of the trail. We follow the stream for a distance and arrive at the point where it widens and bubbles around a mass of large stones. Some are flat and wide, others round and of varying sizes.

"Looks like a path made just for us, doesn't it?" I ask.

"Yes, made just for us," Katteryn echoes.

"But wait." I open my arm out to stop her from crossing. "I've fallen into the stream here many times. Just when you think you know where you should step, the stream changes the footing underneath the stone. Some footings will always be solid, some change regularly."

"So you'll tell us where to step?"

"No I won't."

Katteryn's eyebrows dance about on her forehead before they settle into a frown.

"I can advise you on preparing herbs, and there are certain rules and methods to follow, but at other times, you'll need to trust yourselves and what you believe about the experience you find yourself in, and what your next step should be. In the same way, you can follow my advice and stand on the rocks I suggest, but I don't wear the same shoes as you, or have the same legs as you, so mine's a unique experience to yours. The only way you'll learn which ones to rely on, is to test them for yourself and, if need be, fall into the stream. You could always waste time and wait around to watch another go before you, but you'll only learn by feeling the firmness under your feet, and making the decision to move forward, or rushing across and feeling the splash of water around you. Either way, you need to experience it for yourself to know it. Don't rely on what I tell you, or what anyone else tells you. Rely on what you know. And that often takes practice and lots of falling in."

We cross the stream with much wobbling, swaying, testing, and laughter, and everyone remembers which rocks are steady and which only pretend to be that way. I could never have told them all the information they gathered about each stone for themselves, and no one would be able to convince them otherwise. After we cross, Wren bounces across the rocks as if they don't even exist.

A short distance away from the stream, we duck under some low-lying branches and make our way into a large open space entirely covered by the high tree canopy above us. It always reminds me of an enormous cavern. Gnarled roots pop up here and there out of the damp ground and delightful mossy rocks brighten the ground with their greenery.

A squeal and a thump breaks through our chatter.

We rush to our companion's side. Blood spills from a gash on the side of her knee.

Leaves are pulled from baskets and applied to the wound and she tries to stand, but fails.

We're still closer to Awenmell than we are to the yarrow. "Maybe we can carry you back." I say.

She sits on a large rock. "You go on ahead and I'll wait for your return."

"It may be dark by then."

Katteryn stands over her, "And then you'll slow us down further once we arrive back here."

I'd been waiting for Katteryn to come up with a statement of her own so I could praise her for her originality, instead of her defense of copying everyone around her. But I'm not about to praise that statement.

Katteryn puts her hands on her hips, "I'll go back to Awenmell for help."

"Are you sure? That seems like the perfect solution."

She nods and lifts her chin.

"You'd remember every detail of the way to this spot with that memory of yours."

Her eyebrows bounce with delight. She's probably thinking up all the stories that might accompany this bravest of adventures.

With our course of action decided, we continue on our way. I call to Katteryn to remind her to bring vinegar for the wound when she returns and she waves above her head.

Wren watches the scene from a short distance away. She runs back toward Awenmell the moment our agreement is made. She will undoubtedly beat Katteryn back to the lodge, but what could she say once she got there?

We tread carefully on our way back through the cavern. Thankfully, our journey to the yarrow and back again has been uneventful. In the soft earth around the large rock, boot shaped prints confirm she is safely back at the lodge. Little footprints on the periphery confirm Wren oversaw the whole procedure too.

Everyone has a role inside, and I imagine eventually outside, of Awenmell. Their own reasons for being here, and their own reasons for leaving. The souls that walk with me through this cavernous part of the forest all have their own dreams of their futures. Some plan to return to their villages, some have no villages to return to, but are hopeful nonetheless. Some are more interested in the plants and healing those who ail, others get lost in the world of hornets, bees and hives. Thomas calls me a dreamer, but this goes beyond fanciful dreaming; it's their actions that will make their villages healthy, and it's their action that proves their intention as serious. What do my actions prove? I never thought I'd be training nurses as Martha trained me. But unlike Brenn, it's not about prestige and silver. It's about a willingness to go where you're needed.

An early evening breeze passes by us as we cross the lower field. Our chatter drops to mumbles, then a rich silence. You can't mistake pyre smoke for anything else. We must become accustomed to it when we're working in this open part of the valley as it sweeps in from the terrors on the other side of the range. It's easy to become accustomed to chaos and think it normal, whether it's in the air, or buzzing through our veins, and I wonder if the whole unrest is simply all our insides, escaping to the outside.

Thomas stands with another ahead of us in the field. They're both earnestly looking at the person's hand. He's often comparing hands and palms with just about everyone at all strange times, in the field, in the lodge and around the fire. As I get closer, it looks like he's drawing on their hand with his finger.

"What are you doing?" I ask him as we walk past, "We weren't with the Tallefix long enough for you to take up telling fortunes."

Thomas shrugs. "Just explaining power."

"You must show me one day."

"Yeah, one day when you have a hand free," he calls after me.

I look at my hands. They're always busy, but they're never free. The realization hits me as dizziness sweeps over me and I stagger a couple of steps. No one else notices the truth that surges from my feet to my head and back again. Then it's gone. But it's taken something with it. Like the magnets that drew my feet onto this land have lost their strength; that I might float away at any moment.

There's just enough light for us to spread the plants we've gathered for drying, and to meet with the others around the fire. I scoop my own meal and secure a seat across the fire from Thomas. Katteryn hovers over the lady with the bandaged knee, telling everyone within earshot how she saved the day. The flames flicker on Wren and Oren, eating together. She even scoops her own meal from the pot and then rushes back to his side.

Silas puts his meal down and roughs the wolf's coat to welcome her. He catches my eye from across the fire. "A wolf took my arm," he explains, "but she wasn't the one who did it." Someone calls his name and distracts him.

"Silas," a voice calls, and distracts him, "Can you help me with this latch?"

"Happy to," he replies, "Let me finish my meal and I'll be right there."

He spoons the food into his mouth and doesn't see the smile on my face. The Silas of old would have preferred starvation than asking anyone to wait for him.

Guthrie rolls his wrinkled eyes at Katteryn, regaling everyone with her stories of valor, and turns his attention to the young man beside him who's asking questions about the stars above us. Thomas listens earnestly to their discussion about mythology and meaning and switches his gaze between the stars and their conversation.

Thomas smiles at me across the fire. He may say I dream, but right now I see us all as bedraggled little seedlings staked by our community. Who knows what any of our yields will be and what they might even look like.

⁂

I flop onto the bed as soon as we enter our cottage. What an unusual day.

Nothing seems out of the ordinary to Thomas. He keeps to his routine of selecting his books and laying out the scroll in front of him. Sometimes I wonder if he's forgotten the magic around seedlings and seeds themselves.

"Everyone is so different, aren't they?" I say, "I mean, I know that, but I think I finally understood it tonight. That everyone is off on their own adventure in this life, taking their unique tools and gifts wherever they're needed. The Hall forces people to be who they require, not who the person wishes to be, or is drawn to be. Guthrie positively glows with a challenge or invention. Can you imagine what a waste he'd be in the fields?"

"Hmm," he says.

And as for Thomas, that individuality of gifts means he pours over the scroll and parchments each night. His air is quiet and still, strong, brave and gentle. For all his maddening behaviors, I trust him. It didn't come easy. Trust is one of those unfamiliar relationships that dashes from my grasp. It's almost there, but not complete. I wish I could trust myself.

"So, what are you doing this time?" I inquire.

"Each time I read the scroll, there's something new. Or a novel way of looking at it. Tonight, Guthrie mentioned the stars, so I'm checking all the things you are."

"I'm not a star."

"No, but you're a storm, and a bridge, and... a river, wasn't it?"

"Don't think I'm a river. Maeve just said my life was *like* a river."

"Same thing, isn't it?"

"I think she meant being along for the ride. You can't really steer a river, can you?"

"Well, rivers carve up the countryside."

"I don't intend on carving anything up. If I can help it."

He counts on his fingers, "So, storms, rivers, bridges, fire..."

"Oh, and dirt, if you're counting the Hall's observations."

"You're very elemental, aren't you?" he twists the page in his hand. "I wonder how it fits together?"

"I gave up wondering about it ages ago. There are better things to do in life than vex yourself over the future."

"You're forgetting about the unrest."

I want to forget about the unrest. I may as well be a tiny leaf held in the eddy of a stream, spinning faster and faster and headed toward an answer I don't want to face. "Can we not talk about the unrest, just for now. Can we pretend it's peaceful here, just for tonight?" I try to ignore the stirring inside me. A sense of foreboding that I hide behind upturned lips. A shield I don't want to drop because of his smiling face. I wouldn't know what to tell him, anyway.

There's that dizziness again. A truth that surges from my feet to my head and back again. There's some kind of understanding missing. There's some other call. I float between worlds, trying to make sense of both of them and waiting for them to join into something solid.

I didn't bring Arrow to the cliff with me this time.

He was busy pulling at some tufts as I passed him, and I wandered rather aimlessly into the forest. I felt lured by something I couldn't articulate, yet I ended up here. Alone. Looking into the vast valley below, squinting through the fog to see the early morning lights of Lewtshire.

They don't need me back at Awenmell this morning. Must be the first time ever. No pressing problems to sort out, no desperation to hover over everyone and everything. Instead, I'm magnetized like one of Guthrie's experiments, bonded to this small rock set back from the edge. A bird tweets his welcome to the morning, a breeze rustles past my ear. It must be the openness that draws all my thoughts from my head. I flick my hand above my head; goodbye all of Thomas's questions I can't answer, goodbye Guthrie's calculations I don't understand. I wave again, and again, but one remains. The sensations and vision of that tiny leaf swirling in the eddy.

I close my eyes and dive underneath the turmoil, to the safe space that waits for me, the depths of the stream where all the activity above is of no consequence. Time passes differently here. Visions and colors swirl together and thoughts waft in and out of my consciousness like smoke; taking shape and then dissipating into nothing.

The sun is brighter when my eyes open. Most of the fog has disappeared from the valley and Lewtshire is a gray misty patch in the distance, framed rather artistically by the branches that drape around the edges of my view.

A shuffling noise nearby snaps me back to this moment.

Oren stands at the cliff edge balancing on one foot, choosing where to place the next on his journey along the precipice. My heart thumps in my chest, and I swallow carefully before I speak.

"Oren," I say quietly, "Come away from the edge."

He decides on his foot's placement and faces me. "You needn't worry. I know the edge well. I'm not afraid of it — and it's time you weren't either."

A lump catches in my throat. I don't remember being afraid of the edge, or telling anyone that I was. I suppose I've never really thought about it.... Oren raises an eyebrow and smiles at my puzzled expression, and a sudden understanding washes away the strain of my questioning. It's not this edge we're talking about. It's the new thing I'm afraid of; the swirling leaf in the eddy spinning faster and faster, the truth that runs up and down my body. A sigh escapes my lips but sounds more like an unceremonious grunt. Ugh. It's that clarity I claim I want to see, when I really don't. And it's veiled behind the next decision I make. *'It's time you weren't afraid either.'* His words feel familiar. Perhaps it's not the child who speaks, but that stillness we both know well. If the Mystery can speak to me—and tell me about life through apple seeds—why can't I be told truth from the mouth of a child? So, is this it? The time I'm meant to look at what I don't want to see? What if I'm not ready?

Oren holds his arms out for balance and wobbles along the cliff edge, watching my changing expressions as I gain control of my worry. "You're familiar with the edge?"

"I know of it." I'm ashamed to admit I've spent little time there, but I suspect Oren knows that, anyway.

"Have you noticed the closer to the edge you get, the more it demands of you?"

I nod. "It's certainly uncomfortable."

"The edge tells secrets and reveals answers; that's why everyone is so terrified of it. Why people demand we stay away from it... why you called me away from it just now."

Ugh! The sting of correction, but it's blended with a soothing balm of understanding. So opposite from the brutal punishment I'd receive for ignorance. Nervousness rolls in my stomach. Do I really want to have this conversation? I could make excuses and leave. He's just a child, after all. What would he know? Oren watches me closely. It's almost a dare. He stands as still as a road marker that points that clarity is down this path, and though I waver for a moment, I can't turn away. Not now. The leaf spins faster as the eddy draws it nearer. "What do I need to know?"

"Right!" he laughs, and leaps at a bough that hangs above him. He swings toward me hand over hand and drops to the ground with a cheeky thud. "What do you want to know?"

My head fills with questions that I can't form into anything but a tongue-tied mess. I don't even know where to start.

"Want to know what brought you here? Brought everyone here?"

"You mean to Awenmell?"

He juts his chin in the general direction of home. "They all visited their own edge before they came here. Left all they knew and went searching for something that made little sense. They've seen the valley at its darkest; they respect it, but it holds no fear for them now... not once they've been and returned. Few people will stand and take in the view; but once they turn around, the world seems so contrary, so foreign. The edge... it becomes a part of you. People around you who haven't seen the edge are terrified of it. They don't understand because they've never taken that journey."

"So facing an edge brought them here?"

"And what do you think leads people to an edge?"

I think about their stories of pain, terror, and betrayal. They've all experienced it. "Torment, I expect."

Oren inspects the trunk of a nearby tree. I didn't know I wanted him to affirm my answer—until he doesn't. He studies the branches high above him. "You know what makes the trees stand so strong?"

"It's their roots."

"No. It's not the roots. It's the wind. Without the wind, there'd be no reason for the roots to grasp so tightly and become as stable as they are."

"And when we have storms in our lives..."

"It's only when the wind blows, we find out what's worth hanging on to. But we never *thank* the wind, we never *thank* the things that nearly blow us over and uproot us. But they're the things that lead us to the edge and lead us to make choices we need to make."

"The wind brought me here, to this edge?"

"There's less fear of wind and storms when you know their purpose, don't you think?"

I remember sitting sopping wet in a stream, being thankful for a storm. I don't feel any of that now. I think it's easier to pay attention to noisy and persuasive winds than the gentle ones that guide you until you're sitting on a cliff edge trying to decide about an uneasiness that's made its home inside you. With a child as your mentor. And feeling this is all perfectly normal. "So no matter what brings you to the edge, it's your choice to consider the view, and to decide what to do from there?" I speak aloud, but I'm pondering the words myself rather than talking to Oren. The words dance around something specific, but I can't seem to grasp it yet.

"The wind brought you here. It's up to you whether you'd like to open your eyes to the view."

He slides his hand down a large trunk. "Deep roots mean they can stay close to the edge. Where you find yourself now."

"Leading me to a decision that I trust I can make.... because of the roots I've developed. The winds have already shown me what is worth holding onto, and what is worthless to me; perhaps undermining me."

"Exactly."

I study a tree nearby; its roots are heavy in the ground and it reaches over the edge as if peering into the valley. "Why am I scared to look into the valley and see from the edge?"

"Oh, there're all sorts of possibilities available. Some tolerable. Some not so. But once you open your eyes to the view, you can't unsee it. Many prefer not to look."

There's that dare again. "But I don't *have* to look, do I? I can be content with my roots buried deep into the ground just here at the edge, but never venturing to look over."

"You can. But then you'd never know."

"Never know what?"

He raises a tiny, yet wise, eyebrow. I walked right into that one. Guthrie says curiosity is the beginning of understanding. That makes curiosity sound sweet and innocent, not this animal that gnaws at my insides. Possibilities. That's what he's talking about. I look around. It's easier to walk away, think it nonsense, and pretend this moment isn't happening. Curiosity bangs within me, demanding to be noticed. What if I just took a peek, would that be so bad? *I can't unsee it.* That's what he said.

"I'm not good at decisions," I say. "I haven't had much practice. They were always made for me, you see; either by others, or by circumstance. My decisions always had a horrifying weight that crushed others' lives."

"How does that mean you're not good at them?"

There's that sting again. "It doesn't."

"Habits are funny things. Not only the way we do things with our bodies and the methods of our day, but our thoughts, too. When things are shaky, we go back to what we know. Holding onto a branch for support. It's hard to trust and not reach for what we know. It's perfectly normal too."

I'm desperate to know more. Desperate to stop grabbing at branches.

"You know that still place where the Mystery speaks?"

"Yes."

"If you can find yourself nestled there in the midst of turmoil, then you're not reaching for a branch. Your relationship with the Mystery becomes the branch you instinctively hold on to. You not only hold it; you wield it."

"But I've already devoted myself to the Mystery."

"There is always more freedom from the Hall. Not required, not essential, but on offer." Oren looks over the valley. "Many people deny the edge; what they know to be true inside of them. They fear what being so close to the edge will bring up in them. They're terrified of what they'll see there; some want to see the end before they start, they want to be sure of their safety. But where's the excitement in that? So, it seems your first choice is here. Are you willing to face this edge, accept what it shows you, and consider the choice it asks of you?"

The bees are already flooding my system, alerting me to the danger my choice will bring. I'd swallow if I didn't think I might vomit, yet I stand and take two shaky and lightheaded steps toward the edge. I stop short and the bees return in panic, and I force bile back down my throat. I concentrate on my feet and push them so hard into the ground I can feel the little sticks and stones under my soles and breathe deeply and slowly and listen to the bees. I'm determined to stay still. I won't run from them.

Closing my eyes helps. I follow the bees as they race through my system until they've settled enough that I can hear what has upset them.

My voice is raspy. "The bees have their own truth."

"Which is?"

"That these possibilities you speak of will ask more of me than I can deliver. It is safer to hide and continue being small. I'll survive that way. I have so far. It'd be easier to be small, but something needs me to be large. This edge does. They're terrified that something is pushing me toward what I fear. But it's not only fear, it's excitement too." My mind drifts back to Thomas and his satchel before he could write. He was scared, but excited, too. He trusted where his call was leading him. I gasp. "The edge is a call? This can't be right. I already have one here at Awenmell."

"You mean the safe and familiar one?"

"That's exactly what I mean." Sensations stir again, leaves and eddies and spins that make me dizzy. Can I? For a moment, I imagine myself being bold and standing at the edge, yet the next moment I feel myself contract, folding and folding and crawling into a ball, flopping and folding like a delicate flower under an oppressive hand. "I can't. I'll fall short, I'll fail. People will die."

"Why would that be true?"

"It's happened before."

"Grabbing at branches?"

"Yes. I don't know any other outcome. I can't even imagine any other outcome. I flop and fold. Even when I tell the truth, I'm deemed a liar. I manage to get people killed without even trying."

"But you've never tried to stand?"

"Not without punishment, or twisting of my words to cause punishment. It's so much easier to stay silent, to promise myself to never speak again." My mind reminds me of Martha's chained heart, the one kept bound by silence. If my heart isn't free to speak, I may as well be as mute as my behavior makes me appear.

"More choices to make?"

"It seems that way."

"Your choice is your greatest power. That's why they were so intent on removing it from you, and from us."

I'd never considered that. The bees settle and the horror of stepping closer loses its power. I nod; even the smaller things seem clearer the closer I get to the edge.

Oren stands on the edge and lifts his arms from his sides. The wind pats at his shirt sleeves. I don't even think of calling him back. "You don't have to understand it," he says, "You just have to stop fighting it. Accept you're here, a few steps from the edge. Accept it was the wind that brought you here and trust the edge. Stop being afraid. Embrace it."

You need to stop being afraid of the edge. That's what he said at the start. I really didn't know this is where we'd end up, in a place filled with so much danger but also so much comfort. Truth has this funny way of striking true, but never wounding. I don't feel compelled to move to the edge. Not in the way it compelled me to find Awenmell or the way it drew me to Oren. This is different. I need to make a decision; a choice. I trusted the Mystery wholeheartedly, now to decide to trust the edge it had led me to.

Oren looks back over his shoulder at me. "Care to look at the view?" and a dare sparkles in his eyes.

A deep breath shudders through my body. Look at him all relaxed there on the edge, without a care in the world. How does he do that? I look over my shoulder in the general direction of Awenmell, a silly gesture. I can't see anything, but I think of their tales. Maybe it's easier to step up and commit your everything to an edge when it's already been asked of you, over and over again. A habit that grows stronger each time you step up. Into the unknown. Into possibility.

Oren speaks a little louder. "We both know the secret of this edge, don't we? There's really no need to fear it. Because it's impossible to fall."

What were my edges? The times I didn't fear toppling. Where it was impossible to fall? When I stepped up to scrunch all that chamomyle and throw it on Martha's pyre?

Had I fallen then; would I have cared?

How could I have fallen?

I thought I could fly.

He glances over his shoulder, then turns back to the valley. "The edge teaches what can't be taught. Only known. And you've known it all along, deep inside. Behind the denial, and the fear. And the fear? It just drops away, like a rotted robe. You know this already."

I do. My decision fills me with excitement before I can slip the shoes from my feet. I stride the few steps toward him and curl my toes over the edge. I raise my arms and let the wind buffet me and sway me, and I am not afraid. I can't even conjure up any fear at all. I can almost smell the chamomyle on the wind and my heart lifts and swells with wings of its own. It is exactly as this strange young child says. There is nothing behind me, and all is open before me. With the blades of grass at my feet, the breath in my lungs, and the sincere sensation that falling is impossible, I step away from what was old and prepare for the new.

This is more than guidance through a bog, our knowing steps onto Awenmell, or the flowers on Martha's pyre. This is about surrendering to both the view and the fall. This is about refusing to fold and wielding my love as a weapon, not a platitude. Accepting a call wherever it might lead. This isn't a forced surrender. It's chosen. I stand down from war against the Mystery and lay down my ideas of how it should be. In my mind's eye, I de-armor, and I lay down my shields against my own life.

How can something so terrifying be so calming? My arms stretch out in my full breath to receive and I am balanced. The wind buffets my hair, I am riding with Mardu, echoes of my laughter and hope in the back of my mind. A gust pushes my hands and sweeps its way through my fingers; the same hands that took comfort in

Mardu's mane and cupped his blood. The ones that I deemed useless, that now tend wounds and offer comfort and strength. Everything changes at the edge, every perspective is witnessed anew, and the superfluous falls away. Visions dance past my eyes; hope fills my heart as the old and new mingle in a single purpose. As protective as a lover's embrace. I would gladly stay here forever.

The valley is filled with possibility. I can't see it with my eyes, but I know it's there; on its way to me. And I accept it. I refuse to fear it, for it is mine.

We rest on a stone, back from the edge, alone with our thoughts. Seasonal greens and browns fill the valley. Even though I've looked at this scene a million times, I feel like I'm seeing it for the first time. The colors so rich, the texture so vibrant, I can feel it under my touch.

"The valley looks much wider when the fog lifts."

"We can see so much more."

Everything is clear. I can even make out some fences in the far distance. *Clarity.* "You're the clarity I'd been waiting for."

Oren shakes his head. "The clarity you needed was in the action you took; the choice you made." He watches me as I stand and wiggle my feet into my shoes for my return. "So, what do you believe?"

It stops me short. Isn't that what Brenn said to me, when I thought myself some grand leader with proud ideas? This time, the question is more about an undefined path, a willingness to surrender to a mystical plan. "*What you believe about yourself becomes your truth.* Someone told me that once, but I think I'm only understanding it now." Even though I'm at peace with my decision, there's no direction, no guide through the woods. There's no marker, no way I should be going. "So, what happens now, little wise one? How do I move forward from here?"

"First, stop asking questions when you already know the answer. It's a habit you don't need."

And... another sting. "Thomas says in order to move forward *I need an army; I need a plan*."

"What do *you* think you need?... know you need?"

The edge looks empty without us standing on it, but it still exists within me. That deep connection that I will move forward and do what I must do. "I need to listen. And I need to trust what I know."

T he breeze that sweeps into the field and down to my working hands is tinged with the lightest of smoke. So light that you could ignore it, yet heavy enough for me to remember that this valley is a haven from life on the other side of those mountains. I used to gag at the unmistakable stench of the funeral pyres; hastily put together with no aromatic woods or herbs. I imagine there's no time for that now. I also used to hope that the pyres have stopped, and that's why I couldn't smell them anymore. We still see their smoke, but their familiarity of the smell means it doesn't shock us like it used to. I wonder if that's part of the Hall's plan. We can't be horrified about what we don't sense anymore, and the more numb we become to our senses, the further we move away from the Mystery.

I watch until the smoke dissipates in the sky's vastness and brings my focus back to the mountains. A quiet summons builds inside me, calling my curiosity at what lies on the other side. It was smoke that led me out of the forest's safety and into Smoutlea. This smoke bears no resemblance to a feather in a hat, though, or any of its frivolity. I was safe in the forest; happy there. Yet the Mystery led me out. I'm safe and happy here, too. Yet there's a fine stirring in my chest, a delicate balance between excitement, restlessness, and dread.

All around me people are at work in the fields, on the paths or in the lodges. They laugh, jest, and talk among themselves, oblivious to the invisible ropes that pull me toward the other side of the mountains. Katteryn waves her hands high in the air and tells her listener some exuberant story as they prepare our mid meal outside the lodge. Wren and Oren race past them and down to the edge of the forest, where they've been busy collecting kindling. The dull thuds, hisses, and tinks of metal-on-metal tell me Silas is hard at work, and Thomas stands on the open side of the forge watching over their latest creation. No idea where Guthrie is. He's probably muttering away in his new hut, the one he's slowly filling with jars and books and perplexing devices. It's built just behind the main lodge. Close enough to help with night terrors and private enough for him to work on his experiments late into the night.

I glance at the mountains and return to my task. "You're taking me somewhere, aren't you?" I rarely speak aloud to the Mystery, but I can't be overheard here. Still, I almost whisper my conversation. "I want you to know I won't drop to the ground and act like a toddler... like I have before." My cheeks flush with heat when I remember my tantrum in the stream. "Wherever we're going, I have to trust that I'm ready. You see, I'm not ready... but I'm willing. Will that be enough?"

You didn't run from the edge.

"No, no, I didn't."

You separated your past from your future.

"Well, that's kind of an ongoing thing..."

You're prepared to accept whatever lays ahead of you.

The sensation of freedom I felt at the edge rushes my system and cements my answer. "I am."

Do you trust me?

"Yes."

Then that is more than enough.

I try to imagine what may lie ahead; try to figure out scenarios that might await me, but soon realize it's completely pointless. The Mystery could lead me anywhere, to anything. How am I supposed to behave in this 'anywhere and anything'? There are no protocols for mystery. Not as far as I know. "You haven't told me who you want me to be, who I should be on this adventure."

Why do you wait to be told who to be?

I sigh. "Habit. That's that ongoing past thing I was telling you about."

Old habits are like opportunistic thieves. When they're being watched, they don't show up as often.

"So keep watch?"

Always.

"And who should I be then?"

It's not about who you should be, but who you believe yourself to be. Do you believe the words of others, or the truth of yourself? Leave behind everything the Hall told you about yourself. Everything Thomas, Guthrie, the scroll, or Awenmell have told you. Stop viewing yourself through their eyes and see yourself without their bias. Pay attention to your own truth and heed it more than theirs.

My stomach ties itself into knots. My truth's more important than others? The knots squeeze tighter. "You can't expect me to suddenly believe in something that's never been true for me?"

The truth can be strange. It illuminates that which has hidden in darkness, but was there all along. When you're blinded by habit, you can't see rightly to proclaim what is true and what isn't. You have to feel for the truth inside your body.

Can I feel the truth? I close my eyes and concentrate on what's been hidden in the darkness, fumbling around, ready to brave what I might find. I come across some boldness, but I dare not proclaim it, even to the Mystery. It might not be real. Some kind of trickery.

It sits solidly in my chest like an inner armor. Did it come from the edge? I've never noticed it before. Was it always there, existing in the darkness because I didn't believe it was there until now? "So I feel for the truth inside my body? I get to decide who I will be?"

It's important you be who you are. Your likes, dislikes, leanings, and ideas. Stand firmly on them, like you would an edge. Accept them. They make you who you are. Isn't that exactly what you teach the others here?

Katteryn stirs the large pot and calls out orders to her servers as the time for mid meal approaches. Thomas and Silas admire and discuss their work, turning it over in their hands and pointing to sections that interest them, before animatedly drawing charts and diagrams in the air for each other. Oren and Wren are nowhere to be seen, but you can be sure they'll come running once Katteryn gives her call. Others work in the field, or where they can. Some still rest, waiting for their wounds to heal. They've all been to an edge. Every one of them. Maybe not the one exactly like mine, but very much the same. They've let the wind buffet them, and with their toes curled tight on the precipice, they've seen it all. What lay behind them and what lay before them. And they wobbled and wavered simultaneously, just as I did, and the wind held and rocked them as if given over to everything, every blade of grass under their feet and to the expanse of possibility that opened before them. They're not afraid of the edge. It's their home.

And wherever I am, my body knows the truth. My mind may have told me I was balanced on a cliff's edge, but my body told me I was at peace. Yes. My body knows the truth. It always has. I just didn't listen to it.

"Truthful answers are always so peaceful, aren't they? Even when they're challenging—ugh, maybe even terrifying, or confusing... they're still peaceful somehow. Like they belong, like they've always been there."

Katteryn calls to announce mid meal just as a notion enters my mind. They compete for my attention. The smell from her pot is enticing; but not as enticing as discovering if any of this is mentioned in the scroll.

Some days are just hungrier than others, and today is one of those days. Everyone is so intent on feeding their bellies that they don't notice me pass them and head straight into the main lodge. The scroll is battered and marked from being pulled down and studied so many times. Everyone has their own theories and ideas about what it all means. I stare at the letters and markings that still mean nothing to me. Guthrie promised he would teach me to read, but there was always something more important for us to do. Not that it matters. I've memorized most of it, yet there's something just about holding it that makes me feel I'm studying it and helps me to concentrate. Was there anything in here about smoke? Surrender? Edges?... Leaving Awenmell? I run my fingers over the letters. The last time Thomas spoke about the scroll, he was talking about rivers. Could I be a river? No, the river was my life. That doesn't make sense. It'd be nice if something did. I hang the scroll back up on its nail. I suppose it's normal to want to know what you're heading into. If I ask Thomas, he'll want to know what all my interest is about. Not sure he's ready to discuss something like the edge right now.

"Discover anything new?"

I jump at the voice of the youth who carries a bucket of water into the lodge. "No. No. Just checking for any clues."

"Anything in particular? A few of us get together some nights and come up with wild ideas. Might help."

My mind scans for anything in the scroll that's as far away from smoke and edges, "Ac—", I say, fumbling for the word. "Acamar. The star."

"So you know it's a star. Good start."

"Guthrie pointed it out to me a long time ago. Well, it feels like a long time ago."

"It's a guiding star."

"It is? Guthrie didn't tell me that." He seems to have brought a waft of Katteryn's cooking in with him, and my stomach rumbles as I step towards the door. "Is there anything about the star you think I should know?"

"My father studied the stars and knew all their meanings."

"Now that would be a fascinating occupation. And I assume Acamar has its own meaning?"

He joins me at the doorway, "It means the river's end."

I try to comprehend his words, but I must look like I don't understand. He tries again.

"You know, the end of the river."

"Yes, I understand." I whisper.

"Would you like me to tell Thomas about this? He might not know."

"No. No, thank you. I'll let him know."

My bowl is hot in my hands, and Katteryn's vegetables bob up and down inside it, daring me to not find them delicious. My appetite disappeared at the mention of Acamar's meaning. Perhaps it will return with a scoop of food and some conversation. Thomas lands next to me in a cloud of agitation. He mumbles about having to recreate something in the forge and I try to rummage up something that will make him feel better.

"Oh, I remembered to ask Oren about why some people don't come through the bog."

"You mean everyone but me and Guthrie?"

"I suppose so. Anyway, he said they've already been through one, it just doesn't show. They're proven waders, that's what he called them."

"Proven waders? What? So they like traveling through muck?"

"Err, I think it means that they've waded through enough of it, they don't need any more."

Thomas shakes his head. Well, that certainly didn't help. I'm not about to mention my call, or the river, or Acamar, or anything else for that matter. I don't need to upset him any further. *Old habits are like opportunistic thieves. When they're being watched, they don't show up as often.* Habits I watch and am aware of, I can clearly see. I will do almost anything to avoid upsetting Thomas, just as I did at the Hall. The constant fear of displeasing drains my power away from me. It's a habit that I'm aware of. One I can now watch. It's a habit I can change. But when everything is new, nothing is certain. I don't know how any of this will play out. I eat in silence and consider where this newness might lead.

Mystery? Help me.

I am here.

That's good because I'm not sure I am. I'm different, not the same as I was.

Of course. It's called growth.

But I don't know who this new person is.

You saw the smoke, didn't you? Are you ready to find out?

What if I don't like where it takes me? What if I'm disappointed at the end?

How can you be? It leads to you.

I think I can do this.

I don't want you to think. I want you to know.

❧❦❧

I added another ritual to my bedtime routine. Visiting the main lodge before I retire lets me note Guthrie's health, check on the stock in the apothecary and wonder for a few quiet moments why Oren is here with us, resting soundly in his bed and not tucked away anywhere else.

And all at once I understand, though it's a knowing without words and not one I could ever explain, but it blows like a breeze through my mind and clears away doubt and makes things clear. Why the wolf had to bring him, why it pained me to watch him at the gate, and why my heart had almost burst when I held him to me on the road.

"Oren," I say and kiss him lightly on the forehead. His mouth twitches into a smile as I stroke the side of his cheek with my hand, "We're all so glad you're here." He looks deep into my eyes, way past where anyone else might look, but I'm not afraid of his presence. I need to protect him at all costs. "We've been waiting for you."

I run to greet Thomas under the threshold as the sun sets. Three nights of worrying about how he's fared collecting supplies for us is more than enough for me. They both look tired. The donkey and Thomas, and the stacked cart seems a little worse for wear too. I jump into his arms and plant a kiss on his cheek.

"There's dissension among the guards," he grunts.

"Well, hello to you too."

He smiles and kisses me hard; it makes me miss him more, even though he's standing right in front of me.

"Dissension?"

"They've been working with secret symbols and underground movements. They're being clever about it, but it's just murmurs, of course. No one will tell me anything, not without sharing their uniform, but there's hope now the ranks are disintegrating from the inside out." The donkey decides that a short distance under the threshold is home enough, and Thomas tugs on his reins. "It'll be a help if they get to work destroying themselves so we don't have to do it. Come along, you insolent beast!"

With some encouragement, the donkey concludes traveling a little further won't bother him after all, and people surround the cart and carry the goods to where Thomas directs.

He surveys the decorated lodge yard. "What's this?"

Decorated is probably too grand a statement. Some wild flowers and ivy adorn the fence and Katteryn and her helpers are fussing over the baking of a much lighter bread than we're used to.

"Tonight's fare well feast. Well, not so much a feast, but a change of menu, nonetheless."

"And who do we wish well this night? All of them?"

I clench my jaw. It stops me from muttering unwise words. I understand his impatience, given his focus on the army's imminent arrival, but I've only just got him to stop asking people if they're ready to move on, rather than waiting for them to decide their own fate. The army is nearby, and I sense we're running out of time before they make their appearance. The changes they'll bring fill me with dread, not hope. As if their arrival will flip everything here upside down. This time, I don't dismiss my feelings; I honor them. *Trust what you know.*

"No, not all of them, just those ready and brave enough to follow their path." I long to tell him about the edge, but his jaw is set, and he doesn't see what I see. He sees bodies taking up precious beds and shelter.

I see a supportive and happy family. I catch myself nodding. Yes, a *family*. Where every contribution, even Wren's, blends into a sense of belonging. One *I've* never had before, and I imagine they haven't either. Awenmell has become a little nest where we've all grown and learned together. Now some are leaving. Where to? Wherever they're led. Some have said they'll return to what's left of their villages and explain the bees. Others are traveling far away from their villages to begin anew, yet others are going to find carts and heal as they pass through the lands. Nurses are in demand everywhere, but they'll all have to be vigilant on the roads.

Thomas watches the people mill about. "What's with the flower chains around their necks?"

"Wren made them... as fare well gifts."

He shakes his head. "I hope they fare well; it's hard out there."

"They're much stronger than when they arrived. Do you re-member?"

"How could I forget?"

We both chuckle at that one. How could we ever forget? I lean my head into his shoulder. "The mud, the night screaming, the fighting..."

"And that was just Guthrie."

We didn't even know what this place was when Guthrie arrived. We were just compelled to build it; in the same way a bird builds their own nest by following their instincts. Perhaps that's what calls are. Instincts that we've forgotten to listen to, or been scold-ed for paying attention to them, so they don't bother trying to connect to us anymore. I'm glad I followed my instincts. I'm glad Thomas believed what I said, too. I doubt any of this would have been possible without him.

They are much stronger; and so am I. They're leaving with a much different tale than the one they carried under the threshold when they arrived. They've discarded who the Hall told them they were, dumping the identity like an old robe, and brought their bees close to them as confidantes, not terrorists. Every sting and flurry now becomes a place to learn more, to discover more of the power that was stolen from them.

"Look out! Look out!" Guthrie clears a path through the group for his lackeys to follow. They carry poles with torches attached, and once he's confirmed their correct position in the ground, lights the torches to a hurrah from the crowd. For all his amazing inven-tions and experiments, the greatest of all alchemy surrounds him. The changing of one life into another.

Two young girls approach us, arms linked and almost bursting with energy. They'd arrived within a few days of each other, and were now heading back to their villages together. I reach forward to untangle their delicate flower necklaces. "Ellyn! Ryia! Excited about leaving in the morning?"

Ellyn bounces on her toes. "At first, I was worried, but now I can't wait to get walking. My feet won't stay still; like they're itchy. And I can't seem to stop talking."

"Are you headed home?"

"I am," she says unlatching herself from her friend, "I'm going to stand in the town square and speak to anyone who'll listen to me."

Ryia pales and seats herself on a log. "You're not, are you?... really?"

"Why not? It's my passion, and it's so much a part of me I just can't help myself. If I cease to do it, I cease to be me."

"Oh Stars, I'd be horrified!"

"Why? It's so much fun."

I step away from Thomas to join the girls' conversation. "Every one of us is different. Just look around you. Different bodies, different stories, and different gifts. Some are born fighters, agitators, and rebels. Others are orators, inventors, and healers. Demanding that a revolutionist who shouts in the village square to be quiet, does the same disservice as telling the quilter who whispers to her neighbor that she must shout from the rooftops for her call to be worthy. Each has their own tale to tell and way of telling. And please, be sure to do your work safely."

Ellyn nods her agreement. "As long as the message is out."

Message. Martha said I had a message, didn't she? Ellyn continues her chatter and draws me away from my thoughts.

"The answer to the unrest is found in our choices. In that gap of time where we choose to listen to our bees and heal or be carried away by them."

Ryia pipes up. "Guthrie said—"

"Guthrie said our brains know how to better do something simply by watching and learning. If we can do something well, we give others the opportunity to do it well too. If we watch a reaper, we can better handle a scythe because we learn techniques by observing." She draws a breath and turns to her friend. "That's what he called them, didn't he? Techniques?"

"I believe s—"

"Yes. So we learn by observing. We can learn kindness by observing it in others. And we can learn how to listen to our bees by watching other people deal with theirs. We learn to talk about them, when we hear other people talking about them. So that's why I'm talking."

"Without taking a breath."

"There's no power in being someone else. Not a speck."

I can't argue with that. I can't argue with any of it. Neither can Ryia, it seems. I kiss their foreheads and wish them well. I hope their journeys are safe.

When I turn back to Thomas, he has gone.

⁂

I used to think I loved the view of the fields in the morning, when it was quiet and new and full of promise. Now I think I love it more in the middle of the day, with people dotted here and there working and talking among themselves. It's like it's alive and functioning as its own creature. One man rages in the far field. It looks like what he'd planned to happen with his tools didn't happen. Two others gather around him and help him work through what the bees are saying to him. They don't take his rage and use it to justify a rage of their own. Like the spot fires, the Mystery showed me in Guthrie's barn.

I would never have understood it was about bees back then. The Mystery used a vision of spot fires because I wasn't ready to face my own bees. I chuckle to myself, imagining how I might have reacted if it showed me swarming bees instead. In many ways, I'm an apprentice, shown what I need to know to complete a task, and then building on what I know to discover more.

There's only a short distance to the main lodge where I can deliver this heavy basket of gourds to Katteryn. The basket handle digs into the crease of my arm, and I've been swapping it to the other more often than usual. It pinches my skin, and I drop it with a thud. So close to my goal, yet my arms feel joyful to be released from their burden. I shake them out and summon the determination to lift the basket again.

Something pours from the sky like floodwaters. I turn to run, maybe shout out, but it's not water. I stand mesmerized by sparkles that move through the air like sunlight hitting ripples on water. It flows like water, but it's not liquid. It's light. Thomas approaches me, bringing more supplies to the lodge. I don't move a muscle; I don't dare. "Do you see that?"

He casts a glance into the field and then continues past me. "See what?"

I blink hard and it's still there, flowing like a river, or maybe it's a waterfall landing directly in the middle of the field. Like someone pouring a bowl from a great height. Only the splashes join and become trails of brightness that lead across the fields and spread out like their own streams of light. Just like the clasp on Thomas's satchel, or a spider's web. Still, it travels further out of Awenmell. It's definitely not water. The trails move over the mountains and out of sight, all the while sparkling like sunlight on water. Then it slowly subsides, soaking into the earth, leaving only small sparkles where full trails had been. The people in the fields hold most of the sparkle. It still hovers over them, around them, like little fireflies that hang around however much you shoo them away. The sight astonishes no one else. No one else is looking around for an explanation. I'm on my own.

A new waterfall trickles from my head to my toes. Like warm oil.

It's their hands. Their purpose is in their hands. And they have lowered their shields. Their hearts are *naked*. And mine is about to burst.

"Get the scroll! Get the scroll!" I shout at Thomas as he emerges from the lodge.

He jumps and turns to re-enter, but I meet him there and we push through the doorway together. Thomas beats me to the parchment and takes it down more gently than I would have. "Calm down, Calm down. What do you want to know?"

"The hands. Tell me about the hands again."

"Where?"

"At the start, there's something about hands."

"This part? *'The change hid in our hands'*?"

"That's it. That's it!"

"What's it?"

"Hands. It's collective, not singular."

"And....?"

The waterfall floods every part of me, and I feel like I've just discovered the answer to every question I ever asked. I grab his arm and lead him outside and point over the fields. He watches the workers for a while and then shrugs. I look into his completely bewildered eyes. "I'm not the Eariss."

He sighs. "Oh no, not this again, Ash."

"Stop! Just stop. Look." I gesture to the fields again. "I'm not the Eariss.... *they* are."

Thomas looks over the meadow. There's Silas, a one-armed man teaching complicated tasks to people with two hands. Wren flits from place to place. People tremble and are comforted; others react and are shown a new way. He's still frowning. I can only wonder what he sees.

" *'The change hid in our hand'*, it's plural, Thomas. It's not up to one person, it's all of us. All the seeds. All of them breaking open and growing as they should. The bringer of change, the one to set things right, to demolish kingdoms!"

"Shh!" he hisses at me and turns back to the lodge. "You've lost your mind."

I follow him, determined to make my point. "Tell me what you know about the Eariss!"

"What part? Something from the scroll again?"

"The Hall! They said it was evil, that it would end our world."

"Sounds about right."

"What if it only means to end *their* world. The Hall's world and that's why they're so terrified of it?" I can see the field from the doorway. I watch the workers as I ask more questions of our Eariss expert. "The Eariss is to bring about change?"

"Yes."

"And it's unexpected."

"That's what they say."

"What's it responsible for? Discarding what's old and bringing what's new; what's always been, but disregarded."

Thomas shakes his head. "You have to be the Eariss. What about your power, your eyes?"

My heart pounds with possibility, and I have trouble finding the right words. "What was that thing?"

"What was what thing?"

"The thing Guthrie talks about in his experiments, the thing that causes something else."

"The catalyst?"

"Yes. Why can't I be one of those? What if I'm one of those catalyst things? Something small that starts the bigger thing."

"But you're not. You're the Eariss, and you've gone and made yourself all scared about something," he dismisses me with a flick of his hand, "that's what's brought all this on."

Another thought pops into my mind, so I shift quickly from annoyance back to excitement.

"Listen, listen! Martha said something about the Eariss being a mirror. There must be something in that. What does a looking glass do? Reflects, anything in front of it. Allows you to see yourself. What can you do with a mirror that you can't do with anything else? See yourself. But you have to be prepared to look. It's no good to you if you don't look at it, right? So, if they're the Eariss, it means they'll return to the villages and be the looking glass people can see themselves in. It's only when we're prepared to see each other's pain and suffering and acknowledge it as ours too, that we see we are all the same, fighting the same kinds of battles. They're not scared of their bees; they don't let the bees control their lives. They are the safe place for people to recover and tell their stories. When we're all truly seen, there is no need for attack. When we were traveling, do you remember how you asked me if there could be more than one Eariss? There is. Look at them. They are the Eariss, the new way. We just provided the place for them to see it, the breathing space. They are the table flippers of their villages, they are the mirror, and they live it every day. They are the ones to change the land."

"But the battle and the message—"

"They carry it! Don't you see? Everyone is the Eariss, that's why the Hall is terrified. It's not one person doing anything, it's all of us working together to heal. This won't miraculously end the bloodshed in one day, but isn't that how you win a war? One battle at a time. And sometimes the battle we need to win is the one inside ourselves, and we do that one battle at a time too."

"This is Oren's doing, isn't it? Filling your head with childish nonsense, when we should prepare for the army and making plans to attack the Hall. You can't win a war without some kind of power. The sooner the army arrives, the better. Then we can get some proper work done."

"Armies are powerful, aren't they?"

Thomas nods and then shakes his head at me. He might not believe we're having this conversation, but it's real, and right now. "Guthrie once said that genuine power is about the ability to change something. That's why we lose our power when we lose our choice."

"So?"

"Awenmell has changed these people. They've changed each other. They'll change others. I dare say they'll change the world. By doing life a different way; because just look at them, they're different, and they're learning to love their 'difference' instead of hiding it away." My eyes grow wide. "Ohhhhh," I breathe.

"No!" Thomas says.

"But—"

"No! Don't say it!"

"What if they are?"

"They're not!"

"They're the army, Thomas." I stifle the joyous laughter of discovery that bubbles through my chest as Thomas's face contorts in denial. The beautiful simplicity of it all. This army scatters far and wide and infiltrates the entire land. There's no forcing, no pushing, no striving, just evolving with natural growth. We are all inherently compassionate. It's just the bees that make it seem any other way. My hands turn this way and that, and I consider the change hidden within them. That's what the scroll says. Our hands are our purpose. What we set them to in each of our moments is how we define how we show up in this world.

"It can't be."

"The new way differs from what we're used to. Why can't war be battled differently, too? When faced with cruelty, we become more caring. We face the world's pain, and act as it's mirror and offer compassion because we've met with our pain and listened to our bees. It doesn't scare us to see it in others. It changes everything. Can you imagine?"

"No. No, I can't! This is insane. We need weapons and plans, and armed men. Sound men. We will take the Hall by force."

"Ah, you're forgetting that what you think it is, doesn't make it so. Remember, with Brenn? I thought it was all about being a leader like all the others, and it turned out to be something entirely opposite."

"But they're not the army - they can't be! It says no army can stand against it."

"That's true."

"But that means it's powerful and strong and ready to battle."

"Correct."

He shrugs his shoulders. "They just don't seem committed to me, you know, like a real guard or Trothsman might."

I know about commitment. And so do they. We were once committed to our own destruction. Committed to denying ourselves at every opportunity. I strain to hold a civil tongue. What patience I had has worn out and a new urgency that he understands my words overpowers me. "They know more about commitment than you could ever imagine. Don't dare to question what they will tolerate when they believe something. It would astound you." It's a good thing I'm back to clenching my jaw, there's much more I could say. His satchel hangs from a hook against the wall. He must've been in here making notes from the scroll or discussing it with the other young men. I tug at it to see if it's his book's weight that holds the straps tight. I pull it free of the satchel and slap it onto the lodge table. "Write it down!"

"Well, I don't—"

"Write it down! This is your precious story. It's been parading right in front of our eyes the whole time, only we didn't believe it worthy enough."

He raises his voice. "I will do no such thing. You'll look like a madwoman. No one will come to fight with us when they hear of your... ridiculousness." He stabs his finger toward me, emphasizing his words. "*You* are the Eariss! And *you* will raise an unconquerable army that will destroy the Hall's power."

He just can't see it.

I already have.

"Checking again?" I ask as I pass the lodge yard fence.

Guthrie hovers over his weather machine. The little sideways cups spin, and he taps at water-filled vials and readjusts the dials. "Mmn-yah," he mumbles and scratches at his chin. "I've seen nothing like it."

Neither have I. I wouldn't know how to read one to save my life. "But everything is well?"

"We shall see," he says and turns this way and that, looking at the sky from all directions.

Thomas passes behind me, but we don't acknowledge each other. It's easier this way for now. We'll get around to finding a middle ground about the army, but we're both still too tender and reactive this afternoon.

I turn my attention back to Guthrie. "So what's it saying?"

He taps the glass vials and wipes his sweaty forehead with his kerchief. "Tumultuous times ahead." He chuckles and then turns to me and laughs. "But we all know that, anyway!"

I suppose we do. But I don't feel like laughing.

"There's a storm coming," he says, watching the sky again and returning to his dials. "But I can't tell from which direction it comes, or how soon it will be here."

"That *is* odd."

"I'll keep checking and let you know what I discover."

"Please do. But remember, all the good things that come from what we think is bad; extra moisture for the soil, and it's about time that pond had a good flushing. We've only got to make it to the other side."

Guthrie nods and dabs at his brow again. The air feels so thick you could drink it, and he sways and focuses beyond me.

"Are you well, Guthrie?"

"Me? Yes, but I have discovered something new."

"You have?"

He nods to the distance behind me. "You're needed at the threshold."

Four men stand at the threshold. Well, more like lean on or prop each other up. From here, they seem large and healthy, but wounded. I join the others who have gathered to help them to the main lodge. Thomas places himself under the arm of an injured man without noticing I'm under his other arm. He glances at me, knowing we hold two opposing views about the people who pass under our threshold.

We support the injured man; moving gently toward the lodge as Thomas digs for information. "Do any among you know the guard's movements or the processes the Trothsmen are following?"

He finds his information in one of the least injured who holds his hand out to Thomas. "Well met," he says, "Miran."

"Well met Miran, what can you tell me?"

"There's a rumor the Lord is unwell. Each time help is sent to the Hall, it's been thwarted."

"Thwarted?"

"They kill the nurses on the road to the Hall."

I speak over Thomas, but I must know. "Our nurses? How many? Who?"

"Two that I know of. They were from the kinship, ordered there by the Hall. They executed both at the checkpoints. Over some slight misdemeanor, I expect."

I ignore Thomas completely. "Who is doing this? Who's killing the nurses?"

Miran shakes his head. "No one knows who or which group is responsible for their deaths. It's just anarchy and lies back there. All the people are attacking each other and switching alliances, so often there's no way of knowing who anyone is. Uniform or not. Everyone scrambles for what they can get. For what they need to survive."

"But the guards," Thomas says, correcting me with a stare, "What are their movements? Is it true they plan to turn against the Hall?"

Miran nods with more enthusiasm than his words convey. "I've heard the rumors, but haven't seen the evidence." We're almost at the lodge when he speaks again. "But they're kinder in their searching for the Eariss. They trawl the ruins of the burned villages and the forests, hoping to claim the bounty. Even the Trothsmen search more earnestly, as if time is running out for them. They no longer torch as many villages, but move on. After all, if they destroy the villages, where will the Hall get their guards?"

"And their specific movements?"

"They're just beyond that mountain range. Heading this way. They have word what they seek is here."

Thomas glares at me with a mixture of anger and devastation. He'll want to fight, but he has no army. Not the one he wants, anyway.

Guthrie supports the man's arm as they move into the lodge so I can prepare bandaging and balms for the injured.

The sky has darkened and I don't remember which direction it came from or can sense the direction it travels. I gather splints and jars from the apothecary and try to ignore the hole that grows in my belly. Something is missing. Something isn't complete. But I don't have time for that now. I deliver the supplies into the waiting hands of the trainees and give brief instructions. Something draws me to the sky. Guthrie and a few of the others join me.

An ominous flash of lightning usurps the dark afternoon sky and turns the textured mountains to silhouettes. The storm is in control now. We can only see what it wants us to see. Sheets of light echo in the distance and form a gentle back-light to the height and length of the mountain ridge. I watch until the light echoes fade. Slowly beckoning my mind beyond the highest ridge. The wind picks up and makes my eyes water. But I don't turn away.

Listen, and trust what you know.

Oh Stars. I draw a deep breath and release it. It's me, isn't it? But I don't want it to be me, a complaint that falls out of my mouth purely for complaint's sake.

A sensation like silk cloth drapes my head and trails onto my shoulders, yet it glides not only outside of my body but inside, too. It acts as a muted fear, a challenge; a dare only to myself. You can't walk away from yourself when it's obvious. You can't dismiss it without dismissing yourself.

I resented people making decisions on my behalf, and right now, I dare myself to be responsible for my own call. My own life.

I quickly scan my body. There are no bees. I'm not at all scared, just accepting that this is the way it is. When answers come from a place of stillness, they bring truth with them.

Guthrie stares at me and my interest in the mountains. Does he know too?

I don't catch his eye; avoiding all eyes lest anyone see the truth in them. I am leaving soon; and once word is sent of my departure, they will be safe.

Guthrie checks his weather machine. "Ohh, this will be dastardly. Best get in what we can." He waves his hand to get Silas's attention. "Even the exposed items from the forge. Some of you help Silas, won't you?"

We scramble to bring in firewood and stack it in the corner of the lodge. "Will it be that bad?" I ask Guthrie as he passes.

He taps at a little glass container with crystals growing inside. "I don't know how long it will last. I know that seems odd coming from me, but this is an unusual storm; I haven't seen patterns like this before, and I'm not sure what it entails."

"Your machine out there. Could it be broken?"

"I suppose it's possible, but it's too dark to change anything now."

The main lodge is cramped with people eating and preparing for sleep. The injured rest propped up on rolled blankets. Field tools and forge instruments lay on the open floor and between beds.

I step over sacks to join Thomas just as Guthrie arrives holding our bowls. "Are you staying or going?"

We're just taking up precious space here. Thomas is deep in thought and shrugs. I'm not sure he even heard the question. I take the bowls from Guthrie's hands. "Is everything done here? Is everyone prepared?"

"Katteryn is still out counting and collecting her chickens. Everyone else seems fine."

"Arrow?"

"He's with the donkey in the stable behind the lodge. They'll be fine."

"Keep a window clear for Wren."

Guthrie smiles. "Will do."

Thomas and I eat in silence while the candle flame flickers against the cottage wall. The wind grows stronger and sings its mournful song in bursts, sometimes whistling through gaps we can't see. The rain won't be far away. He pushes the food around in his bowl. Silence is peaceful when hearts are connected, it's simply upsetting when there are words unspoken.

"We got everything into the lodge that Guthrie wanted to protect from the storm. Who would have thought we'd have so much room in that lodge?"

"Mm," he says.

I can't force him to believe the army is here right in front of us, and he can't convince me they're not. It seems unfair to launch another surprise on him while we're still not healed from the last one. I've had time to consider it. To prepare myself. My news may very well land on him like one of those flashes of lightning outside. The rain patters on the roof. Nothing too heavy; nothing concerning. I could leave the news until morning. I could tell him in the bright of day when he might be more distracted by his work. Yet each moment counts; the sooner I remove myself from Awenmell, and the rumors follow, the sooner everyone will be safe. I wait until he scrapes the last of the food from his bowl and reaches for his study books and parchments.

"The need at the Hall," I say. "The one Miran mentioned, it's a position that must be filled."

"Mm,"

"The nurse..."

He opens a parchment wider than his shoulders. I can't see his face, "Hm, mm." I don't know if he's listening or not.

I draw a cleansing breath. "It's me. I'm the nurse that needs to go."

The parchment crumples under his hands in his lap, and he stares at me for the longest time.

My throat constricts and my neck muscles tighten to a solid mass.

"No," he scoffs. "That won't be happening."

My words splutter, but I force them out. "But they need a nurse. I'm well trained... the Mystery—"

"Send someone else."

"But I really feel—"

"Send someone else!" he yells and thrusts his beloved parchment to the ground.

I move to pick it up but recoil, concerned that touching his work might cause another outburst.

Thomas paces the small distance between the hearth and door, shaking his head.

I draw in a jagged breath. "Would you at least listen to my words?"

"You jest! Tell me you jest! I thought the most doltish thing you could come up with was that bunch of misfits being an army, but you've surpassed yourself here, you really have. You heard Miran. It's a mess out there. You think you're just going to wander through it all? Stupid! It's impossible; there are Trothsmen actively looking for you." He shakes his head. "Not to mention guards, disease, wild animals. The paths are treacherous, people are desperate. What if you're found or killed before you make it to the Hall? What would be the point of that?"

"I imagine there would be no point if that happened."

"You stand between Feeney and everything he wants. That man is true to his word. We can hide you and protect you here."

Guthrie's burns remind me no one is safe. "Miran mentioned they know I'm here. If you send word I have left, they may leave you all alone. Tell Katteryn; I'm sure she knows who to tell for the best coverage." I meant it as a gentle jest, but Thomas is nowhere near smiling.

"You'd be out there with nothing."

"But you'd all be safe here." A sudden inspiration bursts from my mouth. "Saved by blood, the crown of fire!"

Thomas grits his teeth. "What?"

"He can't kill me, that's what the song says. It's my blood. If he kills me, the laws change, control moves outside the Hall."

"That won't matter anymore, there're no laws operating out there!"

"But the scroll says—"

"What don't you understand? You've heard his version of the Crown of Fire song. People sing a children's rhyme to remind themselves to hunt you. Hunt you! And you want to walk into the thick of it?" Thomas smashes his fist onto the table. Candlelight flashes against the walls, bowls rattle, and I jump in my seat. "You'd be sacrificing yourself? Why would you do that? He points a stern finger at me, "This can't be right!" He shouts over the boom of thunder that rolls above our heads. "If you're hearing this from the Mystery, you're hearing it wrong!"

Thomas paces and I consider his words. He's let me know what to expect and more. Why would he think I *choose* this? Well, I am choosing it, aren't I? To stay is not an option anymore, and I'll travel to the last place they'll look for me. "Awenmell will be fine under your care." He opens his mouth, but I continue. "Guthrie is advancing in age; he can't do it alone. You know that."

"You're going alone? That beats all. I imagined you going with this useless bunch for an army, but you're traveling alone. Of course, you are, because that is truly insane." He waves his hands in mock surrender. "Wait, wait... but don't you believe *they're* the Eariss?"

"I do. But Feeney doesn't know that. Better I move away from them while his focus is on me."

"And you said you're just a catalyst."

"Being a catalyst does not absolve me from playing my part in this war, and this is my part."

He stares at me with such unapproachable anger and disbelief that I find myself offended. It's easy to find the Mystery in quiet times, the deepest part of the stream, when all is quiet and still. Can I sense the Mystery and drop my shield in stressful times? Can I separate myself from what's going on around me to truly listen? I check in with my body. All is calm. There's a little agitation, but I'm not panicked and reacting to his behavior. My feet feel the ridges of the flagstones under my feet. I can move in and out of our quarrel without getting caught up in it. I can move to the depths without being affected by the splashes and turbulence on the surface. Thomas's face flushes with anger. I wish he could see what I see. "Oren would say—"

"Oren is just a child! So you think your life nothing now, to lay it out. To offer it to Feeney on one of the Hall's fine platters."

"I'm grateful for my life, but I've spent it always choosing the less painful option. Never having a choice. This time I will be the one making a choice,"

"Choose to die? Some choice!"

"It will be my choice and my consequences—"

"It's not only your consequences; don't you see that?"

The pain on his face pierces my heart like a poisoned dagger, spreading its ache to every part of my body.

"And what of Wren? Little Wren. You'll break her heart."

I have no answer for that one. I bite my bottom lip.

He latches onto my arm and drags me to the doorway. The rain pelts onto our faces. "Look out there. You would leave this? Destroy it as if it meant nothing?" His head is so close to mine that as he yells, his breath blows the loose tendrils of my hair across my face like a swing. "You'd walk away from everything we've built together to offer kindness to the place that tried to ruin you and now wishes you dead? They're coming, and you're running, like usual."

Water streams down my face, and I spray it as I speak. "No, I'm trusting, it's different."

"You can't do it, Ash! I forbid it. And you know what? You said my soul would be safe with yours. Well, it's not, is it?"

I have no answer for that one either. It eats at my insides. That he believes I am purposefully causing him this pain. I don't know how to make it easier for him. I don't know what balm to apply.

"You know what you are, then?" He shouts above the pelting rain and storm. A flash of lightning shows the area around the cottage. "You're nothing but a liar!"

Another flash and boom shakes Awenmell. We raise our drenched heads to Katteryn, standing a short distance away. In the echoing light, she stands soaked from head to toe, a chicken under her arm and eyes growing ever wider.

Thomas releases my arm and closes the door on Katteryn's bouncing eyebrows. Our quarrel, and the labels Thomas assigned me, will spread throughout the main lodge in moments.

I drip by the closed door while Thomas paces and drags his hands through his hair. What now?

What to do with the churning of emotions inside me. The pain of hurting Thomas, the embarrassment of Katteryn's gossip, the realization that I didn't fold in the face of accusations and adversity for the first time in my life. And it was my staunchest supporter who undermined me. I might never have expected it, but I understood it. The Mystery is now my support, and this is another edge. Do I stand with my arms outstretched to this challenge, or curl myself away from the growth it offers?

Thomas grunts, and his frustration with me is etched in every step back and forth across the width of the cottage. He stops and sucks air in through his teeth. "How am I supposed to keep you safe when you're determined to walk straight into a trap? You're a dolt, Ash. A complete and utter dolt. This can't be right. Oren fills your head with this nonsense when we should fortify and prepare for our attack." He leans over me at the door, his hand on the wall above my head, but I don't feel at all comforted by his closeness. I'd never noticed how powerful he was before, because I'd never needed to be wary of his strength. "Will you stay safe, here, with me? Will you keep to my demands?"

I can barely inflate my lungs. Any expansion makes them feel like brittle shells that might implode at any moment. I force the words from my mouth, using all my available oxygen, yet they drop from my lips in an inconsequential whisper. A whisper light as a feather, rich with power, and made heavy by the utter sadness at the consequences that my words will bring to us all. Like the birth of something new ripping its way through my body.

"No Thomas, I will not."

I hold my breath and open the door a crack. Thomas mumbles in his sleep and rolls over. On the horizon, the dull gray of dawn peeks through the last of the storm clouds. Guthrie's machine must've been broken after all. Thomas rolls to his back and I hold my breath again and wait for his breathing to fall into its rhythmic pattern. I reached out for him during the night, my fitful sleep punctuated by the points we did or didn't make in our quarrel. Yet he recoiled from my touch even while asleep, as if our closeness might somehow poison him. The door doesn't creak as I open it; it must be the way I clench my jaw. If we must force ourselves through this pain of disagreement, I need to know my motivation. Maybe he's right; I'm not hearing properly, but then again, all this churning and uncertainty could be the horror he's dumped straight onto me, his fear and angry words plastered over me like thick mud.

Arrow seems ghost-like in the mist. He lifts his head and walks toward me, just as eager for a run as I am to get away and clear my thoughts. Is that Guthrie? A shape moves about near the main lodge. His gait gives him away and I raise an arm in greeting, which he returns. No need to worry about Thomas waking and not finding me now. I walk at Arrow's shoulder, passing quietly under the threshold, and mount once we're on our forest track. The air is foggy and heavy from the night before, almost as if the storm has some unfinished business. It hangs like a sensory blanket over the valley where there's an entire world under there that can't be seen. On this ride, I used to be able to see far in the distance, now I can't see a single thing other than this moment. I guess that's the point.

Arrow charges into the warm fog, and his muscles radiate strength and trust in his abilities. A little fog won't slow him. He dodges and weaves with precision, snorting delight at his movement. He thunders along the forest track and I close my eyes as we leave everything else where it belongs. The energy of the argument cracks and breaks away from my body, and Arrow's constant pounding and weaving shakes off its residue, leaving me light again and clear enough to hear.

I keep my head down, wary of low branches and needing to be close to his joy and instinct. My mind closes to everything but this moment. There is no Awenmell, no Thomas, no Hall, no unrest, no guests. Only the thumping of Arrow's hooves into the earth, the wind dragging my hair behind me, and the quiet and stillness deep within the Mystery. It never left, places no pressure on me; it is just here, loving me. There are no words, only peaceful communion.

Arrow takes his time slowing down. When he's done charging, he gallops for a while, eases into an amble, and then walks. I move light branches away from me as we pass through a thicket. I don't know where we are, but Arrow does. I part some more hanging vines and we enter a clearing; I squint into the lighter morning. Heavy clouds still sheet parts of the sky, it's not bright but still a considerable contrast to the forest. Both contrasts are good. They complement each other. Sunny days, cold and rainy days; they're both good for a purpose, and each is not without the other. Arrow walks the edges of the clearing and I compare this clearing with its just right amount of color and breeze and refreshment, with the stark stones of Brennyn Hall, dark, cold, and merciless. Without the turmoil of the argument in me, it's easier to see that after any storm, no matter how tumultuous, there's always a new morning. Will Thomas and I be able to look at this new morning together? Can we push through the bramble fence to reach the lush field on the other side?

The rhythm of Arrow's steady walk around the clearing lulls me into introspection. The answers are always inside, in the silence.

There is no doubt. I heard correctly.

But it's different now. It's one thing to make a grand gesture, to stand on a cliff and be beholden to a new life; quite another to live the reality of those vows. Something old has to give way to the new.

It's all around me; this 'giving way'. It's in the old trees and the new; everything changing form. Rain to rivers, leaves to earth, nothing ever really stays the same, it's always in some kind of process, some kind of cycle. I wonder what would happen if the rain refused to become the river, the old branch refused to rot into the ground?

What if I refused to go?

"I could do it, you know," I call to the Mystery. I've done it before. Shut myself down so hard that no one would know what I'm feeling inside. I could stay. Keep Thomas happy and ignore what I know. The thought grabs at my heart and squeezes tight. I suck air into my lungs. "See? I can breathe like this." I could probably live like this. My heart would beat, and I would breathe, and I would eat, and I would find some way to dull the pain. Arrow plods the edges of the clearing and a cool breeze pushes the grasses to one side and then back again. The Mystery lets me answer my own dilemma. "But I'd just be swapping one Hall for another, wouldn't I? I'd be raising my shields and hiding behind them when I've worked so hard to put them down."

Which world do I want to live in? It's my choice. This constricted one, where I play a role for others, or one that's so expansive anything is possible, yet also unknown and risky, where I feel alive.

"I get to choose which world I live in?"

You choose every day.

I suppose I do. We all do. It hides in the way we speak to each other, in our attitudes and actions. But choosing despite the cost is another edge. What of this cost Mystery, the one where you ask me to give up all I know, all I love?

Arrow halts and rain clouds break above us with no announcement. No storm, no rumble, more like a release of something held for too long and poured out all at once in a deluge. He stays still beneath me, and I don't feel any urge to nudge him under cover. And so we stand while the rain drenches us, and misery and forlornness soaks through me on the same path. I don't send my misery away or try to lighten it. In time, it cloaks me and teaches me. It shows me my pain of being misunderstood, rejected, and my fear of compliance. The sting of being unsupported and the threat of being made outcast. Once again, I grieve for believing I was strong, but I am not. My life thus far has led me to this moment. Rain trickles from my head, along my jawline and drips onto my clenched hands that hold Arrow's mane.

"Is this all I am? Who am I without another's support?" I think back to Martha's admonishment. "Who am I when I'm alone? When there's nothing?"

You? You're the Ash of Awenmell.

I think about what might lie ahead, "Will that be enough?"

It always has been.

It's quiet for a while. I don't hear the rain or the trees, just my breath and the painful thumping of my heart.

My hands release Arrow's mane and stretch out to my sides. Only I'm not flying in search of escape this time, this time I surrender. My tears mingle with the raindrops losing themselves in something bigger. Just like my hope that my choice to return will make everything better somehow. Everything. Awenmell, Thomas, the unrest. If I trust and listen. If I surrender. Grief catches in my throat, and I nod my acceptance that this action may shorten my life. The alternative is something I can't live with anymore. I won't be untrue to my heart again, whether my future is delightful or terrible. I have already paid enough.

This intention holds me in place. An unmovable anchor. Nothing will move me. A nervousness flips my stomach upside down. At least I hope nothing will move me.

Mystery?

I am here.

Is surrender folding?

No, folding is forced surrender, it's where you stop fighting because of an overwhelming force. The repercussions force you to betray yourself.

Surrender due to wisdom isn't folding then? It's not forced, but offered; it's considered an easier way. Still sounds like a fine line to me.

If you're confused, the question to ask is, 'Are you betraying yourself? Are you betraying your soul?'

I see the difference now.

Arrow moves off toward home. Yes, it's time to head back. Back to Thomas, back to choices that I've made but not made public. We walk back through the forest and I replay events and conversations in my head. Moving from this moment with Arrow, into the realms of the Mystery, into the past with Thomas, and back again. I'm still disturbed that I thought I wasn't as strong as I thought I should be. If I can be strong now, why couldn't I before?

Mystery, where did my strength go? Was it hiding?

It didn't go anywhere.

Doesn't seem that way to me.

Your strength went where it was needed. You used incredible strength to armor yourself against your life. Huge metal plates that you held in place to protect yourself. It was exhausting, but you did it.

Metal plates, like the Trothsmen's shields?

It's safe to drop your armor now.

If I drop this armor you speak of, won't I be open to attack?

But your safety is no longer in the armored walls, is it?
No, it's in us.
What if I do it wrong? What if people die?
You always manage to consider others before yourself.
You didn't answer my question.
I'm aware of that.

Everything is sopping wet. Me, Arrow, the fields and fences. Awenmell received the drenching too, and the excess water sits in pools and slides across the already primed surface on its way to lower ground. Many faces, safe under the cover of the lodge eaves, watch me return Arrow to the field. Thomas looks up from outside our cottage and waits there as I approach. I suppose it's a good sign. If he wanted to avoid me, he had plenty of time to move. I slosh my way to our door and try to find the balance between protecting myself and reading his mood. Feeling for something that isn't too tender to begin a conversation.

"I wonder what causes the weather to flip-flop like that?"

He makes no response.

I squeeze drips from my hair in the doorway. "Something far away I expect, just making itself known, here and now."

Thomas follows me into the cottage and watches as I change into dry clothes.

"So, you've come to give your confession, have you? You know, before you die."

"I don't plan on dying, but come to think of it — yes. I don't want to leave Awenmell without making my statement to you. Will you accept it?"

His silence is like a blow to my gut. Hearing a soul's confession is a duty beyond clan alliances, beyond stations, beyond any distinction I can think of. It's considered an honor, and he's... he's deciding! I can always go to Guthrie if I must. It's just I don't want to. I want Thomas.

"You've considered the future then?" he asks.

I nod and pull my undershirt into place. "I assume you have too. Does your other work press you for time, or can we talk now?"

Thomas opens the door and watches people walk past the cottage, pretending not to watch our activities and conversations. "I believe Katteryn has made sure they will leave us alone for the time being, but I'm thinking that a walk might be in order."

"Agreed."

He leaves me to fasten my soggy shoes and tie my dripping hair into more manageable plaits.

Thomas waits at the threshold. He leans his back onto one of the poles and watches a worker in a far field. I can feel all of Awenmell's eyes watching me. What did Katteryn tell them? It would've been nice to have him walk beside me like we did at the Kinship. Perhaps he didn't think of that, perhaps I didn't think of that. Besides, I have nothing to prove on this walk.

He pushes himself from the pole as I approach. "Which way?"

When every decision feels like a battle for power, a wrong word or look can be volatile. I push against my learned reaction to defer. "Let's take this track."

Thomas plods behind me and doesn't speak until the track dissipates into leaf litter and the forest opens up and we stroll among the trees a distance apart.

He alternates between watching where he's going and the branches that sway above him. "So, you're leaving then?"

"I am."

He nods as we continue on, deeper into the forest, the thickness of the undergrowth causing us to walk closer together. He holds a branch out of my way. "You're sure?"

"I am."

He nods again, keeping his thoughts to himself. We walk on in silence, past the birch that grows on an angle, and over the dip in the ground that always has a skinny puddle of water along its length. "I don't understand any of this," he says, "But there is one thing I'm certain of."

"There is?"

"You won't be stopped." His smile is forced and his eyes cannot betray the heartbreak that feeds on us both. The world trips and halts its maddening rush. It sucks life from everything. There is no color, no sound, no nothing. Just his eyes that asked to look into mine every day of his life. Just this moment where our eyes tell each other a thousand stories, and this agreement, this acceptance of the future, binds our hearts into a dull ache and dumps them on the ground in front of us.

His voice wavers but doesn't crack. "But why Ash? You vowed you'd never set foot in that place again."

"Vows are powerful, but they form in strange ways. They're only kept alive by the power behind them. I have no wish to honor the fear that created the vow and keep it alive as if it held power over me. I'm no longer the person who made that vow, it doesn't apply to me anymore. We're allowed to grow larger than the promises we made to ourselves."

"But our vows? The ones we made to each other?"

"We made our vows in love and openness, didn't we? Why would they be at risk?"

"They won't exist if you're dead."

My jaw clamps shut. No, no, I expect they won't. Thomas sighs and shakes his head; I wager he's wishing he'd kept his thoughts inside. It feels like we're back to the start again. Not that I blame him. Someone else's decisions impacting your life; it was my daily occurrence.

The sky has almost cleared to blue above us. Yet it feels like last night's storm is still passing through both of us. Lightning flashes here and there. The storm front might have passed, but it still leaves the aftermath to deal with. Like these broken twigs and leaves all over the ground. Fresh and green instead of dried and brown. It looks out of place, like freshness pulled into decay before its time. I won't be sharing that with Thomas right now.

I shuffle my feet through the leaves and observe our emotions at work; and our reactions. A small stream bubbles nearby, and I find myself at its shallow bank. "Storms are tempestuous, aren't they?"

"I imagine Guthrie might say they are one and the same."

I smile at his correction. "But they're needed."

He squeezes his lips together and gives no indication of whether he agrees.

"There's always something under a storm. Like the one that passed us last night. It was created somewhere else but showed up here in its fury." I pat the ground. "Come sit with me."

The stream is narrow. If I reach with my legs, I can almost touch the other side with my toes. A little way upstream, the water is shallower and babbles over the rounded pebbles that bounce the water along its course. "Put your feet in here, it's a little deeper."

I was expecting some kind of argument, some snide remark about the wet ground, but he removes his boots, folds up his trousers and dutifully dunks his feet into the stream. We talk about rapids, and rivers, and the shallow babbling brook upstream. And we talk about the water that's in front of us, quiet and deep enough to soak ourselves almost to our knees. We talk about splashes and the stillness that waits under the surface.

"Oren taught you this?"

I shake my head. "But he knows the stillness as well as I do."

"I do understand what you're saying, you know?"

"I know you understand, but living it... that is something else entirely."

He frowns and tucks some loose hair behind my ear. "Do you understand what you're asking me to do? My world is falling away from me and you're asking me not to grasp at it, not to make any attempt to save it. Do you blame me? If you go, I will lose you."

"If I stay, I will lose myself."

Our foreheads rest together. We're both fighting for the same thing, but in a different manner. Maybe a moment in unison will bring about a new answer. But no answers come. Just because a decision is hard, doesn't mean it's wrong. My feet look oddly shaped in the water, and the current gently pulls at them and reminds me I can make any decision I want.

Thomas pulls away. He's not attacking, just forlorn. "Tell me, how is any of this for the good? What do I put in the book now? That you rode off and left us?"

"Your story will be as you imagined. It will tell the truth; whatever that turns out to be."

"And what is your truth?"

"Leaving Awenmell is how I will protect it."

"And how do I protect you?"

"Perhaps you don't."

"Well, that makes perfect sense!"

"What are you talking about?"

"Every time Ash. Every. Single. Time you've been in danger, I've failed to protect you."

That can't be true. I've always felt so secure. The bandits, the Tallefix, Brenn, Fur-Vest.... maybe he is right. "You didn't fail. Sometimes you simply weren't there, there's a difference."

"Some protector of the Eariss. Now you want me to sit on my hands and watch you wander into the distance."

"The vine."

"What?"

"The vine. When we had to swing across the ravine. I was terrified I'd end up among all that bramble, remember? And you caught me and nearly fell in there yourself."

"That was nothing, the strength was in the vine, not in me."

"But that's when I needed you and you were there for me, not just then, but many times. Not in valiant deeds, but in everyday ones. Your salvation isn't found in keeping me safe. You've never failed. Consider this Thomas of Feldston... what if it's not your task?"

"Don't be a dolt. Of course, it's my task."

"You're a scribe—of that we are sure—but what if it's not your role to protect me? What if the reason you fail miserably at it, is that it's not what you're meant to be doing in the first place? You're putting all your energy into something that you *assume* you should be doing, not what you should *truly* be doing."

He shakes his head as he tries to grasp what I'm saying.

I bump his shoulder with mine lightly. "When we met, what was your only ambition?"

"To find the Eariss."

"What was mine?"

"To be safe."

"Have you not fulfilled your role?"

"And this... running off... somehow fulfills yours?"

"I hope so. I firmly believe the answer lies in listening, not in assumptions."

"Listening?"

"And trusting what I know."

"You *know,* don't you? About all of this."

"I do."

With that, he honors me with a firm nod. We sit in companionable silence, the trickles of the water over the stones, birdsong, and splashes of light coming through the leaves and branches above us keeping our senses company while we sort through our emerging feelings with sighs and smiles. I rest my head on his shoulder. I will leave tomorrow, but for now, tomorrow is a million road markers away. We lay where we are, and just for a moment, it's like it always was. Safe in his arms and wanting nothing more than the best for each other, but this time with heavy hearts. I always thought uncertainty made anything possible. I'm sure it still does, but it can also make everything excruciating. I can't make this better, or make it go away. My cheek rests on his shirt and I close my eyes and try to trap this memory and every sensation into my mind.

He takes my hand in his and matches our binding scars. "Do wishes work?" he whispers.

"I don't know. Maybe sometimes they do."

"Because I wish we were back in the forest together. Before Awenmell, before there was anyone else but us."

"I wish that too."

And so we pretend our wishes are granted just for now, and there is no Awenmell, no tomorrow. We blend into one in comfort and peace as though no one else exists in this world.

Just Thomas and me and the forest once more.

⁂

What do you say to people when you might not return?

I can't remember my last words to Eshnae, or hers to me. It's all a blur. Martha's words live like an ocean inside me; the right ones rise to the surface when I need them, yet I still can't recall our last conversation. Her words would have meant something, though. They always did. But we didn't know we were saying goodbye. I wonder which way is better? Maybe there is no better. Just what is.

People jostle past me in the lodge yard. It seems the whole of Awenmell is busy with preparations for my departure. Young children sweep through the busyness like flocks of little birds. The energy in the air has them all unsettled. Maybe Thomas was right about them. They journeyed so hard to arrive here, only for me to walk out on them. What do I say? How would they even understand? Ugh. How many forced goodbyes have they said already? Maybe Thomas is right. They'll tell stories of me in their future. *I met her once,* they'll say. *She left us all alone.*

A little hand tugs on my skirts. "It's true? You're really leaving?"

Sets of wide eyes surround my waist; their murmuration halted mid-flight by a simple question.

I hug each in turn. "The people that search for me won't find me here, and you can continue on at Awenmell. Be safe. I'll find my way back to you as soon as I can."

That didn't sound too profound. Or anything like Martha's wisdom. She made the word *'stay'* sound magical and important. Yet it was enough for my little starlings and they return to their chasing, dodging, and turning as one.

"Here," Guthrie says, and wraps the black Trothsman's cape around me. "This should do nicely. It won't protect you from the ire of the rebels, but it should afford you some space as you travel."

We used its darkness to protect the seeds for the new harvest and my hands would run along it, feeling its weight. The scent of the seeds is still in the cloth, even though they've washed it for me. I smile. I've never smelled a more comforting perfume. "Thank you." I tug at my plaited hair. "But this. Any ideas on how I won't be seen?"

"From now, I fear you won't have a choice. But this may help." He beckons to Katteryn, who lifts her skirts in her rush to be of service.

I try holding the plaits above my head. "Should I cut it off?"

"No. Leave the Crown of Fire. You won't have to tell people who you are, just be who you are, they'll see it. You're going into dark places, Ash. Your task is to light the torch and hold it high so it illuminates all around them; not to be blamed for what they see in front of them."

"When did you get so wise, old man?" His smile is generous and kind and so unlike the 'smartest man in Sirban' we met all those seasons ago. His night terrors are few now, but he uses his understanding of them to comfort those who still battle for sleep. "Guthrie, I think it's time to—"

"Yes, yes, I know. Lower the dosages of my dwale."

"We need you clear-headed now. They need you clear-headed, and so do I."

He pats my hand as Katteryn puffs her arrival beside us. "It shall be done."

Thomas passes us, his hands filled with vials, bottles, and packages of herbs and tinctures that I hope to take with me. He secures them in the bags that drape over Arrow's hind and returns to the apothecary for more. He doesn't look for me; not once.

"So, do you think it will work?" Katteryn waves cloth in my face.

"Sorry."

"The cap, put the cap on."

Our hands fight with each other as we push my plaits under the cap. Katteryn takes the long back ties and wraps them over the cap and pins it in place, then steps back to Guthrie so they can consider their work. Katteryn's head tilts slightly to one side and Guthrie rests his chin in his hand. "We'll need the wimple," he says.

"Exactly what I was thinking," Katteryn pulls a length of cloth from her belt and strides at me.

Guthrie leaps to my side. "It'll afford you more protection."

"Exactly what I was thinking," she assures me. "Here, hold this on your chin."

I try to listen to all of Katteryn's instructions about tying the wimple. Where to pin it. How to check it covers all my hair. But my mind seeks any glimpse of Thomas, and I nod to instructions I have no intention of hearing.

"There, done," she announces.

"Thank you, Katteryn." My fingers fumble around the wimple on my head, and prick my finger in the process. At least I know where the pin goes now.

Guthrie follows my gaze to the apothecary and considers me for a moment. "Why is it that you're returning to the Hall in the face of mortal danger, yet I feel I've the more worrisome task?"

I smile at him, but it's only my lips that bother to pretend.

Guthrie pulls the cape's black hood over the wimple and makes encouraging sounds as he positions it. "Is that comfortable?"

I move my head around inside the hood. Safety isn't always comfortable. "It's fine, thank you."

Guthrie and Katteryn discuss the virtues of my costume, and Wren surprises me with a quick circling dash around me and settles on the fence behind them. I pass between their discussion, eager to be close to her lightness. Her eyes are always so kind, so forgiving. A sweet smile stretches across her face, as if she knows something I don't. "Ash," she says. Her voice is musical; innocent as the purest crystal and soothing all at the same time. She glances this way and that, and remains calm despite the surrounding commotion. She shuffles herself along the fence to make room for Oren. "Oren says this is how you will keep us safe. That's enough for me."

I don't want to blink. I don't want to wake up and find I'm imagining this. "That's enough for me too." It will have to be. "Do you have a name?" I made the mistake of labeling Silas, and I don't want to do the same again.

"They called me lots of things. I don't need them anymore. My bees say I'm safe here."

"I'm glad."

Oren nudges her shoulder, and she holds her hand out to me. "Well met," she says as my hand reaches hers. It's soft and wise and trusting. "My name is Wren."

They take flight from their fence rails amid giggles and race each other to the forge. Her blue cape growing smaller as they approach Silas. He watches from the open side of the forge and wishes me well with a wave above his head. I'm so pleased he chose for himself how involved he wanted to be in this moment.

"Ready?" Guthrie calls from Arrow's side. They've led him from the lodge yard to the path that leads to the threshold, and he greets me with a toss of his head.

"Now," Guthrie begins as I prepare to mount. "You've food in cloths here, there's ale in that cask there, an extra blanket—" He smiles and his burgeoning tears creep their way into the creases of his eyes. Mine sting, too. His arms embrace me so tightly I fear I won't draw breath again. "Here," he says, and ties one of his most elaborate scroll ribbons around my wrist. A father's blessing. He kisses my forehead and gestures for me to mount and then wipes at his face.

My height advantage from the saddle lets me offer a gentle smile to all around me. This is no celebration. Of all the faces I scan, the ones calling encouragement and kind words, before me and behind me, none is the face I'm desperate to see.

I search again through the crowd.

Do I wait for him or leave now?

Perhaps this is one of those goodbyes that.... just is what it is.

Time slows while everyone at Awenmell waits and watches me intently. Waiting for me to do something. This is when I'm supposed to encourage Arrow on and leave, but I'm stuck. I'm not laden by all the rich gifts they've given; their understanding, love, well wishes, Guthrie's blessing, and the memory of Wren's voice. I'm trapped by my desperation for a gift I can't force and a disappointment that forms a gnawing ache in the deepest parts of my heart.

The reins feel sturdy in my hands, or perhaps it's me that feels sturdier having something to hold. "Thank you all." My thighs tense, ready to urge Arrow on and the reins tug from my hands.

Thomas appears next to Arrow's head and offers him a scratch on the nose. "Come along, Old Arrow," he says, and the beast follows his directions. Thomas offers no smile or encouragement and pulls the reins from my hand. I dismount to walk alongside him.

Are we going to walk in silence all the way to the threshold? My heart still hurts and I don't feel much like talking, anyway.

Thomas checks behind him to be sure we're not followed. Once satisfied at our distance from the lodge, he speaks.

"Don't let him see that binding scar. It might mean nothing to you, but it'll mean the end of his plan for him."

My thumb rubs the scar along my smallest finger. It's still bumpy but numb. I'd always thought it meant more than some kind of contractual obligation, but he's right. This scar drags Thomas right into Feeney's affairs. If it's true that Feeney wants the Hall and the power that goes with it, his problems won't end with killing me. He's most dangerous when he's disappointed. My body shivers, remembering his rage. Why am I doing this again? *Awenmell.* I'm keeping Awenmell safe. I breathe in determination and use it to stand tall; it pushes my panic away, or at least delegates it to the background. It's easier to feel strong when there's a specific task to focus on.

"If you come across his book…"

Not the book again. Feeney's abysmal book of law. Will his obsession with it never end?

"Promise me you won't look inside."

"It's not like I can read it, can I?"

"Well, if he offers to read it to you, decline."

It seems a fair request; I nod. Not that I ever imagine Feeney reading me a bedtime tale. I go cold at the thought. "If I come across it, would it be best to destroy it?"

He stops at the threshold. "Yes. If you can do so safely, and haven't opened it, destroy that damned thing."

Good. Another intention. Although not as important as keeping Awenmell safe, it's another one just the same. Get the book; destroy it.

So, this is it. This moment of farewell or meet-again. When you don't know what something is, how can you relate to it, how can you respect it? I place my hand on his chest, his heartbeat echoes into my palm. "I love you, Thomas of Feldston. You will always live within my heart. Even in death, your soul will be with mine."

"That's not comforting, Ash."

What can I say that's comforting? How can anything comfort us? Doesn't the pain you feel only show how much you care for something? Maybe it's not meant to be 'comforted away' but felt in all its brutal glory. I cling to him, eyes closed. His heart beats by my ear now, I draw in his scent, feel his warmth and accept the kisses he places upon my head. The moment lingers. I understand that from the instant I let go, I will be desperate to return to his arms again. He kisses me tenderly, and we savor every moment until Thomas pushes me away.

"This is not how the story is meant to end. I wish I knew how to—I need to stop the storm."

It was a long time ago we discussed our inability to stop storms. When we first met, in fact. How strange that he brings it up now. If anything, I thought a new battle strategy had overcome him. "I don't believe you can. And as with any storm, it will be good for some, and not so good for others; but always needed."

"You're the storm Ash. *Why would people wail that a storm was over?*"

I close my eyes for fear that eye rolling will infuriate him.

"Guthrie said it. The night he first showed us the scroll. Called it whimsy and said why would people wail that a storm was over."

"So?"

"I want you to hear what I'm saying to you," he takes my shoulders, "Martha said *you* were the storm, do you remember?"

I was once desperate for him to understand me; I'd do anything. Now it doesn't matter if he understands or not; only that I do. I won't plead anymore. "At this moment, I am not a storm. I am a magnet. And I draw the Trothsmen closer to Awenmell." I position myself to mount Arrow as he launches into another speech.

"This isn't bravery, it's stupidity. Doltish behavior if ever I've seen it."

"I don't wish to be brave. I wish to be true."

His eyes dart, searching for a new topic, panic rising in his voice. "You should never besiege a walled city."

"I won't be besieging it, Thomas. I'll be inside." I lean forward to gather the reins, and his agitation surges. He slaps his hand to my thigh and grips so hard each finger stabs pain into my leg. I don't wince at the warning. I know my choices break both our hearts.

I know this is the point where I back down, give in, deny myself... a forced surrender. This part is familiar, like an old friend. It's more comfortable to give in; it's what I know. It's what I do. What I *used* to do. "Your behavior is your choice, not mine. A blessing would have been more welcome."

Thomas relaxes his grip on my thigh. "No!" he shouts.

All movement behind us at the lodges comes to a halt. He certainly got their attention. My face heats with humiliation. I imagine Katteryn's eyebrows dancing, but all I see is Thomas's face, as desperate and heartbroken as I feel.

I know I can stop this pain. As simple as if I had a magic elixir that made the world well again. I can dismount from this horse, dismount from this idea, and answer his wishes. Of course, I *want* to stop his pain; I feel its intensity too. But there's another crucial ingredient, a spice that insists on transforming this want into a form of torture.

No matter how desperately I want to ease the hurt; I need to do this; I need to leave.

And so, I sit tangled between the desperation of the want, and the compulsion of the need.

A want is easy, and once succumbed to quickly soothes its sharp and painful edges.

A need is something baser, something deeper, something primal.

A want stings.

A need aches.

A want grasps for attention, then moves on to the next desire.

A need refuses to let go.

A want is fickle, gets tossed around and changes from day to day.

A need is in the bones, and retires to sleep in the marrow. It might never be satisfied. Still, it remains.

A want feels safe and good, a personal reward.

A need doesn't care what the personal outcome will be.

Thomas is right. There's every chance this journey will kill me. Publicly perhaps, for some kind of entertainment; Feeney gloating over my lifeless body. I can even imagine his words. *This is what happens when you disobey. Here is your hope. Your Eariss.* This uncertainty is not about some grand adventure. It's about trust, something I thought Thomas understood. "Trust isn't something you do. It's something found inside a relationship. I trust the Mystery because I have a relationship with it."

"Some relationships aren't worth trusting." He speaks to the ground this time, but at least he's not shouting.

"I agree with you."

A painful silence dwells between us. Our hearts are splintered and shattered, and there's no offer of repair in sight. With no repair, love leaks through cracks until there is nothing left. A ferocious ache overtakes my heart and I welcome my shields in protection. He raised his long ago.

"You were supposed to be the answer!" He growls the words more than speaks them. "Get down!" he shouts, "Stay. Stay and live!"

I sit stoic in the saddle. The lump in my throat won't let me speak. Every muscle seems frozen in time.

"Do what I tell you!" he shouts.

I have no words, nothing to leave him as a memory. This will have to do. I offer him a nod of respect that I have heard his wishes.

I squeeze my thighs into Arrow's belly and he dutifully moves me away from Awenmell, away from Thomas.

"Do what I tell you!"

And I disobey.

The path to Sirban is narrow and rocky, but Arrow is sure-footed. The track is just as Thomas and Guthrie described it; cut high into the side of the mountain and leads me upwards and toward the clearing where we first met Guthrie and his contraption. The treetops appear just like they did at Guthrie's home, too. Little moss-covered pebbles I try to pinch between my fingers. They weren't soft to land in, either. That was certainly an unceremonious dumping into our new life. Feels like a lifetime ago. How many lives do we live? I've just left one behind me to move into something new. It took a physical beating to get into that valley, and I feel like I've taken an emotional one to get out.

"Mystery, I didn't mean to cause him any pain."

You didn't hurt him; he hurt himself by expecting you to behave a certain way.

"He wanted me to deny my heart."

And when you didn't, he blamed you for how he felt. He fights himself, not you.

"Will he ever understand?"

We shall see.

Arrow's feet crunch into the stones and gravel. Their color changes as we rise. First it was the darker colors of the valley and now they merge into the cream-colored stones and rock of the high hill; of nearby Sirban. Crunch. Crunch. 'Your feet know the way'. That's what Oren said one morning in the field. I wondered what I was meant to do or how I was meant to get there. His reply was as sweet as every word from his mouth. "Remember how you got here? Your feet knew the way."

Did the others who left Awenmell follow their feet? Of course, they did. They took their knowing with them and their bravery.

Although *brave* is the last thing Thomas thinks I am. He made that quite clear. Too bad we disagree on what makes up bravery.

I think he takes it to mean forcing yourself into something you don't want to do at the insistence of something outside of you. To me, it's surrendering to my truth and not demanding it be one way or another. It could mean charging into battle, or it could mean walking into the vulnerable space that is 'shields down' where a heart-to-heart connection leads to understanding. Bravery is fighting side by side with your truth. And that's what they're doing; the ones who leave Awenmell to talk softly, and to shout from rooftops, they're fighting side by side with their truth wherever its passion leads them.

Nothing looks different in the clearing. The tree, the grass, and the road covered in cream rocks of all sizes. Arrow walks along the tracks flattened by cart wheels up the last rise toward Sirban. What? The gate's supposed to be here. That intricately carved gate, all that information... is exactly how Guthrie described his beloved Sirban. *Gone.*

Two blackened stumps hold place for the once dignified threshold. I dismount, remove my cape, and lead Arrow through the broken and deserted streets of Sirban. Homes have crumbled into piles of rubble, some patches of cream dare to show through the blackened char of fire, and yet some things remain unscathed; a section of fence here, a signpost there. Guthrie's home is broken and empty; wind whistles through broken windows and plunders the last of the dust and dried herbs that scatter across the floor. I place a rainwater pail at Arrow's feet. Blackened timbers form the outline of Donkey's old stable, and among the ashes I find pieces of Guthrie's contraption. I hold the lenses up to the sky, hoping it will act as a filter and allow me to see the Always Star. The one that promised stability; the one that seems to have forsaken Sirban.

Arrow follows me down the path to the market square. In my mind, I see the buildings as they once stood; how I sheltered in the shade of the one on the corner and ran my fingers along the bumpy edge of its low garden wall. Someone has scratched a large symbol into the stones of the square. It looks familiar; maybe it's one of Guthrie's strange letters. I step over it and all around it, but can't make sense of it, like any of the lines and dots in Guthrie's books, it feels like it's trying to teach me something, but I simply don't understand the lesson, lost somewhere between the knowing and the deciphering. It could be a—

Movement. There, behind that pile of rocks. I crane my neck to see around it. "Hello?" I call. A gray-haired head bobs around behind the rocks. "Err, well met?" I say and round the pile. Behind the cascade of stones lies a small house; well, part of one. Fallen stones form one side wall, and blackened timbers lie together to make up the roof. Little green sprouts rise from the decay and bounce happily in the sunshine. At least something good had come from the ashes. There's no fence for the yard, but a gate hangs askew on one hinge and forms the garden perimeter. On the other side of the gate, the crotchety old lady from the markets. I smile in remembrance.

She leans forward to consider me, studies my face until her eyes widen with recognition. "Oh, it's you again", she wags a dusty finger at me. The dirtied lace on her cuff jiggles along with the action. "If you're looking to be of service to the Sirbahn, Guthrie has left... along with all the other simpletons." She brushes at her ashen skirt and lifts her nose; the sun catches her spectacles. One lens is missing, the other cracked. "Only the most superior, the worthiest, have stayed." With the sweep of her hand, the gate falls at her feet. Her lower lip trembles, but still she refuses to acknowledge the surrounding bedlam. Her front door, if she had one, would face the old Hall of Records. What a sight to wake up to each morning.

"I'm assuming this is the Trothsmen's work?"

She rolls her eyes at me. "Of course, you clod." Her sigh is so loud it releases some dust from her hair, which she waves away as If I'd caused it. She tuts as I step towards her, as if being closer is some kind of major inconvenience. She places her folded hands on her sternum, holding her pious position in the dust.

I place my hand on hers, stand on tiptoe, and kiss her forehead.

"Stupid, stupid, girl," she whispers. Her tears run clean tracks down her dusty cheeks.

"Wait here," I paid little attention when Guthrie listed what he'd placed in Arrow's packs, but remnants of his conversation were returning to me. Here they are. Parchments and writing tools. If I'd known the quickest way to render a member of the Sirbahn speechless was to place some parchment in their hands, I would have done it long ago. "I know it's not much, but it's a beginning. You can start afresh. No need to sit in your ashes."

She nods, but there's no other sound, no other movements other than the tears tracking down her face.

"Mistakes are good for us..." Her eyes glare as if I've spoken the most offensive words in the land. Oh, I just did. "Mistakes are where we learn the most about ourselves; and our village."

Her eyes narrow and she holds the parchment rolls so tight they crumple in her hand.

"Write about the mistakes, don't cover them with perfection. If you give them air, we all learn, and those same mistakes won't be made again."

Her eyes move about while she considers my proposal. She focuses behind me, on the rubble of the Hall of records, then to her dusty garden, then somewhere inside herself, to memories old and new. "For a simple lower girl, you're quite easy to understand." she wipes at her tears with her apron and smears mud over her face.

According to the Hall, I'm meant to feel disdain for her; to find the lowly status of her once brilliant village something to mock, to jest at her misfortune. I'm expected to take my opportunity to make her feel worse. Seek revenge for the insults she hurled at me in the past. But I can't. Her heart is broken too. It lies here somewhere among the ashes, and she'll keep searching until she finds it and can give it life again. Her seed still waits for discovery. Charred and aching, but alive. She might even find time to acknowledge its presence now that its outside husk has been stripped away. She pushes past me and disappears among the maze of rubble; the parchments clenched tightly in her hand.

"Well, Arrow," I take his reins in my hand, "That was something Guthrie would describe as... hmm... telling. Or perhaps a potential radical stimulant," I mimic Guthrie as we move back toward his home, "More like a perfunctory apprehension proved wholly via positive causatum." My laughter hides how much I miss him already. "Is perfunctory even a real word?"

"It means done without thought." Eugenica stands outside Guthrie's home, her cream robes decidedly brown and tatted. Her voice tired but still as musical.

Without thought? Of course it does.

"Geerta said it was you, but I could hardly believe it. I had to come and see for myself."

Arrow and I halt on the road. "Here I am."

"Is it true what they say about you?"

"It turns out it's a bit more complicated than that." She nods, but it seems like I've bored her already. A light dust settles on everything in Sirban. I wipe my hands on my apron. How does she manage to make dust look ethereal? "Do you have enough food and water here? Geerta disappeared before I could ask."

"Traders stop by occasionally. There are only a few of us here, we do well enough." She focuses on Arrow and my packs. "Traveling? And dear Thomas isn't with you?" A single eyebrow raises in a graceful arc.

I want to lie. Didn't I just leave him in anguish and in need of comfort? "He's busy. In the valley. Working." I survey the village of Sirban and shake my head. "As are you, I see. Why did you stay; of all people?" *Of all people.* Why did I say that aloud? Am I deliberately trying to offend her? I need to keep my mouth shut.

"Someone had to stay. It's the ones you least expect who proffer themselves in trying times." Eugenica sizes me up. I don't feel as intimidated by her, but she watches me as if she's trying to work something out. She gestures to the rubble that was once Sirban. "And all of this? This was a message. There was a rumor, did you know? The Hall wanted the brown lower girl. But we scoffed. I mean, why would they want *you*? The Sirbahn made sure the Hall knew its folly... and then they were sure to remind us of ours."

"Where is everyone?"

"Dead. Or scattered. Sharing our knowledge before it can be taken forever."

I imagine the Sirbahn, engraving their wisdom into pots and scratching truths into mirrors, a new and novel way to protect rather than hoard their insights. All those brilliant minds no longer in the Hall's service. Many wonders await us, if we can work together, if we can survive.

Eugenica strokes Arrow's neck. She speaks softly, almost reflectively. "I've discovered something I should have seen before. I was blind and I'll admit it. We believed the Hall worked for us and protected us, while we focused on our learning and discoveries. But new knowledge scares them, and they attack what they don't understand. It's important they feel safe and in control, and this is how they make sure we will obey them and take comfort in what went before, and shy away from anything new." Geerta scurries from mound to mound, the parchments still safely tucked under her arm. "It's in every village. This conflict between those who welcome the new, who have been waiting for it, and those who are desperate for everything to return to how it was. But it can't possibly return. No matter how fearful we are, how can you unsee once your eyes are opened?"

I blink hard and hope she doesn't notice. Eugenica breaking with her tradition? Dissolving all she is to welcome the new? "This new way is frightening to those who only see the bad in change and aren't prepared to consider the good."

"Then that will be my task. To make the new palatable." I'd never noticed how a smile could be so determined before.

"I don't have more parchment. Perhaps you and Geerta could work together?"

"Old and new. Like a transition. I'd enjoy that."

"You are still Sirbahn. Be sure to record your insights accurately."

"There are no books left here. I expect the only one afforded exemption is that wretched book of law. One sided and patronizing."

"Like your old books?"

She releases Arrow abruptly. "You mean for us to forget?"

"We never forget. But we can rewrite the way we view anything. That in itself is new."

She nods and smiles at me as if she's discovered another wisdom and holds Arrow's reins while I mount. "I know better than to ask where you are headed, but if your plan is to disrupt them, I wish you well."

"I'm doing what I must do, just as you are. Turns out that's the only matter we need occupy ourselves with."

She squeezes my hand, and I look ahead down the road leading out of Sirban. I want to get away from here and the dust and dirtiness and pain, but I worry about what lies ahead. If the unrest has reached all the way to the mountaintop of Sirban, what might it have done to those on lower ground? I drag the cape towards me and secure it and begin to fumble my fingers over the wimple. They feel around the edges, pulling loose fabric over my curls.

"There's a stray bit there," she points, "Yes, there. You got it."

"Fare well, for all of us," I say.

"And you also," she replies, "May we all fare well."

A rrow stays to the cartwheel paths on the descending road from Sirban. Eventually, the cream gives way to darker stones and then the earthy scent of the lower lands brushed with grass and tree groves. It feels familiar here, even though I haven't traveled this part of the road before. I think it's simply the surrounding greenery; dry mountaintops won't ever feel like home to me.

There's so much you don't see on horseback; the way some grasses sprout from a centerpiece, like upturned spiders you can use as stepping stones on wet ground, or the way the breeze winds its way through a grove. It provides another perspective. What people see depends on where they view it from. The grass and breeze are still the same, but this time I'm observing it rather than being part of it. I wonder how differently I'd view the forest if I hadn't ever been deep inside it? Is this what all horseback riders see; something green over there, as they ride past? The road opens to a vast area of fields, and I pull the Trothsman's cape around me and ease Arrow into a gentle run. It's best to act like I have somewhere important to go.

I smell the salt in the air as the road forks to the left; that smaller road must lead to Ferce Point. We travel over a rise and pass another road marker before the air hints of death and I spy Ferce Point's walls in the distance. Their gleaming white perfection is gray and charred, and the image of broken mirrors fills my mind. It seems even the freshness of the waves on the point, no matter how unrelenting, can't wash away the sadness that hangs in the air.

Muscone's pots are worthless. So are their protective gates we simply walked through. The shiniest copper pots now lay in the mud. There's more glass on the ground beneath the windows of the once showy houses than the windows themselves. The houses appear to be burned at random. Destruction here, pillage there. I hope everyone escaped with their lives. I hope they all hold a black pot close to their chests, and that they're holding onto each other as they watch me cross their silent village square. A Trothsman's horse is a convenience when you want to be left alone.

The road out of Muscone narrows and passes between two steep hills. Wind channels through the pass at great speed and cools. I drop my head and let Arrow lead the way through the forming drizzle. The drizzle turns to larger droplets, yet not quite rain as we reach the other side of the pass. Rest and protection are in order. There were ruins in this area. I squint through the breaks in the forest, looking for shelter. There. Deeper in. I wheel Arrow toward the stone ruins set a distance back from the road. I wouldn't have seen them if I wasn't looking in earnest. I hope every other road traveler passes them by.

The stones sit low. Probably only a half wall of what was once here. But the ferns and vines form a type of roof that covers it nicely. I could set a fire on the other side and it wouldn't be seen. It might be smelled, though. Fair enough. No fire today. A tall oak spreads its cover wide over what I imagine was the yard of this little cottage. It would have looked pretty in its day. Being tangled and hidden means it's not a threat to the Hall; there's no need to destroy quiet compliance.

A shrub shakes. It's not an animal. My heart pounds in my ears and every muscle tenses and transfers the energy to Arrow. His ears prick high on his lifted head. How far from the road am I?

"Mystery?"

Remain alert; not fearful.

Alert. For what? Not fearful... you mean they fear me? I've done nothing to—oh.

I untie the cloak and let it fall from my shoulders onto Arrow's flank, and hold my arms out to my sides. "I am not a Trothsman, see? Would a Trothsman be seen in clothes such as these? What a sight!" I laugh nervously at my jest, helped by imagining a Trothsman in underskirt and apron with a wimple atop his head.

A small snort and giggle emanate from the branches above me. I move Arrow in a circle so they might see me from their hiding places. There's a chuckle from behind the oak, followed by open laughter as a small band of travelers emerges from within the ruins, trees, and shrubs. They stay their distance while I dismount. Mothers shield children behind their skirts and while at first glance the men look relaxed and happy, tension still lines their faces.

The oldest among them, a man not quite as old as Guthrie, greets me with a firm handshake. "Well met,... Mericus."

He bids the others to come from their hiding places. Soon, a mixture of all ages crowds around me. It seems he has a large family, and he appears to have added others to his tribe for mutual safety. They all wear freeman's attire, but as I have recently proven, no one you meet on the roads is as they seem. The only other freeman I've met was Galen, and I imagine they've never seen a costume like mine.

Mericus shakes his head. "Why would you travel the roads with such a disguise?"

"I am a nurse, traveling as best I can, in the safest way I am able."

After much eyebrow raising and nodding, they welcome me to eat with them and offer water to Arrow, who is content to graze among the ruins.

"Here," Mericus shakes half a loaf of bread at me and I tear some and thank him profusely. It's surprisingly fresh. "Good, isn't it?" he nods. "We cook by night when the roads are quieter. Come." The large sparse droplets settle into rain and we take cover inside the makeshift shelter of the ruins.

There's the finest of lines between cozy and cramped, and we all balance it beautifully. Lots of 'pardons' and shuffling ensure we're all dry and comfortable.

"So where are you traveling, young nurse?"

"Just today I passed Ferce Point and Muscone."

"Ah, the poor souls of Ferce," another says amid nods and tsks from the others.

"Please tell me what happened."

The older man wiggles to make some more room for himself. "They were a special lot, our Fercies," he says to sad murmurs.

"Were?"

"Few escaped Feeney and his Trothsmen."

My stomach lurches at his name and the remembrance of no escape.

"Those Fercies," he smiles, "Always with the primping and preening, lovely folk though, perhaps a little self-obsessed. Trothsmen lined them up and burned them. But just their faces. Just to cause them pain. Many jumped from the cliffs. Some escaped without harm, but as you can imagine, there's not a lot of primping going on now."

The rain drums on our makeshift roof without vigor. It falls windless and without direction while we silently consider the fate of the Fercies. Feeney understood what meant the most to the Fercies, but used his understanding to find the best way to hurt them. A deliberate act that he'd blanket in a charge of treason so it couldn't be questioned. "And you?"

"We were burned out long ago, and it seems we've slipped through his hands like grain. Look at us. We're not pretty, nor rich, or clever. We own nothing for the Trothsmen to take. Simple freemen, but we wander without a purpose for now. We're still waiting to be free."

"Trapped freeman," another pipes up, "A valid tale."

A woman cozied in the back corner, removes a dripping vine from the top of her head. "Yes, but the Hall has its way of getting to our kind too, remember—don't be too proud now."

"It's true," the older man speaks again. "They force freeman into guard service and hold their families to ransom. We've just made it through Smoutlea. Everyone is angry there. Such lawlessness I've never seen."

"I've heard some of these stories. But living a far distance away wasn't sure what to believe. There are so many rumors..."

"Believe this one. We've seen the damage ourselves." He looks at the solemn faces of his extended family. "But!" he announces, "There are whispers attempts have been made on his life; yet he's always made aware. Gossip, fear, and a love of silver will do that. Other quiet rumors suggest the elders are turning on Feeney," he claps his hands for good measure, "How good it will be to see him lose his alliances."

I pull a smile for the old man, but it's not exactly a 'good' situation. If Feeney's world is crumbling around him, and he fears he's losing control, he will be more unpredictable and savage than ever before. "You said earlier, that you own nothing for the Trothsmen to take. So they take your families, just as they took what the Fercies cared most about."

"So the way to be safe is not to care about anything?"

"I used to think that myself, but it's not the answer. There's a child I know. A young boy, so much cleverer than anyone I've ever met before. I don't know if it's because he pays attention to the tiniest details, or because he simply sees the world in a clearer way. Before I left my home, he came to me with a message that I didn't understand until now." Every face turns to mine. The rain is lighter now and I don't have to speak loudly to be heard. "He said, 'You are in danger'. And I replied to him that yes, my journey would be dangerous, but he was not to worry about me. 'No, you didn't hear me properly,' he said. 'This is another kind of danger. You're not *in* danger. You *are* the danger.' Me? I said, and he replied, 'Yes. To them.' He explained how when we see the games the Hall plays, the ways it manipulates and turns us against each other, we're no longer at the mercy of their lies and tricks. They can try to scare us, but we see through their plans. We refuse to be commanded and led about like livestock and can show others how to leave the mayhem of the crowd behind, to think for themselves and not be coerced into reacting the way they expect us to."

"If we can't be exploited, they'll have no control."

"That's why we are a danger to them; why they will do anything to subdue us."

"The more fearful they are, the more finger pointing and scare-mongering; the tighter the controls."

"Exactly."

Arrow looks ready to ride again. The bags on his flank are a little damp, but Guthrie oiled them so well I won't bother checking them. Someone's thoughtfully scraped his coat, and he struts with an air of importance of his personal care. Mericus chuckles at his antics and strokes his neck. "Where are you headed next?"

"I'd like to make it through Smoutlea."

He shakes his head. "Will you reconsider? More than half the day has passed and you still have many road markers to travel. Why arrive there verging on darkness? That place is dark enough already."

His words are truth to my body, and I'm done ignoring truth.

"No need to find safety elsewhere. Stay here with us."

I nod. "You really don't expect me to forego a night that offers fresh bread?"

The family works together to free Arrow from his tackle, and he returns to grazing in the surrounding forest.

T he next morning, I bring Arrow to a halt in the presence of the tall gray mountain. "See that?" I whisper, "Smoutlea lies at its base." My stomach churns and gurgles, and Arrow changes his gait beneath me. "You heard that too, didn't you? I told you I ate too much of their fine bread." Talking to Arrow while each of his steps brings us closer to Smoutlea soothes my nerves, if not my stomach. "And did you notice, as we left, they swept the campfire clean? Did you see what was under it? I did. It was that symbol again, only it was laid out in stones at the base of their fire. Whatever it says, whatever it means, it brings me comfort. And you?"

Arrow tosses his head. He's tense but not agitated. He's 'prepared'. It makes me feel hopeful; at least one of us is.

Once through the last of the fields, the trees transform from a grove here and there to more connected tracts of forest. Oh, Smoutlea with your one road in, and one road out. I draw a deep jagged breath, hold it and release it slowly. This time there will be no carts, no market days, no distractions, and no Thomas. Intention has kept me moving forward, and danger has kept me on guard, yet in slivers of quiet time, I'm reminded I can easily turn around. All would be forgiven; he'd be happy to see me. They all would. I imagine them running into my arms; sweet Wren, Oren, Silas, Guthrie, and my Thomas. I draw another deep breath, it's that whole want and need thing again. My stomach flips as the gray butte and its checkpoints loom ever closer; yet I can't deny the unwavering matter that lies on the other side of them.

The Smoutlea I remember had planks for fences, a bustling market, and children sang in its streets. I once imagined it as a jeweled bracelet on the side of the mountain. Now it seems more like a wart. No checkpoint exists on this side of the village; it seems like there's freedom behind me and a set trap in front. The gray mountain once appeared as a monumental guard. Now it hovers over the dull village, plastered with mud, manure, and breathable tension. The ale keep, Winnie, wasn't it? She's gone, so has every other trader. I crane my neck to see down the lane. There was a special little warm straw house down there too, with awful tasting bread secreted in its walls.

Travelers move as a crowd through the open square, caught up and funneled together into a line and hoping for individual pardon. No one speaks, no banter about their travel for fear of being misconstrued. Shouts ahead claim misunderstanding and offer panicked explanations. I pull the cape closer and try to appear ceremonial, isn't that what Trothsmen do? No, they appear sure of themselves. Unfortunately, my nerves have escaped my stomach and shudder their way up and down my arms. Wafts of urine and rotting foodstuffs weave between people, beasts, and carts. Although I gag occasionally, the breeze is still something to be thankful for. That, and fresh air on the other side. Do Trothsmen gag? This one does.

I dream for a moment of fresh air and fields, something to distract me. There's fresh air on the other side, at least I hope there is. Fields and cottages. Playing in the stream with little Joss, telling her a story before bed. How many summers old would she be now? Oh, and the baby... Glynn. The brief smile of remembrance drops from my face. Will they be there, in their sweet little cottage, or have they been sent away, burned out of their home like the others?

The guards wave a Trothsman ahead of me through, might I be so lucky?

Bloodstained spikes point outward from either side of the threshold, aimed at a devastating angle for both beast and rider. A forceful reminder that a charge is futile. Arrow jostles, bouncing from foot to foot. I hold his reins close and once we're at the checkpoint; I lean forward to stroke his neck. We both need to calm ourselves. A gust of wind pushes my hood back and my hand catches my wimple in its rush to catch it. Where is that star-forsaken pin? I pat my head. The wimple slides, and my hope lands at my feet. No one will wave me through anything now.

A short, bearded man shouts instructions. "Get off ye charger — Now!"

I comply and dismount gently, holding my head still as possible. I keep a calming hand on Arrow, searching for a position out of the wind.

He looks me up and down. I wish to avoid his eyes, but I fear lowering my gaze could cause the wimple to fall. "What ye be doing leaving the village of Smoutlea?"

"I am a nurse," I choke on my in-breath, the putrid fumes lining my lungs.

"Eh?"

"I am a nurse, being placed into service," I say it louder but am drowned out by shouts behind me and a horse rearing attached to a cart.

He grabs both of my arms and pushes me to the side while he attends to the commotion behind me. "Here! Take care of this — another nurse she says."

I land into the grasp of another. My head down; the wimple barely holding on. Blood covers his hands. Dried, caked into the lines of his skin, and fresh, pooled and dripping groundward. I can't hear what he's saying. Muffled words made worse by the surrounding chaos. I plant my feet firmly in the mud and lift my chin. The Stars can take care of my wimple.

Galen!

I'm face-to face with Galen. Both our eyes widen, both still alive. His guard's uniform doesn't hide his fearful and angry eyes, not those of the proud farmer I met only a few summers ago. He is not the same, and neither am I. Life has a way of molding us to what it requires. I wish I had something to offer him, some bit of hope, but I have nothing. The bearded man shouts abuse at the horse, the cart, the owner, and anyone within range. Barrels now fall about beside us. Landing with a splat in the putrid mud and bouncing off each other and into other travelers and their beasts.

Galen pulls my hood over the wimple, helps me onto Arrow and ushers me through. "I don't know what you're doing, but go!"

I wish I could tell him I don't know either. I wish I had time to explain I'm following the same sensation that sent me from his home in a sack robe, and this time it leads me back to the walls I escaped. Instead, we bolt. Faster than we've ever moved through the forest at Awenmell. Smoother than the way we round the pond. Arrow's hooves pound into the forest road toward the Hall.

Galen's a guard? What of Maeve and Joss and Glynn? Determination pushes my fear aside. I don't know what I have to do to help end this madness. But I will do it.

The forest road is smooth and Arrow charges ahead, each stride pushing Smoutlea further behind us. All that bristling energy explodes through his muscles and diminishes into the surrounding air. Sometimes freedom is quiet and secretive, other times it's irrepressible. My breath winds deep inside my body, like a gasp taken when you thought you might drown. I'd never noticed how sweet air could be, much like anything denied and then miraculously welcomed again. Strands of his mane swat on my hood and face as he swerves to move around new debris on the road. Stones and rocks fill large holes dug into the road; an unsuccessful ambush? Now an upturned cart here, some burned timbers there. He storms further, almost spent, but his gait is unnatural.

"Whoa. Come now, Arrow. Let me see what's happened."

I slide from the saddle and lead him off the road. We wander into the underbrush until we're far enough in to be hidden should anyone pass. His legs appear undamaged, and he doesn't tense under my hands. Warm muscles, twitching, no cuts. I use a sturdy stick to check his hooves. One by one, I clean them as best I can. Ah, here it is. A rock lodged into the soft pad of his hoof. I dig under and flick it out, relieved it didn't take more effort to dislodge.

"Well, it's gone now, but I wager that still hurts." I don't want to walk the road. Even though it slows us down, a rest is in order. The trees grow thicker the further we move from the road. Large boulders and mossy mounds block our view. "The other side of this boulder", I say, leading him through trailing vines, "We'll stop there." Then I need to find a stream.

I round the boulder and squint through the trees. White flashes between their trunks. I've seen this before. The lake!

"Forget the boulder, Arrow. Come along, you'll get to soak your foot in more than a puddle of cool water now."

He limps along the uneven path I make through the forest. I choose paths that contain the most moss, balancing the danger of him hurting his pad on stones and slipping on the moss-covered rocks that scatter the forest floor.

"Wait, wait." I pull him back from the shore and remove his bags and tackle and slap his hind. "On your way then." Arrow stands knee deep in the cool waters of the lake, drinks and snorts his approval.

The water is an open expanse. A breeze caresses the ripples and blows its coolness into my face. This is where I was brought back to life, way down there, where the old log still lays in the water. I dried my clothes on it. The smaller trees that run along the water's edge are taller, and the seasons have altered their shapes, but it's still as beautiful and peaceful as it was several summers ago. Before I had met Thomas, or understood anything about the Eariss. I've learned so much about myself, about others. From one end of the lake to the other, there was no one there then, and no one now; just the wind blowing across my ears.

The reeds beside me sing. I hadn't noticed it before, there were fewer reeds at the other end. I sit beside them and imagine Guthrie telling me how the wind blows through them to create the sound.

And I'd dismiss him and tell him it was all just a beautiful form of magic however it happens, and can't we just enjoy the music it makes? And he'd pat my shoulder and say, "Of course we can." I wipe the tear that turns cold as it falls from my eye. The wind always makes my eyes water.

Wood spider! That's what Arrow needs. It grows in the driest parts of the forest, yet there's so much moss here I doubt I'll find some. Maybe over there, where it looks sandy and rockier. Looks like a landslip. If there's none there, it won't be anywhere else. I skirt the slip; it looks dry enough to support some wood spider; it'll just mean I need to keep my eyes peeled. I climb higher up the slip and find a small plant hidden between some rocks. The root bulbs aren't very big, but will be enough for Arrow's predicament. The lake's lovely from up here. Bluer now that I'm above it. A nearby log leads like a path into the woods and then back to the shore. How convenient that it passes by some berry bushes. Good thing I don't fall off logs so easily now. The berries pop in my mouth. I'd shoved a handful in my mouth for convenience's sake, and now their juice trickles from its corner and I scoop it up with my fingertip.

The top branches of the surrounding trees frame a gap through the canopy. My breath catches in my throat and I almost choke. The gray turrets of the distant Hall. Right there. I swallow my mouthful before it kills me and cough away the irritation, and my knees feel suddenly weak. How quickly bravado turns tail and runs. Bees at the ready, converge on the inside of my skin, a light buzzing; a gentle warning.

Thomas might be right after all. What if it ends now? What if, finally, being happy causes it all to end?

Wait. I had intentions, bold ones, but they're in the back of my mind somewhere. I search behind the fear to find them.

Keeping Awenmell safe. Determination numbs fear. Like a soldier pulls rank on a lesser being.

There was another one. What was it again? *Destroy the book*; for Thomas. I try to conjure up a happy moment, but all my mind recalls are his angry words and the bitter rock that sits in my stomach.

✦

My feet kick the water as I stroll the lake's edge. If I focus on its coolness and the way the sunlight flashes on the moving water, I can forget the bile that rises in my gullet. I thought the lake would soothe me, but instead it's pulled me back to who I once was.

"Everything was so different then. I don't wish to become their prisoner again, but it seems simpler. Easier to fall back into my role."

Looking back can be difficult.

"Difficult? Well, that's one word for it, I suppose. I feel utterly doltish for not seeing what I can see now. But how could I, if that was all I knew?"

Correct. Shaming yourself for the impossible serves no one.

"This is one of those 'past' things, isn't it? How I tell everyone at Awenmell that if we ignore our pasts, they only rise and torment us in this day. Like the turrets are doing to me now. They make me sick to my stomach and I wish I'd never laid eyes on them." Something deeper than the fear spirals inside my chest; an understanding, a knowing. "My past has made me who I am this day. If I deny my past, I deny who I am. I vowed I wouldn't do that again. But my stupid, doltish self—?"

Survived the best it could, and needs to be celebrated, not rejected.

"So all the broken pieces can come back together."

Only they were never broken; they were just hidden under the noise of the bees.

"Just like everyone at Awenmell." I flick water high in the air in some kind of victory kick. My mind was prodded with fear, and

I've found my balance again. "You know, Thomas once said to me, 'You have to know how amazing you are.' I could never see it, but I can now. I am amazing because my story is amazing, just as anyone at Awenmell is amazing because of their story, or anyone I pass on the road and their story. It is our stories that make us amazing. Our entire stories, our entire lives, not the parts we pick and choose. If I deny my past, I deny who I am, and I deny my story - the most amazing and powerful part of me! Now I understand Martha's lesson about the dilution of the herbs; all the parts must be used to be powerful."

All the lessons that have been taught to me merge into one picture, one story, one power. I'd come here to solve Arrow's problem and end up solving my own. Yet the turrets still confuse me, like they have a pull capable of shattering anything solid inside me. When I walk through the gates, will I automatically become Lady Ashling of Brennyn Hall; here to do anyone's bidding but my own?

I believe you are the Ash of Awenmell, are you not?

I'm numb as I compare the two choices and understand it is a choice and only mine. Martha was right. What you believe about yourself is what you will become. Who do I want to be? I know who I don't want to be. "I am the Ash of Awenmell. I surrender to who I am."

At this moment, what is important?

"You and me."

When we met in this lake?

"You and me."

Martha's pond?

"You and me."

Now?

"You and me."

Let everything fall from your shoulders. Every bee that threatens to buzz right in your ear and flood your body with fear and trepidation. Focus on me. Tell me the possibilities.

"I know the possibilities are endless, and I also know you've brought me here to do something I've never done before. I need to know I won't fold in their presence. I always gave in too easily. There's more than me at stake now. What if I fold, what if I only think I'm strong, but I'm really as weak as they say? I need to know what I'm made of."

What you're made of? You are made of me. Now, what if you don't fold, what then?

I hadn't considered it. And suddenly it's scarier than folding, like there's no ground under me. I don't know what my life would look like without folding; it's my pattern. I'm safe in my pattern. I know what to expect. I wouldn't know what to do. Everything would be new and unknown.

A new life, you say?

"But that's terrifying. There's nothing there. I'd have to learn everything from the start; what I like, what I don't like, without someone telling me."

You've shown such courage to be the first before. Explaining the bees, living at Awenmell. Why shouldn't you be the one to do new things at the Hall?

I can think of a million reasons, but they're all excuses and won't stand up to the Mystery's scrutiny. "It's the not knowing what's on the other side, I think."

And what do you keep telling Thomas?

"Uncertainty means anything is possible."

Tell me the possibilities.

"They're immeasurable."

❦

Arrow wanders the shore in the dusky half moonlight and I curl at the mossy foot of an ancient and feel its protection and love. It's been a long time since I've slept in their arms. The stars brighten one by one as if there might be some magical being floating around up there with a candle, tenderly checking in on each one and coaxing the slow burners to life. I search for the Always Star in particular and wonder if Thomas and Awenmell think of me, too.

An unusual peace settles over me and I could easily float among the stars myself, all expansive and light; a reprieve from the heaviness of the world. It brings with it a determination to embrace my story, who I am and who I will be. A new solidity forms within, and I'm aware I return as a remarkably different person than the one who left the Hall. I once told Thomas I felt empty, like a forest that had been cleared. I still feel that same emptiness but it's filled with the Mystery, less hollow, more purposeful. This time I will choose my behavior and not be forced by others.

A sleepy smile pulls on my lips, and I don't fight the tiredness that drapes like silk over my body. A blissful interlude before whatever comes my way begins.

I can think about tomorrow when the sun rises.

For now, I am protected and at peace. I will sleep.

What matters?

You and me.

❦

O w! What's that?

The blasted pin. A dot of blood emerges on my shoulder. A small price to pay for being able to secure my disguise today. Mist hangs over the surface of the lake and I wish Guthrie was here to tell me why, and Thomas here to keep me warm. The sun's rays haven't made it over the treetops yet. Its light is here, but not its warmth. I whistle for Arrow. He's at one of the far reaches and walks back with no sign of being lame. Our day has started well.

There's no rush on the road. I don't know what awaits me, so I focus on this moment. This day. I am atop Arrow, being gently swayed by his loyal, unwavering steps that carry us towards our future. The trees clear enough on the side of the road to catch glimpses of the gray outer walls of the Hall in the near distance. I pull the cape from my shoulders and roll it into a wad and jam it between the pommel and arrows shoulders. Now is not the time to be caught 'impersonating' a Trothsman. When I try to swallow, I realize just how dry my mouth is. I think back to how I drank from the cool lake this morning and before we got on our way, the mist settling just atop the lake like it was admiring it but not daring to touch it.

I smile to myself when I realize how easy it is to romanticize the past. To think that our best times are back there when really, they are ahead of us. The past doesn't actually exist. I am no more drinking from the lake at this very moment than I am lying in my bedchamber crying from hunger. The only place it might exist is in my mind. The only part of my life I am living is right now. I'm not living in some imagined future, whether good or bad. It doesn't exist.

The sun breaks through the leaves of the trees above me and sprinkles me with dots of warmth and promise. I breathe in the scents of life along the winding forest road. The sun has burned off the morning mist, and the morning is clear, but my mind clouds with a shadow of fear.

The pummel of approaching hooves shoots that fear right through my system. Arrow reacts to my nervousness and shies from the road. We might not see them, but there are many, and they move at speed. I steer Arrow to the edge of the road; perhaps they'll charge right past us. Guards barrel into view. I drop my head as they rush past, shouting instructions to each other. Hopefully, their task will preoccupy them and they might pass me by, but two horses slow at the back of their group. I fumble to ensure my wimple is secured. They slow to a walk as they reach me. I exhale heavily. At least they're not Trothsmen.

The first guard is older, solidly built and annoyed. "This road leads to the Hall. Why are you on it?"

"The Hall called for a nurse, and I responded."

They pass glances at each other. I imagine there have been many attempts on the Lord's life, and on their own. Suspicion has a malicious way of creating situations that don't need to exist. It isn't based in deep knowing, it's based in fear. It's this fear that makes these men and their decisions unpredictable.

The younger guard dismounts and signals for me to do the same. The older guard corrals us to the center of the road and circles the meeting, eyeing the saddlebags. "What's in there?"

"Herbs and oils for the Lord's recovery."

"Recovery!" the younger one laughs right in my ear, "I think he's beyond that."

The older one chuckles, too. "You do know you weren't supposed to come? No help was meant to reach him. It was by order."

"So what will happen now?" I squeak.

"The Hall will keep up the show. They ordered you. Personally, I thought it was a jest to make the Hall look like it cared about its leader. It will surprise everyone someone cared enough to come."

"I don't know that care is the right word."

The solid one dismounts and opens the saddlebags as the younger one pats my body in search of weapons. His hands venture a little too long and they don't bother to hide their lewd facial expressions. So much for the wimple offering social protection. I scan for anything that I might use for a weapon against them should they decide on an attack.

The solid guard closes the saddlebag. "Nothing here. Surprised she made it this far."

The patting ceases as they converse. "They actually sent someone?" The younger laughs and faces me. "You lost the wager, then?"

The older guard mounts his horse and holds his eager charger steady. "This road is no place for a woman. Get yourself to the Hall,"

"The Hall is no place for a woman either," the younger guard laughs and seats himself in his saddle. Their raucous laughter trails them as they disappear around a bend.

I mount and hold my trembling hands to still them. Arrow moves off at a faster pace toward a place I don't wish to arrive at. My mind reels. I'll be happy not to meet another soul here. The road forks and the path ahead leads further into the forest, perhaps even to Lewtshire. The other path to the Hall on the hill, my stomach turns. Not only because I'm returning to the Hall, but the incredulous notion that I should seek my safety there.

The Hall looms high above me. I shrink so tight I have to look at my arms to not believe I am the size of a hare and about to leap from this saddle and zigzag through the surrounding fields.

What are you made of?

I suck in a deep breath and nod to myself. I am made of you.

The air is different here. I fold my arms but can't seem to rub away the chill. Its coldness comes and goes with the wind that circles the walls, but the chill sits deep within me. The closer we get, the Hall seems smaller than I remembered it, weaker than the monstrous personality I'd given it a lifetime ago. It was the ogre that held me captive and never warmed me, physically or emotionally, yet now it seems adamant I see it as I once did. Not as I see it now.

I revive myself with Guthrie's lesson on observing the patterns formed by our behaviors. He said it would be easy for me to return to the role of an obedient and terrified child within those walls; that the familiarity of a place can change how we feel about ourselves. My body trembles and reminds me how true his words were.

I've never stood on this side of the gate. I spent my life watching people approach it from those small windows up there.

A sliding peephole scrapes open on the side door. The gatekeeper's eyes dart back and forth. "Is it just you?"

An absurd question. If I had an army in hiding, does he imagine I'd declare it? "Yes. Just me. The nurse."

The door creaks open and a skinny young man steps into the light, checks this way and that, and once convinced I am as alone as I said, returns through his door and pulls the gates open for me to pass through. He rushes to close them behind me as I enter the courtyard. Weeds grow through the cobblestones, it's amazing what will flourish when not continually quashed. Some even bear tiny yellow flowers.

My feet hit the ground and the world spins. If not for the gatekeeper, I would have fallen. "There, Miss. Are you well?"

I hold my wimple against the stiff wind passing through the courtyard. "A long journey is all."

"I see." he has a kind and boyish face. Far too kind to be working among the scoundrels in the Hall. "My name is Walt; you can call on me for anything. Should I stable your horse now?"

"I'll need to keep the saddlebags close by."

"They've tidied a room for you. I'll bring them to you once I'm done—" A rabid scream interrupts our conversation and gurgles its way into my body. Walt doesn't even blink, but lifts his eyes and waits for a lull in the noise. "Or I can show you to your room."

I scan the walls of the Hall and tremble. "I'm happy to wait."

Walt escorts me through the doors of the Hall. "You'll be glad to hear the physician arrived not long before you. You can talk about all your potions and bleeds with him. I expect—" More screaming funnels its way through the hallways, bouncing from stone to stone. "—he'll want to see you."

There are no servants, no guards. Just the stench of a dirty hallway and the sound of our footsteps filling the gaps between the screams.

"Here's the room they set for you," Walt pushes the door open on my little cell.

A small bed, a table pushed into a corner, and a tiny window.

Walt lays the saddlebag on the bed. "This used to be the larder. I suppose they figured it'd be the best spot for a nurse, being between the Lord and the kitchen." There's a longer lull, and Walt considers it with his head cocked. "Sounds like they finally knocked out the old bespawler. Just in time for your meeting with the physician. A quiet one it'll be now."

"Where will that be?"

"In the great hall."

I feign ignorance and Walt issues directions. I nod, knowing I could walk there blindfolded; and often did. "Thank you, Walt. I'll be there shortly."

I touch the walls; they're as cold as I remember them. The gap that acts as a window lets in just enough light, and if I stretch, I can see the distant green fields that rise above the walls and a group of treetops. Better than looking at stone. I unpack the herbs and tinctures and arrange them on the table. Have I brought the right ones? What ails the Lord? I expect the physician will tell me.

There... hidden in the darkest corner of the table. More a shadow than a solid object. I tap it gently, expecting it to turn to dust at my touch. It's real. I snatch the key, embedding its imprint into my palm. I open my hand again to be certain. It brings many memories, how many times I'd wished for this moment. I'm dizzy with pleasure. The Hall's greatest possession is finally in my hand.

A shadow passes my door, "Don't keep him waiting." Kind but stern advice from Walt.

I brush my skirts and close my eyes to help me concentrate as my fingers wipe over the wimple, checking every fold, tucking away every strand of hair. I fold the key into my apron waist tie. I'll find somewhere more secure later. For now, the physician.

I always knew the doors to the great hall were heavy, but I didn't expect to change my stance to pry them open. The scattered straw on the ground doesn't help with a grip for my feet either. A rush of stale and dusty air greets me as they open, followed closely by the odors of stale urine and dogs. The tapestries still hang, browned and decorated with spider webs, and cloudy light seeps through the once grand window. There's no sign of the physician. At least I've not kept him waiting.

I drag my finger along one of the waxed tables. They're clean under the dust, as shiny as when I imagined a crone's fingers writing her missive with the light. Again, they'll be no missive today. Just survival. Echoes of the commands and threats I heard here sound distant and of another world, another time. The fears I thought would consume me are covered in just as much dust, and just as cloudy. I wonder where they're holding council now. If they're holding council at all. The room is still lifeless, it's just the dust and grime are visible now. Nothing here is changed. But I am.

The doors creak, and I snap to attention. The physician strides forward, his momentum lifting the dirt and straw in his wake. He sneers at me with his nose pinched. Is it the smell, or me? "You're the nurse?"

"Yes."

He considers me, as it seems everyone does, and makes his assessment. "You'll have to do. I'm surprised they even sent you." Feeney needs to look as though he's making an effort, I expect. He looks around impatiently and tuts when Walt trips into the great hall carrying his riding coat. The physician snatches it before it's offered and slams his arms into its sleeves. "I'm needed in Lewtshire, so do whatever it is you do with your herbs and grasses. If you can't knock him out yourself, ask a guard if you can find one. The gatekeeper here will help too."

"How often do you render him unconscious?" I shouldn't have asked that question. There's anger in the physician's face, and Walt's eyes might pop. Perhaps I'm not meant to ask questions at all.

The physician speaks through clenched teeth. "He is a deranged madman." His riding coat creates a swirl of dust at his eagerness to leave. He doesn't bother with my impudence anymore, but directs his last instructions to the ceiling. "If you need anything, best send for a man called Feeney and *not* me!" and with that he is gone. Every bodily sensation drops into my stomach.

Feeney.

Where is Feeney?

I wander back toward my room, deep in thought. How am I meant to find out where Feeney is, without coming straight out and asking? Would that look suspicious? A breeze through the hallways blows dust into the air, and I gasp and cough as I pass the kitchen.

A lady's voice tuts and murmurs. "Just look at her, the piddly weak thing. She won't last a day."

The kitchen looks the same, but only half its space is being used. There's more than enough room for a cook and nurse to work together. Walt stands beside a stout lady who wipes a ladle on her apron to hide the embarrassment of being overheard. If we're the only workers here, of course, they have no need for a larder.

Walt looks a little sheepish too and speaks with the muffle of a full mouth. "This is the nurse I was telling you about, Aigneis."

Aigneis checks me over, sure that her first impression is correct. I stifle my coughing and do my best to appear healthy.

"The physician said I should call for someone named Feeney. Is he around?"

Aigneis drops her ladle and rushes to take my hands. "You don't need him, do you? I'm sure you don't. We can solve it. No need to call for Mr. Feeney. What needs to be done, we'll all help, won't we, Walt?"

"It's all right Aigneis, I don't need Mr. Feeney right now, I just—"

"We have all we need right here. Don't need to be disturbing him."

I squeeze her hands in return to get her attention. "I. Don't. Need. Mr. Feeney."

"You don't?" she stops her fussing and exhales. Nice to know Feeney has lost none of his charm.

"I just want to know where I would find him…"

Aigneis flusters and holds her breath.

"If… *if* I did."

"Oh, he's never around here. He stays in a large house over the way. Lots of servants and fine food. Not like here. He says this place is a dog kennel. He only comes if we summon him. Oh, but no one ever summons him… or we try not to."

"I see."

Aigneis releases my hands and considers me again. "And what do we call you? We can't keep calling you *the nurse*."

"Call me Ash."

"Like the tree?"

"So I've been told."

Aigneis collects her ladle, and Walt makes a dash to the door. "Never in the right place, that one," she says. "At the gate when I need help, and in here when they come checking on us. Makes him flighty I expect."

The bread on the counter is freshly cut. I won't tell anyone she feeds the lanky gatekeeper at odd times, and she wouldn't believe me even if I promised her.

Pots, jars, small bottles. I could make most brews right here in the kitchen. A deep pot brews over a separate fire and I stir it with the large ladle resting in it.

Aigneis jumps and knocks the ladle out of my hand before I can lift it from the surface. "Don't be touching that! Strict instructions! That's the Lord's healing broth."

I sniff the steam coming from the pot. "Who creates the healing broth, is it the physician?"

"Oh no, only Mr. Feeney has this recipe."

"How long has Mr. Feeney been preparing the Lord's broth?"

"All the time I've been here. He makes enough or sends the herbs for us to add, it's a very important brew."

"I'm sure it is... you have taken none of this broth, have you, Aigneis?"

"No, Miss! I'd never!"

"Well, be sure you don't offer it to anyone else; even a sample. It must remain for the Lord only."

Screams echo throughout the hallways.

He must be awake.

I clench at the key in my apron band and the nib digs into my hand. I thought nothing much had changed here.

But he's the one who screams, not me.

He's the powerless one.

I hold the key.

Even the walls look peculiar, as if I'm seeing them for the first time.

If I'm going to be found, it'll be now.

In his presence.

Aigneis waits for a lull. "Sounds like he's ready for you, and your concoctions. But are you ready for him?"

The thin soles of my shoes pad along the stone hallway in a different rhythm. I'd always walked them begrudgingly. I don't know what drives this rhythm. Some kind of urgency? Perhaps panic. Maybe horror... and purpose. I reach my chamber door and swing into the room just as another scream reverberates down the passageway and into my spine. The unknown. That's what rattles through my trembling fingers as I gather bottles and herbs and salves and bandages. What will I find in there?

My feet hurry towards the lord's chamber, and their quickened pace didn't keep the cold from seeping through the floor. A bottle wiggles from my grasp and in reaching for it, I almost drop another like an out-of-control novice juggler. I haven't thought this through.

I haven't thought this through.

My shoulders quake as panic rises through them. "No," I whisper to the overbearing door that marks the lord's chamber. "I haven't thought this through."

Another scream. I start and juggle my bottles again, bang my elbows and possibly my head on the door, righting myself and my collection. There's no way they would have heard me over all that. I squeeze the jingling bottles closer to my chest and lean my body into the door. This dip is not in deference. My elbow catches the ornamental latch and I tumble my way in.

The room is dim and indescribable odors assault me. I regroup and quickly gather my balance and will my eyes to adjust. Two guards armed with clubs stand at the foot of the bed, their muscles tense and ready to attack... or is it defend? The lord screeches from his perch. He stands high on his bed, his filthy bedclothes flapping about as he swats at unseen assailants. Far from being gluttonous and strong, he's weak and feeble, terrified and cursing at things only he can see. His face and arms are heavily bruised. I've seen those patches on bedclothes before. He has wounds, and they are weeping through his clothes.

The guards raise their rustic weapons and ground themselves into their stance should he lunge at them. How can such noise and piercing screams come from such an emaciated body? Surely he'll exhaust himself before they need to subdue him.

I've entered unseen, and definitely unheard. My mouth is open and dry by the time a guard addresses me.

"You're the nurse?" He doesn't move his eyes from the lord's antics.

The lord now prowls and roars like a lion. An old white lion. But I think of it more like a weasel's coat, brown to white with seasons. The guard waits impatiently for my answer.

"Erm. Yes, yes I am." One of my loose bottles rattles onto the floor.

The Lord rises to his feet, his roar transforming from angry beast to a scream of terror.

"Eariss! Eariss!" he cries, and shifts his weight from one foot to the other, and points an accusing finger at me. "Earrrriss!" He tries to get the men to see as he does, pointing earnestly but not being able to clarify any more than his curdling screams of "Eariss!" A wet patch forms on his nightdress and his leap to safety toward a guard only provides him with a cracking blow that flops him to the bed and renders him silent.

Hair stands on the back of my neck. Do the guards see me, too? My arms are full. Can't check my wimple. Can't swallow. Can't do anything but watch the silent guards as they look at each other, then at me.

Raucous laughter erupts from their lips and covers the sounds of me gasping for air. I manage a half-lived smile.

The guard who asked for my position shakes his head. "Haven't heard that one before!"

"Eariss," the other says and lays his club by the covered window. There's a brief moment of silence before they laugh again.

They nod as they pass me on their way to the door.

"So what do I do when he wakes up?"

"You're the nurse."

"Yes, but his delusions make him much stronger than me, won't I have any help?"

"There's Aigneis in the kitchen."

I try to imagine Aigneis and I bringing him under control in a fit like that. We'd have to find a way. Somehow.

The guard watches my open-eyed stare and relents. "Fine. Let's tie him to the bed until you get used to his capers - and there will be many." The men use cloth to tie his arms and legs to each corner of the bed.

"Make sure he can move, just not launch himself from the bed."

The men nod and finish tying their knots.

"How long has he been like this?"

They shrug. "Don't try too hard. The sooner he dies, the sooner you get to go home."

While the lord lies in his stupor, I sit in mine. A self-imposed cocoon while I rethink events. What a debut! The whirlwind of my introduction replays and I consider all I've witnessed. I was sure this was the moment I'd be discovered, and I was. But not as I expected. He knows who I am, and I won't know what that means until he wakes.

Aigneis brings dark bread and a small bowl of stew. I pick at it, but I'm overwhelmed by the oppression in the room and move about for fear the stagnation might be contagious. It creeps after me if I sit too still.

The knots at his wrists are tight in themselves. Dirty strips of cloth that fold in on themselves in fine lines so you can't tell where one edge of the bandage begins or ends. The smell of infection wafts over his entire body. Perhaps the guard was right and there's not that much time for him after all. His dark features have given way to an impotent white; long scruffy eyebrows and deep lines of scorn now belong to valleys of worry and sadness.

A slash of light falls across the bed. If there was a breeze that moved the covers on the window, I didn't register it at all. That was his window, the one where he used to watch all the comings and goings from the Hall. The room needs light, but he may be sensitive to it. So he must lay here in the dark for now, a pathetic shell of a man whose death will move the land into Feeney's hands. Energy buzzes through me at the thought of his name. I pace and sit. Then pace again. I must do something, not just sit here.

All patients need fresh water. The pitchers Aigneis and I rummaged from the storeroom, stand in a line alongside the well in the courtyard. Dark patches pool around them; I was never a good server. This next bucket should be the last.

"Can I help?" Walt's away from his post again, and turned up with the impeccable timing Aigneis knows him for.

"Thank you, Walt, but no. I'm done here." I splash the last of the bucket into the pitchers. "Now to get them to the sick chamber."

He can't take a hint either. Walt's already taken leave, waving over the top of his head. "Very well then. Glad it's you and not me in there." He saunters toward the gatehouse.

Should I call him back?

Probably simpler to do it myself.

The three pitchers fit nicely on the dresser in his chamber. Aigneis was grateful for the other two in the kitchen. He still sleeps, I suppose it's a forced sleep, but I'd rather think forward. Martha always said to focus forward. I brush my hands on my skirts. What's next? My collection. I've no need for remedies in my chamber and I can reach them at ease if I set them here.

The little cloth satchels filled with leaves and tied with string, just as Martha showed me, have made the journey well. The rest of Guthrie's tiny bottles stop rattling in my arms when I place some satchels between them.

"There you go Guthrie," I whisper, "A little softness to soak up all the noise." I smile when I think of them together. They would've made a great team. They still do, only inside of me. I suppose everyone lives on this way. Martha would know what to do here in this Hall; she'd say *listen*. Guthrie? He'd have charts out and tell me to *think*. But they'd both want to know... *what does your heart say, child?*

"Allium and wine... minted wormwood... vinegar," I name the bottles and satchels as I position them in my arms. "And dwale." I'll try the allium on his wounds first. Whatever his ailments, I should have something to work with among these.

The bottles and satchels have loosened their hold by the time I reach his chamber. I almost drop one to the floor but make it to the large dresser in time and they fall quietly onto an old runner. It would've been an extravagant piece of fabric once. Now it's more dust than tapestry. I push it into a mound beside my goods and busy my mind with the order I place the bottles in. The runner will make a good dust cloth and I grab at it. There's something beneath it; longer than my hand.

A dagger emerges from the dusty cloth. It must have been hidden here long ago. The handle is plain, no ornamental show here. They made this dagger for work. I should keep it, lest I need it for defense, but in truth I'm more enamored with its possibility of splicing leaves. I lay it alongside my satchels. A knife is excellent, but will never be more valuable than a key.

So I am done.

Prepared.

I wait.

The heaviness seeps into my skin again. It must be in the air, particles of sorrow and melancholy that I breathe in and out, simply being in this room. Perhaps I should leave. There's no doubt the entire Hall will hear when he wakes.

But I want to be here when he opens his eyes.

Yes. That's why I wait. To be attentive to his needs, make notes on his reactions and use them as a base for his first treatments.

I snort. That's a lie. It's easier to lie to myself than face the difficulty bound in the truth.

I want to be here to see his face when he wakes.

To remind him it wasn't a dream, I am his personal nightmare. And I stand in his beloved Hall.

I try so hard to listen to the gentleness that calls, the quiet silkiness that reminds me to trust what I know.

But there's a pull, a craving, almost delicious, yes that's what it is; enticing. Its richness consumes me so that the gentleness acts like an echo in a dream, there but not quite, gone now, and inconsequential. Darkness seeps over me like a silent wave and drags me into a heavy place. One that won't let my eyes move from the glint of light that reflects off the blade that waits for me on the dresser.

I tap my foot earnestly and cough to remind myself to stay here - inside my body. I willfully ignore the pull, but there's a longing that grows, a delicious surprise hidden within the ignoring, that makes it all the more enticing. The agitation returns in more forceful waves and demands movement. Any action to relieve this tension. I tense and untense my muscles, but it demands more. Perhaps if I just hold the dagger, squeeze my hand around it, this agitation will be satiated.

Somewhere in the back of my mind, almost ghostlike, I can see a deep stream, the calmness beneath, but at the surface! Oh, the surface! There's passion and power, waves and turmoil. A constant delight one after the other. How wonderful to give in, to lose control, to drown in these sensations.

The bees rush into my system as my hand latches onto the dagger. I'm deaf to all but their accusations of injustice and vengeance. The first stings come as a delicious longing, a craving to hand over to them and their power. To fall into the desires of my own righteousness as anger sears my muscles into tight bands.

A smirk covers my lips. What do my bees tell me?

I can read the beat of their wings. They promise ease; they promise joy on the other side. That this act is my balm. Their insistent charge urges my grip on the dagger to be tighter and tighter again.

The dagger feels solid in my hand. Like it was designed to be there. Made for this. Made for me. Beside his bed. He moans in his sleep. Fights to wake up. What if he didn't wake up? Ever.

Maybe that child was right. This is the river's end. Yet, there are no guards here. Would they kill me; or congratulate me? No-one will ever know it was me. I smile at the tip of the blade. My, how power shifts so easily; and now it's all mine.

The blade disappears under the bristles of his beard. Just here. Right across the neck. I balance the blade and pay homage to every moment I had dreamed of this. Press. Tiny nicks in the blade create little dots of blood. Just like my shoulder this morning.

Press. That's all I need do. Press hard and draw the blade. My arm tenses solid, waiting for the command to pull back.

Deep. Hard. Firm. And slice.

Then I can do what the guard told me.

Then I can go home.

Ash? Beloved?

Mmm

If you find the tools you seek, will you be brave enough to use them?

Mmm...?

Listen carefully. The tools you seek are not in your hands. The tool is in your heart. Will you be brave enough to use it?

I frown at the intrusion. I want to do this! Petulance shocks me from my actions, and I step back from the flurry within me. The bees rage and sting, oblivious to my observations, their behavior so similar to the querulous child I thought I'd left sitting in a stream somewhere. It's not their fault. They think this is the answer. That it will make me feel better and return my stolen power, but all it will do is bring a new set of bees and I will fight with those too. Nothing will end until I take responsibility for what sets the hive off, and not simply react to the energy of the bees.

I scrape the blade over his whiskers, and it bounces over them and ripples the skin underneath.

"Oh, I'd love to do this." I can barely hear my own words. "But I won't do this to myself."

I slump back in the seat, astonished. *I won't do this to myself.* A flush of pride warms my body. I've never thought so highly of myself. I've done many cruel things to myself, but now I feel compassion. I won't do this to me. I choose myself.

⁂

The knife rolls from one hand to the other. Pain is an awful thing, but it teaches so much. I may have enjoyed a victory and some happiness for a while, but the pain would still be within me. It's something I carry that has nothing to do with him.

If someone speared me, I could rail all I wanted at them, even hire a guard to spear them a thousand times in a thousand ways more painful than mine, but it would do absolutely nothing for the spear lodged inside of me. I am the only one with the power to remove it, not them. What I cling to controls me; and that goes for stories, too.

Power. That's what this is about. And we're only powerful if we can affect change. What changes can I hope to witness here?

The lord snorts and stirs in a dark and dusty room, and I can only trust this moment is somehow part of my story. Martha reminded me I can't deny any part of my story, that its strength lay in the whole, but I can certainly deny my ending and make any choices I need. That's what I told every soul that walked under Awenmell's threshold, that we get to choose who we are. Am I the kind of person who deliberately causes pain or takes advantage of someone in a weaker state?

No. I won't ever be like him.

But I'm not so righteous to never understand the weaknesses of our hearts and the power of the bees.

The Hall's weakness is in thinking that all are like him, and will act accordingly.

I turn the knife over in my hand. I'm not the same as him, but none of this pain is new. It's just been passed on from generation to generation. No, the pain isn't new; only how aware I am of it.

The light that stretched across the bed is now dull. The sun will set, and darkness will be here soon enough.

The lord stirs, and it seems I will get what I want.

His face when he wakes.

What if I held the dagger above him as he stirs? It'd be the first thing he sees. He frowns in his waking, the weak old man that I can't torture physically or even mentally. I sigh and drop the dagger on the dresser as I pass it on my way to the chair by the unopened window.

He groans as his eyes open in the dim light and pulls lightly on the bands and slumps, defeated. This is not an unknown occurrence. He lifts his head to look about the room. Slowly. This way and that, his gaze passes over me, then returns with a flash of recognition.

His wail is pitiful, his terror quite palpable. He tugs at his restraints, his screams cycle between anger, fear and panic; and then back again. His voice is growing hoarse, but still he shouts.

Aigneis arrives in the chamber holding a cup of healing broth and waits for a lull in the noise. "How are we feeling now?" I wouldn't have heard her if she'd knocked. She places the healing broth among my herbs and gives a curt nod of approval at my display.

I give her a knowing smile. "As expected."

"Tsk. Still so dark in here." She uses a long stick to light the candles on the walls while holding one free hand over an ear. "Young Walt was just saying he hadn't heard him this upset before."

The Lord strains against his ties and his eyes widen at Aigneis' presence. He lifts his head again and shouts to Aigneis. "Her!" he screams. "Her!" He nods violently toward me. "She means to kill me. I need protection. I need my guards. Get the Trothsmen! Now, woman!

Aigneis stifles a giggle, rolls her eyes. "Yes, my Lord."

"Do not tarry!"

"No tarrying here, my Lord," and winks as she closes the door behind her.

If only she knew.

If only someone listened.

It's not a pleasant situation to be in. But it's truth from any angle. What anyone sees isn't always what they get.

Now there's only panting coming from the bed. Desperate, panicked panting. I rise slowly from the chair, keeping my movements calm and predictable. At the dresser, I arrange some scraggly flower heads I thought might serve as some kind of bouquet as he grunts and whimpers against his ties. If I stop, he holds his breath and waits for my next move.

The pitcher is cool and heavy. I pour a cup of water rather dramatically, side on so he might watch every action. His earlier screaming and babble made me consider the blows to his head may have caused some irreparable damage, yet he just ordered Aigneis to rescue him with alarming precision. I drink the water while he watches, then slowly pour another from the same pitcher and move silently to the side of his bed. He whimpers as I get closer. I do feel compassion for the man but wish he understood how close he was to waking up with a dagger in his face. I offer him the cup. The choice to drink is entirely his.

He sips without taking his eyes from me.

I return the cup to the dresser and go about mixing and measuring infusions and syrups. He watches intently and stops pulling on his ties. I've almost finished when he clears his throat in a low grumble.

"Why are you here?" he rasps.

There are so many answers to that question, more than I could count, but he's only concerned with how my presence affects him. "I am your nurse."

"And what is the reason for your return?"

"I choose to be here."

"To torment me?"

I leave him to wallow in the possibilities for longer than is kind to. "I'm not sure yet."

His eyes narrow.

"If you would prefer, my Lord, I can call back the guards and their clubs?"

"No." he turns away from me, "No, don't do that."

Apart from a slight slur of his words, it appears he's escaped severe damage. He's been extremely fortunate, although I'm sure he wouldn't see his predicament in the same light. Surely it would be kind to release his bonds? A firm *'No'* radiates through my body and I concede to tending to him myself and bring the cups closer.

"What's this?"

"Early leaves from the silver tree and a decoction from lion's tooth greenery."

He doesn't look impressed.

"And I have root here too, from the great dragonberry. It'll help with your pain and send you to sleep. Drink up." I push the cup to his lips and tip its contents into his mouth. It's strong, short and sharp. Better than a jug of it made weaker and palatable, if you ask me.

He gags, but it's too late. "Gah! It's bitter. You've poisoned me."

"You'll have to trust me."

"Trust gets you killed!"

"Ah yes. One of the Hall's great mottoes. One that I am most familiar with." I hold another cup to his mouth. "You still have a choice to make. Here. Some water to flush the taste from your mouth."

He pushes the cup away with his head. "Where is my healing broth?"

"There will be less healing broth from now. Drink the water."

His eyes widen in panic and desperation. "But my broth."

The candlelight flickers on the walls. "Let us bargain to wait a little longer." I strike a line across the candle. "When this line disappears, I will prepare your healing broth."

He nods and stares impatiently at the line until his eyelids droop. His hands relax on the straps that hold him down and a raspy snore signals my release.

My shoulders drop with relief.

That is all for now. And I have survived.

The Lord wakes gently as I enter his chamber.

"How is your head this morning, my Lord?" I carry another pitcher to the dresser and pull the corner of the window cover up and fasten it with a shawl clip I found in my pantry room. Even though the day is cloudy, the thick shaft of light sparkles the dust I've moved in my wake. There's a pyre out there, nestled in the grass, waiting. Does he know? Would it surprise him?

He squints at the brightness. "Better than yesterday." He shrugs as best his ties will allow him. Will I release him? Fear catches in my throat. I thought the fear was gone, that I had grown strong despite it, but it was really only tempered by the presence of his ties. Time slows. Will I release him, will I step back into the fear?

"Would you prefer to clean the mess I am about to make in this bed?"

I'm still dumb and trying to sort through this decision. For all my waking thoughts on today's preparation, I hadn't covered this most obvious one.

"Very well then. Let us bargain for my right to toilet."

I pull a half smile to the window and hope he didn't see it. This is the most doltish conversation I've ever had with anyone. His right to toilet. There isn't a definite 'no' reverberating through my body like yesterday, just confusion among my thoughts, pitting my heart against my mind.

Although weak, he is still trained in battle. He could kill me with his bare hands.

Trust.

What if he hasn't been sleeping but spent his night conniving this moment?

Trust.

He wishes revenge for me tying him to his bed.

Trust.

I do suppose he truly needs to relieve himself.

Trust.

Will I regret this? Should I get Aigneis?

Trust.

Ugh. What should I do?

Trust

Mystery, bees hover under my skin, about to fling me into panic. I'm not ready to trust or battle my body in order to do so. We will meet halfway.

I pick at the cloth strips tied around one wrist until it loosens and move on my intention to 'half trust'. The chair becomes an easy ladder to reach one of the ceremonial swords and spears that dot the more regal parts of the Hall. I grasp a sword and almost drop it to the ground. It's much heavier than I thought. Maybe not so ceremonial after all.

The old man hasn't noticed. He scrambles desperately to undo the knots, his wiry old fingers more bone than flesh tug and pull until they release him. He puffs and grunts, his imminent freedom making his need more urgent. The old man almost stumbles from the bed, his body weak and seized from moons of healing broth. He clings to the side of it, as one might embrace a cliff edge.

"You'll have to bring the screen and pot to me. Or else supply healing broth to restore my strength."

My shoulders sting with the weight of the sword. I move the screen with my foot and watch its decorated boards diligently, holding my stance as he disappears behind it. His sigh of relief muffles the sound of his steady stream. At least that's one thing we don't have to worry about.

The screen shakes as he holds it for balance. "Kindness is a rarity in these walls. Thank you. You may tie me again if that is your preference."

He's weak without the broth; almost bedridden. My tired arm drops the sword by my side and I collect and rearrange the cushions, throwing them one handedly from around the room and the bed to make it more comfortable. The bedding is disgusting. Aigneis and I can change it later. I lift my sword as he appears from behind the screen and falls into the bed. Sitting up is too taxing for his lungs and he settles into a low recline against the cushions. I release the sword and collect his morning cup.

"Your healing broth; but not as strong as you like it."

His skinny fingers clasp around the cup and he gulps its contents, desperate for its familiarity. He wipes his lower face with the back of his hand. "More," he rasps.

"Have some sweet tea." I hold another cup to him and he sips. "I've prepared some vegetables, and then there will be more herbs. Remember? The ones to make you sleep? You'll recover quicker that way."

He eats well, almost sucking the vegetables from the spoon. In between passing him cups and bowls, I eye the room, searching for the club. There it is by the window. If he is not asleep by the time his healing broth takes effect, I may have to use it. I exhale quietly when his eyelids droop.

"You," he drawls, "I thought you were going to kill me."

I push down at the cushion behind him to help support his neck and his breath and whisper into his ear. "I was."

The effects of the herbs sweep his shock and frown away and his eyelids lose their battle with the root medicine that overpowers his senses. His jaw drops open in a stupor and he snores lightly from the back of this throat.

To me, the room is dark. To him, that corner of light would be piercing. I shut down the only light source in the room and creep to the door. I squeeze the key, still buried in my apron fold. It feels like taking hold of my entire life somehow; the very meaning of it. What does this simple key give me I didn't have before? The past, present, and future embodied in a piece of old metal. Keys provide choice. My sovereignty over my life becomes solid in my hand. What will I do with it?

Day dreaming is a welcome escape. But there are still many chores in the kitchen. Roots to grind and dry. I need to find a place to hang those herbs from this morning's gather. The Hall is so dark. Walt spends most of his time outside, he'll know where the sun—

I click the door closed just as a wail breaks in the hallway behind me. Aigneis charges me, axe above her head. "AYYYYYYY-YY-EEEEEEEE!!"

Has the whole world gone mad?

"Aigneis!" I dodge one of her swings.

No recognition at all; her face etched with nothing but horror.

She swings wildly to save herself from whatever her terrified eyes have transformed me into.

"Aigneis!" I tear through the hallways; grateful I know where each one leads, with her cursing and swinging behind me. How can a woman of her age be so sprite? I pass another ceremonial weapon and know I can fight her, if I must. *If I must.* Some choices aren't so grand. I scramble up stairs and through corridors. My lungs burn and my brain is running out of ideas. How can we all be safe from this?

There's no time for recollection as I burst through the doorway into my old bedchamber. Aigneis swings wildly behind me, the blade tugging at my skirts in the slightest catch. I draw her around the bed and leap over it, returning to the door while she stumbles over my course across the bed. I dart back to her and wrench the axe from her hands. Her grasp surprises me and I lose my grip, sending the axe handle into the side of her face. I lunge again while she responds to the shock, snatch the axe away and fumble for the key, only taking a breath when I hear that ominous click falling into place. I slide down the door as she wails in rage and panic safely on the other side.

I catch my breath and rest my head on the door. I have no idea what's going on in this wretched Hall.

But there's one thing I'm certain of.

She can't escape that room.

My ankle stings on the way back through the hallways. Must've twisted it in the mad dash. It won't take much to recover, just a little rest. My limp allows me to take my time. The calmness reminds me there's no reason to jump at every noise, or be afraid of every room.

It's quiet in the kitchen without Aigneis's usual banter, just the soft bubble from the pot on the hearth and the scent of the dark bread she'd pulled from the fire. On the table, some cut parsnips and roots rest in their scattered positions, and her favorite knife lies alongside them. Here's her unfinished cup of sweet tea. Another cup stands empty beside it. I draw it to my nose, already knowing what I will smell. I nod to myself. The healing broth.

I pour myself a sweet tea from a pot that has sat for too long and collapse into a chair. The tea's no longer sweet, but it's acceptable. Just like the way I rest my ankle on another chair. Acceptable.

For now, everyone is safe. Isn't that what I'd hoped for?

A cup of tea and a brief rest is magic. Did Martha tell me that, or did I just realize it myself? I strain to hear any noise from either chamber. Sleep is a wonderful equalizer too.

Aigneis's knife doesn't feel sinister in my grasp, just purposeful. The vegetables still need chopping; she won't need the additional stress of being behind in her tasks when she wakes. I slice a parsnip.

Is it just time and sleep that's needed to help people recover from their reactions and addictions to his insidious healing broth? Maybe so. But the poison he spreads among the villages will take more than simple remedies to overcome. Some react violently and take up arms in the direction he chooses, others slowly succumb, their minds made supple by constant lies until they're incapable of any challenge. I hack at a parsnip and notice the whites of my knuckles on my grip.

Someone steps through the doorway. My knife protects me, held chest high, and my stance is firm; every muscle twitching, ready for defense.

"Oh Walt," I say and readjust myself, my cheeks flush with heat. "Sorry—wasn't expecting you."

He raises his hands. "Sheesh. Who were you expecting then?" and steps back.

"No, no. Come in."

"I was, err.. just a tad hungry," he looks around the room, "Where's Aigneis? She's always in the kitchen."

"We got a late start to the stew so it might be a little undercooked." I slide the rest of the vegetables, including the hacked parsnip, into the pot. "Aigneis was feeling... unwell, so I sent her to rest in one of the chambers."

He frowns with concern. "That's not like her."

"Not like her at all, I'm sure. But have no fear, she'll be back in the kitchen before you know it."

"Bet she put up a fight. It's not like her to rest." He offers me some dark bread from the table and tears a piece for himself. "Bit of a turn up, her being cared for by someone."

"Has she no family?"

"Oh, she's family. They just don't care. They're from Grandkith, just outside Lewtshire. Have you been there?"

"Never had the pleasure."

"Most people try to avoid it, but there's lotsa people say it's the best way out of Lewtshire."

"Lewtshire. Isn't that where your Mr. Feeney is?"

"Pfft. He's not my Mr. Feeney." Walt sits and rests his feet on the chair as I had before. "Nor is he anyone else's really. Even the fancy people of Lewtshire don't care for him. That's what I've heard, anyway."

"People do like to talk, don't they?"

"That they do. But there's a lot to be learned from tales too. I've heard some tall tales, absurdly tall, but at least they keep our minds from the pyres."

I nod at him; I can see how that'd be true.

"And if I need to know anything, I can find out just by asking around. Like how many nails the blacksmith used when he shooed my neighbor's mare."

Why would you want to know something like that? I stop the words before they leave my mouth. "That is an impressive amount of detail. Do you think they might make up numbers like that?"

"Why would they want to do that? They'd be no benefit in it, would there?" he scoops another bowl from the pot.

"I suppose not. And while we're speaking of benefits, I plan to work in the kitchen so when Aigneis returns there's not so much to catch up on."

"Grand idea. Count me in." he raises his bowl and grabs at some bread. "I'd best go back to my post and finish this first."

Walt shoves bread into his mouth and strides from the kitchen with all the determination of someone who plans to abide by his promises but always gets distracted. I won't bother waiting. I'm not sure which kind of help I prefer. The one where you know you're on your own, or the one where it's promised and never shows.

My mouth's salivating. It must've been from watching Walt eat his stew. With no one around, I choose my favorite pieces from the pot and stir them around in the bowl as I wait for them to cool. Today's danger didn't come from anywhere I'd expected it. I think of all the expressions Thomas's face will pull when I tell him about this morning's adventures. He'll want to know how I did it, and I'll say when you're chased by someone with an axe, there's no time to think about anything. And I smile.

But my happiness fades. I wish there was some way to let him know I am well, and I am safe. Would he want to know? Or have I let him down so badly he'll want nothing to do with me. Tears sting at my eyes and I don't bother trying to convince myself it was the steam from the bowl. I must keep busy.

❧❦❧

It's much later when I hear Aigneis stir. At least I think that was it, and I follow the noises to my childhood chamber.

Is it safe?

I press my ear against the door.

Bewildered sobbing and the softest wails melt my heart.

The lock clicks open, "Aigneis, I'm here."

She sits among her soiled clothes, confused. Her blotchy eyes seek answers and hide in shame simultaneously.

"I—," she begins, but frowns in confusion and doesn't know where to go from there.

I kneel beside her and hold her hands. "Go now, and clean up. I'll explain when you are ready."

She nods, bewildered, and heads out the door, looking behind her incredulously.

❧❦❧

I retire to my room early.

I firmly believe there are some days that stay way past their welcome. Today was one of those.

Aigneis remained slow for hours and was compliant when I asked her to drink a soothing tea. I don't expect her to wake until morning.

The Lord remains ravaged by the effects of moon after moon of Feeney's healing broth. All we can do for now is attend when he calls, bring him food and settle him for sleep. He sweats and aches and longs for more healing broth to ease his misery. I comfort him, and myself, that he should feel better before the next full moon, and the seizures that grip his muscles might soon end. Sometimes I think it might not be more than hope that drives our comfort.

The tiny patch of night sky reminds me of an expanded life outside these walls, and I turn away from it before my thoughts linger to Awenmell. The tingles across my shoulders turn from nuisance to ache and I toss in the bed and try to find a comfortable position to sleep. My eyes close and I mumble a reminder to myself, "Must get the Lord and Aigneis back to themselves tomorrow..."

I want you to trust me.

I hear the words of the Mystery, but I am too tired to answer.

Walt wasn't at the gates when I passed through them this morning. I'm not sure what his actual task is around here. A sentry in title, I suppose, not in deed. Life's full of people who present as one thing, but are truly another. I snort as I enter the forest canopy. Presentation. Isn't that one of the biggest illusions ever?

I tap the dew from the leaves and flowers I collect so the cloth lining my basket won't be overwhelmed. The earth is cold, rich, and damp. I run my fingers through the litter and loamy surface, and feel it quench the thirst deep inside me. The air tells me a million secrets and brings a slap of coolness to my cheeks. I bet they're as rosy red as Thomas used to describe them. What would he think of my plans here? What would he think of my recent behavior?

A patch of morning sun brightens a trunk, and I sit with my back against the ancient, face to the slightly warming sun, enjoying the splash of red and pink through my eyelids. Birds sing and converse with each other. The whizz of bugs pass near my face. They just travel about, unconcerned about whether this is a good day or a bad day. Never making judgements about whether it's too windy, too hot, cold, or wet; they accept the day and move on.

I wonder where we got the notion to label everything- to decide how something should be according to our preferences? When did we get so ungrateful that it's normal to complain about everyday gifts? Nature doesn't try to stop the wind. It bends with it, floats on it, moves with it and glides upon it.

Dark branches frame the Hall on the nearby hill. The overgrown grasses surrounding it were once lush fields, not the view I was hoping on when I opened my eyes. What kind of day lies before me? Will I choose to label it good or bad, or will I accept whatever comes my way? Anything could come my way.

I take another moment in my sunshine bliss, then gather my basket to return. There's lots to accomplish today and these flower-heads will balance the Lord's sweet tea nicely. I fill a pitcher with cold stream water. The Hall looms as I draw nearer, but it doesn't hold the same terror it once did. Good days and bad days; the Hall doesn't decide that for me; I do. Even with its cold stone and unyielding traditions.

I want you to trust me

"Trust gets you killed—" Stars! My cheeks flush with embarrassment, despite the cold. I don't need correction to understand I'm not even within its gates and the Hall's mottos seep into my reactions. These tall walls might not hold terror, but they hold patterns that nest inside me all too easily. It's still true though. I correct myself. "Trust *here*, gets you killed."

Even so.

"Even so? What's that supposed to mean?"

Silence.

The kitchen is warm when I return. I only just lay my basket on the table when Aigneis appears nursing a collection of fresh eggs in her apron. Her cheeks flush and she drops her chin. "Good morn," she mumbles to the floor.

"What fine eggs. I didn't get round to them; you do such a grand job with all your tasks. They had me feeling quite overwhelmed."

Aigneis doesn't lift her eyes from the floor.

"I'm glad you took a day for rest. Are you feeling yourself now?" I brush her arm as I pass, and prepare a pot for the Lord's tea, but she doesn't respond.

"Aigneis, I know that wasn't you yesterday. You needn't be shamed by something out of your control. In fact, it's a ridiculous notion."

"But it was in my control—I felt poorly and drank the healing broth when it was forbidden; that's what it was, wasn't it? It's all I remember."

"True. You were in control of your decision, but what you were told about the healing broth was wrong. It's not healing; it's caused the Lord's apparent madness and your behavior yesterday. But yesterday is gone, and we all have learned a great deal. Agreed?"

"Agreed." Aigneis rubs her temples. "I'll get to tossing it out now."

"No. What if Feeney returns? He'll want to know where it is. Continue his routine; besides, I'll need a little to aid the lord's recovery." I scoop a small quantity into the lord's cup and choose some leaves from my basket and spread them out in front of her. "I've brought various herbs from the forest today. These will steep to a bitter tasting tea that you must drink. One cup will be enough,"

"Oh no Ash, no more strange potions please."

"The tea isn't pleasant, but you need to trust me. It will make you thirsty and help your body flush the healing broth away. It may tire you, so be sure to rest." She watches me pour water from the pitcher. "It's the same tea I prepare for the lord, see?"

Aigneis seems satisfied with my explanation.

"Oh, and I'll need your help."

"How so?"

"We need to bring pitchers of fresh water from the stream and store them in the kitchen. None of us shall drink from that tarnished well again. We'll go to the source."

"Right. No more well water then."

The lord stirs, and I hastily gather his morning treatments and set it on a tray. Aigneis exhales before squeezing her eyes shut and swallowing the bitter tea. She tucks a pitcher under each arm and sets off to the stream.

Long-stemmed flowers line the side of the tray. I gathered them this morning at the edge of the forest. They're nothing but weeds, but in some kind of arrangement they might promise life in the death room.

My feet again pad their way along the hallways.

So this is my routine.

Keep everyone well.

Be alert for Feeney.

Only visit Awenmell in my dreams.

And *even so*... trust.

The sun has risen and set five times since I walked through the gates. Each day has brought some kind of blessing, even if I have to dig around among the surprises to find the light. The sun sets away from the little window in my chamber, but the shadows of the trees grow taller and taller along the fields until they disappear into the gray of evening. This night feels still and calm, as if it's holding its breath, wanting to exist that bit longer.

The pillow isn't any more comfortable bunched up, and discarding the blanket, then pulling it to me again does nothing to settle me. Even the crickets chirrup softly tonight. It makes the energy inside me loud and impossible. I toss and turn. Frustration becomes agitation, agitation becomes anger. I discard the blanket with such force it lands on the floor.

"Well then, if you won't let me sleep, you could at least hint as to why."

I hope to remind you.

"Remind me? Of what?"

Of your task here.

"Oh, I see. Well, the lord is feeling much better. And surprisingly, the solutions I offer help everyone. Walt and Aigneis trust my word and don't challenge me or make me feel inadequate. I know I wondered how I'd ever accomplish this, but it all seems to be going well."

But what of your task?

"I don't understand."

You listed the things you've done. Who have you become?

The Mystery always gets straight to the crux of the matter. Yes, I have performed good deeds, but the deeds are not who I am. Just as the deeds I performed here as a child do not make me who I am. Who have I become? What have I learned?

"My power is hidden inside my own beliefs about who I am. Not the Hall's, not Thomas's, or even if Aigneis believes I'm doing well. Whether I'm surrounded by good or bad report, I get to choose who I am. So it seems the more I focus on the new person, and choose what's best for her, the Hall version of myself fades away."

And you're ready to step into this new you?

"There's a final piece of uncertainty that tags along, pulling on my sleeve and asking me not to dare. I'm torn between stepping up and taking its advice. Remember how I told Thomas uncertainty was good and allowed anything to be possible? Look at me now."

Without uncertainty, there can be no faith or trust. It acts as a bridge between the safe and the spectacular.

"I always preferred safe, didn't I?" I'm not the same person who lived here as a child; I'm pretty sure I'm not the same person who lived here yesterday. Like a cicada splitting their shell over and over again. How can it sing if it's crushed into being less than what it's created to be?

"Spectacular possibility sounds adventurous, but I have to step up and choose it. Is that what you're telling me?"

What are you choosing?

"You. Always you." I don't stop and consider the words. They live in my bones now. Martha was right. I will become whoever I believe myself to be, and this choice is distinct. There doesn't need to be trust anymore because there is relationship and knowing. This time I have to be certain. This time I have to vow.

"Mystery? I am the Ash of Awenmell." The title settles into my bones and brushes the last of my uncertainty away.

Even so?

"Even so."

⁂

I'm practiced at opening his chamber door now; a bump of my elbow on the latch and a quick roll to my shoulder and I can back in without disturbing his tray of food.

We haven't spoken. Nothing of any importance, anyway. His eyes narrow as they do each morning as I enter. He watches, deep in thought, squinting and considering. Is he planning my demise? I expect he believes I am planning his.

Some tasks don't need full presence, I can daydream and it's as if the tedious tasks perform themselves. Arranging his food, steeping his tea, lets me adjust to the mood of the room until I am found again. Perhaps that's what he does every morning too, only he finds himself—not where he hoped to be—bedridden, with constant reminders in his face. It seems strange to balance this room together without a word, finding our feet, processing and considering.

I pass him a cup. "You shiver. Did your body ache much last night?"

"A little. No need to call."

He prods at the gruel Aigneis prepared for his early meal, shrugs and eats. This morning, he only sips from his watered-down healing broth. He takes his sleep herbs and downs the bitter tea without complaint. I empty the last of the water into his cup to cleanse the bitterness from his mouth.

I move to the window. "Ah, there she is. Aigneis is bringing more water now."

She moves comically along the road to the Hall. Lopsided and splashing water here and there. I know how her arms must ache. I've walked that walk many times. Yet I'd gladly swap aching arms and wet skirts to spend a moment outside the Hall. The forest stream is lovely and clear. There are sections that bubble over stones but mostly it slides by without a word, deep enough to lie the pitcher in and the water flows into it as if it had been waiting for the pitcher all along.

The lord's voice jolts me from my trance.

"I must speak with you. If you will hear me."

I don't move my face from the window. Aigneis ceases being comical, and the heaviness of his words drags down my face and lands in my chest.

"It's just I—"

"Let me collect the water from Aigneis." I turn on my heels and dash from the chamber, half expecting to have left the heaviness by the window, but it has nestled into my chest and I carry it with every step.

I snatch at a loose cup in the kitchen and pour the cold water from the pitcher, spilling it onto the table. I gulp the water, but its crispness doesn't budge the heaviness.

"Calm down my sweet." Aigneis wipes the spill. "There's more just there in the stream. It's not going anywhere."

Walt appears in the doorway, and their discussion muffles. I have no interest in their words. I have no interest in anyone's words. The lord's? No, not even his, although I know I must hear them. It's the most useless sensation to want something you don't want. Utterly useless. What am I to do with this wretched moment?

I pour another cup, being careful not to spill it this time, and stare at the water inside it. Walt and Aigneis have finished their banter. They watch but I don't care.

A wretched moment is simply a moment with a label.

Crisp water is simply water with a label. I stir it with a spoon.

This situation is neither good nor bad unless I assign it a label.

I won't apply a label. This day is what it is. I can witness the swirling waters of the eddy. There's no need to be sucked into its depths. The heaviness lifts, leaving only a cautionary shadow of what was there before.

I calmly drink the second cup and smile at my observers. They smile back half-heartedly but look too confused to ask questions.

The pitchers belong here. There's a ring that marks their place. The same place I put them each morning. I pour the crisp water into a cup and make my way to his bedside. He's sitting and doing that deep in thought thing again. Perhaps he's forgotten what he said. Perhaps he has no words for me after all and we can pretend he never said them. He sips and clears his throat. His voice factual and enquiring.

"When you left here. Where did you go?"

I pull my energy in, where it's safe; where I can't be tricked or my words turned into something they are not. "I traveled here and there. I learned a great deal in the forest."

"My guards said they couldn't find you. You knew they searched for you?"

A lump forms in my throat but disappears once I've formulated my answer. "I did."

"Hmm." He considers my replies, but doesn't push for clarification. He lowers his gaze and for a moment, I think he's addressing the bedcovers. "Is it true?" he enquires, "You are the Eariss?"

"That's what they say."

Silence is a peculiar thing. It can be fragile like fine glass or thick and foggy. This is a foggy silence, one where the truth of who I am blends with every myth and prejudice about the role of the Eariss and we both get lost in it. I search for common ground and will my heartbeat to soften. I have no idea what he searches for, but he finally stretches his back tall and clears his throat with a strange kind of whimper that I try to ignore.

"So, you will destroy us now?" His words slur slightly as his body battles the induced sleep and he sways. I take his shoulders and direct him to recline. He wails into my ear, "You've come now? My army is not prepared. Destroy us while we sleep, shall you?" The rest of his words tumble into grunts and ramblings as he fights my help and the effects of the dragonroot.

His contorted body lies flat on the bed, deeply under the influence of his treatments. Would it have been better if we conversed for longer? That I'll never know. But I do want to understand the legends and why they terrify everyone so much.

When he wakes, I'll be the one with the questions.

The previous afternoon wasn't one for talking. Well, talking coherently anyway. The lord moved from delirium to hysteria. Even if we'd spoken about the legends, I wouldn't know what to believe.

I'm grateful he's calmer today, accepting my help and edging closer to normality. Exhaustion makes us say things we regret, but it also forces us to release our shields and move closer to the truth. For all his curses and mumblings, he's no different from any damaged soul at Awenmell.

The sun points into his room through the small window, down to where his hands rest in his lap. I don't sense any shields. Pain and exhaustion have a way of pushing self-protection aside. My thumb hooks over the edge of the bowl in my hand and dips into the balm inside. Just as he's relaxed; my treatments will cause him pain. Acceptance is the greatest leveler; that's when the bees tend to give up too.

"Are you able to remove your nightshirt, or would you like me to help?"

His shoulders drop at the sight of the bowl. Smearing balm onto open wounds is never pleasant, but Guthrie and the lord have taught me that old men are stoic. Stubborn, wincing, closed and stoic—and repressed. "I'll manage it." The lord does battle with his nightshirt and triumphs, finally. *So much quicker if I'd done it.*

I resist the urge to roll my eyes and gently check over his wounds and weeping sores. "You may be unwell for a while, my lord. Look at these wounds."

"I didn't notice them when I had the broth. I was stronger then."

"That's because the strength came from the broth, not you."

"I was still strong though."

"Yet behind the broth you were rotting away. What kind of strength is that?"

He doesn't answer, but winces slightly as I apply the balm. I imagine he'd pout if I wasn't in the room.

"Almost done." I swipe the last of the balm into my hand and concentrate on the last wound near his shoulder.

"It's seen!"

"Hm? What's seen?" Two of his wounds have spread into one and I'm not sure whether to apply balm or bandage it.

"Strength. It only matters that it's seen, when it's all on show. It doesn't matter what's going on behind it."

I tap the last of the balm onto his wound, and he jumps. "I sincerely disagree. And besides, a person's strength is like truth." I hand him his nightshirt. "It's always felt more than seen, anyway."

The chamber is quiet while I mix his broth. He grunts occasionally but wins the battle with his clothing again without asking for help. He puffs to catch his breath and speaks as I approach him with the broth.

"I think you're right. I pretended to be strong; laid up in this bed, and the guards only ridiculed me."

I dip my chin. There's no need to verify his discovery.

He sips at the weakened broth quietly. Steeping new thoughts as he watches the steam rise on his sweet tea across the room. To speak would break his concentration, so I quiet myself on the seat by the window and leave him to his thoughts.

"You know the best way to destroy something you're afraid of?"

The lord's voice snaps me from my daydream. I shake the last of it free while considering fear and bees and fire and—

"Ruin it. Ridicule it."

"How so?"

"The Eariss."

I move swiftly from the seat by the window to the edge of his bed. His eyes are clear, his speech isn't slurred and there's no malice in his voice.

"Legends have a way of entering the bones," he says to the ceiling. He sighs deeply before facing me again. "I cannot say I am rid of its treachery, for an old fear still dwells there hidden in the crevices of my bones, but my adherence to the old way is depleted. I lay in this bed for moons, exhausted from upholding something that no longer feels like truth. Some things don't feel right even if the entire land believes it."

My heart flips with excitement. Not only because he speaks of the Eariss legends, but of the way he speaks.

"Your head seems clear, my lord."

He coughs lightly a few times. Must be a tickle in his throat. "Clear, yes. And it's not just from the weakened broth. They have separated me from the busyness of the Hall; the plans, divisions, usurpers, suspicion and watchfulness, when you look at it from the outside; it's a treacherous way to live." His eyes fill with confused wonder, as if he's just figuring out one of the Tallefix's tricks. He wheezes a deep breath. "I'm waking up from the most elaborate play I've ever immersed myself in. What I once thought was truth, now looks like parody. How could I have not seen it before? Such a odd sensation." He glances quickly at me to make sure he has my attention. "A costumed amazement where the players are so brightly adorned, I watched it unfold in front of me, the story and the drama so real you become a part of it—and it of you. But once you are clear enough away, the costumes fall away, leaving only the actors and their exposed intentions. It's quite an extravaganza, you see,... and quite an embarrassment."

"And the role of the Eariss in this extravaganza? Surely it didn't have a 'bit' part for its legend to continue for so many generations."

"Oh, its old. The legends seem like they've existed for eternity, but I would suggest, like most, we have altered them from one form to another, twisted until they become the kind of lore that can't be changed easily. Maybe generations will pass again before we restore its truth."

"So it's possible for it to be restored?"

"Perhaps restored is not the right word. Rediscovered anew might be better."

I wiggle my toes in my shoes. Better my nervous energy be unseen when I am so close.

"I've already said the easiest way to defeat something you fear is to cause doubt to be cast upon it, haven't I?"

"You have."

"But first people must fear it before they ridicule it. They fear the new, its power to change what they have set in place for themselves and their own comfort. Think of the Eariss as a great treasure. A ruler could set it aside, never releasing it lest it ruin what he has created, guard it and be under constant attack, or he could devalue that treasure by stealth."

"If it's devalued, no one will want it."

"We did not simply devalue the Eariss, we denounced it. You can't have people going to discover this treasure themselves! Goodness, no. They must fear it and all the things this monstrous Eariss is capable of and would do to them. You know the stories from your childhood? The scarier the better; they travel through to adulthood and shame anyone who considers the Eariss in a positive light."

"But in the mountain villages—"

"The truth lives there. Where the Hall can't undermine their beliefs, we undermine the people. Do you remember the Hall's edict on mountain villagers and idlers?"

"Unreliable, unsound, and untrustworthy." Even mumbled words have power.

"See, when you make them one thing, you automatically make yourself the opposite in people's minds. Therefore, without bludgeoning a single head, the Hall becomes reliable, sound and trustworthy."

"People will fight to the death if they fear something is being taken from them. I've seen it myself. Heard so many tales."

"Make people fear something enough and they are capable of anything. The Hall doesn't have to lift a sword."

It's strange hearing him speak about a plan that gained momentum until it became fact. It almost feels like a confession, though he is no longer close to death.

"So, you knew the horror stories were untrue? Did everyone in the Hall know?"

"I believe they knew it had power, and that was enough to scare them into following an age-old story that made them feel secure. Whenever the fear became too much, we would focus somewhere else, control the people and become bolder with our attacks so the people would be forced to fight among themselves, keeping themselves occupied and not considering for a moment to question what they were told."

"Like a decoy?"

"Exactly like a decoy."

"Did people ever question the Hall's plan?"

"It was easy to vilify them; dismiss them as nonsensical, shame them into being quiet. There was a time of chaos, just before the invaders came from the North. Their attack brought the people back to the Hall."

"So the legend holds two stories in one. The Eariss is either an attacker, bound to destroy and torture if you stray from the Hall and the Book of Law, or it's a new way that moves away from those things."

"A new way, as you call it, by its own virtue is bound to disrupt the old, even destroy it."

"And what you can't control or destroy..."

"You shame and ridicule and turn people against." He coughs laboriously and turns to lie on his side. He breathes easier now.

The plan worked for generations; through passing of lords and ladies, insurrections and invasions. But something new is passing through the land. The mountain beliefs grow stronger. I think of Bez and his campers in the forest, the way Eugenica's heart softened against the rule of her own law. And the Eariss itself. Connection to heart, healing from the fear and anger of the world, and choosing to operate in a specific way. Now that he's seen. I wonder what he will choose. A new way that will change the old. Seeing his grand play, as he calls it, is his moment of choice. He's no longer blind to the players and costumes.

❧⟐❧

W alt dumps a sack onto the table and a wave of green tumbles onto the table. I rescue my cup from an onslaught of pods that rolls toward me.

"Don't ask, and I won't tell." He winks and collects his morning slab of bread and disappears.

Aigneis scoops the escapees back into the sack amid giggles of delight and then tsk noises. "Peas! And they're fresh too," a pod crunches in her mouth. "Best get to shelling so they'll dry quick enough. There's rain coming." She flusters around me, gathering bowls and jars for her peas once they're dried. "Oh, he's a lovely lad, that one, but not good with timing. I've too much to do today already. Here," she thrusts a bowl at me, "Get shelling."

"But I've arranged a conversation with the lord today, apart from his nursing requirements. Soon as I finish this tea." The bowl is cold in my hand, having been pulled from its place on the floor.

Aigneis pushes her fist into her hip and leans toward me. Peas must be serious business around here. "When did nurses start listening to confessions and such?"

"They don't. I mean, I suppose it's something like that."

My answer twists the scowl on her face into a suspicious frown.

"Perhaps I can do it there? Will it be all right to shell the peas during our conversation?"

Her frown gives way to a smile and a large belly laugh. "You want to shell peas in the presence of the lord of Brennyn Hall? You don't know a thing about this place." She continues to chuckle and shakes her head as she drops a smaller bowl inside mine. "I'll leave a place for you here."

❧❦❧

Who ever thought peas would be a problem? I suppose we can make a problem out of anything we want. The sack is light and the bowls become a tray for the lord's sweet tea. I rap at his door with my knuckle.

"Enter."

I don't know what to expect. Will he vomit at the sight or scent of the peas? He doesn't seem to notice them or the sack and bids me to sit in the seat by the window. "Your sweet tea my lord."

He quenches his thirst while I arrange my bowls by the seat. One for my lap, and one on the ground for the pods that we'll add to the small perpetual pot later.

"What do you have there?"

My hands squeeze into the rim of the bowl, my legs tense, awaiting the 'problem' to force me to scramble back to the kitchen and Aigneis's laughter. "Peas, my lord."

"Peas?"

"For shelling."

He considers me and my bowls for a moment. "I see."

"I confess they have already warned me it's not an appropriate activity to perform in your presence."

"It isn't?"

"No."

"Why?"

"I didn't ask. Although now I wish I had."

He rearranges his blankets and neatens them across his legs. "If you had, you would have discovered it's simply another rule. They hide kitchen activities from the likes of me, but I imagine you're all very busy, and breaking old rules is what you're here to do, I expect?"

I return his half smile. What a weird situation we both find ourselves in yet again.

"I've told you of the old," he says as I grab a handful of pods from the nearby sack. "So this new way... It opposes everything about the old?"

"Most. I've a friend who calls it a new paradigm, but I'm not sure what that means entirely."

"A new pattern. A new way of doing things, so that makes sense as a ruler. But where does its power come from?"

"From within the people themselves. It's always been there. It's as you say, keep them distracted and fearful and they'll never discover it themselves. The old way was clever, but it didn't leave any room for wisdom... or heart." The peas split easily; my thumb glides between their seal and the peas tumble into the bowl on my lap. What starts as a small collection soon grows into a handful. "You know yourself that once fear invades a life, it becomes a tarnish that will only clean with vigorous scrubbing and attention.

How can anyone give attention to the power within themselves when they, quite rightly, need to focus on the power that roams around outside of themselves?"

"Quietude and safety; just like my confinement to this chamber allowed me to make its acquaintance?"

"For me it was the stillness of the forests."

We are both quiet for a while and the only sound is the gentle tumbling of the peas into the bowl. His face is relaxed, a slight smile on his lips. I wonder if he's thinking of the quiet discoveries he's made about himself, away from the tyranny of his position. Me? I'm thinking of waterfalls and windflowers and ferns and—

"What do I do now?" he announces.

"Whatever you want, my lord."

"There's a fork in the forest road on the way to Lewtshire. Have you seen it?"

I shake my head and pick some wayward peas from the floor.

"It's a wide, very wide fork, and I feel like I'm there right in this moment. I can choose to return to the way of the Hall. All its traditions and rules, the constant fear and suspicions, yet I know it well. I have a role here. It feels comforting because it's familiar. It tells me how and what to think! What to celebrate. Doing anything else seems like hard work."

I nod. He has no idea the amount of hard work he is in for if he chooses the other road. I understand why it's easier for him to stay aligned with the Hall and forget all about this fork he imagines. "I once had a role here, too. They designed dresses for me that didn't allow me to breathe and rules that didn't allow me to speak. When I discarded the dress, I discarded everything the Hall told me I was; everything I had believed I was. All the things I learned about my life I had to un-learn, and then practice truth. It's very hard work, done a little at a time. But anyone who has done the work, will tell you it's worth the pain."

"So you don't care about the Hall at all?"

"Not really."

"But how, when that's all you knew?"

"Deciding to move is the hardest leap because you don't know where you will land. It's terrifying and you wonder if you might die, but something inside urges you on and you find your leap is what has made you come alive!" I close my eyes and swear I can feel the breeze at the edge brush my cheeks. "To be alive, you have to declare the old frightened and controlled part of you dead."

"Your words feel familiar but nonsensical at the same time. I've never considered anything else was available. Yet I want to be alive more than anything."

"Then you must die."

Most of the peas break free with little coercion. Others need more force. Still, others need the pod almost destroyed before they will loosen their grip. There are plenty still left in the sack and the lord and I have taken to sharing the biggest, smallest, and greenest I find on the tray that holds his empty cup. Another pea pops in my mouth and takes me back to Awenmell. I like to imagine that sunshine is trapped inside each one and that burst of sweetness on my tongue is what sunshine actually tastes like.

For all our conversations, the lord seems more interested in the Eariss. He asks many questions and I deliberately suppress my old patterns of expecting a trap and guarding myself. We begin to converse more as equals and less as lord and nurse, master and servant, or even father and daughter.

"So, how do I choose this new paradigm? How do I choose to follow the Eariss?" He asks with such nonchalance, I wonder if he understands the question. That the acknowledgement of his crimes and injustices will undoubtably rip his insides apart, that the Mystery will suffer no fools, that in order to know the brightest sunshine, he must accept himself in the slimiest depths and own his role in their making. He watches my face as I consider his question. "Ah, you don't believe I am brave enough."

I can only offer him my truth. "I don't know."

He lifts his cup without a smile. "More tea... please."

I back into the lord's chamber carrying sweet tea and some sliced bread on a tray. There was no butter, so Aigneis smeared it with some gravy. I lick some gravy from the corner of my mouth. As the nurse, Aigneis suggested, I checked my own slice, for taste of course. But I think she was rewarding me. She seems deliriously happy about not having to shell those peas herself.

The Lord sits up and prepares his lap for the tray. His eyes widen at the gravied bread.

"I can vouch that it is as good as it looks."

"I see."

"Do you remember the hunter's tales in the council meetings?"

"They were always entertaining."

I take my place in the seat and let the sun stream onto my legs. "Remember the pits they would tell us about? The deep holes they dug and tricked the animals to fall inside?"

"Mm" is all he can manage with bread in his mouth.

"Consider yourself in one of those pits."

His eyebrows raise, but he doesn't interject.

"Only this one is filled with scratchy bracken and sharp thorns. Everywhere you turn, whatever you try to do, results in torn flesh and pain. You're trapped. But then you spy a ladder, it's just a makeshift one, made of thick bracken and tied together with strips of vine, and miraculously, it reaches to the top of the pit and sunlight.

You fight your way through the thorns and get to the ladder and begin to climb. But you're so focused on your freedom; you don't notice the ladder's covered with barbs and prickles that tear at your hands and body as you climb. It gets too painful and you let go and drop back into the pit of bracken. Here's your choice. You can stay in the bracken, being torn apart by every move you make, or you can face the extra pain, and climb your way out. The choice is yours, of course, but what you must understand is, the only way out is up that ladder."

He considers my words as he chews his bread. The Mystery thought it more fitting to describe his dilemma as a hunter's pit. For me, it was the hedge Martha described, and instead of a ladder, I had to force myself through a painful hedge to reach the lush field. I suppose it doesn't matter how we see it, only that we know what we must do to reach the truth and clarity on the other side.

"And at the top of the ladder?"

"Whatever is meant for you. Not as the Hall dictated, but what your soul decreed from before your birth. I'm still working out who I am in this new world. But I can tell you it felt like discovering I'd been fragmented into a million pieces, and becoming whole again, along with the broken world around me. It's so very hard to explain. I'm sure I'm not doing the process any justice."

"Why the pain?"

"We never discover how tightly we hold on to things until we're asked to release them." My voice squeaks at the end of my words and I pretend to cough and hope the motion will dislodge the memories of Thomas that seal my throat. "Excuse me, my lord." The cool water helps with the aggravation of the contraction, and gives me a moment to compose myself, yet the suddenness of missing him surprises me.

"Look around. They haven't left me much to be holding onto."

"It might surprise you what arises. It's not only the things we see, but what we feel too. Some notions become parts of us we must release; like fears, biases, and pride. All the parts we like to keep hidden away, and some we display to keep everyone away from the hidden ones."

This keeps him quiet for a while. I tidy his room and replace his water, moving from the kitchen and back again before he speaks. "You said 'arise'. What arises? How?"

I think I had some strange notion that bees only gathered around those at Awenmell. But the more I think about them being everywhere, the more sense it makes to me. Farmers, Tallefixes, Idlers, Lords and the 'smartest man in all Sirban' all have bees that need tending. If Guthrie could see me now, and know what I'm about to explain, he'd wink and smile. I know he would. Some things you just know, and hold close to your heart.

"First, you need to be still. Are you in the mood for stillness now, my lord, or should we try this later?"

"This is when this 'arising' happens?"

"Well, I expect so."

"Go ahead. Arise me."

Arise Me? I stifle a snort with a bite to my lip. "It's not quite like that, my lord. You'll be the one doing the work, not me. Do you still wish to proceed?"

He gives one curt nod. "Proceed."

He sits like he's in judgement on council day. Arms placed stiffly by his sides. His legs stretched out under the covers in parallel. If you tipped him over, he might stay at that angle. "It might be best if you lay down. It's best if your body relaxes."

He shifts down, wiggling side by side under his covers until he rests flat on the bed. "There."

"Now please relax, my lord. Close your eyes. Maybe some deep breaths, like you're preparing for sleep."

His breath acts like a marching army. In and out. Ordered and measured. "Nothing is happening."

"Concentrate on relaxing. When you're calm, we will begin."

"What did you *do* to him?" Walt stares down the hallway.

"Not a lot." A rush of guilt's heat prickles my neck.

"He hasn't stopped moaning and cursing all day. Hope we get some respite from the noise this evening."

"I know." I breathe through the guilt, knowing there was no other way. The guilt is fake and sticks to me like tar; a leftover from the Hall, this wretched place that seems to destroy every life that comes in contact with it. I don't meet Walt's, or even Aigneis's eyes. "He might be like this for a while. It could get worse."

"You know what you're doing?"

"Yes, I do."

They shrug and give half-hearted nods, and if I wasn't trying so hard to look competent, I'd do the same.

It took a while, but the lord found a trail of bees in his body. An intelligent and curious man, he didn't blame them, and understood the concept of the hive, the bees and the hornets well.

The hornets didn't take kindly to their plan being found out. He tipped his hat to them for showing the way to the bees. And he surprised me with his bravery in following them into the dark and painful crevices in himself. He found pieces of himself hidden in the darkness, attackers and controllers that kept his soul in line through threats and shame. The bees did as they directed. Many times, he clutched at his chest and buckled over. The pain of their stings and the truth of what they told him unbearable. But still he stayed, willing to learn about the patterns that had ruled his life.

"You look forward to this torture?" he gasped.

"It gets easier. It'll feel better on the other side."

"You mean once I've climbed this Star forsaken ladder?"

"At least then there'll be no more briars."

"Until I fall in another pit."

How perceptive. It usually takes a few ladder climbs to understand life is one pit after another. I smiled and hoped to encourage him. "Everyone falls into pits. Some falls are accidental, some are laid for us, and some we jump into. Remember to meet yourself at the top of the ladder with compassion. You've not only realized something trapped you in a pit; you faced yourself in a terrifying process and come out the other side."

His straining calmed, and his breath returned to normal. Not once did he open his eyes, so deep somewhere within himself. Tears slid down the side of his face, and I left him alone with his own relationship with the Mystery that he'll find in those silent and restful places. There are many shields to drop, but the one between your soul and the Mystery is the most important. I felt for him distantly, not getting caught up in his pain. Understanding the pain of another needn't be exhausting. It can't be if my energy comes from the Mystery, and not from my own limited resources.

I'd grown used to the rough blanket and the lumps of straw in the mattress. It was home for my weary body and signaled rest at the end of a long day. Outside my window, the moon only used half of her light in the sky. Some shadows and outlines were all I saw. The Mystery reminded me that's often all we need, a hint, a shadow, to know which direction to turn next. I thought about how our best decisions are made in the dark, when we can't rely on anything else but what we sense. We must feel our way through, caressing the tender parts of us and accepting every lump, bump, crack, and horror, and feel the story it needs to tell.

At night when it's quiet I dream of grassy fields and Wren and Oren, and the way the dew outlines a spider web just outside our cottage door. I miss Thomas's arms around me and hope that one day he'll forgive me for what I've done.

I dreamed I came across a leper with stars in his eyes and I was compelled to embrace him, to stand with him in his pain, to see the stars grow brighter. And in my dream, they did... the longer I stood alongside him.

The morning sun warms my sleeve, and the breeze sneaks the heat away before it can settle into my skin. On the other side of the courtyard, Walt tugs on a particularly stubborn weed. "You were right," he says and tosses the woody stem onto the barrow, "It feels less chaotic without all the weeds here."

Roping him into doing this chore was a feat in itself. I have to busy myself with something and pulling the mini forest from between the paving has a calming, tidying and newness about it. I squint into the cloudless sky. It's warmer now, not that the lord would have noticed anything this last half moon. I warned him to take his enquiries gently. To follow his bees quietly, but he felt an urgency that bade him to enter over and over again.

He cried and wailed most days and an anger seared through his body and echoed through the passageways. He struggled terribly through the conviction that madness was upon him when it seems that the world turns on its head and then back again. It was during this time he developed a deep hatred for me, the Mystery, and the Eariss. He refused to see me and toiled alone, with only Aigneis bringing him food and his concoctions when he called for them by name. In all the noise and purging, he didn't waver from his task.

Another wail flows out the open door to us in the courtyard.

Walt leans against the barrow. "Hm. That one was... anger, frustration, with just a hint of woe."

Walt's taken to dissecting the noises. I suppose it makes it lighter than listening to a man in pain, but I've not found merriment in his descriptions. A flash of color along the distant forest road gets both our attention. Looks like troops, maybe some horses. Another soft wail, more like a moan, creeps through the door.

Walt steps closer. "If Feeney were to arrive right now and see the state of the lord, he'd have you for sure."

My throat dries. "I know that well enough."

The lord wails louder this time. As long as the wind is in our favor, his voice shouldn't carry to the road. I hope.

"How much longer does this go on for—this treatment of yours?"

"I don't know. Each person sees what they need and it must be done alone. He has to face himself without assigning blame to others."

"That's a tough call for any person."

"Indeed."

The wailing grows stronger, louder; as if it's grown legs and is traveling down the hallways. Aigneis shouts amid the noise that rushes out the door, and we make for the entrance.

The lord trips on his nightdress and tumbles through the doorway and scrambles on all fours across the courtyard to my feet, weeping and gibbering nonsense. Only it's not nonsense, he can't find any words to describe what he's feeling. Aigneis appears covered in flour with a rolling pin in her hand. She slaps it into her palm, eager for a chance to keep him quiet for a short while.

"What kind of nurse *are* you? Here, use this."

"No need Aigneis."

The lord squints into the sun, exhausted from his stagger through the halls.

"Walt, get the weeds out. We'll lift him into the barrow."

Aigneis speaks before Walt takes a step. "The old pushchair in the stable might be more comfortable."

It takes the three of us to position him comfortably in the chair. Aigneis provides a cushion from within the Hall and tucks it under him. There's no sign of the wooden pin. "Comfortable my lord?"

He looks at me, still squinting in the daylight, "Don't make me go back."

"A short dose of sunshine will do you good. I'm not strong enough to push you anywhere but the courtyard."

His eyes are closed to the warmth of the sun. "That will be delightful."

'Delightful', Aigneis mouths, and they both take their leave within the Hall.

The chair is old and clunky and Walt's fingerprints are embedded in the dust that covers it. Guthrie would be in his element redesigning it for 'optimum efficiency'. My smile connects straight to my heart and spreads a welcome warmth there. After a few strenuous steps, I position it next to the barrow, we'll have sun for a while here. The lord rests with his eyes closed and so I wait with him, surrendering to whatever this moment will bring. The sun is nice, though. Its warmth stays on my skin longer, now it rises a little higher and the winds are less blustery. I plop into the barrow, the crunch of healthy weeds under my seat.

"I don't know..." he begins in a whisper. "I don't know how to recompense. Or even if it's possible. How *can* it be possible?"

I leave him with his thoughts and return to my own. Thoughts of a one-armed blacksmith who understood the power of regret and its merciless sting.

"Contrition is a powerful force, my lord."

"It consumes me."

"What consumes you is the conflict that rages inside your mind and body. You're trapped between two separate beliefs. What *was*, and what you wanted it to be. It happens to all of us in one degree or another. Our demand that our past be something other than it is, drives us to madness and grief. Have you felt the conflict?"

"There are times I can't take another day alive with myself."

"If you spend time with the resistance that refuses to accept the past won't be changed, feel into its wanting, the struggling and the true permanence of the past, you'll discover the only thing you can change is how you relate to it. As long as you fight what *is*, you're in an unwinnable battle. The more you accept it can't be changed and stop wasting energy there, the more you move out of regret and it loses its hold on you."

He pulls a small smile to the sun. "You appear to know this path well."

"I have regretted who I was on more than one occasion."

We are silent again, letting the conversation soak inside us, and he pats my hand. It's not condescending, it's more in unity and understanding.

Birds glide on the high winds, diving and being lifted again with no effort. I could easily spend the day with such entertainment. The lord looks restful, almost as if he's sleeping. "Are you well, my lord?"

"Much better." He shields his eyes from the sun. "May I deeply apologize for my treatment of you earlier? In fact, all my treatment of you?" His voice squeaks and he tries to hide the inner pain that causes a wince to cross his body.

I would normally brush such apologies aside as inconsequential. Diminish their effect on me and not wanting to feel another's guilt;

let them know all was well. I don't do that anymore. I make sure he can see my eyes. "Thank you."

I pull at a high weed alongside the barrow. "It seems only the weeds grow green around here." The fields are yellow, more like straw than the green that should have flooded them by now. Maybe they're holding the middle balance, like Guthrie's scales, green on one side, brown on the other and yellow, deciding which way it will dip this season. "Do people still believe in the myth where the kingdom will suffer wherever the leader has a wound?"

"I expect so."

"Remember King Derek and his bad leg?"

"His army never could march for long periods."

"Maybe there's some truth to it then?"

"Maybe."

"And where's your wound, my lord?"

He taps his chest and squeezes the word "heart" from his throat.

"When you are fully recovered, do you think you'll be whole enough to lead? Or will your kingdom only further expose your wounds?"

He pulls himself to upright in his chair. "If the myths are true, wouldn't they work in reverse?" He looks at me hopefully. "It seems whenever anyone sets out for war, they're waging a war against themselves; against their wound. Exposed for all to see. But to stop the wars? We need to stop them inside ourselves first."

It's the most animated I've ever seen him; the moons of his wretched despair have created a wise man before my eyes. "Only the bravest will hear that kind of charge, Lord."

"It's only the brave we need." He stares at me until I become uncomfortable and step away from the chair and barrow. I'm still not comfortable being scrutinized. Perhaps one day I will, but for now I force interest in the flower atop a weed until I get sick of pretending and turn to face him.

He's frowning, but it's more melancholy than angry. "I'd never imagined you'd become an enemy of the Hall."

"An enemy? I suppose that's exactly what I am to them."

"No one had ever seen a storm like the one that kept us from you." He pauses to check if I'm interested. I am. "We couldn't reach you until it was too late, you see. Too late for your mother, too late to check your eyes for the Eariss. And too late to stop the celebrations around your birth. We were never sure, you understand, and there was much treachery and pressure to deal with. My rules were designed to keep you quiet and away from any gaze of suspicion."

"You made rules supposedly for my safety. Yet, you didn't protect me at all."

He is sullen for a while and nods slowly. "I did not." He weeps again and groans a little. It's his pain, not mine. I don't need to partake of it. It's only when I understood this myself that I stopped going to war with myself. Maybe the lesson hides in that compassion and understanding. My suffering was never recognized; to not acknowledge another's suffering is an insidious form of violence, and there's been enough violence here already. It's not up to me to decide a satisfactory level for his suffering, just to acknowledge it for him, so he can begin to heal.

So we sit again in silence. Acknowledging there is no magic that will change the past with a wave of the Tallefix's wand, no potion to drink that will make us forget forever. All we can do is accept and live with it and the pain that it brings. Accepting the pain loosens its hold on us. And as Martha said as I twirled in the forest, we get to celebrate who survived. Even if celebration feels a long way off.

He wipes at his face with the back of his hand. "I think I should rest now."

"The sun has colored your face enough for today."

It takes all three of us to lift the chair into the Hall, and I take him to his chamber. He curls into a ball under the covers and I close the heavy curtains and listen to his sobs and wait for the mercy of sleep to arrive.

"Mystery, it's hard to remember pain once filled me so completely, too. That my heart was so heavy I could barely stand and the battle within it never ceased. Transforming hate into compassion is an unusual branch of alchemy. A kind of magic that I didn't force on myself, it just happened when I faced my own darkness. I hope the lord learns that those who show no compassion for others have experienced none for themselves. It's one of the first understandings when we begin to embrace our own story."

The only way to win the war in your heart is to lower your shields.

In your heart.

Of your heart...

with your heart.

Honesty, vulnerability, openness, and acceptance hurt. But you can't connect to another heart through shields. They must come down. Compassion isn't about who is wounded and who is the healer. It's a relationship between equals. Only when we're comfortable and have sat with our own darkness, can we sit with others in theirs. Equal in the darkness, equal in compassion for each other. If you don't know your own darkness, how can you understand another's?

"I wouldn't have healed without compassion. Without Thomas's, without Martha's; they didn't judge or berate me. They witnessed my pain."

Just as you did today.

"It makes sense, this lowering of shields, being open to another's pain, however uncomfortable it is for us. Then they are safe to follow bees, to understand themselves and how their sorrow molds their tale into honey, forever expanding and sweetening the lives of others."

The Mystery nudges at my heart.

"You want me to what?"

You heard.

So, I sit beside the man who sobs in his sleep, and transmute his pain as he releases it. I feel it, acknowledge it and return it to the Mystery. He will learn soon enough how to do this himself.

For now, he is brave to allow the pain to the surface and no longer pushing it away and hiding it. The pain is crushing and twisting, and at times excruciating, but with each acknowledgement it grows softer.

We've developed a happy routine in the kitchen. Aigneis and I move like we're involved in one of Bez's dances; a step this way, a twirl around each other, and we complete our chores without getting in each other's way. Walt joins us for tea most mornings and our days now start with chatter and laughter.

Walt is the last to sit at the small table. "Hey Aigneis, did you hear there's talk of Mr. Feeney moving through the far valley?"

Aigneis frets and oohs and ahhs at his second-hand tale. Her hand wringing and wide eyes tell me more than her words ever could. Not that I can hear them. Bees charge up and down my limbs, stabbing into my stomach and rendering me motionless, trapped like a statue; deaf, dumb, and almost blind. I'm surprised by their ferocity, but even more surprised that the mention of his name causes such a reaction. Walt and Aigneis talk among themselves, alternating between faces of alarm and concern, and don't notice my distance. Once I acknowledge the bee's presence; they release me from my stupor. I don't want to talk about Feeney.

I push my hands on to the table and stand. "I'll do that threshing now."

"There's only a small amount left to do."

Walt shakes his head, "It's pretty wet out there."

Aigneis brushes his concern away with a backhand to his arm. "When it's wet, we thresh in the great hall." She giggles. "Well, it's not used for anything much now, is it?"

She offers her well-worn instructions. "And be sure to open the doors at each end. On a day like today, you'll get a nice stiff breeze."

The flail whips past my ear on the way to the husks on the ground. I thought this chore would distract me but in reality; I stand in the cold and treacherous great hall, listening to the familiar sounds of my beatings whizz past my ear. Bees line my arms and my hands tremble on the flail. Now is not the time to deal with them, but I thank them for showing me the way to something unhealed and waiting for compassion.

There must be something else here to think upon. What else can I sense? Wheat.

It's easy to conjure up memories of threshing wheat at Awenmell; how Wren would run between the threshers, and we'd jest and laugh as we threshed and winnowed. I keep my mind on the fields and scents and sounds of Awenmell, even when Aigneis's 'stiff breeze' almost blows the tossed grain away. I leave the chaff on the floor with the rest of the mess, present Aigneis with a large bowl of grain, and prepare the lord's mid meal.

I scoop a small amount of healing broth into his cup, he's almost down to nothing and his aches have ceased considerably. His outer wounds have healed, but swarm after swarm of bees arrive to exhaust him. I'm glad he finds comfort in his bed. The bees take much energy from us and he'll recover well if he can sleep the effects of his inner revelations off. We aim for balance, but any forward growth and recovery is perfect for now. He needs to let the newness of life settle before he attempts to strengthen his physical body, which is a whole other set of bees that he's not yet prepared for.

The curtains open to a stream of dull light that we both take time to adjust to. His face is a little pink from yesterday and gives him a healthy glow.

"Good morning, my lord. If you're feeling up to it when you've finished, I have a question for you."

"Of course," he says and eats while I wipe dust from the windows just as some sunshine breaks through the clouds. It's an unpredictable kind of day; heavy cloud, rain, and drizzle that breaks into bursts of sunshine that make you forget all about the rain until you turn your back and it appears again.

He doesn't wait to finish his meal before lifting some bread toward me in a gesture that enquires about my question.

I take my seat by the window, and even though I practiced speaking gently, the words fall out in an accusatory tone, and that's not what I mean at all. "Who is the 'we' you spoke of yesterday?"

"I don't understand."

"After my mother's death, you said 'we' couldn't tell if you had the Eariss."

"Oh, Feeney and I—For some reason, it's always been Feeney and I."

"Who is he? I mean, where did he come from?"

"Ah, he's been here so long it sometimes feels like he was always here. He came to the Hall as a child, about 10 summers old; an orphan of the bloody uprising."

"A foundling then?"

"Not quite. He was from a landed family—out to the West, I believe. Carries that air with him all these summers later. Always a strange young man. Obsessed with law. The old and the new."

"New?"

"The changes made after the uprising, when the invaders were chased off."

"I remember now."

"He began his Eariss project shortly after that. Accumulating law, learning it by rote, he became a self-proclaimed expert on the Eariss and with such a powerful demeanor that shouted anyone down, no one questioned it. He was determined to put an end to the Eariss once and for all. If anyone raised questions, he labeled them a traitor and put them to death."

"He wrote the book of law?"

"No one questioned him."

I raise my eyebrows at him with no concern of protocol.

He shuffles his hands about and drops his chin. "Not even me."

"So a landed foundling rules the Hall and writes its laws and decides who dies?" I'm perplexed. How could that happen?

"It wasn't a coup. It was a reliance there, an intrigue here, a confidence there... soon I relied on him more and more for advice, knowing the law so well you see."

He delves back into his meal, slowly lifting the spoon to delay the conversation. I don't mind. I'm still trying to make sense of what he's told me. If the Hall and its generational history were meant to be overly protected, how did Feeney simply walk in and take control of it all?

"It's rather easy, you know," he says, sensing how ludicrous it sounds. "Easy to delegate decisions to another, one at a time, increment by increment." He exhales. "And when you see clearly, it's as if it happened overnight, and you wake to find yourself exhausted and in chains. Before long, you're a Lord with no control or power over your own kingdom, other than your role in the grand show, and another owns your soul. I imagine you think I'm pathetic."

"Not at all." I assume Feeney made everything appear shinier and more advantageous than it was. Like his jeweled book of law. He had a way of making me believe all manner of things. "Feeney seems to have that effect on many people, making them feel a certain way to debilitate them, or believe things that aren't true. But seeing clearly is the biggest step you can take. It removes his power because you've seen him for the shyster he is. How did your men react when you told them of his treachery?"

He bows his head. "By the time I woke up, the men were already his."

We sit in silence for a while. Loss is a devastating emotion. It's made worse by loneliness, no one understanding, and the shame that settles over the loss so it can't be spoken about. But to speak breaks its power over the tongue, and in turn over the heart.

"He once told me, 'If they don't fear you, create a fear for them. Keep it in their minds, and they will become pre-occupied with it, wasting energy on useless tactics and rumors, feeling brave by fighting among themselves, when the whole circumstance is an illusion.' Then he laughed loudly and spoke about how he toasted himself whenever he heard news of another outbreak of violence between the villages."

Just like the gossipers of Sirban. Creating something from nothing. But his monstrous plan sweeps across the entire kingdom.

He rubs his chin sadly. "He's quite clever. I'll give him that. If you create two sides to a non-existent problem, and spread rumors about the evilness of the other, they can only battle and cause bloodshed, believing they're on the side of good. When they're unsure, he is the one with the answers. Everyone else is considered duped and a liar. Much evil is done in the name of good."

"So that's his plan? Bloodshed and confusion? To what end?"

He shakes his head. "Distractions. So many distractions. Why do you think he uses distractions?"

"To keep the people from something."

He nods.

"It would have to be valuable to him or he wouldn't put so much energy into it."

"You don't put your whole life into something you don't value. You put parts, you do your duty, but your whole life doesn't revolve around something you're not passionate about."

It reminds me of the edge, but I don't think Feeney's been to my edge. Maybe an angry and defiant edge?

"He demands everything be returned to him, and he believes he deserves it, being a child of the uprising. Lost it all you see, family, land, who he was. The Hall probably served as a place to re-invent himself, gain what he had lost."

"But the Hall isn't his."

"He believes he's entitled to it."

"And I'm in the way."

"You're more than in the way. You're the Eariss."

"I'm part of a larger whole. He won't be able to stop us all."

"He won't tolerate defiance. It upsets him the most. When you left, he became a madman. Spreading incredible stories about you, even for him. But who could deny him? He had the book of law. It was incredulous to him that anyone would not listen to him and his laws. I wondered for his sanity, but could do no more than wonder. Many were punished. Some were killed."

Heat rises from my body and bursts into uncomfortable pain around my chest and face. It squeezes my throat. Martha's words appear like a breeze that blows it away *'And who holds the cup?'*

Surely there's some who have seen their folly in following him. "And his men aren't defiant?"

"I'm afraid they can't afford to be."

"So it's true then?"

"That he holds defiant men's families as ransom to get them to obey?" he nods but says no more.

It's not just me he hates. It's anyone and anything. Defiance equals punishment, but to continue without defiance creates a slower death where the soul dies and purpose shrivels to dust. A trap where confrontation and death seem the only way out. The lord looks more exhausted than usual. Perhaps the topic drains more from him than I expected. It's easy to judge him as a wretched old man who was more concerned with his image than where Feeney's parade was leading his people and his land. But this is where we find ourselves, and this is the only place we can move from.

"I am yet to meet a person who doesn't have a 'Feeney' in their lives—some type of fear or obligation that keeps them from themselves. Held hostage by a force that drives them or denies them. It doesn't need to be a person. Some can't stay away from the marketplace. Heavy ale, chewing roots, even gossiping can be soothing. That's what Feeney did. He offered you something that made your life seem easier, but it only lasts for a while. Anything that crushes who we are until we can't hear our soul anymore is a 'Feeney'. Destructive voices that drown out the voice of our souls until we claim 'Feeney' as part of our identity, obeying it proudly as if it is us. Or we hide from it, denying its existence in our lives. Either way, the Feeney gets the power, and the destruction goes on."If he wants the Hall, he can have it.

Thomas was right about Feeney, and I've no way to tell him I was wrong.

⁕

I do my best imagining late at night, when the Hall is quiet, and the candlelight creates long flickering shadows on the wall of my chamber. I tuck the blanket under my chin to conserve warmth and let my mind wander down brightly lit paths. There's no use wandering and pacing the dark paths. They lead nowhere profitable.

The Lord has made significant progress. He sees his wounds and is prepared to feel his way through them. He's being open about his role in the kingdom's fall, and judiciary stuff about Feeney. No doubt there'll be more secrets. There always are the deeper we go. Secrets and shames we didn't even know were buried. He may need to speak to another. Perhaps our one-armed blacksmith might enjoy a visit to these walls; he's a good listener and versed in the pain of regret. Once the roads are safe, of course.

I sigh. Will the roads ever be safe? Not while Feeney's in control of them.

A bright light flashes in my mind and I check the candle to see if it's brighter, but it's just the stub that burns low. Perhaps once the lord is well, he can work on restoring his rule. Yes! What a benefit to have a leader with a soulful connection to the Mystery, one who understands bees and the power they hold over people.

What an amazing thought. To have the Hall operating from a contrasting set of rules, an opposing outlook, attending to their bees and working together.

Unease causes me to shuffle in my bed. This scenario feels suspicious, rather like me dreaming of a small house in the valley with Thomas when I was in Sirban, as if there was some straight and easy road to happiness. What a thoughtless fool I was. But I didn't know any better. Am I being naïve again? My heart warms at the thought of our cottage. It spreads to my limbs and there it aches. This is what it feels like to have a home. To miss a place and its people, to not be quite yourself like a piece is missing. I close my eyes and take myself to Awenmell, and deep inside my dreams I close my eyes to the sunshine and smell the breeze pushing its way up the field to the cottage and Wren skips past me with her blue shawl flying out like a cape behind her.

The morning is a little warmer. I wonder for a moment whether the stones have softened, but even I know that's one of those dreamy things Guthrie tries to correct in me. Walt's voice travels from the kitchen and meets me in the hallway. It's not raised in anger, just louder than is usual.

"I'm telling you it's true."

Aigneis looks at me and shrugs as I enter the room. Her eyes are wide and her hands twist at a cloth until it is hard.

Walt faces me and speaks as if I'm some kind of translator that will help Aigneis understand. "A rider came through the village and said the Trothsmen are on the move to Feeney's land."

"Lewtshire?" I squeak and pretend it was my morning voice.

Aigneis rolls and unrolls her cloth. "It's not good news for us this morning, I'm afraid."

"The village is a mess." Walt shakes his head. "Everyone is battening down, ready for his tantrum. Some have packed up, citing important markets they mustn't miss. Others are visiting relatives far away and taking their chances on the road."

Aigneis flicks her cloth gently at my arm. "Have you met him? I don't wish to put you off your first meeting, just preparing you to be on guard for any tricks he might play on a young girl like yourself. They say he loves the ladies you know, but I think he also hates them too with the way he treats them."

My mouth dries. "Thank you for the preparation, Aigneis." Bees fling through my body haphazardly as I try to take control of them.

I don't want to follow them now.

I want to pretend Walt got it all wrong.

He always gets things wrong.

Feeney isn't coming here. He can't.

My work isn't done yet.

I push the bees down and ignore Aigneis's frown that settles on my trembling hands. I don't owe either of them an explanation. I need to know the Lord's plan for the future of his land. The others watch me while I gather his food early and leave for his chamber.

"Walt?" I call over my shoulder in the hallway, "Please bring more water to the lord's chamber."

L ight streams into the Lord's chamber. It's true I pushed the curtains open with more gusto than before, and he blinks hard, although he's already upright in bed. I serve his food and ignore his concerned frown as he studies my face and behavior.

Stretching to my tiptoes at the window doesn't bring Awenmell into view as I wished it would. Some form of hope, Thomas to hold me while the bees dissipate, an understanding nod from Guthrie, a hug from Oren and Wren, and a fresh breeze rolling across the tops of the green crop, just crisp enough to shiver and look forward to the fire.

"Is it far away?" the lord asks. "The place you would prefer to be?"

"Far enough away. A few valleys to the west."

"No details then? It's sensible to hide your treasure." He slurps at his gruel while I stand with one foot here and one foot in Awenmell. A dream state of rebelliousness where I don't have to acknowledge Walt's news. I don't like it; I don't want it, so I fight it. But not for long. That folly left me long ago.

Acceptance comes quickly, dripping into my body like steps of a forward plan more than a sense of defeat. "It's called Awenmell."

He dabs at his mouth with a cloth. "Once I am well, may I come to your Awenmell?"

My stomach clenches. It's fine to watch him heal within these walls, but to invite him to the place where I am truly alive? Where my guard is always down, where I actually live and not just exist? "I fear you are used to some manner of opulence, my lord and Awenmell and its lodgings are quite rustic."

"Whatever you need, we will take there; anything here is yours."

"We *need* nothing there. Everything is found within its boundaries."

"It's magical?"

"Perhaps it is." I know I'm being wistful, imagining the welcoming oak just over the next rise, but whatever I need, I can find in Awenmell. If I need support, it is there. Kindness as I've never known, love, confidence and acceptance. I place my hand over my heart; and yet it's still with me at the same time as if I've brought that here with me too. If I feel this way, what of the others who left and travel the lands? The Eariss. The Army. No wonder the scroll says no army can stand against it.

"Well then, what must I do to be considered worthy of a visit."

"It's not about worthiness, my lord. We're all worthy by virtue of our existence."

"What's it about then?"

"It's many things to many people. A place of peace. Safety; definitely safety, and that safety allows room to heal and grow. It's a place to meet with the Mystery, to discover who you were meant to be, not what the Hall told us we should be." Words can't describe depth. They just brush past the surface of a meaning and all we can do is hope that our understandings share the same intensity. "When you peel everything else away, it's about restoration. Restoring relationship, with the Mystery, yourself, and those around us."

The lord defers a nod. "I can see that."

"The Mystery is the greatest example of relationship. It acts as a template for us and our relationship with others. But we can't do that by *imagining* a relationship with it. We have to know the Mystery and trust its leadings. Then we begin to care, really care about what's going on around us. Many still talk of the traditions and call for peace, but it's difficult to care for things that you don't know intimately. How can you care about peace if you don't know what it feels like in your soul?"

"What is this Mystery and how do I find it?"

"Everyone finds it in their own way. But be assured, it searches for your reconciliation just as much as you do. It's the stillness between heartbeats. The notes played behind the music, the life inside the no breath."

"So it's always been there?"

"Truth is like a rock. It doesn't move. It waits calmly in all its power for you to see and acknowledge it. It needs no song, dance, or grand costuming—or jeweled books for that matter."

"I may have lived my life in this Hall, but you mustn't let me die here. Will you take me to your Awenmell?"

"When you're well enough, let us travel to Awenmell. There's a man with a brilliant mind called Guthrie who'd love to be involved in your plan to turn all of this around. And you must meet Silas..."

"Ah, that's better. See how your eyes sparkle when you speak of the place? But if it's as magical as you say, Feeney won't be happy about it. Then again, he's never happy about anything."

The lord chuckles at his jest. My throat dries and my mind whisks me away from the fields of Awenmell and back into the tale I heard in the kitchen. I rub the cold from my arms and collect his plates. I answer the concerned look on his face.

"Feeney plans to return here, my lord. His Trothsmen prepare the way for him as we speak."

The door opens, and Walt enters holding water jugs and panting, but with a smile on his face. "A horseman rushed to me while I collected water. I ran, then when he called me by name, I recognized him as an upstart from my village who likes to think himself better than others. He made some veiled threat that the Hall should be prepared." He spills the water as he sets it down and tries to mop it up with his shirt, but just spreads it further.

The Lord sits upright, more at Walt's words than his improper entrance. "Feeney knows she is here?"

"He knows of a nurse who has made you well, my lord." His grin would have disturbed me if I didn't know he holds no malice toward me. "He plans to visit here tomorrow after important meetings around the mid-meal I'm told, no doubt to congratulate the nurse…" He leans forward and whispers. "I was told not to mention it, but I know Ash hates surprises. You mustn't let them know it was me."

The lord and I exchange glances with a sadness that goes deep to our bones. *He knows.*

Walt remains oblivious. "Our Mr. Feeney. Very obnoxious, but very powerful. I bet you're excited to meet the man."

I have no words.

Walt nudges my shoulder. "Of course she is, look she's all a quiver."

The Lord coughs to clear the air. "Please leave us so we may prepare for his arrival."

"Of course, my lord."

I fall into the seat as Walt closes the door. The Lord remains upright, deep in thought. As much as I hate to admit it, we're alike, him and I.

Two statues that sit with our hands in our laps, sitting in silence with our own thoughts, our own reasoning and our own plans, weighing up odds, and considering the aftermath of each move.

There's no profitability in words when thinking and sensing must be done. I regain a sense of integration and given the predicament we find ourselves in, I'm eager to move forward. Feeney could have sent the Trothsmen, but I imagine he wants to make a grand entrance himself in pursuit of victory.

"Are you well?" I ask of the lord after a time.

He nods. "And you?"

"Any conclusions?"

"Stay. Leave. Attack. Retreat. Hide. We're not short of options," I nod to the truth of his statement. "Just of expected outcomes."

"Indeed."

⁂

Light spills through the tall fragmented window and warms the great hall. The table the elders would bang makes for a hard bed, but a restful place to watch the light change in the window above me. Tiny angles cut in the glass hint at a range of colors that disappear when I focus on them. I can still make out the gentle crone's fingers of light that reach inside, made whole by the dust from the threshing chaff I disturbed when I entered.

It's an odd but productive position for thinking. Strangely quiet and almost peaceful, lying here in the only place I could never connect with my mind or conjure a rational word. I panicked far more than I did any thinking in here. But I can make up for it now, and remember that terrified girl with compassion. I was surviving, and that's all I had to do, no matter how I did it.

The door cracks, and I jump to sitting, startling Walt as he opens the door. "Err, someone's here for you."

Fear shoots through my body. *No one knows I'm here.* Feeney? I almost gag.

Walt pulls a face at my reaction. "Says her name's Katteryn, and she's on very important business."

Katteryn. I close my eyes and take a deep breath. Is there any other type of business she could be on? The fear disappears within my delight and I bounce off the table. "Where is she?"

"I led her to the kitchen. Is that all right?"

I push past him, "As long as she doesn't go anywhere near that broth it is!"

I move through the hallway at a fast walk that intermittently skips into a brief run. *Katteryn?* The biggest mouth is on the loose and travels the roads knowing who I am and where I am. How many would she have told on her way?

My angst drops from my shoulders like an old robe and while she holds her hand out in greeting, I embrace her in a warm hug, as if I was holding Awenmell itself.

"Sit, sit," I gesture to the chairs at the table and pour water for tea.

Katteryn plops into a chair, weary. I'm surprised she hasn't removed her coat; it looks bulky and difficult to move in. "I could have traveled straight through to the village and visited with you in the morning. That would've been better, don't you think? It would give us much more time together."

The sun has already lowered in the sky. "Oh, this is perfect, Katteryn. It is a joy to see you!" I can't see much of her under her coat and large traveling hat. Her face bears the marks of tiredness, more lines than I remember, but her countenance remains the same. Wait. Did her coat just move?

"They chose me, of course."

"Yes, they did, dear Katteryn. How could they choose another?"

She eyes the larger cup in my hands and I set it quietly beside her. "Important business."

"So Walt tells me."

She sips at her tea, and I long to hear anything she can tell me. Is the important business about Awenmell? I pull myself back from leaning over the table and try to be patient, but she keeps sipping. She can't be that thirsty. "You have news? Of Awenmell?"

"Oh yes. Important business. I have messages I must deliver to you."

"They're safe? Everyone is safe?"

"Oh, yes, yes."

"Thomas.... and Oren, and Wren?"

"They're all well. In fact, that was one of the very messages I was to bring to you." I breathe a sigh of relief, but she doesn't seem to notice. She's far more interested in the half loaf of dark bread on the hearth. I don't know why she just can't tell me the message. Why her need for importance drags out every morsel of her influence during this mission. I think it's a game she likes to play. I'll join her and not fight. I'll play the game lightheartedly. I slice the bread, offer her a slice, and smile as she feigns surprise at my offer. It makes her feel good to play this game, she's traveled so far. Why not reward her with some indulgence. "So there's more than one message. That's exciting."

"Oh yes, they have trusted me with many."

"As you should be, dear Katteryn. Now, who was the first message from?"

She's fired up and leans forward. A gurgle comes from within her coat and a chicken's head pops out at her neckline. "Pardon." She shoves the chicken's head back inside the coat and wiggles her body until it's back in place. The heft of her coat now makes sense. I don't want to know how many chickens she's traveled with, or why, or even how.

Katteryn clears her throat. "Oren."

His name brings peace to my heart, and I'm surprised by the sting of my clouded eyes.

"He said it was very important, and I wasn't to forget it. You know how he gets all serious and stares into your eyes so you won't forget the message?"

"And?"

"Oh, oh. Let me think. 'People talk', that was it. People talk, mostly about you, and they know more than you think."

I smile to hide my frustration. I wanted to hear something tangible. Something that would bolster me. Not something that Thomas had already told me about gossipers, and by a gossip herself. I'm sure my smile looks fraudulent. A knot forms in my stomach, but it's a question I need to ask. "And Thomas. Does Thomas send a message to me?"

She reaches for my hand and squeezes it. "Yes, my dear, he does. Something about battles...."

The knot and my stomach fall to my feet. After all this time and distance, is he still arguing with me about battle plans?

"Now, battles... no.... no, it was shields. Positioning the shield or something."

"Shields down?" My clouded eyes spill over.

"Oh, and this." She reaches into her coat and pulls out a crumpled iris bloom, petals soft like fine cloth, its color—a chicken pops out from her coat and pecks the iris and disappears again. We jump and laugh at the surprise and my tears drop onto the table. Even pecked, it's the most wonderful thing I've seen. My heart blooms. News from Awenmell from the least likely person I would have expected. My heart is full. They are safe.

She chomps on her bread while I admire the softness of the petals and how it has held its color. They grow in the pond, where the agitation from the waterfall settles into a soft flow of water; you can barely discern its movement. Katteryn's words snap me back to the kitchen.

"Now what was it? Something about a cliff?"

"Who? Thomas?"

"Yes, yes.... a cliff,"

"Cliff?"

"No, the edge."

I'm on my feet so quickly my chair topples backwards. "The edge? What about the edge?"

Katteryn reels and almost loses her balance on the chair. I reach to her, fearful of a fall and dealing with her damaged chickens, but she rights herself without incident. "He said to tell you Oren is safe because it was important you hear that. They've been spending quite a bit of time together, those two. Once I saw them working together on Guthrie's weather machine, they got it fixed and then it broke again. You know, I've heard that the reason it breaks so often is because—"

"Katteryn please! The message."

Her caterpillar eyebrows bounce and I feel I've offended her. I've demanded information. Letting someone know what I wanted was always a way to be sure they denied it. Katteryn's face softens and her frown disappears. "Of course, my dear." She concentrates, and I accept it as a sign of her affection, wanting to be sure of passing the correct information. "He said the view is so dramatically different from the edge, he's seen things he couldn't see before and that he earnestly hopes your heart will return to his."

Katteryn becomes a blur of brown, and I wipe at my eyes. "Thank you."

"He said he'd tell you all about it when you get home."

I nod and run a finger along the bent but beautiful iris on the table. *Home.* I can see them at the edge. Thomas would argue and try to be logical and Oren would dive straight into his heart and show him the truth. I wonder how he handled the dare to stand at the edge and what wondrous things he saw. I'm now desperate to get there, but there seems to be too much in the way. I sniff and wipe my face clean. "What do you know of the Trothsmen Katteryn? Did you see any?"

"I'm one to keep on top of everything, as you know." Her coat clucks. "Not much passes me by. Some are headed this way, but many stay back in the valley."

"Our valley? Awenmell's valley?"

"I expect so."

"Why would they split in two?"

She shrugs and reaches for more bread. "All this coming and going. It's rather exciting, isn't it? I came across a troop resting on the road and passed them some fresh eggs for favor and safe passage. Tried to make polite conversation; you know how I'm a gifted conversationalist, and I enquired about what they were doing there. Do you know what they replied? 'Waiting.' What a silly answer. Don't you think? I think so."

Walt waves as he passes the door. The daylight has become gray enough for him to leave.

I stand, and my movement catches his eye. "Wait!" I take Katteryn's hand and ignore the way her coat rolls as she stands. "I'm so glad you came to see me, Katteryn."

"I was chosen because he said I'd be sure to get the message to you. I'm exceptional in that regard."

"You understand the importance of a good message and always carry through."

"He said he could trust me above all else."

"And I agree with him." I nod toward Walt. "You must let our guardsman escort you to the next village. I can vouch for his kindness."

"Very well then." She embraces me then with a look of surprise in her eyes, flips my hand over and draws on my palm with her finger. She smiles. "And that was the last one. Almost forgot it." I clench my hand tight as she leaves the Hall and I wave to the wobbly brown figure with a bemused Walt at her side. Then I turn heels and run to the lord's chamber, faster than I have ever run within these walls.

I don't knock, and the lord jumps as I enter and break his thoughts.

"I've just had a visitor."

"Who?"

"A soul from Awenmell."

"Not a trickster? Not working with Feeney?"

"No. I don't think they'd cope, to be honest."

"News?"

"Some good. Some confusing." Forgive my pacing, my lord. I find it comforting at this moment.

"Certainly. Does this news change any of Feeney's plans?"

"I doubt it; but it may alter ours."

"Very well then. Tell me."

"There are still Trothsmen in the valleys. They have not all returned to Feeney."

"Knowledge is always helpful, even if it's not what we want to hear."

"And there's something else that's come to my attention, my lord, although I'm not sure how it fits with any plans. Ours or his."

The lord's hand is cold in mine. Feeble, white, and almost waxy to touch. I flip it over, just as Katteryn had done to me, and circle his palm with my finger. I'm sure I won't explain it as well as Thomas does, but it's straight from the heart of the man I love. It's almost as if he stands beside me as I speak.

"We are here; this oneness in our palm, we use it to give and take, making decisions that affect all others around us. Life can make it calloused, that's for certain, but generally it's soft and any harshness that forms is protective rather than attacking. But we dwell here, whatever we put our hands to becomes our purpose."

The Lord observes his hand and raises his eyebrows.

I open his fingers and encourage him to stretch them wide. "It's always right in front of us, you see. A reminder of our own power, hidden in plain sight. Not powerless, just... inactive. We're fragmented, you see, and we have to be brought back together again."

The lord considers me with a side glance. "I don't see it."

"See the spaces between your fingers when you open them wide?" I mimic his hand and we compare the shapes made between our fingers. "They're the same size. Balanced. A reminder to provide equal care to the three parts of our lives that require our attention, our bodies, our intellects, and our soul. We need balance."

"True."

"And here," I tap the tops of his fingers, one after the other. "The four tips remind us of the four elements. They may change and alter their physical state; outside circumstances affect them, but nothing ever truly changes their essence, nor what they are here to perform. We find the greatest lessons in the world around us, within the forests, streams and mountains. Seasons change, birth follows death, and life flows with times of fruitfulness and times of rest. To fight against what is, is pure folly. The elements stay true to themselves, just as we must stay true to our own essence to regain our power. Water changes its form, but it doesn't change its essence, what it truly is. Its essence is unchangeable. We are the same. We might not change our physical form readily as water, but we change and move away from our truth in other ways. Others may tell us what our essence is, or should be, often for their own motivations, or to fit with the story they have told themselves. We dress up stories about ourselves, believing ourselves to be bigger and better than others. We hide our essence in the collection of pots, or wear fine costumes, but deep within, our essence hasn't changed. We must find that essence and be true to it."

The lord flexes his thumb. "And this?"

"This brings it all together. Some call it light, because nothing can exist without it, some call it truth. I prefer to call it love. Whatever you name it, nothing can change it or its essence. It takes love to balance ourselves, to accept our nature, and have compassion on ourselves and others." I bend his thumb and lay it across his palm.

"And there it is," he says. "All along, right before my eyes. Whatever we lay our hands to, is our purpose. We must choose every day what we lay our hands and heart to."

I push his fingers together and close the gaps. "Where there is balance, there's unity and wholeness." I roll his fingers down and he forms a fist himself. "And when you know all this, you have found your power."

The lord is astonished and opens and closes his hand several times; fast, slow, and at odd angles. "You can't make a fist without bringing them all together."

"Exactly, my lord."

He draws on his palm with his finger and traces the gap in between each finger. Frowns and then taps the tops of his finger. "I won't remember this." He scans the room and settles on the wall in front of him. "Draw it. Scratch it into the stone."

How am I to draw an idea? The old dagger becomes the perfect stylus and I brace myself for the stone's resistance, but it falls away, crumbles at my determined pressure. I'd prepared my stance for a fight where there was none. First, I scratch the gaps between our fingers, then use the tip of the blade to twist four little dots into the stone about them. As I start work on a spiral for the palm, a sense of knowing comes over me and courses through my veins like silk.

This is the symbol. The one I'd seen scattered on trees, etched into posts and rocks, and hidden under fire pits. Thomas must've used the hands of all who'd left Awenmell, and in turn, they'd used the hands of others to explain their need for wholeness. I brush dust away from my design. And here it is now, scratched into the walls of the Hall at the lord's request. But why would Thomas—?

Ah, he was forming *his* army, he just didn't know it.

The lord looks pleased with my scratchings. It's no work of art, but tells a story he wants to hear repeatedly. He compares his hand with the etch on the wall and then wipes it on his bedclothes.

"So?" He asks, "Trothsmen in the valleys."

I really want to tell him that Katteryn is known for false reports. But all she's known for is elaborated, truthful ones. "It definitely narrows our chances."

"Chances of what?"

"Of making it to Awenmell."

"I was hoping you'd say that."

"Few of our other options won't end in death. There's an old cart in the stables. We can lay you on it. My horse is used to pulling."

"We can't leave now."

"First light?"

"Agreed."

I feel like we should shake hands or something; some ritual that signifies comradery. I prepare his chamber for the night and bring him a hearty meal. We can discuss any thoughts we have during the night in the morning.

"Will the others help?"

"No, we'll send them home before we leave. They won't be here for his arrival."

"He'll still find them."

"They won't know anything. Besides, I think Walt knows a thing or two about hiding."

"He won't stop, you know that."

I nod. Of course, he'll come after us. Sometimes I think it will go on forever, this battle between us. Standing now isn't an option. What on earth could I do, anyway? This way might give us a little time. I don't know what for, but at least there's a plan for our rattled energy.

"First light then?" he whispers.

I nod and carry his plates from the chamber.

The Hall is so still and quiet, my chamber door clicking closed sounds like a smash of iron and wood through the hallways. The candle flame bends with the gust caused by its closing and settles into a bright column of light when I set it on the table.

There. Right there. My finger rubs a marker into the stone where the morning light first hits the wall. It's easier to scrape the symbol into the stone here. The more you do anything, the easier it gets. Now I'll see it as soon as I wake. I open and close my hand into a fist. *Power when we've come together.* Everything makes sense but the timing.

I smooth my hand over my newly swollen belly. Would I have come if I had known? A moot point. A 'what if' with no answer. There's no magic that changes past decisions, no wishing hard enough that something wasn't so. This is now, and this is the only place I'm alive and can decide anything.

The bed offers no comfort and I change positions constantly seeking a peace that's just out of reach. How can I sleep knowing his love for me is waiting? How long will it be until morning? Far too long. Time is the strangest thing. The idea of time only exists when we think about the past or the future. We use it to measure how long ago something was, or how long until the next. It only exists as a measure of our longings. Not for anything else. I watch the candle stub burn. There's a measure of time. How long until morning, dear candle?

❦

I wake into darkness with a gasp caught in my throat.

What was that?

Footsteps. Many of them. Boots.

My clothes get tangled as I dress. I sit with my back to the chamber door, stuffing the last of my hair into the wimple and straining to hear. Bandits? A family looking for lodging? They'd most likely use the stable, not rush into the—

Light and shadow pass under my door and the smell of torches burns my nostrils. The voices carry further down the corridor. Should I chance a look? My hands smooth over my head, searching for stray hair, find their way to the door and tremble on its handle. I listen again, voices, deep and curt; and not a sound from Aigneis's chamber.

The door creaks and covers my gasp, but none of the Trothsmen's backs turn. They congregate near the lord's chamber. Should I approach them?

My mind mumbles something, but any concern fades as bees sting my entire body, leaving their most ferocious attacks on my fingers and toes. I retain the presence of mind long enough to close the door quietly.

I return to the floor and scrunch the wimple to my face; at least if I cry out, it may help muffle my distress. If only my trembling hands would hold it still enough to do its job. Sharp, determined steps tap into the floor outside my door. Familiar sound, familiar pace. Feeney? What if he calls for me?

I launch myself to the table. The key shakes in my hand. Why does every cursed step feel like I'm clattering through pots and waking the dead? *Click.*

It's safer on the floor at the base of the door. My ears strain so hard to hear, I fear they're creating sounds of their own. My hands fold over my belly and calm my racing body and thoughts.

Why am I hiding behind a locked door? Fool! Why don't I go out there?

It's true. I've never been bold. Ever. The only times I might consider myself bold are when I've been desperately trying to hide my cowardice. I'm a coward. I wipe a tear from my face and my hands continue to tremble. Nothing like a warrior. Martha got it so wrong. I want to hide in my shame, but Martha's lesson about each of our stories plays in my mind. I can't remove it. *Your story is unique, she tells me. You mustn't dilute the herbs; you lose the power.* I clench my hands into trembling fists and hold them against my lips.

I understand the need for wholeness, but my body reacts as if it's shattered into thousands of pieces. And other times, my body feels at complete peace about something my brain panics about. Who tells the truth here? Mystery, am I losing my mind? Do my body and brain take turns mocking me? How can I find the truth?

Your body always tells the truth. Your mind helps you decipher its message; meaning whether its message is true for this moment, or true for a moment in the past that you haven't yet healed.

Other than the danger on the other side of the door, I am fine here right now. I can breathe. No one beats me or attacks me. My bees and body reacted to the thought of what might happen. My mind slowly calms and the bees settle into an unpleasant hum. At least I can think again. Just a thought did that?

Not 'just' a thought. A thought or memory acted as a hornet and sent the bees into your body, and you reacted to the bees. It's never just one thing.

Does it work the other way? Is that what the honey is? Healing and replacing the old thoughts with new? I think about that for a while. That would mean training the bees to settle, to not pay attention to hornets. Mystery, you always told me who I was. Now I have to remind myself who I am.

"I only cowered because I believed he was stronger." I whisper. "In fact, I thought everything outside of me was stronger than what's inside of me; and it's not true."

When I'm in charge of how I feel, not him and his games, I regain my power and I am no longer afraid. He has taught me to be wary, but I don't need to be afraid.

I leave the door and rest on the bed, listening to the sounds and shuffling of feet in the hallway. "Mystery, I will walk the hallway through those Trothsmen and enter the lord's chamber this moment if required."

It is not required.

I close my eyes and let go of everything my mind is trying to hold on to. Not because it doesn't matter, but because it does. This is a different type of edge, a different kind of surrender. This one says you'll be fresher in the morning. You can't do anything now. The one that parents you into sensibility instead of childish brawling. Grief and worry do nothing for me. The Mystery floods in as I release myself to it and wraps me like a blanket into deep sleep.

❦

First light's gentle form rouses my eyes. *Feeney!*

Was it a dream? I brush my hands over my sleep crumpled clothes and snatch at my wimple. I open the door a crack, and Walt appears from the other side of the hallway.

"About time," He groans and tilts his head toward the Trothsman standing guard outside the lord's chamber. "Said he's to leave at dawn."

The lord calls from his chamber and I nod and move past Walt toward the kitchen. Walt won't know that plans made for first light take a drastic turn when delayed until after dawn. I'd prefer to be in the lord's chamber, working out where to stop along the way of our journey, but I must pretend that the activities of the night before are nothing to be concerned about, and that this day is no different to any other. I light the fire in the hearth. It's usually Aigneis's job, but the Trothsman won't know that.

"Where's Aigneis?"

"She was feeling poorly and warm to touch. So I told her to rest some more. This day is extraordinary, and it hasn't even started."

If only he knew. "It is a strange day, isn't it? If she remains unwell, could you escort her to her family in the village?" I answer his questioning frown, "The lord's treatments have used all the coriander, but I'm sure she'll find some there."

"Ah, I see."

Walt's always eager to head home. I expect he'll be checking on Aigneis often, so he can 'help' her back to the village as soon as he gets the chance.

It's well past dawn, and the Trothsman hasn't left his guard. I can't wait any longer. Each moment the sun moves higher shortens the time until Feeney's return. Walt creeps beside me at the kitchen door and watches the Trothsman too.

I lean my head closer to his. "Have you ever been in a tussle with a Trothsman?"

"I'm breathing, aren't I?"

"So that means, no?"

"You're not planning on attacking him, are you?"

"No," I lie. "I just want him to leave the way clear. It's getting late."

"For what? Oh, concoctions. Surely his orders don't deny a nurse tending to the ill."

That's right, I'm a nurse, not a fugitive. I collect the prepared tray from the table behind me. "We're about to find out."

The Trothsman wears a sneer with no effort. It's not often you get to see their faces. His seems made of steel, and impenetrable as his armor. He looks at the food and medicines on the tray, and then at me. His sneer seems carved into his face.

"It's dawn." I remind him.

"Not yet, it isn't."

How do you argue with nonsense? He shuffles aside, and I close the door behind me.

The Lord looks pale and doesn't react to my entry.

"You're unwell my lord?"

He wakes and reaches for the silver chalice beside him.

"A drink, my lord?"

He slumps back into the bed and shakes his head.

"Here, I've brought you some hearty broth..."

He turns his head away from me, and I lean against the door to hear the Trothsman shuffle his feet. I lower my voice as I approach the bed. "We must be going. As soon as the Trothsman leaves. What were they doing here last night?"

The Lord shakes his head again. He seems so weak, like he's about to sleep. "Are you unable to speak? Grunt. Make some kind of noise, my lord. They've stolen your voice?"

How can you direct an army with no voice? Guthrie may know. We must be on our way.

The lord again shakes his head and looks sad. "No." With labored breathing, he props himself on an elbow and points to the chalice. His lips are dry and even though he refuses as best he can, I hold the chalice carefully to his lips. The chalice matches a line, not quite a scratch, perhaps a bruise that runs from his mouth upward to his cheeks and the distinct scent of pine needles reaches my mind and my memory.

I gasp, and he relaxes, knowing I understand his message. It's too late for him and we both know it.

The lord beckons me with a slightly bent finger and speaks in almost silent whispers. "He's terrified of the Eariss. He's terrified of..." he points, having run out of breath. "What... terrified... do?"

"Attack."

"Be... ready."

He sighs heavily and draws another breath after what seems like an eternity. Everything's uncertain apart from his death. And so I sit with him again just as I did at the beginning alone, hoping and waiting for I don't even know what.

His breath becomes a bridge between what was, and what is to come. He breathes in the past and exhales the future and I wait somewhere in the middle. A moment where every part of me is thrown into the air. A waiting game with nothing to tie me anywhere. I normally panic at uncertainty, there's no what, when, or where. Just his breath rattling unrhythmically in and out of his body. Soon enough, his breath will stop. But for now, for this moment, I am no one, resting in uncertainty, embracing it, and accepting that anything is possible within its boundaries. Nothing can move on until he breathes his last. There will be no escape to Awenmell. Not for him, anyway.

W ho am I now? Lady Ashling of Brennyn Hall, or the Ash of Awenmell? I close the lord's eyes and consider my choices. How am I to battle Feeney? I stroll to the window. "The fields are green again, my lord," I say. Of course, he offers no answer and I wonder what it all means now, anyway. I imagine they'll soon shrivel back to yellow without his arrival at Awenmell, and the plans he'd made to renew the land. I didn't expect the end to be so mundane. There's nowhere to go from here, anyway. I've failed completely, hiding in my room when I could've stopped this. The lump in my throat stings as I open the chamber door and the Trothsman raises his eyebrows. Walt approaches from further away carrying unneeded water.

I provide the report the mask of steel waits on to relieve him of his post. "The lord of Brennyn Hall is dead."

Walt gasps and removes his hat, and the Trothsman steps into the chamber to confirm my report. He returns to me and snorts and laughs in my face.

My open hand strikes his cheek before I'm aware. I stand firm, waiting for the return blow. "You Star-forsaken foolish dolt of all fools! He was the answer!" I strike again, only he grabs my arm and impatiently flings it away, sending me to the ground. His boots stomp into the distance.

Walt kneels beside me as I scream. *No!* The word echoes around inside my head repeatedly and bees strip my veins of any sanity. My body boils. It keeps coming, this anger and rage as if a wild animal had been unleashed. I don't have the strength to contain it and surrender, wondering if my screams will ever end. I didn't want to see my anger, or deal with it. Anger is truth, and I'd been running from it; afraid it would consume me and alter the me I knew forever. The rush ends, though the continued boiling makes my curled body tremble against the stones.

Listen to your bees.

What are the bees saying? My intention is important. I know that. I close my eyes and follow their stings and frantic buzzing, and recall them to hear the wisdom they offer. The truth of me. Together, we move through the loud reactions, anger, frustration, panic, and rage, and as I sit with them, feel them and understand them, other feelings surface. They sit behind the loud ones, wounded and hiding within dark and heavy robes. When it's safe, they come out and tell me their names. Pressure, blame, inadequacy, always found wanting. And here it is, petrified and hiding in a corner, never wanting to be exposed. Powerlessness.

I sit in silence with my powerlessness. Accepting it and letting it feel safe to be seen. I listen to the stories it tells and feel the pain and fear it has hidden within it. I promise to visit with it again soon. We have a new understanding, and I have much to do.

Walt's concerned face hovers above me. "Are you well?"

"I'm not quite myself, but I am well. Thank you." I sit and extend my arm for him to help me up, but he refuses.

"The Hall is yours now, my lady." He shuffles his feet around like a child being scolded. "I imagine Mr. Feeney might be upset about that."

"I imagine that too...." Did I whisper that or say it in my mind? It doesn't really matter becau— "How do you know who I am?"

"The Trothsman. And there's something else you should know. Feeney left word. With the Trothsman. He told me while we waited for you to come from the chamber. He mentioned a town, or maybe it was a village.... called Awenmell."

"Awenmell?"

"Yes. Apparently, it's surrounded. You will meet with Mr. Feeney or he will send the Trothsmen in like a flood with torches lit."

The fire. It stings in my belly. It heats me from the inside out. The slashing and the burning of the scroll.

Walt's face looks as pale as mine feels. It's not his fault he had to deliver the words. To him they're simply words; not images of people not yet recovered, and a little girl running through the fields in a blue cape.

I'm glad Walt didn't help me to my feet. I would've fallen here, anyway. I have no more energy to fight Feeney. He'll do it, anyway. And he leaves the decision with me. The guilt and the blame with me.

Who holds the cup?

That doesn't matter anymore, when I'm the one forced to control the arm.

At least we didn't have to source wood for the pyre.

The smaller sticks pop and crackle as the fire takes hold. Warmth comes in thick waves depending on whether the stiff wind collects the heat and delivers it to our bodies or whips around us like an icy shawl that seeps into our bones.

I don't grieve the lord; only for what his life might have been. We only grieve for the things that are valuable to us, and I grieve the loss of how change might have come to this land.

Walt watches the fire and shivers and relaxes according to the gifts of the wind. I expect he's witnessed many pyres. His brows furrow and he seems distracted.

I pull my cape closer to me. "What are you thinking about?"

He pulls a half smile. "To be honest, Aigneis."

"Ah, of course."

We're only standing here to be sure the fire takes hold. I doubt I'll need him after that.

He watches me for a while and I let him think I don't notice. "What will you do?" he asks.

"I don't need to *do* Walt; I need to *be*." He's no idea of what I'm talking about, but I think I needed to say it for my own benefit. Time to be clear-headed. "A friend of mine, Thomas, once told me the only way to end a battle without a fight, is to break their will to fight. I have a sense that this is true, and it's what I will see this day."

Walt is back to shuffling his feet, "Well, I don't know if—"

"Please send for Mr. Feeney."

"But Ash..."

"I will meet with him here. In the great hall."

"What can I do?"

"You will take Aigneis to the village and stay there."

"But you'll be here alone."

Silence makes the sounds of the burning kindle louder than it is. "That's correct."

Walt prods at the pyre and moves things as I step away from it. For all the times he's disappeared when we needed him, I'm grateful he's here now. It's time for us to both leave the pyre and attend to the next parts of our day. Walt shakes my hand in farewell, but there's no reason for words.

He strides in front of me, and a sudden realization makes me call to him. "Walt, before you leave..."

"Anything."

"Move my horse." I ignore his surprise and continue, "To the farthest field. It still has water year-round?"

"Nice plump grass too."

"In case I don't..."

He stares at the ground and nods his compliance.

In just one instant, my mind is back in the Hall of old; reverted to making decisions based on safety, calculating outcomes of each of my moves. Guthrie would be proud of my intelligence, but not of my wisdom. *Trust,* my heart says, but it's just a whimper now as my brain is in full stride, stuffing fear down and controlling my actions.

Cover all possibilities.

Have an answer for everything.

Know your enemy better than yourself.

Plan ahead.

Be safe.

Survive.

⁂

The tea falls from the pot to the cup as it's always done. It sounds louder in the quiet of the kitchen. No Aigneis nattering away, no Walt and the underlying tension of whether he's doing what he's supposed to. So, here I am, soon to meet with a so-called leader again. This time there won't be any served cups of tea and stupid rituals to learn. *Who do you think you are?* That's what she said, but I can't pull an answer from my mind. What do I *know*, then? Maybe there's an answer there.

I'm the Eariss. Well, I make up part of it. What am I to do as the Eariss?

Listen.

Trust what I know.

And what should I do when I don't know; when I'm in the dark?

It's time to stop thinking and start feeling.

I've done all the thinking and planning I can possibly do. All that is left is to observe and trust. An army waits to move on my decision; only it's not my army, but Feeney's.

Who do you think you are?

It's an interesting question. According to Martha, it's who I will become. But it's not just about wishing I was someone else. I have to know it and feel it inside me. It has to be mine alone, so embedded in me that no circumstances can take it from my grasp. No person either.

This will never ever be about Feeney. Or anyone else. This is about me. What I believe about myself. How I feel when I consider the past, and how I define it as good or bad when, like Martha's sunny day, it just is. What you believe about yourself, you will become.

What do I believe?

I dive deep into my heart, to the stillness under the surface of the turbulent water, prepared and surrendered to whatever answer I might find. A sensation bursts from my heart like a thousand butterflies taking flight; each beat of their wings reverberates and lifts me higher. What might feel terrifying for others, I embrace; the beat of those thousand wings, though delicate, is stronger than any fear. Nonsensical, but pure and true. Terrifying, but there's no other place I'd rather be than this moment in time. This moment is true. I have taken the right paths. If this day is my last, I need to prepare for it.

❧❧❧

The forest knows. I'm sure it does. There's a greater sense of comfort, of holding me while I rest beside the stream. Not collecting water today, just being. Just quietly noting the sunshine through the leaves, the soft earth under my shoulders and the way the tip of this fern keeps bouncing and lightly tapping my arm. When I close my eyes, the earth pulls heaviness from me and replaces it with a new lightness. It's a magic I don't completely understand, but don't have to, to receive its benefits. Soon enough, it reminds me it's time to return to the Hall.

From the gate, you wouldn't know Eshnae's room existed. I can't believe I squeezed through that hole to get away. I clutch the key in my hand. Everything is changed now. I have openness all around me, yet I can't wait to get away. My hope yearns for my escape. I may have a key now, but I'm still trapped by its machinations.

Even in disrepair, the Hall is large and its pastures useable, but I disown it. Could Feeney's fight come from his expectation that I want it? Could I hand it to him and walk away? He'll have what he wants then. Oh, but there's still the issue of my life. He won't let me keep it. Now others know I am alive. We place value on contrasting things, and my value to the Hall differs from my value to Awenmell.

My chamber door swings open and cold air brushes past me on its own escape. Dusty silk dresses hang like flightless butterfly wings, so delicate and pretty but without a useful purpose. My fingers slip between them, yet I have no desire to embrace them or the life I left here. I feel like Martha, preferring her hut to the lodges, and hold my arms up in the looking glass the way I had many times before, *my useless hands flopping at the end of my branches.* My hands were never useless; they contain my purpose. I clench them into a fist. I am whole. This is me.

What a waste had I stayed.

What a waste to deny one's purpose.

The bed puffs a mouthful of dust as I fall onto it. The old dark tapestry still hangs precariously, only I don't wait for it to fall now. It fell and crushed me long ago; and the Mystery heard my cries for help. Awenmell helps lift its weight. And the special souls there. I have to protect it at all costs.

Should I wear a noble dress to present a noble cause? He might take me more seriously. I flick through the dresses again. It doesn't matter what I wear. I know who stands inside the dress now, and this old one of Martha's is perfect for me.

The stones appear as cold and unfeeling as they did every time I walked this path to the great hall. Was it bitter; the taste I left in their mouths by existing? There are parts of me hidden in these walls. Seeped and merged with the toxic stones so it's unnoticeable, but they're there. I can feel them. I didn't know stones trapped more than cold.

If I'm leaving here, I call back all the parts of me that were buried in the cracks of these walls. Every shout, every whimper, every tear, and every wish. Every moment of my power taken from me. I get to call them back to the places in my soul they were torn from, and I pull them to me as I walk; calling the fragmented pieces embedded within the mortar to return to me. They are mine, and I behold them now.

My hands run along the stones that bid me to rest my forehead against them. We are meeting for the first time without a barrier, with no shields in sight. For the first time, I hear them speak. They remain hard and unmoving because it was always their task. They can't be changed, can't be moved, just like the past they come from. They were steadfast, and they channeled me towards this day. This moment. And I thank them for all they taught me.

Without them, I wouldn't be this person who walks toward Feeney and my fate. The whole of my story must be not only acknowledged but embraced, because that story is me.

If I refuse to acknowledge my story, I refuse myself.

I refuse my power.

I become an herb so diluted its magic has become useless.

There's great comfort in the force that leads me down these hallways. I touch the stones again, feeling past the cold, and into the gratitude that floods me. However brutal these walls were, they formed me.

Without these walls, there would be no Awenmell.

No one armed man tending the forge, no Wren running through its fields, and no Thomas waiting for my return.

A weak fire trembles in the great hall's oversized hearth. Must've been Walt. The slight warmth does nothing but release odors hidden among the threshing floor. This place used to be grand. There are still a few remnants of its previous life; dusty ceremonial spears hang at odd angles, and some chairs tipped over near the hearth. Walt probably broke one down for the fire.

That wonderful fragmented window stands alone. What a bond we share, having witnessed injustice here and forced to remain silent. I used to think it wasn't whole, and it distorted the light, breaking it into fingers and beams that would brighten the room more, if it wasn't for all that lead. The light did still come through, of course, but on diverse angles and in varying strengths.

I always thought that if there was no lead, the glass could take that whole beam of light and shine it directly into the room, but what would it be then? Plain, powerless, and bland. With no lead to hold its pieces firm, it couldn't show any pictures or patterns.

It's the lead that tells the story.

All the fragmented and broken pieces come together and form a unique pattern. I used to think scars were always white when healed like Thomas's. But sometimes they're dark like lead and stay dark: they don't whiten up and refuse to be anything other than what they are.

And yet we want to get rid of the lead, the darkness.

The window is in fragments but remains whole because of the lead, because of its beauty, not in spite of it.

Someone has forced the door to the Lord's document room. I've only witnessed the procedures in this room from afar. The large table he used for sealing declarations stands in the middle, not a stick of wax or a seal to be found. Weapons are missing too. Probably taken by opportunistic guards or workers who needed it for protection themselves. It doesn't look like a powerful place, or a safe place in times of trouble, just dusty and dry and past its date. Once a place of power and integrity, I've only known it to host dubious deals and shameful secrets.

I am back in the place and the moment Guthrie said to be wary about; that I might easily fall into the patterns of long ago. As the familiar contempt rises inside me, I understand he was right.

Horses' hooves snap onto the pavers of the courtyard.

It's near mid meal.

My stomach drops to my feet.

Maybe there is a beautiful death after all. One of sacrifice, when it benefits others, a timely bowing out of service, knowing your part has been played.

Underneath the chaos on the surface, there is always a steady stream, pulling me gently into order. A breeze from nowhere brushes my face. I'm on the edge, and with surrender comes clarity. Clarity of truth that lets me see, the crisp clarity of power that lets me know what I'm capable of, and the clarity of love to know all is well.

What do I believe?

I have to believe more in me and this moment, than I believe in him and my past.

"Mystery?"

I am here.

"Then I am ready."

G uards? And only three of them.

Where are his Trothsmen?

They stroll into the Hall uninterested, uniforms disheveled and their eyes weary. They pass me as they head to the fire, only offering me a cursory nod. It's not that cold. Why the concern with the fire? Their hands reach into their pockets and pull out small sticks no thicker than a thumb. Even from here, I can tell they're from different branches, different trees. One by one, they toss them into the fire, raising a small flurry of sparks as the new wood hits the old. It didn't need more fuel. Yet they give themselves summary glances. I've seen nothing like it, but I have a sudden urge that if I had a stick, I would add it too. There's something strong and purposeful about this act.

Every face turns to the sound of determined steps striking the stones outside the great hall. My gut clenches in a familiar twist, squeezing the life out of my breath. I don't resist its warning, but soothe it. What do you believe? My feet press into the cold stones. I am the Ash of Awenmell.

His silhouette at the door catches the air in my throat and my mouth dries. He strides the length of the great hall, his oily hair bouncing with each step. It's grown longer, but still does nothing to hide the scars on his face or soften his features. One hand brandishes white knuckles, caused by his tight clutch on the book of law at his chest. The other swings freely to accentuate his victory swagger, and less than halfway to me, he gives up fighting the smile that erupts on his face.

My arms wrap around me, but nothing can ward off the iciness that enters the room with him. It makes no difference that my eyes see three guards, and a fire; all I feel is that my clothes have been torn from me and I stand naked and exposed. As useless and helpless as I was all those summers ago.

The bees sting me back to life and implore me to run. Shh, I soothe. I know you worry for me, but this isn't what it was. This is now. A settling warmth spreads through my body, aided by the steady rumble of the bees. I am not alone. I know who I am.

Feeney stares, sizing me up. He sniggers, chuckles and laughs.

I lift my chin. "No Trothsmen?"

"For you? Why would I bother? They're more useful a few valleys to the West. Quicker that way, you see?" His fingers caress the jeweled book. "I'm sure you know what happens next."

Why doesn't he just go in there and destroy it? He wants me to wait. The rules of our game are still the same. It's always the others and I am to blame. Thomas is brave, but he can't hold off a troop of Trothsmen. Guthrie can draw up the most impressive battle plans, but without men to fulfill them... and it must terrify the ones inside. A drawn-out affair of all their apprehension. The fear hides in the expectation of the blows, not the blows themselves.

Tears sting at my eyes. I will never cry in front of him. Ever. Besides, haven't I done what he demanded? Haven't I always?

"Look at you," he scoffs, "Still creating problems for everyone where there didn't need to be any."

My voice squeaks into the air. "We remember things differently."

"What was that? Speak up then."

He's lost the look of the squawking raven, and takes on a cat like demeanor; meaning to pat and paw at me until he decides my end. "We remember the details differently."

"You remember nothing properly, and now I'm remembering how whiny your voice was."

"If you can hear me, you can see me. Silent people are easier to erase, aren't they? The people of this land need to tell their stories, they need to heal."

"I can tell their stories for them. On their behalf. Besides, I make up better ones." The guards chuckle along with him.

"The stories are theirs, not yours. They've never been yours to tell. Mine included." I will myself to be tall and brave and unwavering, but I know I tremble, and he sees me. Living so close to my honesty now; I can't betray it and lie as I once did.

"Not mine to tell, fine. Mine to finish. Mine to put an end to all this bloodshed. It's always been my task to tidy up your mess and I'm getting rather sick of it." He paces, becoming impatient and unpredictable. "You must ruin everything, mustn't you? I mean, just look at what you've done now."

My chin lowers. What have I done now?

"All those people dying out there, you proclaim to care about them, yet all the blood that pours onto the land is because you didn't stay where you were told. All those innocent people fighting and dying because of your selfishness. What have you got to say for yourself?"

My tongue hangs limp in my mouth, bees hoist into flight and sever any connection with my brain. Guthrie warned me this would happen. My brain numbs and all I see is spittle forming on the edges of his lips. Am I really to blame for the unrest? I can't even find an answer to that, just the accusing question that spirals in my mind.

"And you left your duty to do what? Live in a meadow like a dog with dregs; I'm told we need to find a new term that means beneath the lowers. And then you returned here to do what, exactly? Have the Lord hear your plea? Be the voice for those who can't speak or some other nonsense?"

"No one is voiceless, Feeney. Just silenced." I swear, a guard nodded.

"For Star's sake, what can you offer them?" He laughs. "People call you all sorts of things. Do you know that? Some say you're mad and rightly so, not to be trusted. Poison drips from your lips every time you open your mouth. Oh, and a bridge. How's that for a noble structure?" he chuckles again, "So tell me, are you a rickety old bridge or one made of bricks? Is that what you consider yourself? No, tell me really. I'd love to hear your views. Perhaps you'd prefer to be a pig trough?"

"A bridge closes gaps that can't be crossed. So in a way..."

"So, you feel loved for this gap closing? You're more of an idiot than I thought. Honestly, the summers have not done your faculties any favors. People don't love bridges, you fool; they use them! No one loves a bridge. They just love what they provide them with, a connection to what they're after, a way to make their path easier. Case in point; your friend, Thomas."

I lose balance as my legs buckle and my stomach reels. *What?*

"Oh, you didn't think you actually mattered to anyone, did you?"

I gasp, but no air makes it to my lungs. *Thomas?*

He laughs with delight. "You did!" he waves his free arm in a gesture that scoops in the great hall. "This nonsense... it's always been between me and that idiot child from Feldston. You think this is about you? Stupid child, still as thick and self-possessed as ever. It was never about you. He used you to get to me, and it worked, didn't it?" He snorts at me. "Do you really believe that he, or anyone else, could care for you? You're broken. Nothing. Un-fortunately, he was smart enough to figure out whoever controlled you, controlled our future. Looks like he's controlled you from the moment you left here."

No.

Yes.

His obsession with the army. Wanting to take the Hall.

"You don't think I had a hand in making our game a bit more challenging? All those silly symbols scratched into trees. It all worked. Nothing of what you believe is real, never has been."

No, it can't be true

He laughs at my reaction; the room spins and I grasp the back of a nearby chair to steady myself. I've fallen into his trap, as if the ground has pulled away from beneath me and drained my body of its blood. Why does he always do this to me? How does he know how to flip my brain upside down and make me unsure of anything I've ever believed? I have nowhere to stand, except where he tells me.

He pulls the chair away from me, a splinter stabs at my binding scar.

"Come now, you can't really believe an illiterate village boy could get his hands on a leather satchel and have a house built of straw without help?"

The pain from the splinter sends messages to my brain of its own accord, and visions of the rock and Thomas. the flames and cords, flashes of sights, sounds, and smells and Thomas's sweet voice above the turmoil in my head. The gossipers of Sirban, the way messages get misconstrued. But how could Feeney know all of this?

"People talk Ashling" Bilious heat forms under my breastbone and threatens to burn its way through my chest. I clench my teeth. "I don't believe you"

"You should!"

A blow to my head sends me reeling, and its momentum slides me toward the wall when I land. Feeney paces toward me. Blood on my fingertips. It was the book. The jewels must've cut into my temple and side of my face. I scramble into the document room. Was the lock broken? Thomas's Five! Thomas's Five! They don't come.

The door slams behind me. It wasn't me. Feeney's feet on the floor. Move. Quick. Off the floor.

Feeney wedges the door locked while guards pommel on the outside of the door.

This was meant to be the Lord's safe place, a room for refuge. The guards shouting and thumping blur into deafness as Feeney smirks and steps toward me. He raises the book above his head and I scramble under the table.

A spear. There. Fallen from the wall and lodged beside a chair. I lunge for it and Feeney's boot lands on my lower arm. The book lands with a thud as he swaps his weapons. He's so distracted by his prize; I wrench my arm away and rise on the other side of the table.

He tosses the spear from hand to hand. It's short. Not like one of the lances. More for personal combat; the length of a man's arm. "Don't tell me you've come unarmed? How stupid can you be? I imagined you far more powerful than this, given the tales I've heard."

"I have all the power I need."

He jabs the spear at me from across the table. "You have no idea. Brenn mentioned you were an idiot who only desired to sit with leaders. Naïve and stupid. Always were. Nothing's changed, has it? Going to rub your hands on your clothes? Going to cry?"

My teeth clench. The desperate have nothing to lose. I flip the table, forcing him to step back.

"Look how feisty you've become."

His lunge was closer than I'd thought. I didn't feel the sting of the blade. Blood drips from the wound on my neck.

He smiles as my fingers check the size of the wound and I dry my hands across my chest. "What matters most, is whose story you believe, mine or that wretched Thomas's."

Why should that matter?

What do *I* believe?

"I believe I'm the Eariss. One of many, many of One. And when I stand, I am not alone. I never was. There's an army Feeney. Neither of us could stop it, even if we wished it so. The Eariss is no longer an infant; or even a child. The Eariss grows. It's far beyond your control."

"And if I kill you now?"

A smile widens across my face. "The army raises itself. Whether I live or die, the army will rise."

He rages, uses the book as a ram and pushes the flipped table aside; I raise the chair between us, using it as a shield. "I know what's in that book." I jab at his unprotected belly with the legs of the chair and duck another of his lunges. "It's not laws that fill it, but blood. Blood and the lies that caused it to spill." Emboldened by my desperation, I continue. "Your lies took my heart from me, and the hearts of the people. In your search for something solid, you pound and pound on anything that crosses your path, weakening it, and then you blame it for breaking. A child shouldn't go to bed wondering if they'll be alive the next morning, and not wanting that morning to come. If death is still currency, I will pay my dues if required. Every accusation you make is a death sentence, there's never a trial, never a chance to listen and observe and consider another view."

He chuckles, "Oh you flatter me."

I rush at him with the chair and he doubles over, winded. The spear rattles on the ground, his grip preferring the book to the blade. My hand snatches at the spear. Got it. The blade pushes against his throat before he's recovered from the fall. Insatiable rage forms an all-consuming fire in my chest with no outlet for the building pressure. It explodes inside my body and transforms into ravenous, never-ending bees, wasps, and hornets. The drumming of a million bees vibrates through me.

But a force stronger than my rage overtakes it, insidious in its power and manipulation. It slides into the moment, silky and slimy. It is his dread. His fear and everyone else's that he feeds upon. The blade holds firm against his throat and I have shifted from rage to repulsion.

A waterfall, gentle and pure, pushes my revulsion aside and leaves a dreamlike state. The blade holds firm, and Feeney quakes, yet time seems to stand still. The Mystery speaks softly, calming me from the turmoil inside.

Ash? Ash of Awenmell?

"Yes."

If you find the tools you seek, will you be brave enough to use them?

I had promised this. I remember. "Yes."

Listen carefully. The tool you seek is not in your hand. The tool is in your heart. Will you be brave enough to use it?

Brave enough to use my heart. Brave enough to feel.

Feeney pushes himself from the floor, snatches at the spear and his momentum drags me up too. Within the dizzying state of the waterfall, Feeney doesn't appear as a man but a swirl of egoic rage, desperation, and fear. There's no connection to be made here, no conversation possible. There is a heart in there and a soul, but it is so seared by the blazing heat of anger, hatred and rage that I wonder if blood still pumps through it. How his chest must hurt. He latches onto his own story for dear life and creates his own prison. How can you find your way to the edge, when you can't even climb or get through a wall you built yourself?

He spins me and pins me to a wall, his breath hot on my face. The spear blade lies across my neck, and his elbow digs into my outstretched arm. He slams my other arm into the wall spread out underneath his.

In an instant, I am in several places at once. I am riding a fat black pony searching for freedom, my hair whipping in the wind, an exposed belly, an open, vulnerable heart, being held down by a campfire, ridiculed by those I trusted and obedient to impossible demands.

But my openness allows a hug from Wren, floating, dancing, landing on the earth, sleeping in the forest, welcoming Oren and drawing the curtains of the Hall to let the light into the dark places. With my heart open, I am surrendering in the rain, its drips tickling me with possibility. I am buffeted on the edge of my possibility. I will not; cannot fold. How can I when I'm connected to the source of my strength? This is my rightful position, not curled into a ball in defense of my life. The defiance I felt on the day I stood in front of the elders returns. My toes feel into the stone.

The blade moves against my skin as I speak. "Without you, I couldn't have risen so strong and determined. You meant to destroy me; but instead, you made me."

Feeney forces the metal tighter against my throat and his words crawl across my skin. "You don't fear death?"

"Of course not."

This is it. The blade flattens against my neck and pushes down. So this is how I'll die. He'll crush my throat. Apt. I can't move. I close my eyes. What's that? My toes curl around something.

I croak in a whisper. "You haven't thought your plan through."

"I've thought of everything that needs to be covered." He booms but releases pressure on the blade.

"If you kill me, you can't get the Hall. The new laws transfer, remember?"

He pushes on my throat again and scoffs, "That's where you're wrong. Thanks to your ruse, I'm not killing Lady Ashling of Brennyn Hall, am I? Just punishing an insolent nurse, and I'm well known for taking my punishments too far. No one will speak of Lady Ashling's demise, just the death of an insignificant servant. And besides, this confrontation will never have existed. I have this ability to wipe things from history, you see." He leans in so close the blade touches both of us at the same time. "So tell me," he whispers, "You weak, purposeless, insignificant sacrifice. Ha! Tell me... what do you believe now?"

"Bees." I whisper.

They surge through me and threaten to overtake. Suddenly I love them, adore them as though I'd been waiting for them all along. With eyes closed, I can follow them closely. I know they're taking me somewhere I haven't been before. I filter it all; the shame, the pain, the wounds, the humiliation, the anger, the panic, and the rage, the blaming. My feet push into the floor. I feel myself in my body. There's that thing under my feet again. A ridge in the stone. My feet wiggle to a place so that the uneven stone floor lines up along the balls of my feet. I curl my toes over.

The edge.

I shed it all.

Every identity they ever labeled me with.

No longer Lady Ashling.

No longer the Eariss.

No longer by Thomas's side.

Only myself and the Mystery.

I am on the edge.

Surrendered.

Mystery? What would you have me do?

Fear and panic scream at me for leaving myself so vulnerable. Protect yourself. Fight, Attack! But the Mystery's still small voice remains clear and centers me to this moment. It whispers softly but firmly.

Shields down. Your power and your healing and the answer is in laying your shields down. Will you be brave enough?

My mind doesn't understand one bit of this, but my body knows the truth. It always has. My arms are outstretched, open heart, toes to the edge. Trust. Surrender, taking hands off what I expect it to be. I am on the edge and I trust. I fall into the edge and all its promises.

The energy in the room changes when I stop fighting him and this moment. He seems disoriented, almost as if he's unsure of what to do next. Whatever he was feeding on has gone.

A waterfall arrives with pounding force. It pours over me, pulling me under and pummeling my breath from me. A sensation similar to the Tallefix camp, where we shared a moment not of this world, but a gossamer shelter created purely for being; for listening and watching. Feeney is taken here too, by what force I don't understand. Staring just as the Tallefix did. Terrified, unmoving, yet curious.

Scenes form like clouds that blend and move into shapes and vistas. Like the ones that played out before my eyes with Awenmell's visitors. They carry as much emotion and churning energy as any of their tales.

A song plays. The gentle melody of a music box, in a grand home. A young child... Oren? No. My heart swells, a mother and a child, and the music box. It's the Crown of Fire tune. Some notes are different, but it's unmistakable. They sing but I can't hear their words, just how sweet they sound together. The melody moves up and down, around the room like silk. She strokes his hair.

Is Feeney watching this? His face is pale, his mouth hangs open. And all at once I understand he knows this scene, the words to the song, and the warmth of singing with your mother.

Cold air blasts the room, shocking them from their melody. The air becomes painful, as if it poisoned the moment with misery. I buckle over. The notes of the song dis-harmonize, forming loud and jagged spears that fly around the room. Even with my hands over my ears, the noise screeches inside my head.

Burly guards push their way into the room. I don't recognize the uniform, but their white hair strings out from under their helmets and they surround the young child, whose terrified screams continue as they drag him from the room.

"Leave him, leave him!" Her panicked voice contains all the power and sacrifice of her world, yet not a single ear hears above the commotion, shoving, and yelling. All the shouting, and she can't understand a word they speak. She understands the blows that send her to the ground.

This can't be happening. The invaders were many markers away. I was told they... I could have sent him away. I could have sent us away.

She doesn't feel the wounds from where her blood trickles and pools, only that a force holds her from her son. She's deaf to the grunts of dominance that invade her and the sound of her own screams. The child is all she hears. Every whimper, every pleading cry, and every scream. Her bright, beautiful boy. She feels his cries clawing at her; they rip at her chest, shredding it over and over and over again.

All the while, the song plays. A distortion of what had been before. Each note shatters inside her, like fragile ice splintering before its time. Her chest! Was it her heart or the box they stomped on? At least the music has stopped, except for that last note. The one that screeches and warps into the sound of a thousand horses neighing. Then silence.

The child sits alone among ashen debris. If he holds the black string of the music box between two rocks, it creates a dull pluck. There's really no point in salvage. Of anything.

He smudges the clean tracks of tears on his face into the ash and dirt already there. Sadness gives way to a burning anger. What did he do wrong that she wouldn't come and save him? Where is she now? Why won't she come for me? His back tightens like a brace. He doesn't need saving.

Bees envelop the small child. Their stings evaporate his heart, as if any moment before this time, including him, didn't exist. In its place, a rage that consumes any hint of his own powerlessness. A child destined to live a life of unceasing terror that he might ever find himself in this place again. Vows made for self-protection are forged in steel.

The child throws the strings and the crumbling remnants of the music box.

What had Feeney called it? *That wretched song.*

The guard's banging on the door brings me back to the document room. Feeney pants and sweat drips down his face. I know powerlessness, just as he does. And I've seen it in Cal too. We'll destroy ourselves just to gain some semblance of it. If you allow me no power, I will grab at the power to destroy myself. I still have that, and I will wield it as I choose. Feeney's terror consumed all he was, and searched outside for destruction to feed its passion. Passion for any device that meant he never felt powerless again. Yet while this energy was trying to destroy itself, needing to find an end to the misery, it created itself anew, a cycle, a darkness that never stops running long enough to consider its existence.

I am hollow, as if a large ladle appeared and scooped my insides out. A nothingness through to the pit of my stomach, cold but crisp. I slump, feeling an internal punch to the stomach of a truth

I can't deny. A realization as pure as it is horrifying. He took his terror outward. I directed mine inward.

Feeney and I.... we are the same.

Feeney stares at me and reels back confused, his soul hacked to pieces and now lies exposed. His eyes hold terror and pain.

I speak in the softest whisper I can manage. "I know the way out."

He lurches at my words, and panics as an injured animal. How can you tend to an injured animal when they won't let you close? A terror mightier than the largest armies trumpeting their charge, an anguish greater than the destruction of all he knows. I know he feels this moment. I have ruined him. He is seen. All the things he shouted at me; he was shouting at himself.

A softer waterfall arrives and clouds my eyes with mist. My eyes sting, but there are no rainbows, just tears.

Our game is over. *And you will weep.*

He was right. But I weep for him, and he knows it. Eyes so deep and dark and still, as Oren's.

He collapses on the floor in a heap, as though the structures of his story that held him in place have given way to truth and no amount of scaffolding can hold him up. It seems cruel to loom over his weakness and I drop to the floor nearby. Just as devastated by events coursing through my body as the pain is through him. The only sounds are the guards behind the door and our rasping and gasping breath. I reach out to him, but the Mystery hinders my actions.

Don't touch him!

I don't have the energy to wonder why. I withdraw my hand and focus on getting air into my lungs.

The door slams open, and the moment of stillness is gone. Guards tumble through the doorway and Feeney scoots past them in a crawl, wailing like a wounded animal. None of them move to catch him. One attends to my neck; another lifts the upturned furniture.

The other looks out the window. "There he goes; onto his horse and gone already. What did you do to him?" he laughs, "Look at him go, he's gone mad. So, what was it?"

My brain engages with their eager faces, but I don't have an answer to give them, not one that will make sense, anyway.

My blood runs cold. *Awenmell.*

"Sit still, child. It's only been two days." Aigneis has a firm hand when required and pushes heavily into my shoulder, forcing me to sit. The kitchen table makes do as an apothecary, herbs and bandages lay scattered as she tends to the wounds on my face and neck. "Healing nicely."

She pats my shoulder and I'm on my feet again. "They did say today, didn't they?"

"Walt took the message, and he was definite it was today."

Elder Ronell wishes to speak with me. The quicker we can organize my way out of the Hall, the better. It helps that he's my favorite. Perhaps Ronell will know. No one else can tell me what's happened to Awenmell.

The Hall has a distinct air now. At first, we waited for Feeney's return, watching day and night for an attack that never came. Now it's slipped into limbo, somewhere between a governing force and a dilapidated ruin. Will Ronell take it from me? I slip into my chamber, determined to present the Hall in the brightest light possible.

The air seems lighter in here too. I didn't expect this sensation. This clearing of cobwebs, a window wiped clean, able to view something from a different angle. I expected to hold on to the dirt and the pain and the sludge. But it simply washed away. Not without pain; yet my groundwork lay in the depths of Awenmell, not here in this Hall. I'd focused on the wrong thing. My experience was always that the Hall was stronger, but now that I see their forces side by side, the Hall's weakness is obvious. I wouldn't have seen it if I didn't come; if I didn't agree to trust the Mystery. Hindsight is hilariously courageous, especially when we act like someone thrown into a stream expecting to drown and find the water only comes to our knees.

Such fine dresses, each a memory in the past. My fingers walk along the colors and settle on the dark blue. It reminds me of Wren. With my eyes closed, I see her running through the meadow. One more thing. One more thing to settle and then I can be gone.

The dress twirls as it always did and only hints at the snugness across my belly. I braid my hair with blue ribbon and search the room for shoes.

"Horses in the courtyard!" Walt's shout reaches me through the open window, followed by the sound of many hooves on the cobblestones.

I hop down the hallway, securing my shoes as I go. I'll greet him in my mother's chamber; it's the one room in the Hall capable of receiving a guest without death hovering in its wings.

The chair we dragged from my chamber makes a comfortable seat for my wait. Yes, we created an acceptable room after all; a desk and chair from the Lord's chamber, a large posy from Aigneis's home garden, and my old tapestry finally on the floor where it belongs. Feeney's book of law rests on the mantle above the hearth. I want to keep it close. Aigneis sprinkled some thyme on the small fire and it's sweetened the room at just the right strength.

Her head pops around the doorframe. "Ready?"

Aigneis signals Walt at the entrance, and we begin. It's a game really, pretending to blend between the roles expected of us, but we've enjoyed rehearsing protocols none of us care for.

But perhaps Ronell cares. And that's what matters this day.

Aigneis gathers his two men to the kitchen and promises them a hearty meal.

Ronell enters the room, older than I remember him. Grayer hair, a few more scars, and more lines on his face. He takes my offered hand gently. "My condolences on the loss of the Lord."

Ah. Fabricated condolences. My acceptance of them is spurious too. There's no sorrow that the lord is gone. How could there be? "Thank you, Ronell."

He takes a seat on the other side of the hearth. "The land is astir with the news of his passing, but also the astonishing events that sent Feeney from the Hall. There are many versions already."

"Stories help people understand their worlds."

"And they fight about their versions too."

"They're feeling unstable. More than ever now. Any news of Feeney?"

"None. The elders have vowed to pass any news on, but they distrust each other."

"The people need to see a leader, to assure them all is well." I hope to see his eyes light up at my offer, but instead, his brow furrows.

"A leader? I don't think they'll look to anyone now. Just look at what Feeney got away with for so long."

"What makes you think he got away with anything? I still believe in reckoning, Ronell. Understanding a behavior doesn't excuse it."

"True enough. The land will be safe with your heart."

"You mean for me to lead? No!"

"It's expected, my lady."

I lower my face to conceal my frustration. "Have you ever noticed how blindly we perform our duty to the Hall—because it's expected? How might it feel to become duty bound to our souls, our hearts, our longings instead?"

He rubs at his chin, but says nothing.

"When we're engaged in what is right for us; true even, we don't attempt to justify it. Yet we'll often justify our uncomfortable plans to others, as if we're trying to convince ourselves that what we're doing is right, even though our hearts tell us otherwise. You never have to justify the truth. It just is. My place is not here. Of all the elders, I hope it would be yours. I won't try to convince you of what you know is true."

He stands and paces in front of the hearth. Stammering and uncomfortable, but never quite forming any words.

"You wish to lead, don't you, Ronell? You feel a call upon your heart? What I said applies to you as well. There's allowed to be a difference between what's expected of you, and where your soul belongs."

He wrings his hands. "I have secrets. Dishonorable ones."

"As does every person who ever lived. Some aren't as large or surprising as the one in torment expects them to be. Some just need air, to be spoken aloud so the wind can carry it away from our bodies. They're poisonous to our souls, and cause us to be at war with ourselves. If you battle with yourself, what can you expect to live outside of you other than conflict?"

"I should make peace with my secrets?"

"Then the land will flourish."

He doesn't seem convinced.

"Our pasts bond to us, create us and our patterns of dealing with the world, and this bond becomes our identity. It's easy to think that nothing exists without who we tell ourselves we are. But if you let go of that connection, something new opens up."

He paces again. "The laws won't allow for anything but the old way, it's what everyone is used to."

"I'm not interested in what has gone before. It just breeds more of the same. We all know that."

"This new way people speak of? Is that what you're talking about?"

"Have you seen the symbols, carved into rocks and trees?"

"It seems they multiply of their own accord."

"For those who understand the symbol, it's not a call to pick up arms and head to battle, it's a reminder of where our power truly lies. The greatest battle is between ourselves and our blind reactions, and we need to win it if we wish to see the land change. We are only responsible for what we have control over, and that's ourselves and how we handle every moment given to us."

"The ones that don't understand the symbol?"

"Will feel as if the past and their identity is under attack. They'll be terrified and lash out at anything new. The past was safer for them. Painful and confusing, but familiar, safer."

"Then we'll demand they learn the new way!" He reaches for his dagger.

"They'll dig in deeper. Fear is stubborn and needs to be heard. Soothe their worry and they are more likely to drop their weapons."

He nods slowly. "That could take a lifetime. I'm not sure I have the patience." He smooths his hand across the mantle, deep in thought, and rests them upon the book of law. He lifts the heavy tome. Maybe he'll read a passage, give me an insight.

"Out with the old then." The book thuds into the small fire, almost extinguishing it. Small flames lick at the sides of the cover as I jump to retrieve it from the hearth. Ronell bends to help, but I have already secured it. Ronell flusters. "Sorry, I—"

Ronell contemplates my reaction and his eyes narrow. I knew the moment I first touched the book. It contains answers, but I can't explain that to him. He knows I'm incapable of reading.

"There may be clues here." I wipe the ash from the back and side of the book. Tiny white dots of ash covering the jewels disappear as I blow them away. "I know someone who can help me decipher it."

"I see." He doesn't seem convinced of my story, or why I would protect an item so horrendous.

"In the deepest depths of our fears lay the power to destroy them. Fear built and layered the old laws. We have to see what has caused it to unravel it." I wrap Feeney's book in sackcloth. For all its jewels and importance, it's ugly and brutal. "How can we know light if we refuse to understand and accept the darkness? A full day is composed of light and dark; a day is not whole if we only acknowledge the sunshine."

"True enough." Ronell gazes out the window and smiles at the blue sky. "Enough talk of darkness. Will you walk with me outside?"

"As a child, I remember this courtyard full of black horses. I always admired the Trothsmen's steeds."

"They're a fine sight when they gather."

"Do you think the elders will work together again, toward the new way?"

"The elders." He sighs and looks to the sky. "We have failed too. Feeney set us against each other; rumors mostly."

"You were the most respected among them, Ronell. You must make them see they've been hoodwinked. The new way will be much harder without the elders on board as an example."

"They may turn on me. Just another fact to consider."

He deliberates as we walk further outside the gates for a view of the field.

"Have you ever seen measuring scales, Ronell?" Of course, he has. As a landholder, he would use one to count out his silver, or watch as his servants do. "One day they will tip in peace's favor. One brave heart at a time."

He watches over the vastness of the field and shakes his head. "What you're suggesting sounds mad."

"It's only madness because it hasn't been done before and I can't offer proof to sway your mind. Once there's proof, it ceases to be madness. Without proof, it becomes a moment of faith. Everything that was ever new was once considered insanity."

He wanders around thinking, kicking at tufts of grass and shaking his head. He would be marvelous in this position, I know it. I also know there's nothing more I can do but wait.

Ronell needs to reply to his heart and its calling. Not me and my explanations.

He rubs at his hair and checks the sky, paces the fence line and follows me back to the courtyard. His men are watering their horses and he stops to see how they fare. He sighs and rubs his temples, then sits beside me on the barrow with an undignified plop.

"I'll have to call for my family. I have good men who will follow me here." He lifts a hand to the men and they return his familiar salute.

"Good." My heart rests. "I'm sure Aigneis would like to stay on, and Walt is... young and... knowledgeable."

"There's no one to tend the land, though. I can't spare anyone from my holdings."

"Send word to Smoutlea. There's a guard there by the name of Galen. Return his family to him and settle them here. He knows good workmen, is a thinker and of noble character."

"There are brave men everywhere, doing everyday things in the bravest of ways. I know of one myself."

"See, you've noticed the new way already at work in the land."

He calls one of his men to him. "What was that guard's name, the one who started that resistance among the guards?"

The man nods, "Tabar, my lord."

"Of?"

"Tunstream, I believe."

"Take a horse. Find him and bring him here."

❧❦❧

Moonlight reflects off the fragmented glass window. It must be the bevels that capture it and transform the window into a giant spider's web. Or perhaps it's also the ale we've been drinking with one of the finest meals Aigneis has prepared.

Ronell pushes his plate away and reclines on his chair. "When do you travel?"

"In the morning." The roll in my belly must be nerves. "I still don't know what I'm heading to."

"There's fighting near the lip of the valley. We have heard nothing from the valley itself."

I nod. Maybe it's just trepidation that weakens my limbs. "Is that kind of delay expected? Is it normal not to hear a thing?"

"Take comfort. It can take a while for news to arrive at the correct place. Particularly given the chaos out there."

I consider his words. He's trying to bring comfort and I appreciate his experience in these matters. I nod and prepare to leave.

"I'll send for guards to travel with you."

"Thank you. But I prefer to travel alone. I have a fast steed and can protect myself. I'll send word when I arrive."

"Regardless of the outcome?"

"Either way. I will send word."

❧❦❧

It would be nice to say that the flowers automatically bloomed and sunshine and happiness floated on the breeze today, but everyone seems mostly tired. Even so, blooming flowers seemed to be in the air, not that far away. There was hope. Yes, that's what it was. And it blew on the breezes and swept through villages and walls and gardens and chasms and cliffs. I imagined it sweeping through the burned remains of Sirban and lifting the spirits of the Fercies.

The jewels on Feeney's book of law capture the light from my chamber window and reflect shapes across the wall. What if I didn't wrap it in the Trothsman's cape? Not just yet.

My finger bumps over the jewels. Dried traces of my blood cloud some of them, and darkness outlines the seams where it was caught between them. The cover is stiff and heavy and I expect it to creak like an old chest.

Feeney's writing is flourished and fancy; yet not as solid as Thomas's hand. I turn heavy pages, looking at squiggles and lines that mean nothing to me. Guthrie must teach me when I get back. I run my fingers over columns and lines and wax seals. Over dark brown smears and smudges. It's blood. So much blood. The smears are thumbprints. Collected against their will.

I hover my fingers over the words and see flashes of history play out before me. Just like the stories of our guests at Awenmell. The thumbprints hide stories of their own and beg to be told. The pain and anguish of the accused, the confusion. My thumb rests just above a print and almost touches it. Fire burns my nostrils, wails sound in my ears, my heart aches with betrayal, injustice—hatred. Dirty and scarred faces flash in front of me—*Thomas!* I slam the book so quickly it catches my hand and I toss it to the other side of the bed.

He told me not to read it.

And I didn't.

Not the way he expected, anyway.

Deep breaths help me recover from my shock. Once I've wrapped the book in the sackcloth again, I cover it with the Trothsman's cape. I fold it quietly and tenderly, with awe. Not from fear, but respect. There are lives within these pages that must be honored.

A rrow is packed and ready. No matter how skilled Ronell's men might be, I still check his tackle quietly as they help Walt muck out the stables. Ronell was right. He has good men. A bay stands waiting, ready for travel. Perhaps she'll be off in search of Galen. I know he'll love it here.

"You're on your way then?" Walt squints into the morning light while Aigneis fusses over her new charges and requests their favorite foods. The fresh energy within the Hall has made its way into her life, too.

Feeney's book! "I must collect something from my chamber first."

"Well, hurry along then."

My rush through the hallways is different this time. Just as everything is. Being waved off is different to being hunted off. And listening and obeying is different to listening and choosing. Feeney's book lays waiting on the bed. I'm not sure what it holds. Before I touch it, I make a vow to follow those thousands of butterflies taking flight, to stay sensitive to them and the beloved voice of the Mystery. No matter how frightening or ridiculous it seems to anyone else.

Even so, dear Ash of Awenmell?

My heart swells. "Even so."

"Horse in the courtyard!" Walt's voice echoes around the yard and up and down the halls. "No, wait." He laughs, "Donkey in the courtyard."

I chuckle to myself. *Donkey?* Who'd ride a donkey?

My feet move so fast I don't feel them on the stones and the wrapped book drops from my hands as I reach the courtyard. I leap into Thomas's arms. He staggers back, still recovering from his ride. He smells like Awenmell; he smells like home.

I contort his face between my hands. "You're safe? Oren is safe?"

He looks deep into my eyes, relieved. How I've missed those eyes. "Everyone is safe."

I laugh and sniff through my tears. "You rode the donkey?"

"More trouble than it was wor—"

"But you were surrounded! The Trothsmen. How did you get out?"

"We were never surrounded. Where did you hear that from?"

He'd fooled me again. But I'm too delirious to care. "Ugh! A proven liar!"

"My love, are you safe? Are you well?"

I nod, eager to be on our way. "Will you take me home?"

"I'd be honored."

I wave to one of Ronell's men, "Please prepare one of the strong bays." He doesn't hesitate to lead the ready horse to us.

Thomas watches me wrap the cape tighter around the book and slide it into his saddlebag until it's snug and safe. "What have you got there?"

There're so many things I could say. The importance of opening painful wounds in order to cleanse them, how something can hold both horror and freedom simultaneously. That treasure lies hidden in its pages.

Darkness. Pain. Truth.

"It's a gift."

A NOTE FROM THE AUTHOR

Thanks for reading *Rise*. I hope you enjoyed Ash's story and that you'll continue to follow her journey through the Awenmell Series.

I truly appreciate the feedback I get from my readers. If you enjoy my work, please consider leaving a review at your store of purchase and on review websites such as Goodreads.

Reviews not only help other readers find books they might enjoy, they can be instrumental in a book's success.

You can also share your Awenmell experience with friends and on social media. I love it when my friends recommend books to me, don't you? #awenmell #rise

Acknowledgements

I used to have this naïve idea that books were written by solitary writers, slaving away under their own compulsions. What I found is that any form of art is birthed through a community of support. Practicalities that keep artists and writers almost human through the creative process.

There's the person who drops by with coffee, the one who sends a joke through email, or the sender of an *'I was just thinking of you'* note through messenger.

It's the supporters who send interesting articles and anecdotes about their day, sometimes resorting to threats of *'Step away from the keyboard, and no one gets hurt'* when I'm overwhelmed and need to be shaken till my teeth rattle, or hugged until I cry. Their feedback, both good and bad, is a requirement of fashioning these stories together. To all of you, I say an unequivocal thank you from the bottom of my heart.

It's not just those with a physical presence in my life, either. My global online friends are known to drop a kind or encouraging word at just the right time. All these people have inspired my heart in myriad ways as I worked and felt my way through *'Rise'*.

To my lovely team who is always on board
to rally me through. Thank you.

Big thanks to my alphas Michelle Capper, and Sarah Patterson. What a crazy disjointed ride we went on! Thanks for begging for more when I was sure I was spewing forth complete crap.

To my courageous and insightful betas, Pam Gainer, Heather Musingo, Cindy O'Donnell, and Siobhan Pope. Honestly my lovelies, what would I do without you? I love you all to bits.
And to Joanne Smith, proofreader extraordinaire, who always lends an ear to my frustrations and bewilderment.

A blessed thank you to artist Heather Musingo, who embeds an amazing amount of talent, energy, and thoughtfulness into each of the covers of the Awenmell Series.

Thank you. Now to get writing again.

How does 'A Taste of Burnt Honey, Awenmell Series : Book Three' sound?

Acknowledgements

I used to have this naïve idea that books were written by solitary writers, slaving away under their own compulsions. What I found is that any form of art is birthed through a community of support. Practicalities that keep artists and writers almost human through the creative process.

There's the person who drops by with coffee, the one who sends a joke through email, or the sender of an *I was just thinking of you* note through messenger.

It's the supporters who send interesting articles and anecdotes about their day, sometimes resorting to threats of *'Step away from the keyboard, and no one gets hurt'* when I'm overwhelmed and need to be shaken till my teeth rattle, or hugged until I cry. Their feedback, both good and bad, is a requirement of fashioning these stories together. To all of you, I say an unequivocal thank you from the bottom of my heart.

It's not just those with a physical presence in my life, either. My global online friends are known to drop a kind or encouraging word at just the right time. All these people have inspired my heart in myriad ways as I worked and felt my way through *'Rise'*.

To my lovely team who is always on board
to rally me through. Thank you.

Big thanks to my alphas Michelle Capper, and Sarah Patterson. What a crazy disjointed ride we went on! Thanks for begging for more when I was sure I was spewing forth complete crap.

To my courageous and insightful betas, Pam Gainer, Heather Musingo, Cindy O'Donnell, and Siobhan Pope. Honestly my lovelies, what would I do without you? I love you all to bits.

And to Joanne Smith, proofreader extraordinaire, who always lends an ear to my frustrations and bewilderment.

A blessed thank you to artist Heather Musingo, who embeds an amazing amount of talent, energy, and thoughtfulness into each of the covers of the Awenmell Series.

Thank you.
Now to get writing again.

How does 'A Taste of Burnt Honey, Awenmell Series : Book Three' sound?

About the Author

Lisa King is an international award-winning author and amateur nature photographer who lives near Brisbane, Australia. When she's not writing, you can find her hiking though lush rainforests, and exploring the wide open spaces of the Scenic Rim, taking notes for her novels and capturing the diverse and complex ecosystems where she feels most at home.

Lisa loves to transport readers to worlds where the heroes have everyday struggles, flaws and inner conflicts, and the natural world is part of the nurturing and healing process. As an advocate for education and empathy for trauma survivors, Lisa hopes her books will encourage readers on their own healing paths.

You can connect with Lisa on social media @lisakingauthor and join her readers circle at www.lisakingauthor.com

ALSO BY LISA KING

AWENMELL SERIES
Crown of Fire - Awenmell Series : Book One
Rise - Awenmell Series : Book Two

AWENMELL CHARACTER SERIES
Magic Man - Awenmell Characters 1
Eshnae - Awenmell Characters 2

STANDALONES
Dandelion Wishes – The Untold Story of Coral Maxwell-King